GRIM RISING

An Aisling Grimlock Mystery Book 7

AMANDA M. LEE

WinchesterShaw Publications

Copyright © 2016 by Amanda M. Lee

All rights reserved.

No part of this book may be reproduced in any form or by any electronic or mechanical means, including information storage and retrieval systems, without written permission from the author, except for the use of brief quotations in a book review.

❃ Created with Vellum

PROLOGUE

17 YEARS AGO

"I'm the prince."

Jerry always demands to be the prince. He thinks there's something cool about being a prince (I think it's the crown and froufrou pants, but you didn't hear that from me). That means – even though we're best friends instead of boyfriend and girlfriend – that I must be the princess. These are Jerry's rules, mind you, not mine. But there's no way I'd consent to being a princess in the middle of a zombie apocalypse.

I turned an incredulous stare toward my best friend as I perched on the edge of my bed, butcher knife gripped firmly in my hand. "Why would you possibly want to be a prince when we're about to fight zombies?"

At eleven, some people would argue that Jerry and I were too old to play zombie invasion. Luckily, none of those people lived in my house. My parents encouraged us to continue playing as long as we wanted. As long as that play didn't include my father having to sit through another one of Jerry's beauty shop sessions, he didn't care what we did as long as we didn't destroy anything or threaten cranky Mrs. Standish, who lives on the corner next to the really cool willow tree. Dad also wasn't keen on screaming so loudly that we forced the neighbors to call the police. He's kind of a baby about that one.

"I always want to be a prince." Jerry smoothed the front of his blue shirt, making sure there wasn't a wrinkle or stray piece of lint to mar its pristine appearance. It had been my idea to play zombie apocalypse. He'd wanted to watch makeover shows on Lifetime but ultimately gave in because I was feeling dominant today. "I don't see why a prince can't survive the zombie apocalypse."

He had a point, but still ... . "You're ruining the game, Jerry," I complained. "We're supposed to be hunting evil undead things and jamming this knife into their brains." My father let me watch several old zombie flicks the week before and I'd been obsessed with them ever since. He was in trouble with my mother because I had a few nightmares – and blabbed about him letting me watch the movies – but I was mostly over the terror. "If you want to survive the zombie apocalypse, you'll have to let this prince thing go."

I'd known Jerry was different from the first day of kindergarten. I wasn't big on making friends – heck, I wasn't big on attending school and suggested my parents do something bold and tell the district that I was already smart and didn't need any learning – when he walked up to me, announced I needed a makeover, and then refused to leave me alone for the next six years. I barely remembered a time when Jerry wasn't in my life. Despite his determination to whine on odd occasions, I generally enjoy spending time with him.

Tonight was one of the rare occasions I wanted to punch him in the face and make him cry.

"Why would I possibly want to survive the zombie apocalypse if I can't be a prince?" Jerry wrinkled his nose. "Bug, that doesn't make any sense. I'd rather let the zombies get me than give up my crown. If we're going to play, you have to be realistic."

I narrowed my eyes to purple slits. "You can't call me 'Bug' in the zombie apocalypse," I argued. "That's not the sort of name that a zombie fighter would have."

"I've been calling you that since we were five." Jerry planted his hands on his hips. "I'm not changing it now."

"You have to." How did he not get this? "I can't be 'Bug' in the zombie apocalypse. I need a cool name that strikes fear in the hearts of the screaming mortals we're trying to save."

Jerry crossed his arms over his chest. "Like what?"

"Like ... Chainsaw. You can call me that."

Jerry rolled his eyes. "Chainsaw is a stupid name. I'm not going to call you that."

My temper fired. "It is not! It's a cool name."

Jerry shook his head. "Stupid."

"Cool."

"Stupid."

"Cool!" I considered hopping off the end of the bed and throwing myself on Jerry, holding him down until he admitted Chainsaw was the coolest name ever, but I didn't get the chance because my father swooped into the room and snagged me around the waist before I could do it.

"What's going on?" Dad asked, his eyes traveling to the knife in my hand. "Where did you get that?"

I offered up a sheepish smile as he pried the handle from my grip and flipped the item in question over to study it. "I accidentally found it and was going to take it downstairs, but you caught me right before I could do that."

"Uh-huh." Dad didn't look convinced. In fact, he looked agitated. That was his normal face, though, so I wasn't particularly worried. "This knife happens to match the set we have in the kitchen. Do you know how I know?"

I didn't bother to hide my eye roll. "Because you know everything," I muttered.

"No, because a business associate gave me the knives as a gift," Dad said. "They have peach wood handles."

I had no idea what peach wood was, but it was probably some expensive tree that only grew near the wallets of wealthy men. Those were the type of guys Dad surrounded himself with. "So?"

"So I know you're not supposed to be playing with this." Dad carefully rested the knife on my dresser and fixed me with a dark look. "I believe we've talked about dangerous weapons and how you're not supposed to threaten your friends with them."

"Oh, she wasn't threatening me with the knife," Jerry offered. "She was threatening to make me call her 'Chainsaw,' which is just a ridiculous name."

"It's better than 'Bug,'" I shot back, agitated.

"Knock it off," Dad chided, wagging a finger in my face as his gaze bounced between us. "What are you two doing?"

"Nothing." I didn't need to lie – Dad would figure out what we were doing eventually – but I wasn't in the mood for a lecture so I figured it was worth a try. If Dad was really tired he might let us slide without questioning us further.

"What are you two doing, Jerry?" Dad persisted, turning to my best friend. He clearly wasn't in a hurry to escape.

"We're playing zombie apocalypse – her idea, not mine – and she says she needs a cool nickname. But I think that 'Chainsaw' is a ridiculous name." Jerry's expression was serene as he fixed my father with a pointed stare. "I think she chose it because she's surrounded by boys and doesn't get enough female time."

"I see." Dad made a clucking sound with his tongue. "Just out of curiosity, do you want to tell me what 'female time' is?"

"It's time to be a girl."

"I kind of figured that," Dad said. "I thought maybe there was a trick or something to it."

"No, just time to be a girl." Jerry had clearly lost interest in the game. "We should play something else. Oh, I know! We could play beauty shop."

Dad immediately started shaking his head. "There will be no beauty shop tonight. It's late."

"I promise not to touch your toes again," Jerry offered.

Dad tilted his head to the side, considering, and then shook his head. "No beauty shop. You two are supposed to be in bed in twenty minutes." Dad flicked his eyes to the over-sized sleigh bed in the middle of my room. I heard him talking to Mom last week, arguing that Jerry was too old to share a bed with me, but Mom put her foot down and said there was nothing wrong with it and to let it go. Dad argued some more but ultimately lost. For a guy who was used to winning, it had to be hard on him.

"We're not tired," I said, wondering how far I could push Dad. "You could watch a movie with us."

"Absolutely not." Dad tapped my nose as he sat at the end of the bed. "You've been obsessed with zombie movies lately. Your mother won't let me pick another movie for you until you get over it."

"Why would I get over it?" That sounded like a really dumb idea. "I have to be ready when the zombies come, and to do that I need to watch movies to plan ... um ... what's the word I'm looking for?"

"Strategy," Jerry automatically answered, staring at his fingernails. "We definitely should've played beauty shop. I need a manicure."

Dad pursed his lips as he regarded Jerry, shaking his head as amusement lit his eyes. "You'll know better for next time. As for zombies, what exactly is it that you think you must be prepared for, Aisling?"

I answered without hesitation. "The invasion."

"What invasion?"

"The one where we all die from zombie bites."

"Well, kid, I hate to burst your bubble, but there isn't going to be a zombie invasion because zombies aren't real," Dad supplied. "They're made-up things – like from books – and you'll never have to worry about a zombie invasion."

"How do you know?"

"Because I know things."

"Is this like when you knew the Tigers were going to win their World Series and you made that bet and Mom said you're not allowed to bet at work anymore?" I challenged.

Dad's smile slipped. "You must stop eavesdropping. I happen to know for a fact that we had that discussion in our bedroom, which means you were listening to a conversation that didn't involve you."

"That's how most of the conversations in this house go," I pointed out. "Zombies are real. They wouldn't have made so many movies about them if they weren't real."

Dad ran his hand over the top of my head, smoothing my flyaway black hair. "Zombies aren't real. They're movie monsters. You don't have to fear movie monsters."

I knew he was trying to make me feel better, but he was doing a terrible job of it. "Not all movie monsters are fake, so you don't know that zombies aren't real."

"What movie monsters are real?" Dad challenged.

"Vampires."

"I've never met a vampire. Have you?"

There was no way I was going to let him get away with such a simplistic argument. "Maybe they're wraiths," I suggested, referring to the soul-sucking beasts that plagued grim reapers from time to time. "Maybe vampires are really wraiths, and instead of blood they suck souls and people got confused in olden times because ... well ... they were stupid or something. Did you ever consider that?"

Dad arched an eyebrow, the corners of his lips twitching. "No, but you have a point."

"I always have a point." I sank to a sitting position. "Zombies are real."

"No, honey, they're not."

"They are too." I refused to back down. It wasn't in my nature. "One day you're going to see that they're real and I'm going to expect a big, honking apology when you do."

"Fine." Dad held up his hands in surrender. "If zombies ever appear, I will apologize. They're definitely not going to appear tonight, though, so I think it's time you two went to bed."

"I'm down with that." Jerry offered Dad an awkward fist bump. "I need my beauty sleep."

Dad smirked. "I think you're plenty beautiful, Jerry, but make sure you brush your teeth before going to bed."

"I will." Jerry's smile was so wide it almost swallowed his entire face. "I have to floss and rinse with mouthwash, too. I know the drill."

"I know you do." Dad tousled Jerry's hair before pinning me with an expectant look. "You need to brush your teeth, too."

I stared at him for a long beat, agitation rolling through my tummy. "Zombies are real. I've seen them in movies. They have to be real."

Instead of telling me I was wrong, Dad adopted a quizzical expression. "Why do you think that?"

"Because it's the only thing that makes sense," I replied. "They wouldn't have made all of those movies if it wasn't true."

"They make a lot of super hero movies and those aren't true," Dad countered, going for the pragmatic approach.

"You don't know that superheroes aren't real," I argued. "Sure, they might not shoot webs from their hands or fly, but they could be real. You're real."

"I'm not following you."

"You're a different kind of superhero," I supplied.

"Really?" Dad looked pleased. "I believe that's the nicest thing you've said to me in weeks."

I returned his smile. "You're definitely a superhero. I think you're even the type of hero who won't tell Mom I accidentally found a knife and brought it to my bedroom."

Dad's smile slipped. "You're a master at manipulation. Has anyone ever told you that?"

I shrugged. "No. You won't tell, will you?"

"Of course not." Dad shook his head. "Do I ever tell?"

"When she makes you sleep on the couch."

Dad scowled. "You need to stop eavesdropping. It's not an attractive trait."

"Whatever." I mustered a sunny smile. "Will you read to us before bed?"

"Aren't you too old for me to read to you?"

"No."

Dad heaved out a sigh. "What story do you want? How about some *Lord of the Rings*?"

I shook my head. "*Carrie*."

"Oh, I hate it when you want me to read Stephen King," Dad complained. "If I read *Carrie* you'll spend three weeks running around the house pretending you have telekinetic powers."

"It's better than when you read *Christine* and she spent all her time spying on the cars in the garage," Jerry noted, striding out of the bathroom.

"You have a point." Dad grinned at Jerry before shifting his eyes to me. "Fine. *Carrie* it is. Brush your teeth and get in your pajamas first. I'll be back in five minutes."

I couldn't help being suspicious. "Where are you going?"

"Someone has to put the knife back in the kitchen so you don't get caught, don't they?"

That hadn't occurred to me. "Good point." I smiled as I hopped off the bed. "You should probably get us a snack while you're down there. Reading a story is much more fun when you have a snack."

Dad stared at me for a moment, and shook his head when I risked a glance back to see if I'd pushed him too far. "One of these days, kid, I'm going to find my spine and tell you no."

"Let's hope it happens before the zombies eat your spine."

Dad snorted. "You're a menace, kid, but you're my menace. Brush your teeth and change into pajamas. I'll be back in five minutes to read your story."

I mock saluted his retreating figure. "I'm still going to want you on my team during the zombie apocalypse," I called after him. "You can't join anyone else's team. Don't forget that."

Dad stilled near the door. "I could never forget that, Aisling, and I would never want to be on anyone else's team."

"Do you mean that?"

"I do." Dad smiled. "I'll always be on your team ... even when you're a pain in the butt and steal knives you've been expressly forbidden to touch."

Strangely enough, I knew that. "Don't forget the snack."

"Don't forget to brush your teeth. I'll be right back."

I scowled at his retreating form. "Never say that. If you say that you won't survive until the end of the story. Don't you know anything about surviving the zombie apocalypse?"

"Don't worry about that. I'll be around for a very long time."

"You'd better be."

Dad winked. "Right back at you, kid."

ONE

PRESENT DAY

"Absolutely not."

Serafina York crossed her arms over her chest and glared at me, screwing up her pretty face into a grotesque imitation of something straight out of a horror movie. Sadly for her, she was trapped in her own horrific version of *Friday the 13th*, even though she refused to admit the obvious.

"You don't have a choice." I tugged on my limited patience and feigned friendly interest. "I know this comes at a bad time for you ... ."

Serafina cut me off with an indignant screech. "Bad time? Bad time!" She gestured wildly, her ethereal spirit floating next to the kitchen table where she had died. Her body remained at the table, her face planted in a plate of egg whites and tomatoes, and the room was starting to smell.

Okay, I could've been imagining the last part. Whenever food is involved in a death, I can't stop myself from thinking about potential bugs and scavengers. It's a mental thing that I can't explain.

"Fine. It's a terrible time," I conceded. "You had your whole life in front of you. You were ... what ... twenty-nine?"

Serafina narrowed her eyes. "I am twenty-five."

That didn't sound right. I lifted the iPad I carried – the reaping business was going completely green these days, so I didn't have to worry about leaving behind one of those pesky files I always had to tote around – and tapped the screen to scan Serafina's file. She had died only thirty minutes earlier – although it felt longer – yet I was already running behind. I had a full slate of souls to collect. I knew better than to engage in conversation with the recently deceased, but apparently I never learned.

"This says you're twenty-nine," I countered, ignoring the way Serafina's spirit glared at me. She wasn't a threat. There was nothing she could do to hurt me. Even if she screamed and carried on – which she'd been doing since I turned up and told her she was dead and it was time to chart a course for the other side – the neighbors couldn't hear. As a reaper, I could hear, but no one else had the ability. That was both a blessing and a curse in this instance.

My name is Aisling Grimlock and I'm a reaper by trade and birthright. I wasn't always part of the family business, but a downturn in the economy forced a change in professions and now I suck souls for a living. It's honestly not that bad – other than complaining spirits, annoying brothers to work with, my anal-retentive father breathing down my neck when he's determined I did something wrong or purposely courted danger, and the occasional wraiths and monsters that try to kill me on what's turning into a monthly basis. Other than that, things were peachy keen.

Wait ... did I just use the term "peachy keen?" That couldn't be right. That was a Jerry saying. Clearly we'd been spending too much time together. Wait ... what was I supposed to be doing again?

"I am not twenty-nine," Serafina scoffed, bringing me back to reality. "Clearly your file is wrong."

"Possibly, but that rarely happens."

"And yet it's happened this time. I'm twenty-five."

She said the words, but I had trouble believing her. Ever since introducing myself to Serafina York – the daughter a rich real estate developer in Detroit – I'd rather abruptly come to the conclusion that she was a total pain in the butt and most likely a pathological liar.

"You should probably go back to your office and make sure I should really be dead," Serafina suggested. "I'm assuming they've made a terrible mistake and you'll have to return and resurrect me." The longer she talked, the wider she smiled. "Yes, that's it. I'm accidentally dead. I'm sure you'll realize the paperwork error quickly and get me back on my feet as soon as possible."

Serafina slid a sidelong look toward her body, tsking as she shook her head. "Speaking of feet ... I'm due to get a pedicure today. If you could hurry this along I'd be forever grateful. I'm supposed to have fresh toenails for the big day."

I pressed my lips together as I regarded her. She really was a piece of work. I was used to souls trying to bargain their way out of death, but Serafina was tackling it in a new and unique way. I had to give her credit for trying.

"I don't give and take life," I pointed out, doing my best not to stare at the way her body shifted a bit, internal gasses dispensing and making things worse (if that was even possible). "I collect souls. There's a difference."

Serafina wasn't ready to give up. "Well, you need to go to your boss, tell him there's been a mistake – I mean, I do not look twenty-nine – and have whoever handles death reversal come to the house and fix me up."

I stared at her for a long beat, dumbfounded. "I know you think you're fooling everyone with the Botox or whatever else you're getting – and you really didn't need it because you were already pretty – but you look your age. I'm sorry, but ... it's true."

"I do not!" Serafina shrieked, stomping her foot on the floor. Because she lacked corporeal form she didn't make a sound when her foot struck the carpet. Instead of pitching a fit, she looked as if she was rhythmically challenged and had been selected to line dance to a rumba on *Dancing With the Stars*.

"Whatever." I was in no mood to put up with a meltdown. I had my own issues to deal with and none of them – other than the obvious strain she was putting on my time management skills – revolved around Serafina York. My eyes drifted to the stack of magazines and the over-sized binder sitting on the counter. "You were getting married, right?"

"I am getting married," Serafina countered. "I am getting married in a few days to the most wonderful man in the world."

"Hmm." Given Serafina's attitude, I had my doubts anyone halfway decent would put up with her. "What's his name?"

"Skylar Worthington."

I stilled, flicking my eyes to her, incredulous. "I thought Skylar was a girl's name. Don't get me wrong, I'm all about sexual equality and stuff. My brother and best friend are gay. In fact, they live with each other. I was weirded out at first – not because they're gay, but because we all grew up together – but now I kind of like it."

Serafina worked her jaw but no sound came out. I figured that meant she wanted me to continue talking.

"So how does a lesbian wedding work?" I asked, flipping open the binder and glancing at the organized items inside. "Holy crap! Are these your wedding plans?"

"They are," Serafina confirmed, floating to a spot behind me so she could look over my shoulder as I paged through her binder. "Don't mess anything up. I've been planning this wedding for more than a year. If you mess it up I'm going to mess you up."

I wanted to remind her that she couldn't make fists so she had no way to mess me up, but now didn't seem the time. "You've been planning your wedding for a year?" My stomach somersaulted at the thought. "Why?"

"What do you mean?" Serafina was haughty. "A year is the bare minimum to plan the proper wedding. You need to think about caterers, a location, a minister, music, the perfect dress, which bridesmaids you want to reward and which ones you want to punish ... it's a lot of work."

It sounded like a lot of work. "And your girlfriend left everything for you to plan?" That didn't seem fair.

"Skylar is a man," Serafina shot back. "He's a very rich and powerful man."

I noticed she didn't say "sweet" or "handsome" when describing her intended. Heck, she didn't even say he was "loyal." That had to be on purpose. "Skylar and Serafina, huh? That sounds like a very milquetoast union."

Serafina openly glared at me. "Our napkins are beautiful thanks to the alliteration. I can't wait to use them."

"You can keep saying that all you want, but it's not going to change the fact that I don't have the power to bring you back," I said. "I'm sorry but ... you're dead. It's done. There is no reversal department."

Serafina's mouth dropped open as abject horror washed over her features. "That cannot be right. Do you have any idea how long I've been working toward this day? Heck, I snagged Skylar Worthington, for crying out loud. It's a big deal."

"Why is he so important?"

"Because his father owns the new skyscraper complex on the Detroit River."

That meant absolutely nothing to me. "So ... he's rich?"

"He's extraordinarily well to do," Serafina corrected. "Only crass individuals would say 'rich' like you just did."

"Yeah, well, I'm fine with being crass." I unconsciously flexed my left hand, the one that boasted my new engagement ring. I was still getting used to the weight even though Griffin had slipped it on my finger weeks before. It made sense to say yes when he proposed – my family looking on and smiling – but once the novelty wore off the terror took hold.

I had absolutely no idea how to plan a wedding.

I grew up with four brothers. My mother died when I was a teenager, long before things like this appeared on my radar screen, although she was back and straddling the line between human and wraith these days. She was possibly eating people, too, but that wasn't something to dwell on now. Sure, my best friend was diving in and planning the cake and shopping for dresses – he had the Bridezilla role down to a science – but I wasn't exactly certain what I should be doing.

"So where did you start when you decided it was time to plan your wedding?"

Serafina's expression was hard to read. I couldn't tell if she wanted to answer the question or strangle me with my winter scarf. Winters in Michigan are brutal, so the scarf was necessary. Serafina's attitude was not, even though I had a feeling she knew much more than I did about matters of marriage.

"I see you're wearing a ring," Serafina noted, inclining her chin toward my hand. "It's cute. Quaint, but cute."

I flicked my eyes to the ring and scowled. It was beautiful. Griffin Taylor, the man who gave it to me, did a bang-up job when he selected it. The ring was everything I ever wanted – solitary stone, platinum setting, not overbearing – and yet the idea of what came next was enough to freeze me in my tracks.

I was afraid ... and I had absolutely no one to admit it to.

"I can help you," Serafina offered. "If you spare me, I can help you."

"That's sweet, but I still don't have the power to save you." I flipped through her wedding binder. "What the heck is this?"

Serafina made an annoyed sound as she focused on the binder. "That's the seating arrangements for the reception."

"You have to do your own seating arrangements?" That sounded awful. "Why?"

"You can hire someone to do it if you have enough money ... ." Serafina broke off and surveyed my outfit, taking in my simple jeans and Ugg boots with mild distaste. "I'm guessing money will be an issue for you, so scratch that."

Was it? Would money be an issue? As Cormack Grimlock's only daughter, I didn't think that was true. We'd never really talked about it, though. Perhaps that was something I should do before making decisions. Except ... I was a grown woman. I should pay for my own wedding, right? Isn't the idea of expecting your father to pay for a big wedding old and antiquated?

Ugh. I'm so confused.

"Money isn't the issue," I gritted out. "Money is the least of my problems. It's ... this. How do you know to do this?"

Serafina's expression was blank. "What?"

"This!" I tapped the binder for emphasis. "You've got everything in here from the caterer to the decorator. You have different designers for the wedding dress and the bridesmaid dresses."

"Well, they're my friends, but I don't want them to look nearly as good as me," Serafina sniffed. "Trust me. That's non-negotiable. When it comes time to pick bridesmaid dresses, make sure they're ugly. Then tell everyone they're cute and they can wear them again. That's the only civilized thing to do."

That sounded fairly diabolical. "I don't even have female friends," I admitted. "How am I supposed to have bridesmaids if I have no friends?"

"You said money wasn't an issue." Serafina was in pragmatic mode. "I'm sure your father can pay someone to stand up for you."

"That sounds just ... lovely," I muttered. In truth, the only reason I let Serafina York start yapping in the first place was because I saw the wedding gown hanging on the back of the kitchen door. I needed someone to talk to, and while I was certain she was a total narcissistic nightmare within thirty seconds of her opening her mouth, that didn't change the fact that I was a bit lost. "I don't know how to do any of this."

"Tell me about your fiancé," Serafina prodded. "What is he like?"

I smiled at mention of Griffin, remembering the way his tousled hair accented his face when I rolled over to find him staring at me this morning. "He's perfect."

"No one is perfect," Serafina countered, dismissing my comment with a wave of her hand. "My Skylar is as close to perfect as possible, but he still has a third nipple."

I wrinkled my nose. "Excuse me?"

"It's true." Serafina bobbed her head. "He's pasty, pale, and has a third nipple. He's also sickly. And I'm pretty sure he's banging his secretary."

"How is that perfect?"

"He's rich."

Serafina's answer was so succinct and matter of fact that all I could do was shake my head. "Griffin is none of those things."

"Griffin Walters?" Serafina perked up. "Are you engaged to Griffin Walters?"

I had no idea who that was. "Taylor," I corrected.

"I've never heard of him," Serafina said. "Is he one of the Grosse Pointe Park Taylors?"

"He's a cop," I supplied, biting the inside of my cheek to keep from smirking when Serafina's face fell. "He's a police officer who doesn't make a lot of money and puts his life on the line every day. He also puts his life on the line for me because I always find trouble, but I've been good for weeks and we've decided not to talk about it."

"Oh, well, how great for you." Serafina was quickly losing interest in the conversation. "Why would you marry a cop?"

"Because I love him."

"Why else?"

Someone like Serafina would never understand true emotions, real love, but I gave it a shot anyway. "Because he's a good guy who listens when I talk, always tries to make me laugh, and never makes me feel bad when I do the girly thing and cry."

"I always cry to get my way," Serafina said. "If you want the perfect wedding, you'd better learn to cry so you can manipulate your father. You said he has money, right? You'll need it if you're marrying a cop. Start negotiating your future allowance now."

"I don't want the perfect wedding," I countered. "I just want a nice wedding. I don't want to screw it up. I'm not sure how to do that, though. I've never been the type of girl who dreams about a wedding."

"Why is that?" Serafina seemed legitimately curious.

"Because I never thought I'd find someone willing to put up with my lifestyle," I replied, opting for honesty. "Griffin actually accepts the fact that I am who I am, that my family is what it is, and he doesn't ever ask me to change. He deserves a nice wedding, right?"

"Honey, he's a cop." Serafina didn't bother hiding her disdain. "Give him a hot dog and a beer and call it a day. He'll probably be thrilled with that."

Sadly, I had a feeling she was right. Still ... I wanted the wedding to be pretty and memorable. I wanted it to be a day Griffin and I would always look back on and enjoy. That meant I had to make sure I didn't screw up things before the fact. That seemed out of my wheelhouse.

"So, where did we land on you calling the reversal team?" Serafina asked, her eyes bright.

I forced a smile for her benefit as I dug in my pocket for the scepter that would absorb her soul. "I wasn't lying about not being able to help you. Believe it or not, I'm sorry. I wish you'd lived to see your big day."

Serafina was positively apoplectic when she saw the scepter in my hand. "But ... I can't be dead. I'm young. I'm twenty-nine, for crying out loud."

"I thought you said you were twenty-five."

"I lied. Sue me."

I chewed my bottom lip to keep from laughing. "No harm, no foul. Continue."

"I can't die," Serafina lamented. "I'm not ready. I haven't gotten everything I wanted yet."

"There's no going back. I'm sorry."

Serafina heaved a sigh. "Can you at least tell me how I died? I deserve at least that."

"Sure." I smiled as I turned back to the iPad, momentarily wishing I'd kept my big mouth shut for a change. "Oh, well ... ."

"Was it a tragic heart condition?" Serafina looked hopeful. "That will read well in my obituary."

"No, your future mother-in-law slipped poison in your coffee creamer." I faked a bright smile. "Apparently she didn't think you were destined for happily ever after with her precious Skylar. It's over and done with, though. There's no reason to fret. Are you ready to go?"

I hoped I'd be able to slip that one by Serafina, but her screech told me otherwise.

"I knew that old bat hated me," Serafina bellowed. "I can't believe she murdered me!"

"Yes, well, we all have struggles. Come on now, you're going to a better place."

Serafina didn't look convinced. "I need to talk to your boss."

Yes, this is why I'm supposed to suck and run. Conversation – especially with belligerent spirits – is highly overrated.

❧ 2 ❧
TWO

"There's the love of my life."

Griffin, his shoulder-length brown hair tousled from the wind, was all smiles when he walked into the townhouse we shared – which was conveniently located next door to the one Aidan and Jerry shared – until he realized I was already in my fuzzy pajamas and thick socks.

"Perhaps I should call you the dark shadow over my heart today judging by that expression on your face, huh?" Griffin switched gears smoothly, shrugging out of his coat and hanging it in the hallway before grabbing the one I discarded on the chair at the edge of the living room an hour before and putting it away. "I believe we talked about you picking up after yourself, didn't we?"

I slanted my eyes so he could see I was agitated and held up my hands in front of the gas fireplace. "I hate winter."

"I can see you're in a wonderful mood." Griffin dropped a kiss on the top of my head before sitting next to me on the couch. "Do you want to tell me about it?"

We'd been together for months. I was comfortable sharing my feelings – or whatever dumb chick stuff I was supposed to do to make the relationship thrive – but I didn't think he'd take the admission that the idea of planning a wedding, of flipping through endless magazines and giggling over fabrics with Jerry, filled me with a lump of sick fear in the pit of my stomach, so I decided to be evasive.

"I made the mistake of talking to one of my charges today and it was a nightmare," I said, offering a petulant pout for his benefit. "She wouldn't shut up, and kept demanding to see the 'man in charge,' and I was almost late for my third job. Plus, the lady at the doughnut place on Main Street did not salt her front walk, and I fell."

"My poor baby." Griffin lifted my hand and pressed a kiss to the soft skin along the inside of my wrist. "At least you got a doughnut, right?"

"I did, but don't tell Jerry. If he finds out I went to another bakery he'll have a fit."

"Why did you go to another bakery?"

I went to another bakery because I didn't want to listen to Jerry gush about wedding plans. There was no way I could say that to Griffin, though, so I lied. "I wanted one of those chocolate cake doughnuts with sprinkles, and Jerry's sprinkles bug me."

"Oh, well, as long as you have a good reason." Griffin's hands were cold as he pressed them to my neck.

"Brr." I made a face. "That's another reason I hate winter. Don't you have gloves?"

"I do, but I forgot them on my desk."

"Well, remember them next time." I knew I was being unreasonable. It wasn't Griffin's fault that I was the worst girl in the history of girls and had no idea how to turn myself into a better bride-to-be. He wouldn't understand, and could very well get hurt if I wasn't careful. I wasn't lying when I told Serafina he was perfect. He was so perfect I couldn't figure out what he was doing with me. I generally have high self-esteem, so I wasn't sure what to make of my newfound self-loathing.

Griffin, ever calm, arched an eyebrow. I swear it mocked me. "Aisling, do you want to tell me what's really bothering you?"

I pasted an innocent expression on my face. "Nothing is bothering me. My life is perfect." I held up the ring he gave me for proof. "See."

"Yeah, well, I've known you long enough to realize you're lying,"

Griffin countered. "I can't help you unless you tell me what's wrong. And before you think of another lie I won't believe, remember that I love you and we promised to tell one another the truth. There's nothing you can tell me that I won't understand."

If I were a betting person I'd lay some heavy odds against exactly that. "I'm fine."

Griffin didn't look convinced. He stared at me long and hard, as if he was drilling for oil in my soul. Finally he exhaled heavily and shook his head. "Fine. What do you want for dinner?"

That's it? That couldn't be it. He never lets me slide that easily when he knows I'm being less than honest. Notice I didn't say "lying." I wasn't technically lying. I was merely skirting the truth. "I can eat anything."

"Yeah, we both know that's not true," Griffin said. "I'd rather not suggest Thai, have you agree to it, and then be forced to watch you make faces while you're eating Pad Thai. What do you want?"

I wanted to curl up on his lap, put all the wedding decisions in his hands so he'd get exactly what he wanted, and weep. I couldn't explain the feeling, but that's what I wanted. "Thai is fine."

Griffin narrowed his eyes. "Aisling, you're really pushing it. If you think I can't tell something is wrong you're deluding yourself. You're not fooling me, no matter how much you think you are. It's starting to get ridiculous."

Starting? Where had he been the past six weeks? "I'm ... ."

"If you say 'fine' we're going to have a fight. Now, I don't want a fight because it's cold and I'd prefer eating and cuddling in front of the fire all night. I will fight if it comes to it, though."

Oh, geez. He was going to make me say it.

"Are you having second thoughts about marrying me?" Griffin was calm when he asked the question, but I didn't miss the exaggerated way he swallowed as he waited for an answer.

"No," I replied hurriedly, fear crowding my heart. "I want to marry you. It's just ... ."

"What?"

"I don't know how to plan a wedding. I think I might be missing the girl gene that's supposed to know how to handle that. I'm pretty sure my chick pod is defective."

I expected an explosion after I blurted out the words, but Griffin's expression softened.

"Oh." Instead of yelling — or even giving me that disappointed look that he rarely whips out because he reserves it for special occasions — Griffin slipped his arm around my waist and tugged me so I was practically on his lap. "I see."

He was apparently feeling succinct. "Griffin ... ."

"It's okay." Griffin pressed a kiss to my cheek and rearranged us so we could lie comfortably on the couch, my head on his chest. He grabbed the afghan from the back of the couch and placed it over us. "Why didn't you tell me this was bothering you?"

"Because I can't tell you that."

"Why not? Just two days ago you told me that you were convinced the old guy who lives in the end unit was staring through the sliding glass doors because he wanted to see you naked."

"I haven't been proven wrong on that."

"He's mostly blind. He even has a service dog."

"That's why he has to get so close."

"I'm pretty sure he's also gay," Griffin said.

"Then perhaps he was looking at you instead of me." My voice hopped as my irrational anger came out to play.

"Calm down." Griffin stroked the back of my head, organizing my long dark hair – which was shot through with streaks of white because I wanted to look different from my brothers – and brushed his lips against my forehead. "You need to tell me these things so I can help you before I overreact to your overreaction and my head goes to a weird place."

I tilted my chin so my eyes locked with his. "Where did your head go?"

"I was pretty sure you thought you made a mistake when you agreed to marry me and were trying to find a graceful way out of it," Griffin replied. "I thought maybe you were going to break my heart."

"You can't be serious."

"I'm serious. I was a little worried. You've been acting like a nutball the past two weeks."

I let loose a groan. "That's because I don't know what to do. Am I supposed to talk to my father about money? Are we supposed to pay for it? Am I supposed to pay for it?"

"I don't know." Griffin chose his words carefully. "What do you want?"

"I want you to get everything you want for a change."

"Oh, baby ... ." Griffin's lips curved. "You don't have to kill yourself with preparations. We both need to get what we want out of this. It's not about one person."

"How do we do that?"

"Well, for starters, we need to talk about things," Griffin replied. "What kind of wedding do you want?"

"Honestly? I want to get naked on the beach and have it just be the two of us."

"I could live with that."

"But my father can't. Jerry can't. And my brothers? No matter how big and macho they pretend to be, they'd kill you if we slipped off and eloped."

"Good point." Griffin seemed more relaxed now that he knew what was really bothering me. I internally kicked myself for making him worry. That was the last thing I wanted. In fact, that was the thing I'd been working so hard to make sure didn't happen. "Do you want a big or small wedding?"

I answered immediately. "Small."

"We agree there. See, we're already rolling. Do you want to get married in a church?"

I tried to picture myself walking down an aisle, a steely-eyed priest staring me down as if he knew all of the dirty things Griffin and I did on a daily basis as nuns readied rulers to crack across my knuckles for untold transgressions. Yeah, in my fantasy every religion overlaps in weird and innovative ways. The answer to that was a big, fat no. I had no idea what Griffin wanted, though. "Do you?"

"I asked you first."

"Yeah, but ... I can't make a decision until I know what you want," I said. "I don't know how to explain it, but I keep having these panic attack nightmares where you show up for the wedding and then walk out because you didn't get what you wanted."

"Aisling, all I want is you."

"Then it seems like you're getting the short end of the stick. Although, you know what? I've never understood what that saying means. If I were getting the short end of the stick it would be something to cry about. From your perspective, I'd think you'd want to avoid the stick at all costs."

Griffin barked out a laugh, his entire body shaking. "Good grief. Is it any wonder that I love you the way I do? How could I be getting the short end of anything as long as I get to keep you for the rest of our lives?"

He made it sound so easy. I was dumbfounded by his relaxed nature. "Aren't you worried at all that I'm going to screw this up?"

"No. I'm worried you're going to make yourself sick over certain things, because that's your way. But I'm not worried you're going to ruin anything. I really wish you'd stop worrying about stuff like this."

I tilted my head to the side, considering. "I don't think I'm going to be able to tell you what I want until I know what you want."

"I don't like that idea, because, given your mood, I can already tell that you're going to give me whatever I want no matter if you want something else or not." Griffin fell silent, his hand busy as it rubbed my back. "I have an idea."

Griffin left me on the couch and shuffled into the kitchen, returning with a notebook and two pens. He started writing – concentrating for a long time – and then finally ripped off the sheet of paper he scrawled across and placed it on the coffee table.

"Can you think of any other immediate questions we need to tackle?"

I wasn't sure what he was getting at, so I peered around his shoulder and read the words. It was a list of questions regarding the wedding, including queries on venue, colors and food choices. "I'm not sure what we're doing."

Griffin ripped off another sheet of paper and handed it to me before carrying his notebook to the chair on the other side of the table and settling. "We're going to write the answers to the questions and then compare answers. This way we won't sway one another."

"What if we don't agree?"

"Then we'll talk about it and come to a compromise," Griffin replied. "I am not going to let you mold this entire wedding into what you think I want. This is supposed to be a beautiful day for both of us."

I studied the questions for a moment. I hated to admit it – mostly because it wasn't my idea – but it made sense. "Are you sure about this? We can do whatever you want."

"I'm sure that's the last thing I want," Griffin said. "Now, write down your answers. When we're done, we'll compare and talk about our choices. Whenever we have things to decide for the wedding, this is what we'll do."

It sounded rational. Er, well, kind of. "It's like a really important test that I haven't studied for," I muttered, clicking the pen so I could write. "I'm going to need food after this, just so you know. I'm already feeling weak."

"Read the last question," Griffin ordered, his eyes never drifting from his answers.

I did as he instructed, smirking when I saw it. "Oh, well ... ."

"Focus on your answers," Griffin ordered. "I want to see where we land. We can't move forward until we see how far apart we are."

I exhaled heavily through my nose and then focused on the questions, losing myself in my answers once I realized that no matter how hard I craned my neck I couldn't see what Griffin wrote. Once I was done, I shifted my eyes to Griffin. He sat quietly, his eyes expectant, and flashed a smile when he saw I had finished.

"Ready?"

I nodded.

Griffin moved over to the couch and sat beside me, collecting my paper and imitating a professor as he started. "Okay, so we both would prefer an outdoor wedding. No church."

I couldn't hide my relief. "Really?"

"You're really a bundle of nerves about this, aren't you?" Griffin was amused. "I'll rub you down later to relax you."

That sounded nice.

"We both want small weddings, with prime rib and chicken. I suggested adding salmon and you suggested adding lobster. If you want to spring for lobster, I think we'll have to bring your father in on this."

I pursed my lips. "Aren't I too old to expect my father to pay for a wedding?"

Griffin shook his head. "I think you'll hurt his feelings if you don't. It's up to you, though."

"I'll think about it."

"Good." Griffin smacked a quick kiss against my lips. "We both said summer for a wedding period, which is good. And as for flowers, you wrote lilies and I wrote 'Whatever you want.'"

I knitted my eyebrows. "That's not fair. I didn't know 'Whatever you want' was an option."

"Yes, well, I think flowers should be your choice," Griffin said. "I don't know flowers, and you'll be the one carrying a bouquet."

He had a point. "What about people to stand up with us?"

"What about it?"

"I don't have any female friends."

"Oh." Griffin snorted. "You really don't. It's kind of sad. You could have Jerry stand up for you."

"I can?" The suggestion was such a relief that I almost melted into a pool of goo on his lap. "You'd be okay with that?"

"Of course I would." Griffin tucked a strand of hair behind my ear. "He's your best friend. It wouldn't be right if he wasn't up there with you."

"But how will that work? Aren't we supposed to have even numbers of ushers and stuff?"

"Aisling, don't let this derail you," Griffin comforted. "We'll figure it out. I don't want you tying yourself in knots over this. Look at these lists." He shook them for emphasis. "They're mostly the same. You were freaking yourself out about nothing."

That was rich, coming from him. "You were freaking yourself out, too."

"Not nearly as much as you were."

"Whatever." I rested my head on his shoulder. Despite everything,

I really did feel much better. "I'm glad we did this. I feel ... more relaxed."

"I do, too." Griffin rested his cheek against my forehead. "We even said the same thing for dinner."

"We did? You want Middle Eastern food, too?"

"I do."

"Are you just saying that because you figured I wanted Middle Eastern food?"

"Not even close," Griffin replied. "I have a hankering for some hummus."

I pressed my lips together to keep from laughing, love swamping me for a moment when his eyes lit with amusement. "Thank you."

"Oh, Aisling, don't thank me." Griffin shifted the sheets of paper to the table and tugged me to him so he could hug me. "I get to marry you. Shouldn't that be thanks enough?"

"I know you have hearts in your eyes and stuff, but I'm still going to be me when we get married," I pointed out. "I'm difficult."

"Oh, baby, you idle at difficult." Griffin grinned when I pinched his flank. "Everything will be okay. You need to talk to me about these things before you get yourself worked up. It affects both of us."

He was right. I opened my mouth to tell him just that when the front door of the condo flew open and Jerry breezed in. He didn't shut the door behind him or offer up a greeting. Instead, he planted his hands on his hips and glared at me.

"You've been avoiding my calls all day, Bug, and I've had it," Jerry said. "I happen to know you were downtown and bought a doughnut from Mrs. Field's store this afternoon. Three different people saw you, and one said you had chocolate breath."

Griffin buried his face in my shoulder so Jerry wouldn't catch him laughing.

"I'm not going to yell at you for stress eating," Jerry continued. "You're going to be a bride. That's expected. We'll talk about diet options after the weekend."

I stilled. "I am not going on a diet."

"I said we'd talk about it later," Jerry barked. "As for the rest, I'm not going to take it personally. I think you're overwhelmed."

"I was overwhelmed, but Griffin and I talked about it," I said. "We've already made some decisions."

"Great. Good. Outstanding." Jerry waved his hands, impatient. "I think we need to start with the obvious purchase and go from there."

I had no idea what he was talking about. "What?"

"Your dress!" Jerry rolled his eyes. "The dress is the centerpiece of the wedding. We have to pick that first."

A dress. I'd been dreading that since Jerry started pulling out back issues of Bride magazine, forcing me to look at taffeta nightmares from three different decades. "Jerry ... ."

"We'll start tomorrow," Jerry announced. "Come over to our place for breakfast, and we'll leave right after."

That sounded like a terrible way to spend a day. "I have work."

"No, you don't. I called your father and he said you have the day off."

That's what happens when you work with family. They rat you out. "Jerry, I'm not sure that ... ."

"It's already decided." Jerry folded his arms over his chest, as if daring me to argue. "It's going to be a full day of shopping, so make sure you eat a lot. And get plenty of sleep. That means you can't keep her up with your wandering hands, Griffin. She needs to be fresh if we're going to find the perfect dress."

I expected Griffin to argue. Instead he merely smiled. "I promise to keep my hands to myself."

"Hey!" That was so not how I saw this evening going. "I thought we were going to play games in front of the fire."

"We'll figure something out." Griffin smiled at Jerry before lowering his voice. "If you think I'm going to fight your battles with Jerry you're very wrong. I love you and want this to be a perfect day, but where Jerry is concerned you're on your own."

That's exactly what I was afraid of.

THREE

"What do you think of this?"

Jerry lifted a wide white monstrosity – buckets of lace and sparkling rhinestones adorning the bodice – and held it in front of his slim hips.

"I think you would have to kill me to get me into that," I replied without hesitation. "The skirt on that thing is wider than I am tall."

Jerry made a face as he returned the dress to the rack. "It's a bell hoop. They're making a comeback."

"If that's supposed to mean something you missed your mark." I ran my fingers over a nearby dress, frowning when I imagined wearing it.

"Do you like that one?" Jerry was hopeful.

"I'm pretty sure I'd feel as if I was choking if I put it on," I said. "In fact, for all we know the dress is possessed and it really would choke me because it knows I'm a filthy harlot."

"Oh, well, it's good to know you're not freaking out or anything," Jerry drawled. "Since when did you start thinking of yourself as a dirty harlot?"

"In the bathtub last night. There were scented bubbles."

"When else?"

"Every day since I started noticing wedding dresses," I admitted, rolling my neck as I stepped to a different rack. "Have you ever noticed how white they are?"

"Have I ever noticed how white wedding dresses are? Yeah. They've written songs about it. What's your deal? You'll look great in white. You have the perfect coloring for white, by the way. You're going to look like an angel."

"But I'm not an angel. That's my problem. The dresses are too white. They make me feel ... weird."

"Oh, geez." Jerry made an exaggerated face as he joined me at the rack. "I think you're freaking yourself out about this for no good reason. Why?"

"I don't know."

"You know."

"I really don't." I didn't. I felt better after Griffin and I talked the previous night, but the feeling lasted only until Jerry forced me into a Royal Oak wedding boutique on the city's kitschiest street. "Have you ever considered I'm not good enough for Griffin?"

"No." Jerry answered without hesitation. "You haven't considered it either. Not really."

"I'm considering it right now. The white dress makes me feel ... flawed."

"Oh, shut up, Bug," Jerry groused. "You're the least insecure person I know. You're happy with Griffin. He's happy with you. Something else is going on here."

"Yes. I'm not good enough for him."

"That's not it." Jerry tapped his bottom lip as he regarded me with overt irritation. "Oh, I know what it is."

He said it as if he honestly did know, but I had my doubts. "What is it then?"

"You're worried about the reaper stuff."

I glanced around to make sure no one was eavesdropping and pinched Jerry for good measure when I assured myself that the family reaping secret remained intact. "Say it a little louder," I hissed. "I don't think that Stepford wife and *Twilight* teen temptation over there heard you."

Jerry leaned to his right so he could gaze around me and focus on the women shopping on the other side of the store. "Okay, I get the Stepford comment. That woman has so much product in her hair she looks as if she's wearing a helmet."

"Thank you."

"What's the deal with the *Twilight* comment, though? I happen to love those books, and that girl looks absolutely nothing like Bella. Besides that, she's clearly not a teenager. She looks young, but she's shopping for a wedding dress. I think that denotes that she's at least eighteen."

"Not if she's knocked up and her parents signed a waiver."

Jerry pursed his lips and folded his arms across his chest, waiting.

"Fine." I scalded him with a dark look. "She's not a teenager. She looks the type, though."

"What type?"

"The type who will feel at home in a white dress and not worry that she's totally ruining an innocent man's life."

"Oh, well, here we go." Jerry led me to a set of chairs in the middle of the store, pushing me into one before settling next to me. "Talk."

"Fine. I'm not a harlot."

"I know that. Before Griffin I worried you'd ultimately opt to become a nun. I thought whoever your next conquest was might find cobwebs down there."

"Ha, ha." Jerry always made me laugh. Today I didn't seem to have the energy to give in and embrace the surreal. "I'm not a harlot, but I'm worried that Griffin deserves better."

"You've said that twice now and it's ticked me off each time," Jerry snapped. "Griffin doesn't want any of the hundreds of people he could have who are better than you. Wait ... that came out wrong. What I mean is that you're what he wants and he seems to be happy with the total package. Before he proposed, you were happy with the total package, too. What's your damage?"

"It's not me. I know I'm delightful and men everywhere should fall at my feet and tell me so."

Jerry snorted. "So what is it?"

"The reaping thing."

Jerry turned slowly, his face a mask of "I told you so" triumph. "What do you mean?"

"I've almost died four or five times since Griffin and I met," I reminded him. "I keep finding trouble even though I'm not looking for it."

Jerry arched a challenging eyebrow.

"Hey, I've only been looking for trouble like three times when I almost died. It finds me whether or not I'm looking."

Realization washed over Jerry's face. "And you think that Griffin is in danger because of all of this stuff and you want to save him from it, so you're telling yourself you're wrong for him as some sort of penance. Do I pretty much have that right?"

Sadly, he was very close. "If something ever happens to Griffin because of me ... ." I left the sentence hanging because it was too terrible to finish.

"Well, it's too late for that, Bug," Jerry said, remaining calm despite the fury in my eyes. "If that was really a concern you would've sent him on his way after you got down and dirty a few times. You couldn't, so ... it's done."

"But ... ."

"No." Jerry made a clucking sound with his tongue. "It's too late to turn back. No matter what you're feeling, I know you. You wouldn't want to turn back anyway. You love Griffin."

"I do love him. That's why I don't want him to die."

"He doesn't want you to die either, and there's no way you'll ever shake him now," Jerry said. "The thing is, Bug, you both have dangerous jobs. He's a detective with the Detroit Police Department, pretty much one of the most violent cities in the country. You're a reaper. You have wraiths coming after you at every turn and crazy freaks dropping out of mirrors to get you. You don't live normal lives."

"Doesn't he deserve a normal life?"

"Don't you think you should've thought about that before he proposed?"

Jerry had a point, but I couldn't shake the worry weighing heavily on my shoulders. "I love him. I don't want to give him up."

"That's good, because he's not going to let you. He's smart enough to realize when you're being a schmuck. But don't ever tell him I said that."

I snickered. I couldn't help myself. "Your secret is safe with me."

"You two are now officially stuck, Bug," Jerry said. "You love each other. You hurt when he hurts. He suffers when you suffer. For better or worse, your lives are already forever joined. The wedding is just a formality at this point."

He was right. Fighting it was silly. "I won't ever recover if something happens to him."

"He won't ever recover if something happens to you."

I pressed the heel of my hand to my forehead and sucked in a breath. "I guess that means we'll have to work overtime to make sure nothing happens to either of us, huh?"

"That would be nice." Jerry squeezed my shoulder. "Now, it's time to try on some dresses." He was back to business. "What kind of dress do you want?"

He wasn't going to like the answer, but after last night I knew telling the truth was important. "I want something simple."

Jerry groaned. "Simple? Are you trying to kill me?"

"Simple," I repeated. "If it didn't look too white I'd be happy, too. I'm not joking about the whites being too ... white."

"Oh, geez." Jerry pinched the bridge of his nose. "You're going to be the most difficult bride ever, aren't you?"

He had no idea. "Did I tell you that I want a blue cake?"

"Shoot me now."

"WHAT DO YOU THINK?"

After two hours I found only one dress I even remotely liked, and it wasn't something I'd spend money on. Still, Jerry was desperate for me to try on a dress, so I felt I needed to do it for his sake. He was about to swim a lap in the crazy pool if I didn't try on something.

I thought he'd laugh, make fun of my taste or maybe even dive beneath a dress rack to hide his eyes from my hideous selection. Instead I found him sniffling, tears threatening to course down his cheeks.

"Don't you dare," I warned, extending a finger. "If you cry, I'll punch you in the nuts."

Jerry sucked in a steadying breath, but the shimmer in his eyes remained.

"Oh, come on." I turned to look at myself in the mirror, finding I didn't hate the way I looked nearly as much as I'd thought I would. "Hmm."

The quiet moment didn't last long. When I lifted my head I saw the devil's reflection staring back at me from the spot next to Jerry before she even opened her mouth.

"Well, well, well. What do we have here?" Angelina Davenport had a smug smile on her face as she leaned back on her heels and rocked. "Are you two finally admitting that no one else will ever have you and settling for a marriage of convenience? I have to say, I called this in tenth grade."

I narrowed my eyes, debating whether I could jump on her without ripping a dress I didn't want to buy. I didn't get a chance to find out because Jerry was already on the attack.

"I can't believe they even let you in here," Jerry seethed. "I would have thought your foul stench would cause them to force you out of the building for fear of ruining the dresses with that crab odor you always expel."

"Oh, bite me."

"I've already had my flea bath for the week."

I considered telling Jerry that particular burn reflected as poorly on him as Angelina, but there didn't seem to be a need to make the situation worse. Instead, I gathered up the dress fabric and stepped down from the three-way mirror platform so I could meet my arch nemesis – and, no, I'm not being remotely dramatic – on even footing.

"Did you come in here to rub your face against the dresses and dream of a world where a man wouldn't rather cut off his hand than touch you?" I asked, going for Angelina's tender spot right off the bat. "Is your purse full of Kleenex? We certainly know your ass is full of lard, so one would seemingly go with the other."

Angelina rolled her eyes. "That didn't even make sense."

"I don't know. I managed to call you a lard-ass and make fun of the fact that men hate you in one sentence. I consider it a win."

"But what does my purse being full of Kleenex have to do with my ass being full of lard?"

Crap! I hate it when she has a point. "What are you even doing here? Oh, wait, let me guess. You're following women around in an effort to trip them so you can move in on their broken-hearted soul mates after the fact. I'm close, right?"

"I'm here to pick up a veil for a client." Angelina bobbed her head in a haughty manner. "At least I have a legitimate reason to be here. Why are you here?"

"Cillian is getting married and we're picking out bridesmaid dresses." It was a low blow. My brother Cillian dated Angelina for a time – until she cheated on him – but she remained hung up on him as he tried to put the shame of ever touching her behind him. "We're all looking forward to the big day."

The jab hit hard and true, and for a moment, Angelina's face slackened. Then she realized she wasn't nearly as slow as I pegged her to be and gestured toward the dress I wore. "You're wearing a wedding dress to your brother's wedding? Did I slip into an inbreeding wormhole when I wasn't looking?"

I had to give her credit for the wormhole reference – however grudgingly – but the inbreeding joke made me want to kick her in the vagina while simultaneously punching her in the boob. What? She's horrible. She has it coming.

"I saw the dress and wanted to try it on. It's no big deal."

"No, it's a really big deal," Jerry corrected, shooting me a hard look. "Aisling is the one getting married."

Whatever she was expecting, that wasn't it. When hearing about my good fortune, Angelina's features twisted even harder than they did when faced with the thought of losing Cillian forever. "You're getting married?"

I nodded. "I am."

"Show her the ring," Jerry prodded. "That will make her green with envy instead of puke for a change."

Angelina shot Jerry a withering look. "What does that even mean?

Am I green because I want to puke or because someone else puked on me?"

Jerry looked to me for help, but all I could do was shrug. "I want to argue with her because she's Angelina, but our insults haven't been great today. I blame the dress."

"Don't blame the dress," Jerry hissed. "It can hear you. You don't want to hurt its feelings before the big day."

"Jerry, I'm not buying this dress. It's the closest to what I like, but it's still too frilly." I tugged on the fancy skirt. "I want something simple."

"That's what your fiancé probably said when he proposed, huh?" Angelina's eyes gleamed. "Who's the lucky fellow? Let me guess; did you find a bum on the street and bribe him to get your father off your back? I'll bet your father is thrilled to get you out from under foot."

"She's engaged to Griffin, you ninny," Jerry snapped. "You know very well who she's engaged to."

"Seriously? He proposed?" Angelina didn't look happy with the tidbit. "I guess I should be surprised, but he seems to have legitimately fallen under your spell. How did you do it? Did your brothers threaten him? Did you father bribe him? It probably cost a pretty penny, but I'll bet that's what happened. Your father came up with a dowry to make sure he wouldn't be responsible for taking care of you forever, right?"

"Actually, I bribed him myself," I retorted. "It only took sex and a lollipop."

Jerry cringed. "That was worse than mine, Bug."

He was right. Seriously, I was totally off my game today. Most days I can make tossing zingers in Angelina's direction look effortless. Today, though, I clearly had other things on my mind.

"Yes, well, I have what I came for." Angelina held up a small garment bag by way of proof. "I have better things to do than hang around with you losers. In fact, I have a very important meeting. I should be going."

"Wait, we haven't come up with any good insults yet," Jerry groused. "You can't leave."

"Write them down and have them ready for next time," Angelina suggested, cackling to herself as she swept toward the front door.

"Don't worry, Aisling. I'm sure Griffin will realize his mistake before the wedding. If he doesn't, I'll be on the lookout to make him feel better after the wedding."

I knew exactly what she meant by the insult, but she was already gone before I could think of a quip. "Son of a ... !"

"Maybe we need some sugar or something," Jerry suggested. "I'm sure we'll think of loads of things to insult her with once we're riding high on mocha frappes."

I'd had worse offers. "Okay, but I have to get out of this dress. I can't believe she beat both of us. It must be a full moon or something."

"Not for a couple days. What? You know I keep track of that stuff. Astrology is more than just magic in paragraph form."

I heaved a sigh. "We definitely need sugar."

"We'll get some of those cake pops, too."

The day was already looking up. "Just let me change."

4

FOUR

"Stop pouting, Bug. You'll get her next time."

An hour later, Jerry and I sat at a window booth in one of our favorite coffee shops as he flipped through a bridal magazine and I stewed about the lame insults I came up with when faced with Angelina's stupid face.

"I usually get her every time," I pointed out, gripping my coffee mug tighter as I stared into it. "Do you think I'm slipping?"

"I think you have a lot on your mind and you need to talk to Griffin about it." Jerry kept one ear on the conversation but was clearly more interested in the magazine. "He'll want to know what you're feeling."

"I can't tell him what I'm feeling," I scoffed. "He'll get angry and yell."

"He always gets angry and yells."

"Yes, but this time it won't be funny or sexy, because it will hurt his feelings," I pointed out. "That's the last thing I want to do."

"Bug, I've decided you're panicking because you need something to do," Jerry said after a moment. "It's been a quiet six weeks. Ever since you ended that mirror monster thing and recovered from your injuries, it's been calm. The only thing you've had to focus on is the fact that Griffin proposed.

"The problem is, you're convinced something else bad is going to happen and you can't seem to stop yourself from focusing on that," he continued. "That means you're creating scenarios in your head that aren't going to happen."

I sipped my coffee and stared, unblinking.

"Stop doing that," Jerry muttered, averting his gaze. "You know I hate it when you do that."

I did know that. When people don't blink it freaks him out. He's convinced that's one way to recognize the oncoming zombie apocalypse. We're both still waiting for that, by the way. We've upped our planning a great deal.

"I'm not creating scenarios," I said, batting my eyelashes before holding open my eyes again, taking perverse pleasure when Jerry involuntarily shuddered. "The odds of me making it through the next ... um, let's say month ... without getting attacked are pretty slim. I can't help wondering if Griffin deserves a better life than what I can give him."

"Oh, stuff it." Jerry made a disgusted sound in the back of his throat as he turned back to the magazine. "You're a drama queen. Has anyone ever told you that?"

My eyebrows migrated up my forehead. "Excuse me?"

"You heard what I said." Jerry refused to back down. "You're a complete and total drama queen, and you make me look rational and sane."

"I think that's the most ridiculous thing you've ever said to me," I shot back, tapping an anxious finger on the table. "By the way, you once told me that you dreamed of being the next Dolly Parton and moving to Nashville so you can live in the Grand Ole Opry. I still think that is the most ridiculous thing you've ever told me."

"Hey!" Jerry extended a warning finger. "I still maintain that's a viable life choice."

"You can't sing."

"I sing like an angel."

"You can't play an instrument."

"I can learn."

"Well, I doubt very much they have anything like the Fox Theatre in Nashville," I snapped.

"I could live without that," Jerry said, his eyes flashing with impatience. "I didn't move to Nashville because I didn't want to be away from you."

My irritation flagged as warmth washed over me. "Oh, that's kind of sweet."

"That was before I knew you were crazy and trying to sabotage your own happy ending," Jerry said, his expression serious. "I'm not joking, Bug. You need to tell Griffin why you're worried – and I will check to make sure you've told him the whole truth, so don't even think of doing one of those half-lie things you're so fond of – because he's better than me these days at talking you down from a ledge."

There was truth in Jerry's words, but it was obviously hard for him to admit it. I impulsively reached over and grabbed his hand. "You'll always be the best one at talking me off a ledge. You're so good at it you should be able to list it under 'special skills' on your résumé."

"Thank you, Bug."

I returned his heartfelt smile. "I'm not telling Griffin what I'm worried about, by the way. That will upset him, and I hate upsetting."

Jerry's smile slipped. "Oh, you're going to tell him. If you don't, I'll tell him. I'll get extra points for being his hero and everything, because he thinks I always take your side."

"You do always take my side," I huffed. "That's why you're my best friend."

"No, I'm your best friend because I always try to do what's right for you," Jerry countered. "What's right for you is to be with Griffin. You're happy with him, content. He makes you smile. Heck, he makes you giggle. You've never been a giggler even though I tried for years to transform you into a girl's girl. It's nice to see that when you're with him."

I opened my mouth to protest, but Jerry silenced me with a look.

"I'll tell him because it's the best thing for you," Jerry continued. "You need to get it off your chest. You told him about your wedding fears yesterday – that he would somehow be unhappy with your choices – and you're already over that. You'll be over the fear factor of your job just as quickly if you tell him what you're feeling."

Part of me believed Jerry's assertion. The other part clung to the doubts fueling me. "If you tell him, I'll wrestle you down and give you a swirly."

Jerry didn't so much as blink. "If you try, I'll pick out your wedding dress myself and it'll be nothing but ruffles and lace. Scratchy lace, to boot."

"That's just mean."

"I'm feeling mean," Jerry said. "I don't want you to ruin this, Bug. Griffin loves you. I get being afraid that something is due to happen with your job. Something always happens with your job, for crying out loud. Don't let it overtake your life. I don't like it. I want you happy."

I contemplated what he said, draining the rest of my coffee and considered ordering another – they were seven hundred calories each, and despite what I'd said about watching my weight, I didn't think it would hurt to cut back on a few daily calories – when I caught a flash of violent pink through the window. I turned in that direction, mildly curious about who would purposely wear that color, and frowned when I saw Angelina strolling by. The pink was from one of the shopping bags she carried.

"Well, well, well," I muttered, slanting my eyes as I watched her head toward the kitschy voodoo shop across the way. "Perhaps we haven't lost out on our chance to land a few solid zingers on Angelina after all."

Jerry followed my gaze, blasé. "She went into the voodoo shop."

"I noticed. She's probably buying dolls that look exactly like us."

Jerry's eyes widened. "Do you think that's really a thing?"

"Probably not," I conceded, "but it might be cool if that's what she was doing."

"I don't think it would be cool to have a witch like Angelina sticking needles in my chest."

"It would be a doll that looked like you, not you. You wouldn't feel anything."

"Um ... I think that goes against the very tenets of voodoo."

I'd actually done a bit of research on voodoo at one point – mostly because I was curious about various religions because of my job, and I'd yet to cross a voodoo practitioner – and I figured I should explain that the doll wasn't really a big part of the voodoo faith. A religious history lesson sounded more boring than anything else at the present moment, though, especially since the sugar was kicking my system into overdrive.

"Let's go over there," I suggested.

Jerry wasn't nearly as excited by the prospect. "Why?"

"Because I want to get back on the right insulting track. I have a reputation to uphold."

"But ... it's cold out." Jerry adopted a whining tone. "Do you really hate Angelina enough to bundle up, cross the street and go into a voodoo shop just to mess with her?"

"Did you just meet me?"

Jerry stared me down for a long time before heaving a resigned sigh. "Fine. I'll go with you if you agree to tell Griffin what's worrying you."

Wait ... he was blackmailing me? "I just said ... ."

Jerry cut me off with a wave of his hand. "Those are my terms."

"Fine." I forced out the word even though I wanted to kick him. "I'll tell Griffin what worries me. Will that make you happy?"

"For the moment." Jerry tossed a tip on the table and grabbed the magazine before standing. "I won't truly be happy until you're married and I know you won't do anything dramatic to torpedo yourself. But this is a nice start."

"Whatever." I theatrically threw my scarf around my neck, hitting Jerry in the face with the end of it as I headed toward the door. "I'm going to make Angelina cry before the day is out. I promise you that."

"I have absolutely no doubt."

JERRY AND I WERE careful as we let ourselves into Voodoo Vacation, a colorful shop with shrunken heads in the window and a flamboyant middle-aged woman behind the counter. I cast a quick look around the shop searching for Angelina, but I didn't immediately see her. The shop was big enough that it boasted three rooms, so that wasn't a surprise.

The woman behind the counter had light brown eyes – they were almost gold – and caramel skin. Her hair was completely covered by a bright satin scarf, and she wore an ankle-length skirt and white peasant blouse as she fixed me with a bright smile. She looked to be in her fifties – maybe even sixties – but her skin was smooth despite the age reflected in her eyes.

"We're just looking around," I answered automatically.

"Actually, we're looking for dolls so we can stick pins in them," Jerry corrected, beaming at the store clerk as he immediately headed in her direction. "We have a lot of enemies and it would be easier to torture them from the safety of our homes than venture out when the weather is cold."

Instead of being offended, the woman let loose with a sparkling laugh. "I think we might be able to arrange something. I'm Madame Dauphine. Welcome to my shop."

I cocked an eyebrow, genuinely amused. "Dauphine, huh?"

She nodded. "That is correct."

"It's a lovely name," Jerry enthused. "Do you have potions here? Can I curse people with potions if they do something I don't want?" He spared a quick glance for me. "I'm not talking about you, Bug."

"Whatever." I skirted around the front display shelf, casting a sidelong look at the pretty pottery but keeping my attention on Dauphine. "It's an interesting name. A dauphine is the wife of the heir to the French throne, right?"

Dauphine nodded. "Yes."

"It's also a street in New Orleans," I added. "I read about it when I researched Marie Laveau's history. Her father reportedly lived on it, which I believe means she lived on it for a time if I'm not mistaken."

Madame Dauphine beamed. "Tres bon! It's not often that I find someone in this area who knows anything about New Orleans history."

"I happen to have a unique interest in religion," I supplied. "I like learning about all of them."

"And which do you practice?"

"I'm kind of lapsed."

"From what?"

It seemed like a dangerous question to answer given the circumstances. "Just lapsed." I forced a smile as I circled a small display shelf. "Someone came in here a few minutes ago ... tall woman, long hair, a face that only a mother could love. Do you know where she went?"

"It's not my job to babysit customers," Dauphine replied. "She'll show up when she's ready."

Hmm. That was an interesting way of looking at things. "Well, I guess we can wait for her outside." Dauphine's presence made me uncomfortable. She wasn't the only "madame" in town with the ability to do that. She made Madame Maxine look downright friendly, though, and there was something about Dauphine and the way she carried herself that set my teeth on edge.

"You don't have to leave," Dauphine countered, tapping her long fingernails on the counter. Jerry, bless his heart, remained oblivious to the tension roiling between us. He was much more interested in the potions he perused. "In fact, I've been searching for a way to introduce myself to you."

"Oh, really?" I arched a challenging eyebrow. The woman was good at unnerving people, but I grew up with four brothers and prided myself on the fact that I could derange strangers in five minutes flat. She was no match for me. "That's ... interesting. Why is that?"

"Because you straddle two worlds, like myself, and I'm always looking for others who can see death and walk beside it."

I stilled, her words washing over me like a cool breeze in sub-zero temperatures and causing me to involuntarily shudder. "Excuse me?"

"You peddle in death," Dauphine noted. "I do, too. I have for a very long time."

There was something about her voice, the way she carried herself, that had me flashing to Marie Laveau. I'd seen photographs and depictions in the various books I'd read when I resigned myself that I would have to join the family reaping business. This woman was doing a fantastic impersonation of the television variety, not reality.

"I see. So ... you believe in all this?" I held up a pair of odd-looking sticks and made a face. "What are these?"

"Chicken feet."

"Gross." I hurriedly dropped the feet where I found them and moved forward enough to search the room to the left. It was empty. No sign of Angelina. "What was I saying?"

"You were asking if I believe in voodoo." Dauphine's smile was eerie as she watched me move to the room at the right and scan it. "You're the only ones here."

"Yes, but we saw Angelina Davenport come inside," I argued. "She didn't leave. We were watching the front door the entire time."

"Perhaps I have more than one door," Dauphine suggested. "Perhaps your friend was merely picking up an order she already placed and didn't have time to waste talking about ... perception and religion."

Dauphine had a way of talking down to me that grated. I was sure Angelina would enjoy it – she often talked the same way, after all – but it made me want to start throwing punches.

"Well, in that case, we really should be on our way." I turned to Jerry, but he didn't so much as glance in my direction. "We need to go."

"Just a minute, Bug. She has love potions ... and money potions ... and potions to make people you don't like itchy."

Oh, well, that was interesting. "Grab one of those itchy ones. I want to use it next time my brothers get full of themselves."

"I already grabbed four of them."

"Good thinking." I kept my gaze focused on Dauphine. She studied me with undisguised interest. "Is there something you need?"

"I believe you came in here because there's something you need," she countered. "You're at a crossroads in your life and you have questions. I have answers. Although, you might not be ready for them."

"You're good." I wagged a finger, my heart rate speeding up. I had to give Dauphine credit. She was excellent at manipulating people. I wasn't sure how she was capable of reading people the way she was, but it was unnerving. "Why was Angelina in here?"

"I really cannot say," Dauphine replied. "Everyone is entitled to privacy, are they not?"

"Not Angelina." I shook my head. "She's evil."

"She's something other than evil," Dauphine corrected. "She's neither good nor evil. Most people aren't one thing. They are many."

"I'm good," Jerry said, raising his hand to get Dauphine's attention. "I'm so good I should have a halo and wings."

Dauphine beamed at him. "You truly do have a giving soul. There is no doubt about that." She flicked her eyes back to me. "Your friend is more ... ambivalent ... about things like that. She bounces back and forth between beliefs and philosophies."

Jerry stared at Dauphine for a beat and then shook his head. "No. She's good. She's just good in a different way. She's good with minor lapses into evil."

Dauphine smiled. "That's an interesting way of looking at it."

"I like to think outside the box." Jerry carried his cache of potions to the counter. "Now, talk to me about voodoo dolls. I want, like, ten of them."

Dauphine widened her eyes. "Ten? How can a good person attract so much negativity?"

Jerry wasn't bothered by the question. "Just lucky, I guess. We should get to it. We have more wedding dress shopping to get to this afternoon."

I groaned at the words, flicking my eyes to the window at the front of the store. A light snow fell outside, leaving me feeling bereft and longing for spring. "I thought we were done dress shopping today."

"You're not done until the dress finds you," Dauphine said. "If you want the marriage to work, you need the perfect dress, right?"

Jerry snorted before I had a chance to answer. "She'll be fine whether or not she finds the perfect dress. The perfect dress is for me. Everything else – the marriage and love – is them. They'll be fine."

"You seem pretty sure about that."

"Sometimes you recognize power when you see it," Jerry said. "I don't know how to explain it, but it happens. There is power in love, and when you see it you want it."

"It is always illuminating when you recognize power in others." Dauphine's gaze was weighted as it landed on me.

"Aisling and Griffin are powerful when they're together," Jerry said. "That's how I know they'll love each other forever."

It was a simple and sweet sentiment, and I was going to tell him as much, but Jerry opened his mouth again and ruined the spell.

"I need a book that tells me how to curse people I don't like, too," Jerry added. "There's this woman at work who is driving me crazy. I would love to make her hair fall out."

Dauphine stared blankly at Jerry. "I see."

"Move." Jerry made small shooing motions with his hands. "We don't have all day." He flicked a glance to me. "Sheesh. Can you believe this?"

I really couldn't. "Hurry up," I said finally. "I want to get out of here and grab more coffee." I had no idea why, but Dauphine's mere presence made me uncomfortable. There was something about her, something almost familiar, and yet I was sure I'd never met her before.

"I'm on it." Jerry tapped his fingers to prod Dauphine to move faster. "You have to try on another dress at the other store, though. It's only fair, and I'll whine if you don't."

I would do just about anything to get out of this store. I grew more uncomfortable with each passing second. "Consider it done."

FIVE

Griffin suggested a nice evening out – romantic dinner and a walk through the fresh snow – so I spent the afternoon at Jerry's bakery while I waited for him to join us. Griffin loved snow, but I couldn't figure out why. Thankfully, we didn't get too much of it in southeastern Michigan, and we were only a month from spring.

I was going to make it. I was almost sure of it.

Jerry worked diligently behind the counter, smiling at his customers and sketching out flamboyant cake ideas for interested parties while I munched on cookies and mainlined caffeine. By the time Griffin showed up, I was practically bouncing off the walls.

"Hey." Griffin didn't seem to be in a hurry when he dropped a kiss on my forehead and took the seat across from me. "How was your day? Find a dress?"

"She didn't, and she was a total monster," Jerry answered for me, pouring a mug of coffee for Griffin before delivering it to the table. "She's agitated."

Griffin studied Jerry for a long moment before focusing on me. "I thought we talked about this."

"We did." I scorched Jerry with a warning look before continuing. "But picking out a dress is a big deal, and I don't want anything overly fancy. Every single thing we looked at was covered in lace. Oh, and there was one covered in rhinestones."

"That dress was fabulous," Jerry argued. "I thought you looked like a princess."

And therein was the problem. "Jerry, I know you have a prince fetish, but I never wanted to be a princess."

"You wanted to be Princess Leia."

"That doesn't count. She kicked ass."

"And she looked pretty – and sometimes even fancy – while doing it," Jerry said. "Why can't you be that kind of princess?"

Jerry's probably thought that was a simple question. For me, it was something else entirely. "Whatever."

Griffin's face lit with amusement as he sipped his coffee and leaned back in his chair. He was used to Jerry's antics, and often found them funny. He also found Jerry's theatrics tedious at times, but this was clearly not one of them. "Have you considered sitting down with a designer, explaining what you want, and having something made just for you?"

I shifted on my chair, surprised. "No."

"Why not?"

"Because I assume that's expensive."

"Okay, well ... ." Griffin didn't finish the sentence, his mind clearly busy as he debated the best way to address the big pink elephant – decked out in a wedding dress, of all things – circling the room. Luckily for him, he didn't have to voice the question. Jerry was more than willing to do it for him.

"Why do you care if it's expensive?" Jerry challenged. "Your father will pay for it."

I clamped my teeth together and focused on a spot over Jerry's shoulder.

"She doesn't know if she wants to ask her father for money when it comes to the wedding," Griffin supplied. "She's ... struggling ... with the idea."

Jerry was appalled. "Why? He's your father. He's also rich. He won't care about the money."

I was fairly certain that was true. "Shouldn't I care about the money?"

"I have no idea," Jerry replied. "Last time I checked, it was customary for the father to pay for the wedding if he's able. News flash, Bug, your father has more than enough money to not only make you look like a princess on your wedding day but actually bribe someone to make you a real princess."

"But ... ."

"No." Jerry extended a finger and wagged it in my face. "Don't make me go around you and tell your father what you're thinking. He won't be happy, and I won't feel even a little bit guilty for telling on you if I have to."

"I hate to agree with Jerry, Aisling, but I think you're going to hurt your father's feelings if you don't involve him in the process," Griffin added. "You're his only daughter. It's not as if he's going to go broke paying for weddings."

"Listen to Griffin," Jerry ordered. "He's wise and he knows what he's talking about."

Well, great. There's nothing I like better than being ganged up on. "I'll think about it." I dragged a hand through my hair. The idea of sitting down with my father and talking about wedding plans filled me with a dread I hadn't felt in ... well, since a mirror monster started stalking me and put me in the hospital. Perhaps that wasn't the best comparison.

"Speaking of things that we need to talk about," Jerry hinted.

Crap! He was going to make things even worse. "Are you ready for dinner?" I asked Griffin, pasting a bright smile on my face. "I thought we could get Italian. That's your favorite, and it sounds really good on a cold night like this."

Griffin's a police detective, so he's good at reading people. We met over a dead body, in fact. I lied and he figured out I was lying with minimal effort. That's one of my least favorite things about him. The look he gave me now was one of mild contempt.

"What's going on?" Griffin asked. "Did something happen today?"

"It did," I confirmed, bobbing my head. "We ran into Angelina, and my insults were terrible. I was embarrassed by some of them."

"Yeah, that wasn't a highlight of our afternoon," Jerry agreed. "But that's not what I was talking about."

"What were you talking about?" Griffin asked, his voice calm even though I sensed the danger lurking beneath his quiet veneer.

"We went to a voodoo shop," I said, desperate to turn the conversation. "The woman who owns it acted weird, and Jerry bought a bunch of curses and voodoo dolls."

"Great. I can't wait to see them." The smile Griffin shot in my direction promised mayhem. "What is Jerry specifically talking about, though? I doubt very much it has anything to do with your stop at that voodoo store, which has been the source of several complaints over the past few weeks, by the way."

Oh, well, that was interesting. I'd much rather focus on that. "Is she a con artist? I'm betting she's a con artist."

"Don't." Griffin flicked his eyes to Jerry. "Tell me what's going on."

"I'm sorry, Bug." Jerry mustered a chagrined smile. "You're going to be angry, but I warned you I was going to tell him. When you take your revenge, remember I'm your best friend and I love you."

"I really hate you right now," I muttered, staring at the table.

"I love you dearly." Jerry patted my shoulder as a form of solace and then immediately opened his big mouth as he locked gazes with Griffin. "Aisling is worried that you deserve better than her because she keeps attracting trouble. I told her she was being ridiculous, but she won't listen.

"The thing is, she has attracted a decent amount of trouble over the past year, but I honestly don't think it's her fault," he continued. "She's worried that she's ruining your life by constantly putting you in danger, and she's feeling sorry for herself while she's doing it."

"I see." Griffin's eyes were dark as they met mine.

"Oh, I feel so much better now that I've told you." Jerry beamed as he moved away from the table. "Does anyone want more coffee or cookies?"

"No. Thank you." Griffin slowly got to his feet. "We're going to head to dinner. I appreciate you telling me, Jerry. I'll fix it before the end of the night."

"See. I knew you would." Jerry's grin was so self-satisfied I wanted to knock it into his mouth so he choked. "Have a romantic dinner, guys."

"I'll make you pay for this later," I called to his back, doing my best to avoid Griffin's heated gaze. "So ... um ... hmm."

"Yeah, you're not getting out of talking about this." Griffin extended his hand. "Come on. We'll get dinner and then have a very deep discussion about what an idiot you are."

I scowled, frustration coursing through me. "I want to point out that I had no intention of bothering you with this. I told Jerry because I needed someone to talk to. He's the one with the big mouth. If he'd kept it to himself, none of this would've happened."

"Yeah, we're going to talk about that, too." Griffin helped me tug on my coat, taking time to wrap my scarf around my neck and help me into my gloves. He then took me by surprise when he gave me a soft kiss, although his expression remained dark. "I love you, but you're a massive idiot sometimes. You know that, right?"

Oh, geez. It was going to be one of *those* nights. "I'm willing to make naked snow angels with you if you forget this whole thing?"

"No."

Crap!

"What about naked bed angels?"

This time Griffin cracked a smile. "Come on. I promise this won't be nearly as painful as you think it will be."

I couldn't help having my doubts.

"THAT WAS PRETTY good, but now I have garlic breath."

I exhaled heavily in Griffin's face to prove my point. Dinner had been a quiet affair, Griffin talking about his day and me re-enacting my lame insult attempt when it came to Angelina. He didn't so much as bring up what Jerry said. I thought I'd gotten away with it – perhaps he'd forgotten – but he was anxious to talk the minute we hit the sidewalk.

"How could you possibly think that my life would be better without you?"

Oh, geez. Jerry is the bane of my existence. I'm going to make him cry for this. Never doubt that for a second. "That's not what I said." I moved to pull my hand from his, but he didn't allow it. "I just meant that ... you're not always safe when you're with me."

"No, I'm not," Griffin agreed, tightening his grip on my fingers. "Stop trying to pull away from me. It's driving me crazy."

There was a double meaning to his words, and I couldn't help feeling a bit guilty. "I don't ever want to pull away from you. But when you love someone you want what's best for them above all else. I'm not sure I'm what's best for you."

"You are."

"What if you die?"

"Then it had better be because I was trying to keep you safe," Griffin replied without hesitation. "What if you die?"

"Then you'll probably be safe again."

"Oh, knock it off." Griffin used his free hand to flick my ear. "You're coming up with every excuse you can think of right now, and it's really starting to agitate me. You said yes. We're getting married. I'm happy. I want you. Get over it."

I sighed. "You're kind of bossy."

"That's rich coming from you."

"Speaking of rich ... I'm uncomfortable talking to my father about this. I don't know what to say to him."

"Do you want me to do it?"

It was a nice offer, but I couldn't help picturing Griffin lying in a pool of blood on the other side of Dad's desk. "I think I'd better do it."

"Are you going to do it?" Griffin slowed his pace. "Baby, I'm not lying when I say that your father' feelings will be hurt if you don't include him. He's your father. You're his only daughter. Do you know what he said to me when I asked his permission to marry you?"

No, but I'd been dying to ask that very question ever since I found out Griffin went the old-fashioned route. "Did he pull a gun?"

Griffin snorted, genuinely amused. "No. He got all misty-eyed and said yes. Then he called me 'son.' Then he told me I was to watch my wandering hands even after I proposed, because he wasn't going to suddenly pretend he didn't see them."

"He got misty-eyed?" I couldn't picture that. "Really?"

"Aisling, of course he did. He wants to be part of this. I don't understand why you're so mental all of a sudden. Don't most women get excited about the idea of picking out a dress?"

"Probably," I conceded. "That was never my thing growing up. All I cared about was being one of the boys. I didn't want to be treated differently."

"And I can see that," Griffin conceded, resuming our walk. "You're still a girl. You can be excited for this, talk to me about it, and still not lose your precious street cred. You know that, right?"

He was so earnest the thing I wanted most was to believe him. "I did kind of get some ideas today while we were shopping. I didn't really like anything I saw, but I got some ideas."

"That's good." We lapsed into amiable silence for a few minutes, Griffin breaking it first. "Tell me about your run-in with Madame Dauphine."

I didn't bother to hide my surprise when I shifted my gaze to him. "You've met her?"

"No. She's technically out of my jurisdiction. However, Brett Saunders – you remember I introduced you to him at the big Christmas party – he's working a missing persons case, and the last place anyone saw his victim was at Madame Dauphine's voodoo shop."

Oh, well, that was interesting. It was also a conversation that didn't make me feel weak or silly. "That can't be her real name. She's trying to run this Marie Laveau shtick with the way she carries herself, but I've got her number."

"Who is Marie Laveau?"

"She was a New Orleans voodoo priestess. She was born in the early 1800s. She had a Creole mother and a free man of color as her father. She gave birth to, like, fifteen kids I think, but only one made it to adulthood."

"Is that why people thought she was a voodoo priestess?" Griffin asked.

"No, she told people she was a voodoo priestess. I've been trying to remember a lot of this since we met Dauphine because I was honestly struck by the similarities. It was obvious that she was playing a part by the way she was dressed ... and the way she talked to me, as if she'd been around a very long time even though she was only in her fifties or so.

"Marie Laveau married a couple of times, worked as a hairdresser because she got a lot of gossip from the rich white women of the time, and she was rumored to have a really big snake that she carried around," I continued. "A lot of the stuff they write about her can't be substantiated, so she's taken on mythic proportions in certain circles."

"And you think this Madame Dauphine is trying to emulate her?"

"I think she's playing a part for anyone who will fall for it," I clarified. "Jerry certainly believed her spiel. He spent like two hundred bucks on voodoo dolls."

"And why did you go into her store when you were supposed to be shopping for a wedding dress?"

"Because we followed Angelina after she won the insult war for the day. We were in a coffee shop and I happened to see Angelina enter the voodoo store," I explained. "I thought that would be a way for me to redeem myself."

"And did you?"

"She was already gone by the time we got over there. I think she must've left through the back door or something. It was odd."

"Did you ask Madame Dauphine why she was there?"

"That's none of my business."

Griffin didn't comment.

"Of course I asked what she was doing there," I said, causing Griffin to chuckle when I changed course. "Madame Dauphine wouldn't say. She said it was private ... as if she was a doctor or something."

"I'm not sure what to make of her, so I want you to be careful if you go back," Griffin said. "My best guess is that she's some kind of grifter. That Marie Laveau thing you mentioned is interesting. I'll have Saunders conduct some research."

"I have no intention of going back. I only went the first time because I wanted to make Angelina cry."

"Yes, well, you're nothing if not consistent." Griffin squeezed my hand. "About the other thing ... ."

"Oh, do we have to go back to that?" I did my best to ignore how whiny I sounded.

"We're not going to argue," Griffin said. "I need you to know that I can't live without you, though. I get that there's danger and you can't always tell when it's going to show up, but that doesn't change how I feel about you. It never will."

The words were enough to make me feel silly ... and a little better. "I'm sorry I'm such a pill. It's just ... this is new to me. I've never done this before."

"And you're only going to do it once, so I get why you're worked up," Griffin said. "Try talking to me instead of freaking out. I know I've told you that two days in a row now, but it would actually make me feel better if I thought you were listening."

"I'll do my best," I said, my shoulder slamming into a man walking in the opposite direction. He didn't even try to avoid the contact. "Hey, walk much?"

The man didn't respond with words. Instead he let loose an unearthly growl and extended his hands toward my neck. I was caught off guard, so I didn't have a chance to plant my feet, and the next thing I knew I was tumbling to the snow-covered pavement.

"Son of a ... !"

6
SIX

The snow did nothing to cushion my fall. Pain ricocheted through my back and the elbow I instinctively reached out with to slow my downward momentum. I groaned as I hit, shifting my hips. I knew I wasn't in danger of dying from the blow but that didn't mean I wouldn't break something.

"Aisling?" Griffin moved to help, reaching for me instead of the man on top of me.

"Dude, get off." I shoved him, rolling my eyes when he made a hissing noise, as if he was expelling gaping mouthfuls of air. "You ran into me. Get off!" I pushed against his chest as hard as I could, but he refused to move, instead placing more of his weight on my achy frame.

"What is your deal?" I tried pushing a second time, but the man only burrowed closer, causing me to slant my eyes toward his neck. He had a weird mark, like a tattoo gone wrong, but I couldn't make it out. I forced myself to focus on his face and I jolted when I found a pair of milky white eyes staring back. At one time they might've been brown, but they were almost completely white now. Instead of apologizing or acting confused, the man gnashed his teeth as he made slurping noises near my neck.

"What the ... ?"

I reacted instinctively, lashing out with my forearm, making solid contact with the man's chin. I heard the distinctive sound of the man's teeth colliding — something I was familiar with from when I used to wrestle my brothers as a kid — and shoved with everything I had to dislodge the heavy interloper.

Griffin, clearly not understanding the situation, appeared mildly concerned as he reached for me. "Are you okay?"

I let him pull me to my feet, my eyes never moving from the man who now lay prone on the pavement. "I think there's something wrong."

"I'll say there's something wrong." Griffin brushed the snow from my back. "You just got felt up by a potential drunk and you didn't even swear once. You're growing as a person. Are you hurt?"

"I'm fine."

"I asked you a question." Griffin grabbed my shoulders and forced me to look at him. "Are you hurt? Tell me what hurts. Do you need to go to the hospital? Do you need me to carry you?"

He was still getting over my last mishap, the one that left me unconscious in the hospital for several days and him a ravaged mess of a man who didn't leave my side, so I took pity on him. "I'm okay." I lowered my voice a bit. "He knocked the wind out of me and you're going to have to massage my back later. Other than that, I'm fine."

Griffin didn't look convinced. "Would you tell me if you weren't?"

"I have no idea, but since I'm fine, it's a moot point." I rubbed my sore elbow and shifted my attention to the man on the ground. "He's another story."

"I noticed." Griffin slid around me and bent over to give our new friend some pointed attention. "Is he drunk? Are you drunk, buddy? If so, you need to get up and go home. You'll freeze to death if you try to sleep out here."

Griffin had handled his fair share of drunken fools over the years. I had a feeling this guy was different.

"I'm not sure he's drunk." I narrowed my eyes as I stared at the mark on his neck. Now, that I had more time to look, it didn't look like a tattoo as much as a recent injury. It was as if someone had carved a childish snake with lines through it – or maybe a gang symbol for all I knew – into his neck.

"Well, he certainly wasn't walking like a sober person," Griffin argued. "He was lurching a bit. I saw him when we were walking but just figured he'd imbibed a bit too much wine or something over dinner and was on his way home."

Royal Oak was a happening hot spot in southeastern Michigan. Many residents lived close enough to the downtown area that they could walk to and from area bars and restaurants. That was a good thing because parking in the small enclave is an abominable nightmare at times ... and that's when it's not snowing.

"He didn't smell as if he'd been drinking," I argued, shifting so I could be closer to Griffin and get a better look at the suddenly still man. "In fact, he looked as if something else was wrong with him."

"What?"

"I ... ." I wasn't sure how to answer. Explaining what I saw in the man's eyes might make Griffin think I was crazy. I opted to split the difference on the truth. "His eyes didn't look right."

"Really?" Griffin rested his knees on the snow and leaned closer, tapping the man's shoulder in an effort to get a reaction. "Sir? Sir, can you hear me?"

No response.

"Sir, if you're in pain or injured, you need to tell me where it hurts," Griffin prodded. "We can call an ambulance ... or perhaps get you a warm place to sleep for the night if that's what you need."

It took me a moment to realize Griffin believed the man to be homeless. An extended look at his clothes, the tattered hems and ripped elbows, made me think Griffin was on to something. Perhaps I was so distracted by what happened I didn't get a chance to smell the alcohol. Maybe he was blind drunk and I imagined what I saw in his eyes. Maybe it was so cold that it dampened the scent of the alcohol.

They were all possibilities, yet none of them felt right. "Griffin."

"Just a second, baby." Griffin put some effort into rolling the man, and when he slid onto his back, his eyes staring at the darkening sky and yet seeing nothing, I had to tamp down the overwhelming urge to vomit ... and then run. "You've got to be kidding me!"

Griffin's expression twisted as he leaned forward and pressed his ear to the man's chest.

"Is he ... ?"

"Dead?" Griffin flicked his eyes to me. "I think so."

Oh, well, and I thought the day was looking up. "What do we do?"

"Call the police."

"You are the police."

"This isn't my jurisdiction."

That made sense. I dug in my pocket for my phone, working overtime to control my shaking fingers. "What do I tell the 911 operator when she answers?"

"Tell her we have a Detroit police officer on the scene and what looks to be a DOA on the sidewalk. I have no idea what he died from, but ... just call. We need some help here."

THE ROYAL OAK Police Department was located right around the corner, so it didn't take officers long to arrive. Griffin's precinct was in downtown Detroit, but he clearly recognized the officers who joined us, and I was suddenly odd woman out as the cops greeted one another.

"Detective Taylor."

"Detective Green." Griffin was grim as he stood. "I haven't seen you around in a couple of months."

"It's been busy over here," Green said. "You know how it goes. What do we have here?"

"I'm not sure." Griffin rubbed his hand over the back of his neck. "We were leaving the Italian restaurant and walking down the street – just talking and stuff – and this guy ran into Aisling. He took her down.

"At first I thought he was drunk, but he didn't respond once I got Aisling up," he continued. "When I got closer to check, well, he's clearly dead."

"Yeah. I noticed that." Green's eyes flicked to mine before focusing on the uniformed officer kneeling next to the dead man. "Did anything else happen?"

"Meaning?"

"Meaning was he active after falling on your woman?"

Woman? Did he just refer to me as his woman, as if I was Griffin's property? Ugh. I hate cops. The only cop I can tolerate is Griffin. I'm not joking. I hate them all ... and that's only partly because I was arrested several times in my youth.

"I don't know." Griffin turned to me. "Aisling, this is Mark Green. Mark, Aisling. Did he say anything to you when he landed? I didn't even ask. All I heard was you telling him to get off."

Hmm. This was a sticky situation. Did they not notice the guy's milky eyes? Wait ... was I the only one who saw that? Crap. I didn't like that one bit. "He didn't speak." My voice was unnaturally phlegmy so I cleared my throat. "He didn't say words or anything. He made kind of a growling sound, maybe even a little hiss, although that might've been because he was in pain."

"He landed on top of you," Griffin pointed out. "You should've been in a lot more pain than him. You went down hard."

"Tell that to my back," I muttered.

Griffin absently shifted his hand to my back to rub it. "I'll get you in a warm bath when we get home."

"Did you look at his eyes?" the uniform asked, causing me to exhale heavily with unveiled relief. At least I wasn't the only one to notice. That meant I wasn't going crazy ... not that I thought I was or anything.

"What is that?" Green asked, leaning closer. "Are those ... cataracts?"

"They're not like any cataracts I've ever seen," Griffin noted. "I didn't really look too closely at his eyes until you mentioned it. I thought it was the snow or something, maybe the way the light hit them."

"That's definitely not normal." Green flicked his eyes to me. "And he didn't say anything?"

No, he just made hilarious "I'm going to eat you" noises and then went for my throat. Hmm. I probably shouldn't mention that part. "No." I shook my head. "Like I said, he made growling noises, but I guess those could have been pain noises. He wouldn't get off, and I panicked a bit because he was moving his mouth around my throat, so I hit him in the jaw. Then I pushed him off and ... well ... he's dead."

Green's eyebrows flew up his forehead. "You hit him?"

"He was on top of me and wouldn't get off." I shouldn't have to defend myself here. I was the wronged party. I did it all the same. "I thought he was trying to attack me or something."

"It's okay." Green's voice was gentle, reassuring. "I'm sure it wasn't your fault."

Oh, geez. Did I mention that I hate it when men talk down to me? I opened my mouth, something snarky on the tip of my tongue, but Griffin silenced me with an imperceptible shake of his head as he slipped his arm around my shoulders.

"She's just cold," Griffin offered. "She doesn't like the snow."

"Who does?" Green forced a smile. "We'll get the medical examiner down here and see what he says. Do you mind going into the coffee shop over there with me and waiting? I have to ask you a few more questions."

I absolutely minded. Griffin, however, was resigned.

"No problem."

"I CAN'T BELIEVE you're getting married." Green's questions consisted of five minutes of lame "who did what and when" before he turned his full attention to Griffin and me. He seemed dumbfounded by the news that we were engaged. "I pegged you as a bachelor for life."

Griffin slid me a sidelong look as I warmed my hands on my mug of coffee. "I thought there was a distinct possibility that I was a bachelor for life, too, but once I saw Aisling I was a changed man."

"Oh, whatever." I didn't bother to hide my eye roll.

"Love at first sight, eh?" Green's eyes filled with jocularity. "Did you take one look at her and say 'That's the woman for me?'"

"Kind of," Griffin replied. "I don't really believe in love at first sight, but we became close pretty quickly. I think we were lucky enough to recognize that we belonged together without a lot of drama."

I had no idea whose life he thought he'd been living, but our relationship (and exterior forces) had been nothing but drama since we met.

"What about you, Aisling? What do you do for a living?" Green turned his expectant gaze to me.

"I work for my father."

"They do a lot of business with antiques and antiquities," Griffin interjected. "You know, estate sales and the like. She's usually traveling all over the tri-county area while working most days."

"Sounds exciting." Green smiled. "It's like you get to go garage sale shopping every day of the week. My girlfriend would love that."

His girlfriend sounded like an idiot. "Yes, it's one big shopping extravaganza every single day. Whee!"

Griffin squeezed my knee under the table to silence me. "Aisling," he warned. "You're being rude."

"Don't worry about it," Green said, his grin never slipping. "She's had a trying ordeal. I mean ... a random guy on the sidewalk knocked her down and then he died on top of her. That's got to be disconcerting. It's not as if it happens every day."

What was disconcerting was two men – one of whom I was engaged to – talking about me as if I wasn't even sitting in the same booth with them. That was both disconcerting and annoying. "How much longer do we have to stay?"

"Are you anxious to get your guy home?" Green asked. "Do you have plans for him?"

"Yes, I'm going to lock him in the basement," I deadpanned. "Then I'm going to put ribbons in his hair and make him watch chick flicks."

"We don't have a basement," Griffin pointed out.

"My father's basement." Because I was convinced my father's basement was infested with snakes, that was a terrible threat. Griffin didn't look bothered in the least.

"How much longer do you think the medical examiner will be?"

"No idea," Green shrugged. "I'll check. You guys wait here."

"We'll do that." Griffin kept his hand light and easy on my knee until Green disappeared outside. Then he began to squeeze to the point where I had to shift because it was becoming uncomfortable. "Why are you treating him like that?"

I blinked three times in rapid succession, debating how to answer. "Didn't you see that guy's eyes?"

"I did. Do you know what caused that?"

I had no idea. I had a few theories, though. "He was probably possessed."

Griffin's lips twitched. "Like ... by the devil?"

"I'm a freaking reaper who sends souls to heaven, hell and whatever falls between," I hissed, keeping my voice low. "Is that so hard to imagine?"

Griffin balked. "I ... did not think about it that way." He turned serious. "Do you know what caused that?"

"No, but what I didn't tell your friend is that I only hit that guy because he was trying to bite my neck," I supplied. "He was making weird animal noises and trying to chew on me. That's why I hit him."

"So ... what? You think he's a vampire or something."

I snorted. "No, but I think there was definitely something wrong with him. Maybe he had rabies. Or, maybe he ran into Angelina and had untreated syphilis and went crazy. Oh, geez. Why couldn't I think of that one when I saw her earlier?"

Griffin was gentle as he rubbed the back of my neck, his fingers tracing a soothing pattern as he stared into my eyes. "I can see you're worked up. I need you to remain calm. The last thing we need is for Green to think you're nuts."

"What about you? Do you think I'm nuts?"

"I think I love you and if you say you saw something then I believe you." Griffin smiled at the waitress as she passed, waiting to make sure she was out of earshot before continuing. "You can't mention that stuff to Mark."

"Why do you think I didn't mention it?"

Griffin tilted his head to the side, considering. "I don't know what to make of it. The medical examiner should have some additional information tomorrow. I guess we'll have to wait until then."

That sounded fairly unbearable to me. "Great. Does that mean we can leave?" I dug in the booth for my coat. "You promised me a massage and a bath, and I really want to get out of here."

"We just have to wait for Mark to come back and cut us loose," Griffin countered. "It won't take long."

"Well ... whoopee."

"I can tell already you're going to be a pain in the ass the entire night," Griffin muttered, shaking his head and plastering a fake smile on his face when Green walked back into the coffee shop. "Anything?"

"Well, we've got something, but I'm not sure what to make of it." Green rubbed his chin, his eyes troubled.

"Just tell us," Griffin said. "If Aisling's blow did anything to him, it wasn't on purpose. In fact ... ."

I was apparently slow on the uptake, because it took me longer than it should have to realize that Griffin was suddenly terrified the cops would try to take me in. It hadn't even occurred to me. Well, crud on a cracker. That was just one more thing I didn't want to fret about given everything going on. Now I had something real to worry about, and it was going to totally throw me off my game.

"I'm not sure her blow did anything," Green said. "In fact, I'm not sure what to make about any of this. The medical examiner is taking custody of the body. You guys are free to go. Um ... I'll be in touch when I have more information."

That couldn't be right. He was acting too weird. "What does the medical examiner think killed him?"

Green held his hands palms out and shrugged. "He doesn't know. Whatever it was, though, killed him about a month ago. Now, I'm not sure what you saw, but that body out there has been dead for quite some time. Do you want to revise your story?"

I risked a glance at Griffin, flabbergasted.

"No, we don't want to revise our story." Griffin was firm. "We told you what happened. There have to be cameras on the street that caught it, too."

"We'll definitely look into that," Green said. "Until then ... I don't know what to tell you. It's going to remain an open case. We'll start investigating as soon as we get the final autopsy results. That's the best I have to offer."

It wasn't much. "So what does that mean?"

"It means you go home," Green replied. "We'll call you when we have more information."

And just like that we were dismissed. Griffin didn't look even remotely happy about it.

7

SEVEN

I was chilled to the bone by the time we got home, the walk to Griffin's vehicle and the drive back to the townhouse done almost completely in silence.

I felt Griffin's eyes on me as I kicked off my boots and stripped out of my heavy coat, sighing as I put away both rather than leaving them out. Griffin's expression was hard to read, but I knew he was worried. I didn't know how to ease that worry, so I didn't even try.

I needed to think. This entire thing was fantastical ... and more than a little troubling.

"I'm going to take a bath."

I didn't meet Griffin's eyes because avoidance sounded easier than discussion, and I headed straight into the bathroom. I dropped a scented bath bomb – one that smelled like cloves – into the water before stripping. I practically sighed in relief as I sank into the hot water, leaning my head back against the ceramic edge of the huge jet-propelled tub and hoping I'd wake to find this day had been nothing but a bad dream.

When that didn't happen, I focused on reality.

I closed my eyes, tilted my face to the ceiling and let my mind drift. I wasn't sure what to make of the night's events, but whatever it was, it couldn't be good. The first thought that came to my head was zombies. Yes, I know how ridiculous that sounds, but I'd seen enough over the past year to tell me that practically anything was possible. Besides, I didn't know how else to explain what had happened. The man had clearly been alive – er, well, at least mobile – when he slammed into me on the sidewalk. If the medical examiner thought he'd been dead for at least a month – and I had to believe the medical examiner knew what he was doing – then something else was going on.

Something strange.

I registered movement in the room even though my eyes were shut, and when I risked a glance toward the space next to the tub I found Griffin getting undressed.

"What are you doing?"

"Well, I thought about letting you shut me out and pout for the rest of the night, but I've decided that I don't like that idea." Griffin put his hand on my neck and prodded me to lean forward. "Instead I'm going to take a bath with you and force you to tell me what you're thinking. I'm hopeful that will head off any potential problems we might have going forward."

I wrinkled my nose as he climbed into the tub, taking perverse pleasure in the way he hissed as the hot water enveloped him.

"Wow! How cold were you?" Griffin's eyes lit with amusement, although the gleam was somehow muted. When I didn't smile, his expression turned rueful. "Tell me what you're thinking."

I remained leaning forward, debating whether or not I wanted to pick a fight that would leave both of us morose until we made up. "I don't think you want to know what I'm thinking," I admitted after a beat. "You'll lock me away if I tell you."

Griffin got more comfortable behind me, moving his hands to my shoulders in an effort to soothe me. "Try me."

I groaned as his fingers dug in to my sore back. "Keep doing that forever."

"I believe that's one of the things I signed up for when I proposed."

And the rest? Did he sign up for zombies? "I'm afraid to tell you what I'm thinking because the odds of you immediately calling my father and telling him I've lost it are pretty high."

"I promise not to do that."

He said the words easily. I couldn't help but wonder if he actually believed them. I guess we were about to find out. "Okay, well, I think it was a zombie."

Griffin's fingers never slowed, but I felt him shift in the water. "Why?"

"Because that guy was clearly moving when he ran into me – I don't think we need to debate that – and he tried to bite my neck. Then, when I smacked him in the head, he went down and didn't get up again. The medical examiner says he's been dead for a month. Do you have another explanation?"

"The medical examiner made a mistake."

"I don't think that's likely."

Griffin pressed his thumbs to the tender spots beside my shoulder blades. "Well, as a duly sworn police officer in the fine city of Detroit, I can tell you that medical examiners make mistakes all of the time. It's not something we like to spread around, but it happens."

"Yeah, but when a medical examiner makes a mistake on a case you're working on, it's usually in the vein of an hour or two," I pointed out. "I doubt very much that you've had a medical examiner overshoot by a month."

"That's a fair assessment." Griffin's hands were relentless as they tackled the tension in my back. He remained convinced that I was still recovering from my near-death experience before Christmas, even though I promised him repeatedly that I was back to full health. He was tireless when it came to making sure I rested and took care of myself. In a way, that was his weakness, just as mine was worrying that he'd grow tired of the supernatural snafus and walk away without a backward glance. Perhaps we were both being ridiculous.

"A lot of things could impact an initial examination," Griffin continued. "Weather is one factor. We have no idea if that guy was homeless or what his health situation was. We need to let the medical examiner have more time with the body before we panic."

"I'm not panicking."

"You're panicking a little," Griffin argued. "I saw it on your face when you heard the time of death. That's such a ridiculous scenario that Mark already knows it doesn't fit the evidence. You're not in any danger of being arrested or anything. You know that, right?"

Part of me knew that. Part of me wasn't so sure. "His demeanor changed after he went outside and came back."

"Of course it did. The medical examiner just told him that a guy who we assumed died minutes before had really been dead for a month. That completely fouls up his paperwork. Trust me. I know how that goes."

"It was more than that."

"I don't think it was, Aisling, but let's pretend he does think we're hiding something for a second," Griffin said. "How exactly does that work? You spent the day shopping with Jerry, which means you have multiple alibis. I was working."

"Yeah, but do you remember what you were doing a month ago? That's when he supposedly died."

"I'm pretty sure I was doing much the same thing. It hardly matters, though. If Mark believes that guy died a month ago and somehow we're involved, that means we would've had to drag a body from a vehicle, carry it down the sidewalk, and leave it there without anyone seeing.

"You have alibis for the entire day, as do I," he continued. "We were seen at the restaurant right before it happened. Quite a few of those shops have security cameras, so we'll have been caught on those feeds. We won't have a body with us in any of the footage."

He had a point. "What if they have video of that guy walking on the sidewalks and the medical examiner sticks to his notion that he died a month ago?"

"Well ... ." Griffin trailed off, hesitating. "Baby, you're very wise and beautiful. Have I ever told you that?"

The fact that he shifted gears the way he did told me he was about to say something I really didn't want to hear. "Only when you want deviant sex."

Griffin chuckled. "We'll see how you feel after your bath. As for the zombie thing, well, I don't believe in zombies."

He said it in a matter-of-fact tone, as if there was no possible way to argue. I'm a Grimlock. I always find a way to argue.

"Did you believe in reapers before you met me?"

"No, but that's different."

"How?"

"I can see how the whole reaper thing works," Griffin replied. "I don't pretend to understand everything you do, but I've seen you in action and know reapers exist. I think if zombies existed we might've seen a few of them on television over the years. It would be impossible not to catch them because everyone carries a phone camera these days."

"How do you explain the Kardashians?"

"Ha, ha." Griffin poked my side. "I'm glad to see you're feeling better. You only make Kardashian jokes when you're feeling feisty."

He was right, but that didn't mean I was going to abandon my zombie theory. "What if zombies are real?"

"Then we'll grab our things, move to Grimlock Manor and wait until the apocalypse ends. If we're going to play that game, though, I want to dress up like Daryl from *The Walking Dead*. I know he turns you on."

"Daryl turns everyone on," I said dryly. "I'm being serious here. What if that guy was a zombie?"

"Aisling, I don't believe in zombies. I don't think you do either. I think you've had a long day and you're exhausted. Why don't we open a bottle of wine and get comfortable in front of the fire? I'm sure, after a relaxing evening and eight hours of sleep, you'll feel differently."

He was trying to placate me. Sure, he was doing it from a place of love. That didn't mean I wasn't bothered by it all the same. "If it is zombies, I'll never let you live down the fact that you didn't believe me."

"That seems fair." Griffin pressed a kiss to my cheek, wrapping his arms around me and settling my body on his so we could soak comfortably in the fragrant heat. "I've learned to adjust my thinking on many things since I met you – and I'm not sorry in the least, so don't do some maudlin moping because I said it – but I have to draw the line at zombies."

"Why? Why draw the line there?"

"Because it's zombies." Griffin tickled my ribs, causing me to giggle and squirm. "You're tired. I want you to put this out of your mind.

"You're fine. I'm fine. Everything is going to stay fine," he continued. "We're going to have a great wedding and extremely loud married life. I promise."

Because I wanted to believe him I let it go. "Okay, but you've been warned. If it's zombies, I'm doing a little dance and never letting you forget that I was right and you were wrong."

"I can live with that."

MY DREAMS WERE turbulent, images from every bad zombie movie I'd ever watched – and that list was long – flitting through my head. By the time I climbed out of the blood and carnage and found myself in the real world, I was almost wearier than when I rested my head on the pillow.

"You look tired." Griffin tucked in his shirt as he watched me fumble with my sweater buttons.

"Thanks. There's nothing a woman loves hearing more from the man she's going to marry than how bad she looks."

"That's not what I meant." Griffin is a morning person and very rarely flies into a rage because I'm not, even though I tend to pick fights before I've had my morning coffee. "You simply look as if you didn't sleep well."

"Weird dreams," I grumbled, abandoning the cardigan buttons and shuffling toward the kitchen. I couldn't focus without caffeine.

Griffin followed me. He wasn't about to leave for the day without doing his shrink routine. "Do you want to tell me about them?"

"No."

"Why not?"

"You'll make fun of me." I flipped the button on the Keurig so it could heat up and filled it with water before focusing on my selection of K-Cups. "I think I've had my fill of that."

"When did I make fun of you?"

I rolled my eyes. "Seriously? That's half of our relationship. The only rule is that no one can laugh when the other one is naked ... at least in a derogatory way. If we're laughing because we're enjoying ourselves, that's allowed."

"Yeah, I'm pretty sure we've never had a discussion about laughing while naked," Griffin countered. "I would have remembered that."

"Not if we were naked when having that particular chat." I was grouchy and belligerent – something he didn't cause – and I couldn't rein in my attitude. "It doesn't matter. It was just a dream."

"I want to hear what it was about," Griffin pressed. "I'm worried. You look ... really tired. Maybe you should call in sick today. I'm sure your father would understand."

He would. Sure, he would grouse and complain and tell me that I was being a baby, but then he would show up with a chocolate malt and soup at lunchtime if he really thought I was sick. Despite my attitude, I pride myself on a good work ethic.

"I'm not calling in sick," I said. "I'm not sick." Griffin opened his mouth to argue, but I cut him off. "If you say I look sick you'll give me a complex and things will get all kinds of ugly."

"I think you're exaggerating, but you always look beautiful." As if to prove it, Griffin leaned closer and kissed the corner of my mouth. "Now tell me what you dreamed about."

Oh, geez. He was not going to let this go. "What do you think I dreamed about?"

"I hope it was a naked rendezvous on the beach – maybe a honeymoon destination or something – but I'm guessing that wouldn't leave you this foul tempered."

"I am not foul tempered."

"Baby, if Jerry didn't keep a calendar I'd be convinced that you have PMS."

I should've been offended. The fact that my best friend, boyfriend and brothers kept track of my monthly cycle so they could hide like little worms when they thought I was most likely to be irrational was not only annoying, it was insulting. Sadly, I couldn't muster the energy to pick a fight over this particular battlefield of nothing.

"It doesn't matter."

"It matters to me." Griffin tucked a strand of my hair behind my ear, his expression gentling. "Tell me. Did you dream about zombies?"

"If you already knew, why did you ask?"

"Because I wanted you to tell me yourself," Griffin answered without hesitation. "You didn't, by the way, so that's still something we have to work on. Tell me about the dream."

"It doesn't matter," I said, placing a mug under the Keurig spout and slapping a K-Cup into the holder. "Zombies aren't real, right? You spent hours telling me that last night."

"And sadly I'm starting to think that none of it sank in."

"I'm fine."

"No, you're obsessed with the fact that you think zombies are real and that they are going to start attacking," Griffin argued. "I want to make you feel better, but I don't expect to get a follow-up report from Mark until this afternoon at the earliest. I'm sure this case isn't a priority for him."

"Oh, what, zombies aren't sexy enough to interest police detectives?"

"Oh, come on." Griffin pinched the bridge of his nose, frustration practically oozing out of his pores. "Are you going to make this a thing? You don't believe it's really zombies, do you? I know you like to work yourself up, but you can't believe it's zombies."

He looked so annoyed at the thought I opted against pushing him. "Of course not." I forced myself to remain calm. "I was just messing with you."

Griffin took a moment to study my face, his expression unreadable. "I'm not sure you're telling me the truth. I'm also not sure if you're trying to convince me or yourself that you don't believe it's zombies.

"I also don't have time to have this argument," he continued, grabbing my hand. "If you want to fight about it some more, I'll try to be home early tonight. Does that work for you?"

I forced a smile for his benefit. "Sure. Do you want me to pick up dinner on my way home so we don't traumatize another delivery guy with our antics?"

Griffin's lips curved. "We have dinner at Grimlock Manor tonight."

Crap! I forgot about that. Having dinner with my entire family in my father's mansion wasn't something I was keen on given my mood.

Still, the food is always good and there was a decent chance Dad would serve prime rib.

"Okay, new plan," I said. "We'll go to dinner at Grimlock Manor, not tell them what happened last night because I don't want to hear any snickers when I mention my zombie theory, grab ice cream on the way home and argue when we get back here."

Griffin buttoned the cardigan for me and smiled. "I will agree to your terms if we can be naked when we argue."

I didn't want to encourage him, but I couldn't swallow my giggle. "Fine."

"See. Compromise, baby." He smacked a kiss against my mouth. "Works every time." He moved toward the door, stopping to gather his boots. "I'll be working most of the day, but if I get word from Mark I promise to text you."

I nodded, trying to force myself to relax for his benefit if not my own. "Sounds like a plan."

"Okay. I love you."

"I love you, too."

I meant it with every fiber of my being. That didn't mean that I wasn't going to obsess about the possibility of zombies taking over. If he thought that I'd simply discard the idea, he clearly didn't know me at all.

EIGHT

I had only four jobs for the day, which was a relief, because scanning every person I saw on the street for signs of zombieism was exhausting. By the time I hit my last charge in Ferndale, I was ready to focus on other things and put this long and terrible day behind me. Even an overwhelming – and unbelievably loud – dinner with my family was better than worrying about random strangers on the street trying to rip out my throat.

Spencer Markham, of the Birmingham Markhams – the people who own, like, eight area malls and fifteen huge business plazas – was dressed in a cupid costume when I arrived at his upscale loft. Even though Ferndale is an older community, it's got something of a hipster reputation. It's also considered the most gay-friendly city in the state. I happen to love Ferndale, and barely put up a fight when Jerry and Aidan take me to whatever club is "most happening" on any given weekend. The lofts were rather infamous for their price tags, so I was mildly curious when I realized I'd be able to see one of them.

That was before I found Spencer's spirit (and technically his body, too, although I tried not to look too closely) in an adult diaper – I'm only mildly exaggerating – and waving his arms about as if he was trying to take flight.

"Calm down," I ordered, internally chastising myself for holding a conversation that I knew would get me nothing but grief. "You're dead. You have to deal with it."

Spencer had a face like an angel (and not just because he was dressed as cupid) and his mournful blue eyes tugged at my heartstrings. "I can't be dead. I'm too young to die."

I shuffled over to the huge windows that made up the entire west side of the loft and looked down on one of Ferndale's main streets. In the summer the area would be flooded with people. Given the cold, it looked mildly desolate. Still, it was a great view.

"This place is cool," I offered, flopping into one of the retro chairs by the window so I could enjoy the open floor plan and ambiance. "It's kind of like being king and looking down on your subjects, huh?"

Spencer scalded me with a dark look. "I hardly think now is the time to talk about that. I think we have a bigger problem."

"I know." I thought that, too. "Do you believe in zombies?" I had no idea why I was having this discussion with Spencer, but the possibility had been weighing on me all day. "My boyfriend thinks I'm losing my mind, but I think zombies are a definite possibility."

The look on Spencer's face was straight out of a bad sitcom. "Is this some sort of prank? Did Chad send you here to mess with me?"

"I have no idea who Chad is."

"He's my consort."

I pursed my lips. "Really? You use the word 'consort,' but it's bad form for me to discuss you thinking of Ferndale as your kingdom. That seems kind of messed up."

"This whole thing is messed up," Spencer snapped. "I am not dead. It's simply impossible."

"You're dead." I tilted my head toward the counter. "I think you did a bit too much blow and your heart couldn't take it. You know, it's not my place to tell you what to do with your life – and it's too late to change anything – but if I had a view like this I'd actually work out at the gym so I could live longer and enjoy it. You had everything, but decided to shorten your life. What's up with that?"

"I am not dead!"

"So ... you don't want to answer my question?"

Spencer made an exaggerated face and gave his crumpled body on the floor a wide berth as his soul floated closer. "It was just a little pick-me-up. I certainly didn't think this would be the outcome. If I apologize, can I take it back?"

"No. Dead is dead." Unless you're my mother, I silently added. She died and came back to life. Sure, she didn't technically die. Someone faked her death and turned her into a half-wraith and she probably eats people when she's hungry, but this was hardly the time to discuss that. "Sorry. You screwed up. If it's any consolation, drug offenses don't get you sent to a bad place. You're going to a good place. I checked."

I thought the information would make Spencer feel better, but I was wrong. "I don't want to be dead."

"No?" I cocked an eyebrow as I scanned his outfit. "Did you have big Valentine's Day plans? You know that's still like a week away, right?"

"Why would you think that?"

"You're dressed as cupid."

"So?"

"So that's a Valentine's Day thing, right? Speaking of that, what do you get your fiancé for Valentine's Day? He got me a big ring for Christmas, and even though he thinks I'm crazy because I'm convinced zombies are about to invade I feel as if I should get him a special gift for Valentine's Day. It only seems fair."

"Are you seriously asking me about shopping?" Spencer was dumbfounded. "Just because I'm gay – and you can't tell just by looking at me, so it must say it on that stupid iPad you're carrying – that doesn't mean I'm an expert shopper. Do you know how prejudiced that is?"

"I'm not prejudiced. I love gay people. My best friend is gay."

"Oh, please," Spencer scoffed. "Is your best friend also black? Now you can say you're not racist."

"What are you even talking about?" I was too tired to get animated, so I leaned back in the chair. "I'm not prejudiced or racist. I assumed you were gay because you have the new Converse gay pride shoes." I gestured toward the high tops on the floor. "Jerry has those, too."

"Oh." Spencer had the grace to be abashed. "Is Jerry your best friend?"

I nodded. "Since kindergarten."

"Does he believe in zombies, too?"

"I haven't really talked to him about it," I replied. "It only became a point of discussion after dinner last night."

"How?"

"I was attacked by a zombie in Royal Oak when we were leaving Marino's on Main Street."

"Oh, they have a delightful spaghetti squash pasta with low-calorie marinara that is to die for." Spencer adopted a wistful expression. "I guess I'll never get to eat that again."

"I don't know," I said. "I'm guessing Heaven has good food. It wouldn't be Heaven without brownies, right?"

"True."

"As for spaghetti squash pasta, that's not really pasta. You know that, don't you?"

"No, but it's delicious, and without all of those yucky carbohydrates."

I glanced back at the counter, confused. "So carbohydrates are bad, but cocaine is good? By the way, when did cocaine come back into fashion? I thought it was all about meth and opiates now."

"You seem to know a lot about the drug trade for someone who claims she doesn't partake," Spencer said dryly.

"I live with a cop."

"Your fiancé?"

I nodded. "He's a good guy, although he doesn't believe in zombies. He tells me about a lot of his cases, and drugs are often involved."

"Is he vice?"

"Homicide."

"Is that better or worse?"

That was an interesting question. "I think he's the type of person who needs to help others, so he's where he's supposed to be."

"With you?" Spencer offered up a soft smile. "You seem pretty unhappy for someone sporting a new engagement ring."

"I'm not unhappy. I'm ... edgy."

"Because you believe the zombie apocalypse is upon us and you won't be able to have your dream wedding?"

"Maybe. I'm more interested in having a dream marriage than a dream wedding, but that's not my big concern right now. That was my big concern yesterday. I thought Griffin – that's his name, by the way – wasn't going to get what he wanted when he married me, but now I realize that's stupid. Who wouldn't want me?"

"You're very cute," Spencer confirmed. "If I rolled that way, I'd totally roll on top of you."

"That's possibly very flattering."

"So now you're worried about zombies, huh?" Spencer made a tsking sound as he considered my conundrum. "I'll have to side with your fiancé on this one. I don't think zombies are real."

"Did you think grim reapers were real before I showed up to transport your soul to its final resting place?"

"Good point," Spencer conceded. "I'd have to say no on that one, but I still think reapers are more realistic than zombies. I mean ... zombies? They'd decay and fall apart before taking over the world. We all know that."

"Maybe the zombies aren't the same as those we see on television," I suggested, doing my best not to stare at the way the diaper dipped low on the body's hip. I could almost see the Holy Grail, although I had no interest in catching a glimpse of cupid's special arrow. "The medical examiner said that the man died a month ago. A body could probably hold together for that long under the right circumstances, right?"

"I'm not a doctor."

"No, but you're free with your body," I teased, grinning when Spencer attempted to shift behind the couch so I couldn't see so much of him.

"This was for a special occasion," Spencer explained. "I was going to be cupid for Chad."

"And where is he?"

"I don't know." Spencer shrugged. "He was supposed to show up last night. I guess he forgot."

"Does he have a key?"

"No. I got burned on that too many times and was tired of paying for new locks," Spencer replied. "He seemed fine not having one."

"Maybe he was here," I suggested. "Maybe you were passed out and didn't hear him knock." I liked Spencer. He was a bit theatrical, but in a good way, like Jerry. I didn't want him to needlessly suffer. "Maybe he's sitting at home right now worrying about you."

"You think he showed up after I died?" Spencer was obviously relieved at the possibility.

"Not died," I clarified. "I showed up right after you died. I'm guessing you could've been unconscious and fighting for your life for hours before then. You probably wouldn't have woken no matter how hard he knocked."

"That's kind of sad." Spencer wrinkled his nose. "Do you think I was brave during my fight?"

"I think you were unconscious and your body did most of the work," I replied. "Still, I think it's sad you died so young. Are you even twenty-five yet?"

"Thirty. I get a lot of Botox."

"Oh, well ... ." I wasn't sure what to make of that. "The cupid outfit is a nice touch, though. Very special. I'm sure you and Chad would've had a lovely Valentine's Day celebration."

"Oh, this wasn't for Valentine's Day," Spencer explained. "This was just because I like the outfit."

Of course. I should've seen that coming. "What were you going to do for Valentine's Day?"

"That's private."

"Fine. Forget I asked."

"I won't tell you exactly what, but I will tell you that it had a cirque du soleil theme."

My head went to a very scary place. "Okay, well, thanks for the talk." I pushed myself to a standing position. "Believe it or not, I feel better about the zombie thing. Maybe Griffin is right. Maybe the medical examiner simply made a mistake. Maybe the cold temperatures made him see something that wasn't there ... or vice versa."

"There you go." Spencer brightened. "You seem to be in a better mood. Somehow ... lighter."

"I am."

"Great," Spencer enthused, miming clapping his ghostly hands. "Does this mean you'll reverse my death? I promise to clean up my act if you do. I only did the coke because I was looking for an energy booster. I'll switch to caffeine from now on. I promise." He crossed a finger over his chest.

"I'm a reaper, not God."

"I know, but ... ."

"I'm sorry." I really was. "I don't have the power to bring you back. I don't think anyone does."

"Well, that bites." Spencer's face fell. "That means we're going to have one heck of a busy afternoon."

I pursed my lips, confused. "What do you mean?"

"I mean that you have to get anything and everything that might even hint that I'm gay out of here," Spencer replied. "My mother doesn't know, and she can't find out this way."

I was understandably incredulous. "No way."

"Do you want to be responsible for her death?" Spencer's voice ratcheted up a notch. "My mother is a good woman, but she doesn't understand things like this."

"So you never told her?" I couldn't help but wonder how he'd managed to hide it. I thought that unless his mother was blind and deaf she had to know. "I think you're probably mistaken on this one."

"She tried to set me up with a friend's daughter two weeks ago."

Hmm. "Well ... ."

"She's known as the country club slut in my parents' circle."

"Yeah, I get it."

"You have to help me get this stuff out of here," Spencer pleaded. "At least the big stuff. I mean ... you can leave the shoes. She won't know what those are. I have a goody drawer in the other room. If she sees that stuff ... um ... it will be Aneurysm City."

He had to be joking. "If you think I'm hauling your sex toys out of here, you've got another think coming."

"Please."

His expression was so hopeful, so desperate, that I couldn't stop myself from agreeing. "Fine. But I want you to know this is even worse than being overrun by zombies."

"I have absolutely no doubt."

THREE HOURS LATER I heaved a garbage bag full of ... well, I'd rather not say what it was full of ... into a Dumpster behind a Grosse Pointe bar that I occasionally frequented with my family. I knew the owner, and if he questioned what I was doing I'd have to answer him. He knew me well enough not ask certain questions, though, which was why I decided to dump Spencer's toy collection close to Grimlock Manor.

The lot was packed, so I had to park on the street. I kept my eyes open during the short trek between the Dumpster and my car. I was almost completely over my zombie fixation. Who knew it would take a nice guy with bad drug habits in a cupid costume to do it? I certainly didn't see it coming.

I fobbed the lock on my door and opened it, sliding behind the wheel and putting my key in the ignition before something caught my eye in the rearview mirror. I kept the car in park as the engine roared to life and took extra time to fasten my seatbelt.

A blue sedan was parked behind me, about two car lengths between us, and a broad-shouldered figure sat behind the wheel. The individual didn't move to exit the car or leave the street. Even though I couldn't see a face, I was convinced that the man was focused on me.

I stayed where I was for a long time, my eyes glued to the window. The figure shifted, although only slightly, but otherwise remained still, as if waiting for me to make the first move. I considered locking the doors and settling in, refusing to leave until he did.

I exhaled heavily as I made my decision and pulled onto the road, internally sighing when the car remained where it was. I was at the stop sign at the end of the street, a white car behind me, when I noticed the car pull into traffic heading in the same direction.

I tried to remain calm as I pulled onto my father's street, opting to take a random turn into the neighborhood as a test. Sure enough, the blue sedan followed. It didn't get too close, always keeping several car lengths between us, but after another four turns it was more than obvious that I was being followed.

I chewed on my bottom lip as I returned to my father's street and headed toward Grimlock Manor. This time I increased my pace, practically flying into the gated parking area in front of my father's house.

I bounced out of the car and hurried to the gate, looking through the mechanically controlled mechanism's slats in an attempt to see the driver. The sedan was gone. I couldn't see it from my vantage point. That didn't stop me from believing that it was definitely following me. I had no doubt about that. The question floating through my brain was the obvious one: Why?

9

NINE

I was still staring through the front gate, determined to catch sight of the sedan so I could get a better look at the driver, when my brother Cillian sidled up beside me.

"Are you considering making a break for it?"

Of all my brothers, Cillian is the calmest and most rational. When I'm in a dour mood, he's the one I gravitate toward. "If I was going to run I wouldn't have pulled into the driveway first."

"So what are we looking at?" Cillian positioned himself so he could follow my gaze. He wasn't wearing a coat, which meant he must've spied my antics from inside and come out to investigate.

"I thought someone might've been following me." I saw no reason to lie. If something was about to go down there'd be no keeping my father and brothers out of it.

"Really?" Cillian arched an eyebrow, sobering. "Why? Did you have a run-in with someone today?"

"No, but I did clear the sex toys out of a guy's drawer because his mother didn't know he was gay. He was dressed like cupid and wearing an adult diaper."

"Huh. Like a Depends diaper?"

"More like a loin cloth made of white fabric. He had huge plastic safety pins holding it together. It was really distracting."

"You know, you wouldn't have these problems if you'd just absorb the soul before talking to it," Cillian pointed out. "Dad doesn't like it when we talk to them."

"Well, Dad wasn't there, and I kind of felt sorry for him. He had one of those really cool lofts in downtown Ferndale."

"Was that Spencer Markham? I figured he was one of the rich Markhams we occasionally run into at those charity events Dad makes us attend when I saw his name on the list."

"Yeah. He snorted a bunch of cocaine and died. It's too bad. I liked him."

"Well, at least you helped him by getting rid of his stash." Cillian's handsome face split with a wide grin. "Do you think someone was following you because they wanted the toys?"

"I'm not sure anyone was really following me," I said. "It seemed like he was but ... maybe I was wrong."

"He?"

"I don't even know that it was a he," I conceded. "I couldn't see his face. He had broad shoulders, though, and he followed me through four turns in the neighborhood. Four unnecessary turns, I might add. If he was going someplace and coincidentally following me he must have a negative sense of direction."

"Like you?"

"Ha, ha." I elbowed his side, my hand accidentally brushing against his. I felt the cold permeating his skin right away. "We should probably go inside."

"That's a smart idea." Cillian slung his arm around my shoulders as we trudged toward the front door. "You seem down, Ais. What's going on?"

"What makes you think anything is going on?"

"You've been pretty happy the last couple of weeks," Cillian replied. "You've been doing that 'floating-on-air' thing I hear about happening to engaged people. I didn't believe it until I saw you do it. Now you're ... down."

"I'm not down," I corrected, following Cillian into the ornate foyer. "I'm just ... distracted." Something occurred to me. "Do you ever worry you're doing Maya a disservice because of what we do for a living?"

Maya, Griffin's sister, was Cillian's girlfriend, so the question caught him off guard. "No. Do you feel that way?"

"Griffin says I'm being ridiculous because he's known about the reaper business from the start, but I can't shake the feeling that maybe he deserves something better."

"Something better than you?"

"No. There's nothing better than me. Something better than worrying if I'm going to die on a weekly basis."

"Ah. You're nervous." Cillian flicked my ear. "I heard you were coming up with outrageous scenarios to justify a bunch of panic attacks this week. It's kind of cute."

I scowled. "I'm not nervous."

"You are. You're going to be a married lady, something you probably thought was a bit further off, and you're nervous. You're so adorable."

I narrowed my eyes to dangerous purple slits. "I am not nervous. I don't get nervous."

"What is she nervous about?" My oldest brother, Redmond, appeared in the archway that separated the foyer from the rest of the house. All of my siblings – me included – boast the same black hair and purple eyes. We look like our father. The only reason I stand out is because I added white streaks to my hair. Sadly, we all have the same overbearing tendencies, too.

"I'm not nervous," I spat. "Stop saying that."

"What is she nervous about?" Redmond repeated, shifting his eyes to Cillian.

"She thinks that she's doing Griffin a disservice because her life is constantly in peril and she's looking for something to pout about and this is all she could come up with," Cillian replied, causing my temper to flare.

"Ah. We saw this coming. Who had this week in the pool?"

"Excuse me?" My brothers are masters at agitating me. Apparently they'd picked today to gang up and do it as a unit. I shouldn't have been surprised. They'd been taking it easy on me since my hospital stay. It was only a matter of time before things returned to normal. I'd had six weeks of bliss. What more could I ask?

"We had a pool going as to when you would freak out," Cillian supplied. "You held on longer than any of us thought. I think Aidan was the only one who said you'd hold out this long, which means he's the winner."

"Whatever." I shrugged out of my coat and hung it on the rack in the corner of the room. "I need a drink."

"Wow. You really are in a mood, huh?" Redmond played with the ends of my hair as he followed me toward the main parlor. We usually gathered for drinks before dinner. "And here I thought you'd gone all soft and gooey once Griffin put that ring on your finger."

"Oh, stuff it," I muttered, instinctively flexing the hand with the ring. I'd become accustomed to it over the weeks and I found myself staring at it from time to time. Of course, I could never admit that to my brothers. I could admit it to Jerry – who would say it was normal behavior – but because he lives with Aidan and they gossip worse than teenagers I had to keep it to myself.

"What's wrong with you, kid?" Redmond's expression shifted from teasing to worry. "You seem ... upset."

"She thought someone was following her," Cillian volunteered, moving behind the drink cart. "Wine?"

"Whiskey," I replied. "I told you that I'm not completely sure someone was following me. It simply felt as if someone was following me."

"Someone was following you?"

The sound of Griffin's voice caused me to jolt. Oh, well, great. Now I was going to have to tell him about my afternoon and never hear the end of it. "Someone might have been following me. Might," I stressed, turning to face him. His cheeks were flushed from the cold, making him even more handsome than normal ... if that was even possible. "You're early."

"I had an easy day." Griffin gave me a quick kiss, running his hand over my hair and tilting up my chin as he studied me. "Why do you think someone was following you?"

I told him the story, conveniently omitting what I had dumped behind the bar before getting in my car. The more I thought about it, the more I looked like an idiot when I told that particular tale. I was hoping to avoid it becoming public knowledge. So far, only Cillian knew, and he was my most trustworthy brother.

"That doesn't sound like you were imagining things," Griffin noted. "It could've been a coincidence. What were you dumping?"

I averted my gaze. "Just ... stuff."

Griffin is an ace detective, so he recognized my attempt to skate around the question. "What stuff?"

"Um ... ."

"Oh, just tell him," Cillian prodded. "I'm dying to see his face when you do."

So much for being my favorite brother. "I'm never telling you anything again," I hissed.

"You didn't say it was a secret," Cillian pointed out. "In fact, it seems to me that's perfectly normal Aisling behavior. It's a funny story. Why are you getting worked up about it?"

"Because I end up looking bad in it."

"Actually, I think you end up looking good in it," Cillian countered. "You have a good heart, Ais. No matter how you try to hide it, you're a sweet girl."

"Oh, well, kick me when I'm down why don't you," I lamented. "That was just ... mean."

"Now I definitely need to hear the story." Griffin wrapped me up in a hug, refusing to let me go even though Cillian was done with my drink and I desperately wanted to down it. "Talk."

"I might have helped a dead guy in Ferndale," I hedged. "He had a few things he didn't want his mother to see, and I did him a solid."

"What things?"

"Well ... ."

Griffin sighed when I hesitated. "Am I going to be upset with this? It wasn't drugs, was it?"

I immediately started shaking my head. "It wasn't drugs. I left those on the counter. He wasn't worried about them. Apparently his mother is fine with cocaine, but sex toys are a big no-no in the Markham house."

"Spencer Markham?" Griffin knit his eyebrows. "I heard about that about an hour ago. They say he overdosed."

"He did ... and in a cupid costume."

Griffin pressed his lips together to keep from laughing. "Oh, well, I guess that's not too bad." He kissed my forehead before releasing me. "I thought you were going to say you hid drugs or a weapon of some kind. I don't really care about the sex toys."

"He was in an adult diaper," Cillian added. "I'm so glad she ended up with that assignment instead of me."

"Like a Depends diaper?" Griffin was intrigued.

"No, it was some sort of cloth. Can we not talk about the diaper?"

"Oh, good grief." My father Cormack Grimlock, always an imposing figure, shook his head as he walked into the room. "Who is wearing diapers? If it's one of my offspring I don't want to hear about it. If it's part of some perverse sex game I definitely don't want to hear about it." He pinned Griffin with a dark look, as if to say "I'm watching you despite the fact that I agreed to let you marry my only daughter."

"Hey, I have nothing to do with the diaper." Griffin held up his hands in mock surrender. "Aisling's charge was wearing one. That's what we're talking about."

"A diaper?" Dad shuddered. "Was he elderly?"

"He was dressed like cupid," I replied. "The diaper isn't really germane to the story. It's simply an amusing anecdote."

"You and I have differing definitions of amusing, kid." He stopped in front of me. "How are you feeling?"

If I thought Griffin was a mother hen since I was injured, my father was ten times worse. "I'm fine."

"Except for the fact that she thinks someone was following her," Cillian interjected, earning a fiery glance from the bottom of my soul. "What? If you're being followed, I think everyone wants to know about it."

"You were followed?" Dad didn't look happy. "Why?"

"Ugh." I related the story for the third time, including the bit about dumping the sex toys, because I knew my brothers would rat me out. When I was done, I grabbed my glass of whiskey from Cillian and downed half of it. "I don't know what to think."

"Well, it was probably nothing." Dad clearly wasn't convinced, but he refused to push me on the situation. "Just be careful when you're out and about. If you sense, even for a moment, that someone is closing in, call me."

"Great. More babysitting." I threw myself in the closest chair. "I'm perfectly fine. I saw the doctor two weeks ago and he says I'm completely recovered. There's no reason to get worked up."

"He wouldn't be a Grimlock if he didn't get worked up," Redmond said. "You should be happy that you're so loved."

"She's not loved; she's tolerated." My brother Braden decided to join the party. We fight more than everyone else, so I wasn't looking forward to his arrival. That feeling only intensified when he added the next bit. "Mom is here for dinner, by the way. She's putting her coat on the rack. Everyone should be on their best behavior."

My mouth dropped open as the news washed over me. Lily Grimlock's return from the dead had held top billing in our lives for months. We'd come to an uneasy meeting of the minds of sorts since Christmas, although I'd only seen her twice. She's been lying low – and hopefully not eating people to survive – but I did my best to refrain from dwelling on her as much as possible.

"Why is she here?" I knew I sounded whiny, but it was too late to adjust my tone.

"Because she's our mother and she wants to see us." Braden's eyes flashed with warning. He had struggled most while Mom was gone, and was desperate to find a way to include her in our daily lives. "She's having dinner with us. I asked Dad if it was okay and he said it was fine. If you have an issue, take it up with him."

I flicked my eyes to Dad, who had the good sense to find something fascinating to focus on at the drink cart. "Coward."

"Let's go back to talking about the diaper," Dad suggested.

"Who is wearing a diaper?" Mom appeared in the open doorway, a bright smile on her face. She looked fairly normal, the bright veins that made her face look unnatural fading to the point where I could barely see them. I wanted to ask how she managed it, but I was terrified of the answer.

"We all want Aisling to wear one because she's such a baby, but she refuses," Braden answered. "It's an ongoing project."

Griffin flicked Braden's ear and gave him a warning look. "Don't make things harder than they need to be, huh?"

Braden rolled his eyes. "Whatever."

"I think everyone should listen to Griffin," Mom said, sitting on the parlor couch across the way and beaming at me. She wasn't Griffin's biggest fan – she hadn't bothered to hide her overt dislike since rejoining our lives – and the fact that she took his side now was suspect. "He's very wise."

"Thank you." Griffin was clearly suspicious, but didn't give voice to his concerns. He sat next to me, plucking my hand up so he could hold it against his chest. "Other than cupid, how was your day?"

I knew what he was asking and refused to embark on the zombie conversation in front of my family. "Pretty quiet."

"Nothing happened?"

"Not really." I was grateful when Jerry and Aidan walked into the room, happy to have something to focus on that didn't revolve around zombies or diapers. The feeling evaporated when Jerry barreled past Cillian, almost knocking him over, and plopped on the couch next to me.

"I got new magazines, Bug." He sounded thrilled as he held up issues of Brides, The Knot, Martha Stewart Weddings and Bridal Guide. "Now we can really start looking for a dress."

I pressed the tip of my tongue against my teeth as I studied them. "I was actually thinking of having a dress custom made," I admitted, risking a glance at Griffin before focusing on Dad. "That is ... um ... if it's okay with Dad."

Dad arched an eyebrow, surprised. "Why wouldn't it be okay?"

"I'm not sure," I hedged, shifting. "It's just ... do you want to pay or do you want me to do it?"

"Of course I'm paying." Dad's face flushed red. "Why wouldn't I?"

"I don't know." I lowered my gaze, discomfort rolling through me. "I thought maybe you thought I should pay for it myself. I don't want to go overboard or anything, but Jerry and I were looking at dresses yesterday and they're all a little bit too frilly – and pricey.

"Griffin suggested I might want to get something unique made, but that's bound to be even more expensive," I continued. "Maybe if you give me a budget I can figure something out."

"A budget?" Dad was incensed. "There's no budget. You may have whatever you want."

"Really?"

"Of course." Dad's voice boomed throughout the room. "You're my only daughter. You're getting the wedding you want. I won't hear another word about it."

For the second time in as many minutes I was beyond grateful. "Thank you."

"Don't thank me." Dad didn't look like he was going to calm down anytime soon. "Pay for it yourself? That's insulting." He grabbed the drink Redmond was pouring for himself. "Unbelievable. You kids will be the death of me."

I chewed my bottom lip as I fought the urge to laugh at his fury. I felt a bit silly for questioning whether or not he would want to pay, but I felt better knowing it wouldn't be an issue. The feeling lasted only until Mom opened her mouth.

"You're engaged?" Now she was the one infuriated.

Whoops. Did I forget to mention that to her? That's probably a big no-no, huh?

10
TEN

"You didn't tell your mother that we were engaged?" Griffin's tone wasn't accusatory, but he looked decidedly uncomfortable.

I rubbed my hand over my forehead as I racked my brain. "I guess I must have forgotten."

"You forgot?" Griffin clenched his jaw.

"Well, the bride is out of the bag now." Jerry refused to let his cheerful demeanor wane. "Isn't it great news, Mrs. Grimlock?"

Mom's expression said she found the news to be anything but great. "When did this happen?"

"Christmas Eve," I replied. "It was after everything that happened with the mirror beast. I guess I forgot you weren't there."

"I see." Mom placed her hands on her knees and shifted a dark look in Dad's direction. "Did you know about this?"

Instead of being uncomfortable – as he was with the conversation about who would pay for the wedding – Dad actually looked amused as he sat in his regular chair. "I did."

"Did you know before it happened?"

"Griffin asked for my permission several weeks before he proposed," Dad replied, refusing to avert his gaze. "I thought it was a nice gesture given the fact that so few men these days do so. For the record, boys, I expect each and every one of you to ask permission before proposing."

"I don't think you have to worry about that," Braden said dryly. "None of us are even close to ready for anything like that."

"I don't believe that Aidan and Cillian agree with that assessment, but that's none of my business," Dad countered. "You and Redmond are definitely dragging behind your siblings, but I expect it to happen eventually. You will show proper manners when the time comes."

"Yes, sir." Braden rolled his eyes as he sat next to Mom. "I might be a bachelor my entire life, though. I think it sounds like a fun way to go."

"Please," Dad scoffed. "You'll find a woman to whip you into shape one day. I have a feeling she'll remind me of Aisling for some reason."

Braden was understandably affronted. "You want me to marry my sister?"

Dad's smile slipped. "Don't be impudent. I simply meant that I think you'll find a woman who is bossy and must always be right. Frankly, I think you've earned it, son."

Now I was the insulted one. "Hey!"

"I didn't say there was anything wrong with that." Dad flashed me a fond smile. "In fact, I'm kind of partial to it myself."

Surprisingly enough, that didn't make me feel better. "I'm not bossy."

Griffin snorted as he squeezed my hand. "You're a sweet and delicate flower. You'll never hear me saying anything to contradict that."

"That's because you know she'll go nuclear if you do," Redmond said. "Still, I think it was gutsy for Griffin to ask permission. I can't believe Dad managed to keep it a secret, but I still think it was gutsy."

"Wait ... does that mean if I want to propose to Aidan that I have to ask your permission?" Jerry asked, running the scenario through his head as he shifted the magazines to my lap. "Will you pay if I propose?"

Dad didn't hesitate. "I will pay. As for asking permission ... ." He glanced to me for help. Dad never once made Aidan feel different when he realized he was gay. He was careful when it came to making sure he didn't inadvertently say anything stupid when it came to his youngest son's sexuality. I knew what he wanted to know. Unfortunately, I had no idea how to answer.

"Don't ask me." I flicked my eyes to Jerry. "Are you supposed to ask permission in that situation?"

Jerry shrugged. "I've never given it much thought."

"Don't worry about it." Aidan obviously wasn't uncomfortable with the conversation. "I have a feeling I'll be the one asking you."

"Will I get a ring?"

"Do you want a ring?"

Jerry pursed his lips. "I don't know. I need to give it some thought. I might want a crown instead."

The room erupted into laughter, the tension easing for everyone but Mom. She remained on the couch, her back ramrod straight. Whatever she was thinking clearly wasn't going to make the room happier.

"I don't understand why you gave him your permission, Cormack." Mom's eyes were like lasers boring into Dad's profile. "Don't you think you should have discussed your answer with me first?"

"No," Dad replied, rolling his neck until it cracked. "You may have given birth to them, Lily, but I'm the parent of note in their lives now."

"Yes, but she's still my daughter."

"And yet you know very little about her," Dad challenged, his temper ratcheting up. "It took a great show of courage for Griffin to ask my permission. I haven't always been ... pleasant ... where he is concerned. He could've merely asked Aisling and then expected me to accept the answer regardless.

"He didn't, although I'm pretty sure that if I had said no he would've asked her anyway because that's how he does things," he continued. "I knew before he asked that they would marry. It was obvious. As for your participation in this blessed event, that's up to Aisling."

"But you're still going to pay, right?" The question was out of my mouth before I thought better of it.

"Of course I'm going to pay, Aisling." Dad shook his head. "Were you really afraid of asking me that?"

"She's been a little ... uptight ... about the planning," Griffin volunteered. "She's working herself into a frenzy daily. I think it's nerves."

"I'm not nervous."

"Oh, you are and it's cute." Cillian patted my head as he passed. "As for permission, I don't think Aisling and Griffin need anyone's permission, Mom. He's already part of the family. They live together. The wedding is merely a formality."

I risked a glance at Griffin and found he looked absurdly touched by Cillian's statement.

"The wedding is a formality," Dad agreed. "I accepted Griffin into this family a long time ago."

"But why?" Mom wasn't holding back now. "He's a police officer. Last time I checked, police officers make very little money and their lives are often in jeopardy. Do you want Aisling to get that call one night?"

"That's the last thing I want. Given Aisling's track record over the last year, though, Griffin could just as easily be getting that call." Dad moved to get up and then settled again, clearly restless. "They love each other. I'm not going to apologize for her being happy."

"That's not what I meant," Mom protested. "I don't dislike Griffin."

"You could've fooled me," Griffin muttered under his breath.

"I don't dislike you," Mom repeated. "I'm merely trying to ensure that Aisling has the best life she can."

I found my voice. "And Griffin will give me that. We're happy. I didn't think I'd ever find someone who would put up with me and this family – including a mother who may or may not be eating people – but I have. Why does that irritate you so?"

"Knock it off with the 'eating people' stuff," Braden warned.

I ignored him. "Griffin is my future. Sure, I'm a little nervous because the idea of standing up in a white dress in front of people and promising to be a better person than I might actually be gives me the heebie jeebies, but I've never doubted that he was the one for me."

"Oh, that might be the sweetest thing you've said in days." Griffin squeezed my hand. "Does this mean you'll stop being a nervous freak of nature?"

"Probably not."

"Well, I can live with it. In fact, you lasted longer with the nerves than I thought you would. I had two weeks in the pool and lost fifty bucks."

I slanted my eyes, irritation returning with a vengeance. "You were in the pool?"

"Hey, does that mean I won?" Aidan looked excited. "I have my eye on a new jacket at Woodward Crossing. It's black leather and fancy. Now would be a good time for extra money."

"You did win," Cillian confirmed. "I have the money upstairs. Remind me before you go."

"You know, I should be offended that you were all placing bets on me," I said. "Do you think that's fair?"

"I think that's human nature," Dad replied. "You'll notice I didn't place a wager."

"No, but you said she'd melt down before New Year's Eve. We all knew that was too soon," Redmond pointed out.

"Stop talking, Redmond," Dad ordered when he saw the look on my face. "Aisling, I knew months ago that you and Griffin were meant to be. Sometimes life works that way. You should consider yourself lucky that it worked that way for you, because it's not always that easy for everyone."

Dad spared a glance for Mom before continuing. "As for you, Lily, I appreciate that you're trying to be involved with the kids and not pushing them to accept things they're not ready to accept," he said. "However, you're not in charge of the decisions in this family. I am."

"I didn't want to make the decisions," Mom said, her voice cracking. "I just wanted to be informed."

"You were informed."

"Six weeks after the fact." Mom crossed her arms over her chest, fury positively rolling off of her. "It's not fair."

"Life isn't fair," Dad shot back. "Deal with it." He flicked his eyes to me. "As for you, don't skimp on this wedding. Make it as big and as grand as you want. If you skimp, I'll know, and I'll be angry. Do you understand?"

I swallowed hard and nodded. "Thank you."

"Don't thank me. You're my daughter. I want to do this for you."

"Since you're paying for a big wedding for Aisling, does that mean you're going to give us extra money, too?" Braden asked, attempting to defuse the tension.

"The only thing I'm going to give you is a boot in your behind."

And just like that, things were back to normal. Er, well, other than the scowl on Mom's face. There was nothing I could do about that, though. Dad was right. She was only tangentially a member of the family. Whether she'd make it all the way back was still up in the air ... as were the lingering questions I had about exactly how she spent her days.

That was a concern for another time. "What are we having for dinner?"

"Prime rib," Dad answered. "I figured it was a good night for comfort food."

"Yes!" I pumped my fist, excited.

Dad smiled. "Did I mention you're my favorite today?"

"No, but I'm always happy to be at top of the heap."

GRIFFIN PARKED AND waited for me in the lot outside the townhouse. He had a bemused expression on his face, one that always accompanies a loud Grimlock dinner, but he didn't seem beaten down by the evening's events.

I slipped my hand in his as we walked to the front door. "How do you feel?"

Griffin grinned. "I'm pretty sure that's supposed to be my line."

"I feel fine."

"Other than the guy you think was following you, right?"

I shrugged. "I could have been wrong."

"You're not usually wrong on things like that," Griffin said. "I know you didn't want me to bring up what happened last night in front of your family, but I'm a bit worried that things aren't going to be wrapped up as easily as I originally thought."

The conversational shift surprised me. I'd almost forgotten about the potential zombie – what with my human-chomping mother melting down over dinner and all – and questioning Griffin on the medical examiner's findings completely slipped my mind.

"What happened?"

"Nothing terrible," Griffin cautioned. "It's just ... when I called Mark Green for an update he conveniently didn't answer my calls."

"What do you think that means?"

"He could have been busy."

"But?"

"But there's a thing called customary courtesy when it comes to law enforcement, and he broke that today," Griffin answered. "I'm guessing the medical examiner's findings are somehow bad for us."

I rolled the idea through my head as I waited for Griffin to open the door, kicking at a set of footprints in the thin veneer of snow that had fallen since I'd left this morning. "Someone was here."

Griffin followed my gaze. "It was probably a solicitor."

That was possible. We got a lot of those in Royal Oak. "Do you think the guy who was following me was an undercover cop?" I don't know why I jumped to that conclusion, but given Griffin's update it seemed a logical assumption.

"I don't know." Griffin ushered me inside, double-checking the lock before following me into the living room. He gathered my coat with his and hung them in the closet before moving to the couch and settling next to me. "I don't want you to worry about this. You didn't do anything wrong, and they have no evidence that suggests otherwise."

"But you're worried, aren't you?"

"I'm more worried about your mother stalking me and putting a knife in my back when I'm not looking."

He meant it as a joke, but it fell flat. "I'll talk to her. I'll make sure she knows that if something happens to you she'll be the first suspect."

"Aisling, your mother isn't going to go after me." Griffin sounded sure of himself, so I wanted to believe him. "She knows that would reflect badly on her. Don't get me wrong, I think she hates me, but she's not dumb enough to go after me."

"I'm sorry about tonight. I didn't even think about telling her the news. I guess I can understand why she's upset, but her reaction was over the top."

"Why didn't you tell her?"

"I don't know. She wasn't there when you proposed. Everyone else was. She's been out of my life for such a long time that I didn't think about it."

Griffin didn't look convinced. "I think you're struggling to trust her, despite what she did to save you a few weeks ago. Part of you wants to believe she's telling the truth, but the other part can't allow it because you recognize the danger associated with it."

"That's true." I stretched my arms over my head. "It's done now. I screwed it up, but now she knows. She'll have to get used to it. I want you. You want me. We're getting married. That's the end of it."

"So the nerves are gone?" Griffin ran his finger up and down my arm. "Does this mean you'll be easier to deal with?"

"No. I can't help myself. I freak out. It's what I do."

Griffin chuckled. "I know. I find it cute sometimes. We'll deal with it."

I shifted on the couch so I faced him. "If I tell you something, do you promise not to laugh?"

"No, but I promise to love you no matter what. That's the best I can do."

It would have to be enough. "I spent the entire day looking over my shoulder for zombies."

Griffin didn't laugh, although he did crack a smile. "I figured. At least cupid and a cop distracted you for a bit."

"I know you don't want to think about it, but I'm guessing that the medical examiner's initial findings held up and now your buddy is trying to figure out how we got a month-old body to downtown Royal Oak without anyone noticing. He won't believe that guy walked there himself, so the only rational explanation is that we did something."

"Except we didn't."

"He doesn't know that and he won't think outside the box," I argued. "You've seen crazy things since hooking up with me and you don't believe."

"I didn't say I didn't believe you," Griffin clarified. "I just said ... it can't be zombies. There has to be another explanation. I don't want you making yourself sick over this. We'll figure it out."

"We'd better. I don't think it'll be much of a wedding if I'm behind bars."

Griffin snickered, sliding his arm around my waist and tugging me to his side. "How about we think about something else for the rest of the night? I think we've had enough drama of the mother and zombie nature for one evening."

I cocked an eyebrow. "What did you have in mind?"

Griffin's grin was devilish. "Well, I've been giving it some thought." He leaned in and whispered a suggestive thought. "What do you think?"

"I think the last one in the bedroom is a rotten egg," I teased, using my hip to nudge him out of the way as I bolted in that direction. "Oh, don't forget the chocolate sauce. I bought a new can. It's in the refrigerator."

Griffin was already heading for the fridge. "I love that we're always on the same page when it comes to stuff like this."

I cast a quick glance over my shoulder and smiled. "You're not the only one."

ELEVEN

I woke, warm and naked, to a pounding sound. I'm not a morning person, so I wasn't happy about the incessant noise.

"Again? What are you, a rabbit? Let me sleep and I'll consider it in an hour."

Griffin was out of bed like a shot, yanking on a pair of boxer shorts and stumbling from the bedroom before I managed to muster the brain power to figure out what he was doing. As if in a daze, I searched the floor next to the bed for something to pull on. All I found was Griffin's discarded shirt from the night before and a pair of pajama bottoms that didn't even remotely match. I tugged them on anyway, and by the time I hit the living room I found Griffin squaring off with Detective Green.

This couldn't be good.

"Is there a reason you're banging on our front door before dawn?"

"It's after dawn," Green said calmly, gesturing toward the window for emphasis. "You need to get dressed and come down to the station. We have a few questions for you."

"Excuse me?" Griffin's eyebrows flew up his forehead. "You're hauling us in for questioning?"

"I am." Mark's expression was cold and flat. "Please don't make this difficult."

"Oh, well, I'd hate to make this difficult for you," Griffin muttered, flicking his eyes to me when he sensed my presence in the doorway between the living room and our bedroom. "Apparently, we're being summoned to the police station for questioning."

I wasn't sure what to make of that. Being questioned by cops didn't exactly fill me with fear. Griffin questioned me in an official capacity before we ever started dating, after all. I also had been arrested a few times during my wild teenage years – I was innocent every time, except for the car thefts, which were misunderstandings – so this wasn't my first go around on the overzealous cop merry-go-round.

"I don't believe you can compel us to visit the police station without a warrant," I offered, dragging a hand through my snarled hair. I knew how I must have looked to Green, but I refused to get myself worked up over it. Whatever he thought of me – and it was obviously bad – it didn't matter. What mattered was being smart about this.

"I can secure a warrant if you like," Green sneered.

"That won't be necessary." Griffin pinned me with a pointed look. "Right?"

I never knew it was possible to love someone as much as I loved Griffin, but I couldn't take his side on this one. This was too important. He was looking at it from a good guy place, believing that all innocent people walked free. He couldn't see what I could: that Green believed we were guilty and was ready to officially start going after us.

"I believe you're going to need a warrant," I said carefully, folding my arms over my chest. "I also believe, while you're waiting to get your warrant, that you should be outside of our home."

Griffin's mouth dropped open at my calm demeanor. "Aisling, he's just here to ask questions. That's normal."

"No, he's here to force us to the police station," I corrected. "That is not normal. That means we're officially suspects."

Griffin slid a sidelong look in Green's direction, his mind clearly working overtime. Green took advantage of the lag in conversation to attempt to smooth things over.

"I didn't say you were suspects," Green supplied. "I simply said we want to talk to you at the police station. If you're innocent you shouldn't have a problem with that."

"You can't run that load of crap on me," I countered. "I know how this works."

"Yes, I've seen your record." Green's teeth gleamed under the muted light. "You have your own special way of dealing with law enforcement, don't you?"

I pursed my lips. I certainly did have my own way of dealing with potential arrest. Before Griffin, I had very little respect for law enforcement. Now, because I loved him, I made myself to look at things from a different angle. I forced myself to see his side of things. It wasn't easy, but he was a good cop. I wasn't sure I could say the same of Green. I was starting to believe he was a lazy cop, nothing more.

"If you want to question us at the police station, you'll need a warrant," I said.

Griffin openly glared at me, shaking his head. "You don't need a warrant for me. I'll willingly go to the station."

The look Green shot me was one of triumph. "Thank you. I'll give you a few minutes to get ready."

"I'll talk to her," Griffin added, under his breath. "She's not a morning person."

Green remained impassive as he stared at me. "I think I figured that out the second I saw the hair."

I ignored his tone and followed Griffin into the bedroom, waiting until he shut the door before bracing myself. Instead of yelling, Griffin merely shook his head.

"Why are you making this difficult?"

"Because I have no choice," I replied. "He's going after me on this. You feel it. I know you do. Why else would he come here first thing in the morning? He's trying to catch us off guard. He's trying to catch us in the act of ... doing something."

"All he caught us in the act of doing was sleeping." Griffin stripped out of the boxer shorts he hastily tugged on before answering the door and strode naked to the closet. "Get dressed. He won't be patient for long."

I did as instructed, but only because I knew Green was securing a warrant and it would save time. I selected an obnoxious T-shirt and basic jeans before heading into the bathroom to wash my face, brush my teeth and attempt to tame my wild hair. I was just finishing up when the sound of voices in the backyard caught my attention. The bathroom doesn't have a window, so I walked back into the bedroom and drew apart the vertical blinds and peered through the slats.

At first I didn't know what to make of the activity. There were at least twenty men – some uniformed cops – standing by the fence that marked the property line. I didn't know what they were doing, perhaps looking for evidence or hidden weapons, but I recognized the medical examiner from the other night, and when I saw him kneel next to something on the ground my blood ran cold.

"Griffin!"

"I don't want to fight, Aisling." Griffin clearly hadn't noticed the activity on the back lawn. His attention was on his belt. "Please. This is going to be hard enough to get through without a fight."

"It's going to be harder than you think," I muttered, my mind firing with possibilities as I released the blinds and headed toward the nightstand that held my cell phone.

"What is that supposed to mean?" Griffin's agitation was palpable. "Please, just answer his questions and don't be difficult. You didn't do anything wrong."

"You keep repeating that because I think you actually believe it," I said, pressing the speed dial button for my father. "I think your world is about to be shaken."

"My world is not about to be shaken, because you are my world," Griffin gritted out. "What are you doing? Who are you calling?"

I held his gaze, sympathy washing over me. This wasn't going to go well for him. My father picked up on the third ring.

"This better be good."

"Daddy ... ."

"Daddy?" I could practically see Dad's face twisting. "Have you been arrested?"

"I'm being taken into custody for questioning," I replied, maintaining an even tone even though I wanted to cry. "I'll be taken to the Royal Oak Police station very soon."

"On what charge?"

"I don't think they're going to charge me quite yet, but when charges do come it will be multiple murders."

"Murders?" Dad's voice echoed on the phone at the same time Griffin asked the exact same question from the foot of the bed.

"It's a long story, Dad, but the cops are in our backyard right now and I'm pretty sure they're looking at a body," I volunteered, watching as Griffin's eyes widened and he started toward the window. "The thing is, even though I know the body wasn't there yesterday I'm guessing the medical examiner will find the individual has been dead for more than a day or two."

"Why do you say that?" Dad was unnaturally calm.

"Because the same thing happened two nights ago in Royal Oak," I answered. "Some guy knocked me over and kind of attacked, so I hit him in the mouth. He was dead. When the medical examiner showed up, he said that the guy had died a month ago.

"Now the same cop showed up at our front door and there are people recovering a body in the backyard," I continued. "He demanded I go to the police station, but I told him that wasn't an option without a warrant."

"That's my girl." Despite the nature of the conversation, Dad didn't sound worked up. I wished I could see his face to confirm my suspicions, though. "I'll get Neil Graham to the police station as soon as possible. You remember him, right?"

Neil Graham had a special knack for getting reapers out of trouble. He was one of the best criminal attorneys in the state, and he was on retainer at the home office because reapers often found themselves in run-ins with cops. "I remember him."

"Don't talk until he gets there," Dad ordered.

"I won't." I flicked a worried look in Griffin's direction, but he was focused on the activity outside the window. "Will you come, too?" I felt like a baby for wanting my father, but I couldn't help myself. I wasn't good in certain situations, and this would be an example of that.

"Of course I'll come." Dad's voice softened. "I'll be there as soon as I can. You remember what to do when it comes to being questioned by the cops, right?"

I did. It wasn't something Griffin would like. "Yeah."

"I'll be there as soon as I can, kid. Don't give them anything to work with."

"Do I ever?"

"No." Dad chuckled. "I can say that of all my children you're the best at dancing around police involvement. You never crumble under the weight of an interrogation."

"At least you're proud."

"Always, kid. I'll be there as soon as I can. Just ... hold it together until I get there."

"Thank you."

I disconnected and fixed Griffin with a calm look. "Dad is sending a lawyer."

"I don't need a lawyer," Griffin barked. "I didn't do anything."

This was going to be much harder on him, although I wasn't sure what to do about it. "If it's any consolation, I think they're coming after me. You should be clear on this, other than your association with me, of course."

Griffin scowled. "We're a unit. I'm not free of this until you are."

It was a nice sentiment. I knew it would change relatively quickly. "You're not going to like how I handle the interrogation."

Griffin was instantly suspicious. "What is that supposed to mean?"

"Well ... let's just say that I have to do what I'm about to do, and it doesn't reflect on my love for you."

"Oh, well, that sends chills down my spine."

I clapped a hand on his shoulder and forced a smile. "It's going to be a long morning. Prepare yourself."

"MS. GRIMLOCK, DO you want to work with me here?"

Detective Green was in the room with me for only twenty minutes before he wanted to pull out his hair. I have a unique way of influencing law enforcement, sometimes inspiring violence, and I can always tell when I'm irritating someone.

"I don't know what you want me to say," I said sweetly, resting my hands flat on the interrogation room table and fixing Green with my best "I'm a stupid woman and you'll have to use small words so I understand what you're saying" expression.

"I want you to explain to me how a body found its way into your backyard," Green gritted out.

"I really have no idea."

"Theorize."

"No."

Green leaned forward, scorching me with a hateful gaze. "I don't know what kind of game you're playing here, but if you think Detective Taylor can save you, you have another think coming."

I remained immovable and silent.

"What? Now you're not talking?" Green practically exploded.

"You didn't ask me a question," I pointed out, shifting my eyes to the double-sided mirror on the wall. "Are people watching us through that, like on television?"

Green spared a glance for the mirror. "Not everything is like television. It's a normal mirror."

"Hmm." I didn't believe him.

"Tell me about your relationship with Jed Burnham."

"I don't know who that is."

"He's the man you claim you ran into on the street two nights ago," Green said.

"I don't believe I've ever met anyone by that name."

"You're sure?"

I shrugged. "The only other time I've heard the name 'Jed' is on *The Beverly Hillbillies*. If I heard that name a second time I'd be making so many cement pond jokes that you'd want to smack the crap out of me."

"I'm pretty sure I'll want to do that anyway."

He meant it as a threat – or at least to be daunting – but all the simple statement made me do was smile. "Oh, just wait."

"You're in very serious trouble here, Ms. Grimlock," Green pressed. "You have two dead bodies and strange circumstances surrounding both that absolutely no one can explain."

"If no one can explain them why do you think I'd be able to?"

"Because you're the only common thread in both deaths," Green replied, his temper flashing. "Well, Detective Taylor is a common thread, too. Perhaps we should be looking closer at him. Is that what you want?"

He was trying to manipulate me. I wasn't dumb enough to fall for it. "Do you have any coffee? I'm dying for some caffeine."

"You want me to get you coffee?" Green was beside himself. "Do you think I'm your waiter or something?"

"I wouldn't rule it out," I said. "You're probably a better waiter than you are a cop."

Green slammed his hand down on the table. "Don't push me!" He expected me to be afraid, but all I did was stare back at him.

"Where did we land on that coffee?"

"You are a piece of work, aren't you?" Green pushed himself to a standing position and paced in front of the mirror. "You're in real trouble here, Ms. Grimlock. You know that, right?"

"No, you're in real trouble here."

I flicked my eyes to the door when it flew open to allow Neil Graham entrance. It had been a few years since I last saw him – an arrest for assault with intent to do great bodily harm after a public fight with Angelina forcing him to plead me down to a public nuisance charge – but he looked the same. I smiled when I caught his eye.

"Long time no see."

"I was hoping the last time would be the last time," Neil said. "I guess I'm not that lucky."

"Probably not." I leaned back in my chair. "This is Detective Green. He has something up his butt and it's very uncomfortable, so he can't sit for more than thirty seconds before doing a dramatic routine in front of the two-way mirror."

"I told you that no one is behind that mirror," Green barked, causing Neil's lips to twitch.

"It doesn't matter if anyone is behind that mirror," Neil said. "The fact of the matter is, you have no right to hold Ms. Grimlock. You have no right to question her. You have no right to invade her home."

"We got an anonymous call about suspicious activities in her backyard," Green sneered. "We followed up on the call and found a body. If that's not a reason ... ."

"You found a dead body in the backyard area she shares with at least twelve other people," Neil clarified. "You have no proof that she or Mr. Taylor put it there."

"Since she had dealings downtown that resulted in another dead body two nights ago, I'm going to argue that point," Green said.

"If I understand the situation correctly, your own medical examiner said that body had been dead for weeks," Neil noted. "If you come up with a firm time of death, I'm sure Ms. Grimlock would be happy to supply an alibi. Otherwise, you have nothing – including motive and means – when it comes to my client."

"I have a pattern," Green challenged.

"Well, take your pattern to a quilting bee because we're done here." Neil nodded, telling me it was time to go. "Come along, Aisling. This police officer will be no further problem for you."

"I'm a detective," Green growled. "And I will be on this case until I close it."

I offered him a bright smile as I passed, unable to let one last chance to mess with him slip through my fingers. "Good luck with that."

"This isn't over," Green warned.

"Yeah, good luck with that, too."

"Come along, Aisling. Your father is waiting in the lobby, and he's most anxious to see you."

I had no doubt about that.

12

TWELVE

Dad was waiting for me in the lobby. He offered me a quick hug before glaring at the officers behind the protective bubble and leading me outside.

"Is your car here?"

"I rode with Griffin."

Dad stilled. "Where is he?"

"Probably answering questions." I rolled my neck as I glanced back at the building. "He's not happy with me."

Dad was calm despite the circumstances. This wasn't his first time dealing with overzealous police involvement and his offspring. Heck, this was probably the twentieth time. "Why?"

"Because he believes in the system. He keeps saying, 'You didn't do anything.' He believes that actually means something."

Dad heaved a sigh. "He'll be all right. He understands how things work. You did the right thing by calling me."

"Yes, I love being a grown woman who has to call her daddy when things go bad."

Dad rested his hand on my shoulder before inclining his chin toward the coffee shop on the next block. "Can I buy you some caffeine? We clearly have things we need to discuss."

It was an enticing offer, much better than braving the cold while waiting for Griffin, but I wasn't sure it was a good idea. "Shouldn't I wait for Griffin? I mean ... isn't that what people who are going to be married are supposed to do? I'm pretty sure he'd wait for me."

"I'll check on his progress," Neil offered, exchanging a weighted look with Dad. "I'm not technically his lawyer, but I'm more than willing to offer my services."

"Do it," Dad ordered. "He won't take you up on it, but it's worth a shot. Make sure he knows where Aisling and I are, and then join us."

Neil nodded, his lips curving as he glanced at me. "You held together well. I almost forgot that special gift you have for driving law enforcement around the bend without even breaking a sweat."

"Yes, I get better with age," I deadpanned, falling into step with Dad as we left Neil to work his magic. I waited until we ordered our drinks and secreted ourselves into a corner booth before speaking again. "So ... how angry are you?"

"I'm not happy, but I'm not sure 'angry' is the word I would use when describing my feelings," Dad replied, sipping his coffee. "Why didn't you tell me what was happening? You had a prime opportunity last night. This situation would've made a great distraction when your mother began whining about the engagement."

"I don't know." It was a terrible answer, one I knew he wouldn't accept, but it slipped out anyway.

"I think you did it because you didn't want me to worry."

"You're probably attaching altruistic leanings to my decision that aren't there," I countered. "I didn't want you to worry, but it was more for my benefit than yours."

"Because you think I've been hovering since you were hurt?"

"Yes." I saw no reason to lie. "I love you, but it's getting to be a bit much. I'm fine. I'm back to normal. You don't have to spend your time worrying that I'm getting into trouble. Even when I do find trouble, most of the time I find my own way out of it."

"You do indeed." Dad leaned back in his seat. "As for smothering you, I can't help it. You almost died, Aisling. You were unconscious in the hospital for days. I watched your brothers, Jerry and Griffin melt down on numerous occasions while I had to pretend to be strong for all of them. I can't simply wipe that from my memory."

"I am okay."

"I'll be the judge of that. For now, tell me what's going on."

I launched into the story, which wasn't very long because I knew absolutely nothing, and when I was done, Dad was contemplative.

"What do you think it means?" Dad asked finally. "I've never heard of a body walking around after death."

"What do I think it means? I think he was a zombie." I had to bite back a smirk at the way Dad's face twisted. "I can tell what you think of that idea, but there's no other explanation. And, before you unload, you should know that Griffin thinks I'm going crazy, too."

"I doubt very much that Griffin said that to you," Dad countered. "He loves you. The zombie theory is a bit much, though."

"Then how would you explain it?"

"The medical examiner made a mistake."

"You sound like Griffin."

"Six months ago I would've taken that as an insult," Dad said. "Now ... perhaps it's a compliment. He's grown a lot in my estimation. The way he sat next to your bed while you were recovering ... well ... he's a good man."

The sentiment warmed my heart. "This is hard for him. He knows the detective. He was friendly with him the other night. He'll be angry that you called in Neil."

"He'll have to get over it. You're my daughter, and I won't let you sit in jail."

"I wasn't technically in jail."

"Close enough." Dad rolled his neck. "Griffin will understand. I'll make him understand, if necessary."

That would be a neat trick. "I'm worried about him."

"Are you worried about being arrested and charged?"

"I'm not sure. I don't think they can pin it on me, but that doesn't mean they won't try."

"Well, I'll have Neil start going through their files right away to see what he comes up with," Dad said. "He doesn't seem especially worried. He even joked about someone pointing the finger at you by making that anonymous call. Any police officer who wasn't blind and dumb should realize that."

I let my eyes drift to the police station and exhaled heavily when I saw Neil and Griffin walk out together. "There they are."

Dad followed my gaze. "Griffin doesn't look happy, does he?"

"No, and I have a feeling we're going to have an argument when we get back to the townhouse."

"Well, at least you won't be bored." Dad grinned as he sipped, sighing when he took in the dark look on my face. "Stop worrying. It will be fine."

I snorted. "Who do you think I learned to worry from?"

"Me," Dad answered without hesitation. "I worry when justified, though. This is not something to worry about. It's ridiculous." He turned his face to the door when Griffin and Neil entered, offering up a bright smile as Griffin slid into the booth next to me. "There's our jailbird."

Griffin slanted his eyes as he grabbed my coffee. "Do you think that's funny?"

"I think your sense of humor seems to be missing this morning," Dad replied, making room for Neil to settle next to him. "What did you find out?"

"They don't have anything," Neil said. "In fact, they have less than nothing. They apparently have a video feed of whatever happened the other night, but they won't let me view it. They claim they need an expert to authenticate it first. That means they don't like what they see."

"There's nothing to see on that video," Griffin argued. "We were walking down the street, a man ran into Aisling and knocked her over. She punched him in the face and he was dead. Now they say he'd been dead for a month. None of it makes sense."

"It does if you believe in zombies," I offered.

Dad offered me a slit-eyed stare. "What did I tell you about zombies when you were a child?"

"To shoot the most annoying person in our group in the leg and leave him behind for fodder as I made my escape."

"That was a joke." Dad's smile was sheepish. "What else did I tell you?"

"That they weren't real," I replied, understanding that was the answer he sought. "You also told me Santa Claus was real, so you clearly can't be trusted."

"Don't push it." Dad extended a warning finger. "You need to stop with this zombie nonsense. I'm sure there's another explanation."

"And I will find out what that is." Neil got to his feet. "I'll be in touch, Cormack. As for you, Aisling, try to stay out of trouble. If the police bother you again make sure you call me."

"I'll add you to my speed dial." I offered up a sweet smile and watched him leave. "Now he thinks I'm crazy, too."

"No one thinks you're crazy," Dad chided.

"I might, but I have bigger things to worry about," Griffin said, sliding his eyes to me. "You know that car that was following you yesterday?"

"It was the cops, wasn't it?"

Griffin nodded. "They didn't come out and say it, but I asked. They evaded instead of answering. That means they were following you. The good news is they seem to have lost you in downtown Ferndale and have no idea you were in Markham's loft."

"Well, I guess I'll have to be careful."

"I think they might've been following you all day," Griffin said. "They asked me if I was aware that you drove all over the suburbs and made multiple stops."

"What did you tell them?" Dad inquired, sobering.

"That she was probably researching estate sales and I don't really keep up with her day-to-day activities because antiques don't whip me into a frenzy," Griffin explained. "I'm not sure they believed me."

"Which means they'll probably have someone following her today, too." Dad rubbed his chin, thoughtful. "You know what that means, right, Aisling?"

"I do. It means that I can't text while driving, because they'll know if I do."

"You shouldn't do that regardless," Dad said. "It also means you can't go out on jobs."

Wait ... what? "Excuse me?"

"You can't go out on jobs," Dad repeated. "If you go to the wrong one and someone sees what you're doing — or worse, a wraith comes calling — we'll be in big trouble. We can't risk it."

"So, you're sidelining me?"

"I don't see where I have much choice."

I turned to Griffin for help. "They won't follow me to jobs, will they?"

"I think that they're going to follow you everywhere," Griffin replied. "I'm sorry. Until we figure this out, you're grounded. You have to stay home and not draw attention to yourself."

That sounded like the worst idea ever. "But ... what am I supposed to do?"

A small smile played at the corner of Griffin's lips. "Well, Jerry brought you a bunch of wedding magazines. Maybe you can get a jump-start on wedding plans."

Dad beamed. "That sounds like a capital idea!"

I didn't bother to hide my disdain. "I hate you both right now."

"You'll live." Griffin patted my hand as he finished off my coffee. "Now, come on. Some of us actually have to go to work today. We can't all lounge around and do nothing but dream about marrying the best man ever."

I groaned as he dragged me to a standing position. "This sucks."

"Yeah, and I have a feeling it's only going to get worse."

"WHAT TIME IS it?"

I paced the living room as Griffin affixed his badge to his belt and watched me go insane. "Five minutes after the last time you asked. Stop doing that. You'll wear a path in the rug."

I scalded him with a withering look. "Ha, ha."

"Hey, this isn't my fault." Griffin's voice was tinged with irritation. "I didn't cause this situation."

"But I did, huh?"

"I didn't say that."

"You're thinking it."

"You have no idea what I'm thinking," Griffin argued. "The fact of the matter is, you're in this position for the foreseeable future and there's absolutely nothing we can do to get you out of it until we have more information."

"You're only upset because I called my father," I grumbled, running my toe over the carpet as I stared at my feet. "You think I should've played nice with Detective Green, even though he thinks I'm a wacky murderer who hides bodies for a month and then disposes of them in downtown Royal Oak."

"I'm not happy you called your father," Griffin conceded. "I think it was completely unnecessary and that you only did it to put Mark in his place. He pretty much said the same to me."

"That's not why I did it."

"Then why did you do it?"

"Because my father told me a long time ago that I had to be careful," I replied, refusing to back down. "I'm a reaper. We do weird crap on a daily basis. If someone were to find out ... what do you think that would mean for all of us?"

"I don't know," Griffin sighed. "I've often wondered if it wouldn't be easier for everyone concerned if you worked in the open. People should understand you have a job to do."

"Oh, please," I scoffed. "If people found out they'd tracking us down and killing us because they'd think that way they could live forever."

Griffin stilled. "I didn't consider that."

"That's on top of the rich ones who'd think they could buy their way out of death," I said. "This house would be under siege from people who want to save a dead loved one from passing over, as if that somehow means they're doing a good thing by ending us."

Griffin held up his hand to stop me before I went off on a tangent. "Okay. You have a point. That still doesn't mean we needed your father to send his high-priced lawyer down to save us. Mark has nothing on us."

"You keep saying that, and I know you believe that means something because you're a good cop and always look for the truth, but Detective Green is obviously looking hard at me even though I have no motive and he has video of the first altercation," I said. "I love that you believe in the system, because that means you're good at your job. You take pride in it, and I take pride in being with you every single day."

Griffin's expression softened. "Aisling ... ."

"I'm not finished." I turned so my shoulders were squared as I faced him. "Not all cops are like you. Detective Green isn't going to stop until he manages to pin this on me. That means we have to figure out what's going on ourselves."

"How?"

"I don't know yet. Apparently I have the whole day to give it some thought."

"Well, let me know what you come up with." Griffin moved toward the door, causing my heart to flutter when I realized he wasn't going to kiss me goodbye. He was putting on a good show of not being angry, but I knew that temper lurked under his handsome and amiable features. He wanted to explode. "I'm sorry this is so hard for you. I'll pick up dinner on my way home and we'll talk when I get back."

I stared at him for a long moment. "Right. Have a good day at work."

"Have a good day looking at the magazines. Why don't you mark anything you like and we'll look at them together when I get back." It was an olive branch. He was doing his best to keep things from imploding in spectacular fashion.

"Sure." I swallowed hard. "One thing before you go."

Griffin stilled near the door, his fingers on the handle. "I'm going to be late."

"This will just take a second." I hated the distance between us. I hated it that it appeared so quickly, forming a chasm that wasn't there mere hours before. "Did Detective Green tell you who called in the body in the backyard?"

"No."

"Did he give you a name?"

"He doesn't have an identity yet."

Hmm. That was interesting. "Do you think you can find out who called it in?"

"Why?" Griffin clearly wasn't in the mood for me to play amateur sleuth, and his expression said exactly that. "You're not to stick your nose into this situation until we have a talk tonight and come up with a plan. Do you understand?"

"I love when you boss me around."

Griffin ignored my tone. "Do you understand?"

"I understand," I hissed, crossing my arms over my chest. "I get it. You don't have to talk to me as if I'm two."

"That's not my intention. I just ... need you to be safe." Griffin opened the door and stepped over the threshold, stopping long enough to give me one more look. "I love you. I'm sorry about all of this. Be safe and ... I'll bring a nice dinner home."

I pursed my lips and nodded. "I'll be waiting."

The second Griffin shut the door I reached for my cell phone. I'd be waiting when he got home, but if he thought I was hanging out in this townhouse all day knowing the cops were outside watching my every move he had another think coming.

My brother picked up on the first ring.

"Redmond, I need you to come pick me up. The thing is ... I need you to park two blocks away in that alley by the market so the cops don't see us. We have a situation."

There was a reason I called Redmond instead of anyone else. He didn't even hesitate when responding. "Cool. I love messing with the cops."

That made two of us.

THIRTEEN

Redmond had the heat blasting and a cup of coffee waiting for me when I hopped into his Ford Expedition.

"Where are the cops?"

"In the parking lot." I removed my gloves and wrapped my hands around the coffee. "They're not even attempting to hide themselves. I think they're trying to unnerve me."

"They must not realize what a hard case you are." Redmond offered up a saucy wink. "Where's Griffin?"

"Work." I averted my gaze and stared out the window. "You should exit this alley from the opposite direction, just to be on the safe side."

"Okay." Redmond didn't put up an argument, waiting until we were on the road and heading away from the townhouse to speak again. "Where are we going?"

"Woodward Crossing."

He furrowed his brow. "We're going shopping? You called me to spring you from the ever-watchful gaze of the cops to go shopping?"

"No, we're going to question Madame Dauphine," I corrected.

"Who is Madame Dauphine?"

"She's a voodoo queen who does this Marie Laveau shtick that's right out of a bad horror movie," I explained. "I met her the day before yesterday."

"Would that be the same day you had a guy die after hitting him in the face?"

I should've known my father would fill in my brothers. Ah, well. It made things easier. "Yes."

"Dad didn't have much time to tell us about all of that," Redmond said. "He picked up your jobs for the day, by the way. Do you want to expand for those of us not in the loop?"

"Not if you're going to make fun of me."

"Why would I make fun of you?"

"I know Dad told you about my zombie theory."

"Oh, that." Redmond chuckled. "Yeah, that's a little crazy, Aisling. Zombies aren't real."

"Most people would say that about reapers."

"We're not most people. We know how the paranormal world works, what's real and what isn't, and zombies are most definitely not real."

"Zombies like we see in movies and television aren't real," I corrected. "That doesn't mean the idea of someone using dead bodies as weapons doesn't have merit."

"Okay." Redmond stretched out the word as he regrouped. "And you think this Madame Dauphine has something to do with it?"

"I think that Jerry and I ran into Angelina the other day and she was acting squirrelly. I couldn't even land a good insult. I thought I was off my game, but maybe something else was going on."

"Like?"

"Well, we saw Angelina go into a voodoo shop, so we followed her."

"And that's where you met Madame Dauphine? What? Don't look at me that way. You're terrible when it comes to telling a story. You get that from Dad. He takes hours to tell one story, and then the end isn't even worth the ride."

"I'm telling him you said that."

"Hey, I pushed off my jobs on Cillian, Braden and Aidan so I could spend the day with you," Redmond said. "I think you owe me."

"Fine." I blew out a sigh. "When we entered the shop, I sensed right away there was something different about this woman."

"You sensed?"

"It's a girl thing," I explained. "She seemed ... keyed in to me, if that makes any sense. She knew I was different. She wouldn't stop staring. Jerry was the one buying everything, but she was much more interested in me."

"No offense, kid, but you seem to have that effect on everyone," Redmond pointed out. "People are fascinated by you because you say whatever comes to your mind and you don't care about making a scene."

"I wasn't making a scene in the voodoo shop," I argued. "I went in because I wanted to see what Angelina was doing. I didn't care about Madame Dauphine or her potions."

"What was Angelina doing?"

"I don't know. She was gone by the time we got there. She went out a side door."

"That's kind of suspicious, huh?"

"Exactly! I've been thinking about this." I shifted in my seat so I faced Redmond. "What if Angelina has been going to the voodoo lady to get spells to mess with me? That would explain why my insults were so lame."

"Yes, because messing with your insult ability is the same as killing a man."

"That's the thing. What if she didn't kill anyone?" I challenged. "What if she merely used a spell or potion on a body that was already dead?"

Redmond arched a dubious eyebrow. "How does that work?"

"How should I know? I'm not a voodoo queen. That's why we're going to talk to a voodoo queen."

"Okay, I guess I can get behind that." Redmond said the words, but he didn't look convinced. "Just out of curiosity, what does Griffin think about this?"

"He doesn't believe me." I sat back in the seat, deflating. "He thinks I'm crazy. He's also angry because I called Dad, and Neil showed up while I was at the police station."

"That's the smartest thing you could've done," Redmond said. "As for the voodoo stuff ... I don't know. The timing is interesting, and I think it's worth a shot to question this Madame Dauphine. Why do you think she's trying to emulate Marie Laveau?"

"It's just this feeling I got when I was in her shop. She has a way of carrying herself. You'll have to see for yourself to understand, but it's weird. She knew what I was. I'm almost certain of that. She said I dealt in death."

"Technically Angelina knows what we are," Redmond pointed out. "She had an idea after that wraith attack a couple months back. She knows Mom came back from the dead. Even though we told her that lame story about how it happened, she doesn't seem to believe the lies we're spinning. Then, of course, she was attacked by the mirror man and survived all of that mess. She might not know everything about us, but she knows enough to make our lives miserable. She could've told Madame Dauphine about us."

"That's possible." I'd considered that, but something didn't feel right about the scenario. "I don't think Angelina saw us following her, though. How did Madame Dauphine know who I was if Angelina didn't tell her about me?"

"Huh. A woman with black hair streaked through with white and purple eyes. I have no idea how she figured it out. It's a mystery."

"Knock it off." I poked Redmond's side. "I honestly think there's something going on in that shop. I can't explain it, but I feel it."

"Well, I have faith in you, so we'll check it out," Redmond said. "What did Griffin say when you told him you were doing this?"

"Oh, I didn't tell him. He's mad at me. Besides, he'd be totally ticked off to know that I crawled through a window to sneak out of the townhouse and then climbed a fence to get into an alley. He doesn't find playing games with cops nearly as much fun as we do."

"So that means he's going to be ticked off when he finds out, right?"

"Yes."

"Are you ready for that? You guys haven't done much fighting of late. It's been quiet."

I tilted my head to the side, considering. "I think we need to have a fight, if that makes sense."

"Not in the least."

"I know that he was upset when I got hurt ... ."

"Wrecked," Redmond interjected. "He was wrecked when you got hurt. He didn't leave your side, kid. He even cried a few times, and he didn't care who saw."

The statement caused my stomach to flip. "I don't want to hurt him. It's the last thing I want. He can't cushion me in bubble wrap and protect me forever. He needs to lose his temper so he realizes he can do it without the world coming to an end."

"And you're going to help him strictly out of the goodness of your heart, right?" Redmond's tone was teasing.

"I'm going to help him for the good of us all."

"You've always been altruistic."

"And don't you forget it."

REDMOND LET ME lead the way to Voodoo Vacation, but the minute we reached the door he put a cautioning hand on my arm.

"Maybe you should let me do the talking," he suggested.

"Why?"

"Because I'm better with people. You tend to be abrasive when things don't go your way."

I was pretty sure I should be offended. "Let's play it by ear."

"You'll let me start, though, right?"

"Sure." Why not? I would take over eventually. I had the whole day to play with Madame Dauphine, after all, because I didn't have work slowing me down.

Redmond's smile was all charm and flirtatious energy as we walked through the door. Dauphine, alerted by the bell over the door, flashed a smile when she saw us.

"Bienvenue! Are you seeking anything in particular?"

Redmond exchanged a quick glance with me, something unsaid passing between us. Dauphine acted as if she'd never seen me before.

"We're just here to look around, merci," Redmond answered. "Your store looks tres interesting."

"Only to those with open minds." Dauphine drifted from behind the counter, barely sparing me a glance as she focused all of her attention on Redmond. "You have a warrior's soul and a romantic's heart."

Redmond blushed under her intense scrutiny. "Oh, well ... ."

Yeah, that was all about all I could take of that. "She's messing with you," I admonished. "She's trying to pretend she doesn't recognize me."

"Hey, I do have a warrior's soul," Redmond argued.

"Whatever."

"I thought you were going to let me talk."

"I changed my mind." I flicked my eyes to Dauphine and found her staring at me. "What do you know about zombies?"

"Oh, geez." Redmond pinched the bridge of his nose. "This is why I wanted to do the talking."

"What do you mean?" Dauphine asked, her demeanor relaxed. "Are you having trouble with zombies?"

"Maybe. Do you have a potion for that?"

"No."

Well, that was disheartening. I wasn't keen on rewarding bad behavior, but if she had a potion to free me from a zombie curse I'd totally pay whatever it cost. "Do you know how to raise the dead?"

"That's an interesting question." Dauphine floated to a nearby display shelf. "You work with the dead, no?"

"See. I told you." I turned to Redmond expectantly. "I was right."

"Yes, I see." Redmond's patience was wearing thin. I didn't miss the fact that he positioned himself so that he could intervene should Dauphine make a move on me. "My sister asked a question. Do you know how to ... harness a dead body and use it to do something else?"

"Like what?" Dauphine was all faux innocence and light. "What do you think I've done with dead bodies?"

"She's not even denying it," I pointed out.

"Will you shut your mouth for five minutes?" Redmond barked, shaking his head as he locked gazes with Dauphine. "My sister was attacked by a man the police say died a month ago. You wouldn't know anything about that, would you?"

Dauphine crossed herself. "Mon Dieu! Why would I?"

"Because I saw you the day it happened," I answered. "More importantly, I saw Angelina Davenport come in here the day it happened. She's clearly up to something."

"I told you, I don't talk about customers."

"She's not a customer. She's evil."

"She may say the same about you."

"Oh, she'd say much worse about my sister," Redmond said. "You seem to be avoiding the question. What do you know about ... um ... raising the dead?" He couldn't bring himself to say the Z-word. I guess I couldn't blame him.

"It is an old art," Dauphine replied. "It is not for the faint of heart."

"That wasn't really an answer either," Redmond pointed out. "Do you have the power to raise the dead?"

"More importantly, did you give Angelina a curse so she could do it?" I asked. "Is she out to get me? Did she steal my ability to utter a proper insult? If so, I totally want that back. I feel naked without it."

Redmond spared me a dark look. "I'm talking. Me." He thumped his chest for emphasis. "We agreed I would do the talking."

"We agreed you would do the talking until I decided I would do the talking," I clarified. "It's time for me to talk."

"That's not how I remember it."

"Shh." I lifted my finger to my lips and glared at him before turning back to Dauphine. "So ... have you been raising the dead and sending them after me?"

"Non! I don't raise the dead and send them after anyone," Dauphine replied, making a clucking sound with her tongue as she migrated back behind the counter. "I only use my powers for good."

"You've got a potion over there that claims it can make people break out in endless zits," I argued. "How is that not evil?"

"It is simply a reflection of one's soul."

"Oh, I hate when your type gets all fruity with your word choices. What does that even mean?"

Dauphine didn't get a chance to answer. The bell over the door jangled to signify an incoming customer. When I darted my gaze in that direction, I found a familiar face staring at me. She didn't look happy. "Oh, man, what are you doing here?"

Redmond brightened when he saw Madam Maxine, the owner of a

different magic shop on Woodward a few miles away. She was tight with certain members of my family — including Redmond — and was often a source of information when we were in trouble. "Hi. We were coming to see you next."

"No, we weren't," I countered.

"We were, and shut up." Redmond squeezed my shoulder hard to let me know he meant business. "What are you doing here?"

"I have business with Dauphine." Madame Maxine's tone was clipped. Either she didn't like seeing us shopping at a competitor's store or she really did have business with Dauphine she didn't want to share. Perhaps it was a mixture of both. "What are you doing here?"

"Nothing," I answered hurriedly. Maxine made me uncomfortable. She often insisted on looking into my future, and she almost always saw weird things. It was disconcerting ... and freaking annoying.

"Aisling thinks she's being followed by zombies," Redmond supplied. "That's on top of the fact that the cops are watching her because she's a murder suspect."

Maxine's expression lightened a bit. "Never a dull moment, huh, baby Grimlock?"

I narrowed my eyes. "I don't suppose you know anything about raising the dead and amassing a zombie army?"

"Only what *The Walking Dead* has taught me."

"And what's that?"

"That it's never wise to be the moral compass when the world around you is falling apart," Maxine replied. "Why do you think zombies are chasing you?"

"I was attacked by a guy the other night and, according to the cops, he'd been dead for a month when he did it."

"Isn't that interesting?" Maxine's eyes were dark as they pinned Dauphine. "You wouldn't know something about that, would you?"

"Ha!" I moved a finger and swung my hips for Redmond's benefit. "I told you the crazy voodoo lady had something to do with this. It's all Angelina. I'm sure she thought it up. We need to find her next."

"Slow your roll, kid," Redmond chided. "We don't have anything concrete to go on yet."

"And that's not what I said," Maxine pointed out. "I merely asked Dauphine if she knew anything about it."

"And as I already told the death dealers, I don't." Dauphine's expression remained serene. "Why are you here, Maxine? I thought we had an agreement."

"Oh, you don't like her either?" That was very interesting. "What did she do to you?"

"I don't make it a habit to like or dislike anyone," Dauphine replied. "Maxine and I simply have different ways of viewing the world."

"We certainly do," Madame Maxine agreed. "Still, if Dauphine says she doesn't know what's going on, you have to believe her."

"Why?"

"Because raising the dead to go after you would offer her very little profit, and she's all about profit," Maxine replied. "I think you're looking in the wrong place."

"What about you?" Redmond asked. "Have you heard anything about the dead rising?"

"Not since the last time I warned you about that very thing and you managed to save a reaper family," Madame Maxine said. "It's been quiet of late."

"That should be suspicious right there," I muttered.

"Oh, little Grimlock, you're always a joy to be around," Maxine lamented. "Has anyone ever told you that?"

"No one worth listening to." I ran my tongue over my lips as I debated my next move. "I'm still not convinced you don't have anything to do with it, Madame Dauphine."

Dauphine held her hands out in a placating manner. "I'm sorry you feel that way, mon cher. It must be difficult to operate without the answers you seek."

"Yeah, yeah." I waved off the kind words. "You should know that I'll be watching you."

"I look forward to your company in the future."

Oh, she was smooth. I lobbed a dark look in Maxine's direction as I headed toward the door. I had a feeling she was here to talk to

Dauphine in private and I wouldn't get more out of either of them given the overt animosity crackling throughout the store.

"I'll be watching you, too," I told Maxine.

"Stop in for a reading later this week," Maxine ordered. "I might be able to help you."

I seriously doubted that was true. "I'll keep it in mind. In the meantime, I'm watching you." I held my fingers up to my eyes before flashing them in Maxine and Dauphine's directions.

Redmond grabbed me by the back of my neck and dragged me out, waiting until we were clear of the battling madames to speak again. "Just once I'd like you to make a situation better instead of worse when you open your mouth."

"I'll keep it in mind as a Christmas gift for you next year." I narrowed my eyes as I watched through the window as the two women gestured wildly. "What do you make of that?"

Redmond shook his head. "Nothing good. This entire situation is surreal."

"You're telling me."

"Let's get out of here. I think we need to conduct some research on this Madame Dauphine."

"Ha! I told you she was guilty."

"I didn't say she's guilty," Redmond clarified. "I'm simply not convinced she's innocent."

Well, that was at least something.

14

FOURTEEN

"What's the word?" My father and brothers were in Dad's office – which actually doubled as an imposing library – when Redmond and I arrived at Grimlock Manor. I didn't bother to hide my surprise.

"Is no one working today?"

"We're done for the day," Dad replied. "We always finish early when you're not on shift."

"That's because she insists on talking to the charges," Braden said. "I don't do that because I'm a diligent employee."

"Quiet, please!" Dad rolled his eyes. "Are you supposed to be wandering around, Aisling?"

I blew out a wet raspberry so Dad would know what I thought about the question. "Oh, now you ask? I happen to know that you cleared Redmond's schedule so he could help me."

"That's because I wanted to make sure you weren't taken into custody twice in one day," Dad said. "I let that happen once before, and I've never gotten over it. I still have nightmares about that legal bill."

"That was a fluke."

"You were arrested for throwing a construction barrel at Angelina's head," Dad reminded me. "You were out exactly five minutes before you took off, and two hours later you were arrested for punching her in the middle of the mall."

He said it as though it was something to be embarrassed about. "You always say that persistence is important for success."

Dad pursed his lips. "I hate it when you repeat things I've said."

"You just hate it when I'm right." I slid into the chair across from his desk. "Are you angry because I called Redmond?"

"No, I expected you to call Redmond," Dad replied. "You always call Redmond when you want someone to coddle you."

"No, I call Jerry when I want someone to coddle me. I call Griffin when I want someone to cuddle me. I call Braden when I want to fight. I call Aidan when I need some twin power action. I call Cillian when I need research or a quiet presence to be around. I call Redmond when I need someone to do something stupid with me because he always thinks it's a good idea regardless. And I call you when I want to be spoiled."

Instead of reacting with anger, Dad smiled. "You seem to be feeling better than you were this morning. Did you make up with Griffin?"

"No. He didn't even kiss me goodbye when he left." I felt stupid admitting that in a roomful of men, but I have no female friends and Jerry was working late.

"Oh, poor Aisling." Cillian slung his arm around my shoulders. "Are you panicking because he didn't kiss you? Are you doing that girl thing where you make up various scenarios in your head – none of which are rooted in reality – and convincing yourself that he's going to break up with you?"

"I wasn't before, but I am now."

Aidan poked my side. "Griffin isn't going to break up with you. He might be a little upset – okay, he's going to be very upset when he realizes you snuck out of the townhouse – but he'll get over it. He always does."

"She says she's looking forward to a fight because Griffin has been holding back since she got injured," Redmond volunteered.

"I told you that in secret," I protested, annoyance bubbling up. "Can't you keep a secret?"

"No one in this family can keep a secret."

"I can keep a secret. I think I must've been adopted."

Dad snorted. "Yes. You don't look anything like us. That must be it."

"No one needs the sarcasm."

"You eat sarcasm like other people do ice cream," Braden pointed out. "As for Griffin, if he breaks up with you I'm sure Dad will let you move back in here."

I formed a fist and seriously considered plowing it into Braden's face before Dad stopped me with a look.

"Now isn't the time," Dad said. "We need to figure out what's going on. There must be an explanation – one that doesn't involve zombies, because I don't want to hear that word mentioned again. Now ... think."

My brothers, in their infinite wisdom, decided to think by sticking their heads up their behinds.

"Maybe it was a dream," Aidan said. "We could still be waiting to wake up."

"Maybe Aisling didn't see what she thought she saw," Redmond offered. "It wouldn't be the first time she imagined something ludicrous."

"Maybe he was a puppet," Braden suggested. "Maybe someone made it look as if he was walking by attaching strings to his appendages."

"Really, Braden?" Dad's tone was dry. "You don't think Aisling would have noticed strings? Think before you speak, boy."

"She thought he was trying to bite her," Braden pointed out. "Maybe she got confused when the strings were cut."

"And what type of giant would be able to control a human puppet without anyone noticing?"

"An invisible one."

Dad dropped his forehead into his hand. "What did I do to deserve this brood?"

"I think that's between you and your god," Cillian teased, grabbing a book from the shelf and sitting in the chair next to me. He was always calm, whatever the circumstances, and didn't appear bothered by the human puppet and zombie talk.

"I think the human puppet idea is idiotic," Aidan interjected. "I'm ashamed to be related to you, Braden."

"I'm always ashamed to be related to him," I offered. "It's a zombie infestation. Why can't you guys just accept that?"

"Because zombies aren't real," Redmond answered. "You must know that, kid. You're dramatic and theatrical at times, but you're smart. Smart people know that zombies aren't real."

He made sense, of course. "Smart people also know that when a woman says 'size doesn't matter' it really does."

Redmond's jaw tightened. "Who told you about that?"

I smirked. "You just did."

"No, who else?"

I refused to look at Aidan, who suddenly found something interesting to stare at on the bookshelf. Four days earlier, while drinking heavily, he'd told me a rather hilarious story about Redmond at the bar, and I'd been waiting to bring it up for days.

"I have no idea what you're talking about," I lied. "I guessed and got lucky."

Redmond made a face that even our mother – the woman who is probably eating people to sustain herself – couldn't love. "Someone told you something." His gaze bounced between our brothers. "Something that was supposed to be private. It was part of the Grimlock bro code ... and someone broke it!"

"I would like to point out that it's very wrong of you guys to cut me out of something like the Grimlock bro code simply because I have ovaries."

"Oh, geez." All four of my brothers made disgusted faces.

"Do you have to say things like that?" Braden whined.

"Ovaries is not a dirty word."

"It's not," Dad agreed. "Don't say it, though. As far as you're concerned, you don't have ovaries."

"I don't have a penis either."

"Don't say the P-word." Redmond extended a finger. "I know that was pointed at me."

"From what I hear, your P-word wasn't pointed at anyone," I teased, grinning at the way Redmond shifted.

"It was cold," Redmond hissed. "I can't control the weather."

"Are you talking about this past weekend when you tried to pick up that woman at the new bar you boys visited in Rochester and you ... um ... failed to rise to the situation on the terrace?" Dad asked, forcing me to choke on my laughter when Redmond's face flooded with color. "It happens to everyone, son."

"I hate this family." Redmond dramatically threw his arm over his face before dropping onto the couch. "I really hate every single one of you."

"But we love you enough to make up for that." I offered up my best "I'm sweet and you have to love me" expression. "You're our big brother and you mean everything to us."

"Everything," Braden, Cillian and Aidan echoed.

Dad didn't bother hiding his smile. "Some days I can't help but love each and every one of you."

"Not Braden," I said, sobering. "He came up with that stupid human puppet idea. That's nowhere near as believable as my zombie theory."

Dad's smile slipped. "And I'm back to wondering why I let your mother talk me into having any of you." He shook his head as his phone rang, knitting his eyebrows when he checked the caller ID. "It's Griffin."

I hopped to my feet, miming a slashing motion across my throat to warn Dad against telling Griffin I was here. Dad made a dubious expression, but otherwise remained calm.

"Hello. Oh, hello, Griffin. How are you?"

I glared holes into Dad as I listened to his side of the conversation.

"Aisling? Hmm. I don't know what to tell you. How do you know she's not at the townhouse?"

Uh-oh. This wouldn't end well for me.

"The Royal Oak Police Department had officers in the parking lot, huh?" Dad looked only slightly interested in the conversation. "They were watching the townhouse and didn't see movement for an extended period, eh?"

Crud. Crap. Crappity crud. My life wouldn't be worth spit when Griffin caught up with me.

"They knocked and no one answered, and then you called and she didn't answer, eh? What? I'm not repeating everything so she can hear what you're saying. Why would you even think that?" Dad shot me a quelling look. "Well, Griffin, if Aisling did manage to sneak out of the townhouse without alerting the police, I'd think that was kind of fun ... and rather ingenious on her part."

Dad always found entertainment in the oddest things. Apparently now he was finding it at Griffin's expense.

"No, I'm not saying I helped her escape, I didn't," Dad continued. "If she asked me, I would've found a way to help her, though. As for where she is now ... I couldn't say. Have you considered calling Jerry?"

I flashed Dad an enthusiastic thumbs-up. So far he hadn't told any outright lies. Sure, he wasn't exactly telling the truth, but he wasn't going to suffer the ill effects of a rapidly-growing nose anytime soon.

"Of course you're not an idiot. Of course you thought to call Jerry first," Dad said. "If I hear from her, I'll certainly tell her that you're looking for her. Yes, I will also make sure she knows that she should crawl back through the window if that's how she escaped. Yes, I'll keep in touch."

Dad dropped the phone to its cradle. "Griffin is looking for you, Aisling."

"Thanks. I never would've figured that out." I rolled my neck until it cracked. "He's going to be ticked. I wonder if he would believe I was next door in Jerry's townhouse all day."

"I'd say not," Dad said. "He knows you're with us. That call was simply a warning that you're to find a way back into the townhouse without tipping off the cops in the parking lot."

"Did he say that?"

"No, but I can tell that's what he was getting at," Dad said. "Still, he said he would be home with your dinner at six. That means we have several hours to work on this."

"So how are we going to do that? You guys won't believe the zombie theory and I'm convinced it can't possibly be anything else."

"I don't know." Dad scratched his cheek as he thought. "Give me a minute and I'll definitely come up with something better than the zombie theory."

"Don't even try stealing my human puppet theory," Braden warned.

"Listen, I don't want to give credence to Aisling's out-of-control ramblings about zombies, but that Madame Dauphine at the Voodoo Vacation store really did react oddly to us stopping in," Redmond supplied, changing the focus of the conversation. "She seems to recognize what we are. Now, if she had dealings with Angelina it's possible that's how she found out. If not, then she can sense that we're different."

"Which means she might be different," Dad noted. "I don't know much about voodoo. All I do know are from case files."

"Voodoo priestesses throughout the centuries were accused of raising the dead," I said.

"Ugh." Dad made a groaning sound. "I don't want to hear you say things like that. It makes me question your sanity."

"You had five children. That makes me question your sanity."

"That makes two of us."

"That makes six of us," Redmond corrected. "I was perfectly happy being an only child. As for the voodoo stuff, I think we need to talk to someone who has knowledge of how it works."

"Other than Madame Dauphine?" I asked.

Redmond nodded. "Until we know more, I also think we should give Madame Maxine a wide berth, too. She acted extremely weird today."

"Maxine was in the shop?" Dad was surprised. "Did she say anything?"

"She fought with Madame Dauphine, but she waited until we left the shop," I replied. "She was kind of snarky while we were inside, but she waited until we left to unleash whatever was irritating her."

"It was a little odd," Redmond conceded. "Maxine usually falls all over me when I visit. She also enjoys messing with Aisling. She barely did either, and seemed eager for us to leave the store. She didn't look happy with Dauphine."

"And Dauphine mentioned that they agreed to stay away from one another," I added. "She seemed surprised to see Maxine."

"Hmm. I don't know what to make of that, but it seems too coincidental," Dad mused. "Does anyone know where we can get a crash course on voodoo?"

"Actually, I think I might," Cillian said, shifting the book on his lap. "There's a section at the back of Eternal Sunset Cemetery. It crowds a small Detroit neighborhood, and the residents there call themselves Catholic but practice a form of voodoo. They bury their dead in that small corner of the cemetery that's cut off from everything but the neighborhood. There are generally a lot of people hanging out in that area. They chant and stuff."

Dad didn't bother hiding his interest. "How do you know this?"

"I collected a soul over there about six months ago," Cillian replied. "The family members were busy sacrificing some animal – I think it was a bird of some sort – in the yard while I worked. I heard them. Other than the animal sacrifice, they seemed mostly normal."

"I don't think anyone in this family should judge anyone else when it comes to normalcy," I said, flicking my eyes to Dad. "What do you think?"

Dad shrugged. "I think if we're going to do it, we're doing it as a family. I'm not sure what to expect, but someone is clearly targeting Aisling. I want her well protected."

"Oh, good, we're back to the babysitting," I muttered.

"You're loved," Dad shot back. "Get used to it. As long as you're a target, we're going with you."

I exhaled heavily. "Fine. We should go now if we're going. I need to beat Griffin home."

"That's not going to save you," Braden said.

Sadly, I had no doubt he was right.

FIFTEEN

Redmond's Expedition was the only vehicle we had big enough for all of us, and even then we had to squeeze in to the point where Aidan and I shared a seatbelt. Dad's big on seatbelts, no matter how uncomfortable, so we didn't really have a choice.

"Get your leg off me," Braden growled, shoving my knee to the side. "I don't want your cooties."

"I'm surprised you're not the one who had performance issues at the bar," I shot back, groaning when Aidan's hip pressed into my side. "Everyone knows you fold under pressure."

"Shut it."

"Both of you shut it," Dad ordered from the passenger seat. He looked perfectly comfortable with Redmond chauffeuring him around.

Despite Dad's tone, I ignored him. "How did that even come up? Were you going to have sex on the terrace or are we talking about vigorous rubbing here?"

"Tell her to shut up again, Dad," Redmond ordered.

"I'm actually curious about your answer, so I'll let her be," Dad countered. "What were you trying to do on the terrace?"

Redmond was caught, but did his best to focus on the traffic heading south rather than answer the question. "It's not even rush hour yet. Will you look at this?"

"If you don't answer I'll make stuff up," I said. "For example, were you re-enacting the final dance scene from *Dirty Dancing*? Were you trying to lift her above your head and accidentally pulled a muscle?"

"Nobody puts Baby in a corner," Aidan mimed, amused with the game.

"Only a chick would know lines from that movie," Braden snarked.

"I happen to like that movie," Dad argued.

"How do you even know that movie?" Cillian asked.

"I was forced to watch it an inordinate number of times when Aisling was younger," Dad replied. "I know most of the words and half of the dances."

"You made Dad watch *Dirty Dancing*?" Braden made a face. "I think someone needs to turn in their man card."

"It wasn't Aisling," Dad supplied. "It was Jerry. He made Aisling watch it. He was infatuated with recreating the dances until he tried a lift with her and almost threw out his back. He was twelve."

"He hurt his back because he lifted wrong," I argued. "He didn't do it with his knees, like I told him. It's not as if I was fat or anything."

"Of course you weren't fat." Dad grinned. "Your mother warned that we were never to use that word around you when you were a teenager because she didn't want you developing poor self-esteem. You merely went through a ... thick ... stage."

"Thick!" Braden belted out a laugh. "There are too many jokes in my head. I can't settle on just one."

"Ignore all of them," Dad ordered. "We're talking to Redmond. What were you trying to do on the terrace, son? I believe I warned you about trying to impress a woman when it was cold outside when you were fourteen."

"I don't remember that." I racked my brain a second time to be sure. "What happened?"

"Nothing," Redmond snapped.

"He tried to kiss Melanie Bernsen but he misjudged the distance between them and when he leaned forward he actually kissed the pole right next to her. It was so cold his mouth got stuck," Dad supplied.

I stilled. "That's a scene from *A Christmas Story*."

"Not quite, but close," Dad countered. "I showed him that movie afterward. He didn't find it funny. Of course, to save face, he pulled his own mouth off the pole and ripped half his lips off."

I wasn't sure I believed that story, or at least how it happened. It sounded much more likely that one of my brothers dared Redmond to do it and they made up the rest of the story so Dad wouldn't think they were idiots. "I'm still interested in what Redmond was trying to do on the terrace," I said. "Why were your pants down? Dad always told us never to drop trou in public."

"Actually, that was just a rule for you," Dad said as Redmond pulled into the cemetery parking lot.

"That's not fair." I was happy to unfasten the seat belt. "Why did I have a different set of rules? The boys were far more likely to drop their pants."

"Yes, but you're a girl." Dad issued the statement as if was perfectly normal, and then hopped out of the Expedition, leaving me to scramble after him.

"That makes it even more unfair," I complained. "I shouldn't have had a different set of rules."

"You were my baby. That's simply the way the world works," Dad said, falling into step with Cillian as he led the way through the gate. "I would like to pretend that I treated all of you equally, but you had a separate set of rules."

I turned to Aidan, aghast. "Do you believe this?"

"What I can't believe is that you're complaining about it," Aidan replied. "You got spoiled twice as much as the rest of us because you were a girl. So what? You got more rules because you were a girl, too. It balanced out."

"I wasn't spoiled more than you guys," I muttered, crossing my arms over my chest as we moved into a section of cemetery I'd never visited. Oddly enough, I'd spent an exorbitant amount of time in this cemetery since joining the reaper profession. For years I'd visited because I thought my mother was laid to rest here. After that, things kept happening to draw me back to the property. Now, it seemed, even more answers might be found inside its stone walls. "Dad, tell them I wasn't spoiled."

"You were spoiled rotten," Dad said. "I couldn't stop myself from buying you whatever you wanted, and you knew exactly how to get me to do what you wanted. Don't bother denying it."

"Whatever." I scuffed my feet along the paved walkway. "I think, once I have time to give this separate rules thing some thought, I'm going to be traumatized."

"You'll live."

"I'm going to need a special gift to feel better about myself," I argued.

"I put a huge retainer down for a lawyer for you just this morning," Dad said. "That's a fine gift."

"Oh, geez." I wrinkled my nose as we walked into an unfamiliar section of the cemetery. The tombstones were all large and ornate, many of them in the shape of crosses. "Have you ever been here before?"

Aidan shook his head. "I'm not big on hanging out at cemeteries. Plus, well, I almost died in this one last summer. I can't say I've been giving it a lot of thought."

"Good point." I split from my brothers and walked to the nearest mausoleum, peering through the stained-glass window to see if I could get a good look.

"Are you thinking of climbing through that window?" Braden asked, sidling up beside me. "I don't think that's the window Griffin was talking about. I wish I could be there when he gets home. I'm sure he's going to pop a cork."

"I've never understood that expression," I said. "Popping a cork is what happens when you have champagne. Champagne is good. Shouldn't that be a good thing?"

"Do you think it's going to be a good thing when Griffin gets home?"

That was a fair question. "No." I knew Braden was trying to bait me, but I didn't have the energy to acquiesce and embrace my inner immaturity angel. "We're going to have a big fight."

"Oh, come on." Braden flicked my ear. "I was just messing with you. You're not really worried about something terrible going down with Griffin, are you?"

"We're in a weird place because of all of this," I replied. "He wants to believe in the system, but I can't because it's never really helped me."

"I believe it was the system that brought you to Griffin in the first place, wasn't it?"

I hate it when Braden makes sense. "Yeah. It's hard for him because he's linked to a potential murderer. That probably reflects poorly on him at the office."

"I doubt he cares about that," Braden said. "I think it's far more likely that he's worried about you being hurt. He's not quite over the last time it happened."

"Tell me about it."

"He'll get there."

"Not before the zombies get us," I muttered, moving away from the window and walking to the front of the mausoleum so I could study the door. "What does that say up there?"

I pointed to the faded words chiseled into the stone.

Braden followed my gaze. "I'm not sure. I think it's a foreign language."

"Like Spanish?"

"It's Haitian Creole," Cillian supplied, his eyes pinned on the words as he joined us. "'Mante nan mouri.'"

"Do you know what that means?"

"Yeah. It means, 'The dead rise.'"

I stilled, a mixture of emotions flowing through me. "Really? 'The dead rise,' huh?" I cast a triumphant look over my shoulder as I found Dad's gaze. "What do you think that means?"

"What do I think 'the dead rise' being etched over the door of a mausoleum that looks to be a hundred years old means? Not much."

"Whatever." He was really starting to irritate me. If he would just admit that it was zombies I would feel so much better. "I think it's a very odd coincidence."

"Good grief. We'll never hear the end of this, will we?"

"Not as long as the dead are rising."

"You're on my last nerve, Aisling," Dad warned, moving to stand next to Cillian in front of the mausoleum. He lowered his voice – probably in an attempt to make sure I didn't hear him – before he spoke. "That doesn't mean what she thinks it means, does it?"

Cillian chuckled, genuinely amused. "I doubt it. Voodoo practitioners believe the dead can rise, but, as you said, this is an old mausoleum."

"You know I can hear you, right?" I was about at my limit with overbearing men. For about the one-hundredth time in the past six weeks I sincerely wondered why I couldn't find a female friend. The closest I have is Maya, and while I like her, I certainly can't trust her to keep her mouth shut around Cillian and Griffin.

"Plug your ears," Dad suggested, squinting as he moved closer to the building. "There's a symbol here. Do you recognize it?"

Cillian leaned closer. "I'm not sure."

Because they were already staring, I decided to join the club. "It looks like a snake with a line through it." Something niggled the back of my brain. "It reminds me of something I saw on Jed Burnham's neck when he was on the ground."

"Jed Burnham is the man who made funny chomping noises after dying a month before tackling you?" Dad asked.

"Yes. And they weren't chomping noises. It was more like he was smacking his lips because he wanted a tasty snack."

"Then why did he go after you?" Braden asked.

"Hey, not that I want to be eaten, but I bet I'm delicious." I realized what I said when it was too late to yank it back into my mouth. Whoops. "That came out wrong."

"I'm pretending I didn't hear it," Dad said. "What do you think the symbol means, Cillian?"

"I don't know." Cillian waved us back so he could take a photograph. "I'll look it up when we get back home."

"What else should we look for?" Braden asked, glancing around. "We didn't just come here for a symbol, did we?"

"No," Cillian replied. "I was hoping someone would be hanging around. The last time I was here it was crawling with people. I thought we might be able to talk to someone who has actual knowledge of voodoo instead of winging things for a change."

As if on cue, a young girl – she looked to be about fifteen – poked her head out from behind the mausoleum. She had long dark hair, wide brown eyes, and a live chicken clutched to her chest.

"Who are you looking for?" she asked.

I forced a smile for her benefit and took a step forward. I figured it was better to present a friendly front rather than letting my brothers run roughshod over her. "Do you live around here?" I asked.

She nodded. "Across that way." She kept hold of the chicken with one hand as she pointed with the other. "My gran is buried here. I visit sometimes."

"Oh, really?" That was good news. That meant she was probably familiar with the voodoo culture. "Are you here to sacrifice that chicken to her?"

"Aisling!" Dad's voice was low and full of warning.

"What?" I risked a glance at Cillian and found him shaking his head. "What did I say?"

"This is Sassy," the girl said. "She's a pet. She escaped from her coop and I chased her over here."

"Oh. So ... you're not going to sacrifice it? That's good. That would've made me sad."

Instead of being offended, the girl giggled. "You're funny."

"You should tell these guys that. They don't think I'm funny at all."

"That's because we've spent more than three minutes with you," Dad said. "What is your name, young lady?"

"Astryd."

"That's a pretty name." Dad pasted a smile on his face that would've made pedophiles everywhere say "too much."

"You're going to creep her out." I edged him away with my hip. "Are you familiar with the symbols and stuff around here?"

Astryd nodded. "Why?"

"Do you know what this one means?" I pointed at the symbol on the mausoleum.

Astryd gave my father a wide berth as she circled to look. She nodded immediately when she saw what I pointed to. "It's the Damballah-Wedo."

"And what is that?"

"He's associated with life and creation ... of birth."

Hmm. That was interesting. "Why is he shaped like a snake?"

"Because when he possesses people he hisses rather than speaks," Astryd replied. "Why are you interested in that symbol?"

"Because I saw it on a person the other day."

"Was the person dead?"

"How did you know that?"

Astryd shrugged. "Just a guess. He didn't ... bite you ... did he?"

"No. Why would you ask that?"

"Just something I heard when I was little," Astryd replied. "We don't embrace the old ways all that much. We're more ... mainstreamed. That's what my mother calls it anyway."

"Have you ever seen anyone possessed with this mark walking around after death?" I asked, going for broke.

"Aisling!" Dad was clearly near the end of his patience rope.

"That's a myth," Astryd said. "My gran said that it happened when she was a child, but I've never seen it."

"Do you believe it can happen?"

"I ... ." Astryd chewed her bottom lip before shrugging. "I guess anything is possible. I'm not sure what I believe."

"Okay, well, thanks for the information." I tilted my head to the side when I heard a voice calling Astryd's name. It sounded like a woman, and she was a fair distance from us. "I think someone is looking for you."

"It's my mother. She's looking for her." Astryd tightened her grip on the chicken. "She needs something for tonight's sacrifice."

"Really? You just said that was a pet."

"Yes, but I wanted to see what you would say." Astryd's eyes lit with mirth as she bolted in the direction of her home, giggling maniacally as she did.

"She's not really going to sacrifice that chicken, is she?"

"I'm pretty sure she was teasing you," Dad said. "Come on. Let's look around and then get out of here. We need to get Aisling back home before Griffin gets off shift if she doesn't want him to take five layers of skin off her hide."

"Ha, ha." I knew he was joking, but it hit a little too close to home.

We spent twenty minutes looking around, Cillian snapping myriad photos, and then we trudged back to the parking lot. I pulled up short as we approached, my stomach doing a bit of a somersault when I found Detective Mark Green reclining against Redmond's Expedition.

"Uh-oh."

Dad followed my gaze. "Is that the detective who questioned you this morning?"

I nodded. "He doesn't look happy, does he?"

"Not in the least." Dad puffed out his chest and stepped in front of me. "Can I help you?"

"You can," Green said, as he held up a sheet of paper. "I have a warrant to take your daughter in for formal questioning. In fact, since you're all here, maybe you want to come along for the ride. How does that sound?"

"As if I should place a call to my attorney," Dad replied automatically. "Does that warrant cover all of us or only Aisling?"

"Just Aisling, but I can get one for you, too, if it's necessary." Green's teeth gleamed as he practically dared Dad to give him guff.

Dad wasn't about to be bullied. "All right. Secure your warrants. I'll call our whole legal team."

Green's smile slipped. "Team?"

"Yes." Now it was Dad's turn to smile. "I think they'll love dealing with you. They haven't had an easy time of it in years. It's like playing a children's video game as an adult. It's ... stimulating."

16

SIXTEEN

Dad wasn't keen on it, but he relented and allowed Green to transport me to the Royal Oak Police Department for questioning. He promised Neil would be there when I arrived, but I understood (better than even Dad probably) how things would go and wasn't worried about flubbing the interrogation. I was worried about Griffin.

As if reading my mind, Dad patted my shoulder before I slid into the back seat of Green's car. "I'll call him."

"He won't be happy."

"That's not your fault." Dad gave Green a steely-eyed glare. "I'll be right behind her."

"With your legal team, no doubt." Green's expression said he didn't believe Dad would unleash a load of lawyerly fury on him. He was in for a rude awakening.

"I'll see you in twenty minutes, Aisling," Dad said, his eyes never leaving Green's face. "Don't worry about anything."

Green waited until he was in the driver's seat, his door closed, before speaking. "You should worry. We have some tough questions for you."

"Bring it on."

At the police station, Green ushered me to the same interrogation room I'd occupied this morning. He made a big deal of showing me in and telling me to get comfortable before leaving me to sit in the sterile room for what felt like forever. I knew exactly what he was doing. He was trying to frazzle my nerves, cause me to be anxious and then hopefully make a mistake under questioning. As Cormack Grimlock's daughter, I knew how that worked. I stole my father's vehicles multiple times as a teenager, even going to so far as to accidentally dump one in the Detroit River during a pursuit one night. Trust me. Dad was much more terrifying than Green.

Neil showed up ten minutes after I was seated, and took the open chair next to me. He didn't spare a glance for the two-way mirror on the wall, instead offering up a relaxed smile as he focused on me. "They didn't mistreat you, did they? I will be filing several nuisance complaints before leaving today. I want to make sure I have all of them lined up."

"They kept their rubber hoses to themselves."

Neil snorted. "I forgot about your mouth. I believe the only time I've ever been speechless was when you told that officer in Detroit that you were sleepwalking when you took your father's car from the garage and you had no recollection of how you got behind the wheel in your Hello Kitty sleep pants."

"I still maintain that's what happened."

"You're good under pressure," Neil noted. "Don't lose that trait. Let me do the talking. If he asks a question I believe you should answer, I will let you know."

I nodded. "Did the rest of the legal team show up for Dad?"

Neil smiled. "I believe they're in the lobby right now."

"Is it an army?"

"Oh, honey, it's a platoon."

Neil rested his palms flat on the table and stared at the door until Green made his way in. Green was cocky, an added swagger to his step, but my ability to read people pegged it as posturing rather than legitimate bravado.

"Well, Ms. Grimlock, you seem to have had a busy day."

"I have," I agreed, answering before Neil gave me the go-ahead.

"Do you want to share what you've been doing?"

"Sure."

Neil arched a confrontational eyebrow but didn't stop me from barreling forward. He knew me well enough to know I wouldn't volunteer pertinent information as much as I was going to work overtime to annoy Green until he wanted to bury his head in a pile of quicksand and cry.

"For starters, I found out my brother Redmond has performance issues," I supplied. "Apparently it's hard for men to ... um ... rise to the occasion when it's cold out, and something happened this past weekend at a bar. But he refuses to tell me what he had planned for the woman he met on the terrace, so my mind is racing with possibilities."

The second he realized what I was doing, Neil leaned back in his chair and relaxed. He was primed to enjoy the show. Green, on the other hand, didn't bother to hide his irritation.

"That's not what I was talking about."

"I'm not done," I chided. "Don't be rude."

"Far be it from me to be rude," Green muttered.

"Great." I plowed forward with enthusiasm, and very little of it was fake. "Then I found out that my father had a different set of rules for my brothers and me while we were growing up. Can you believe that? Apparently I was spoiled more than they were when it comes to money and goods, but they got easier rules.

"For example, there was a 'no dropping your pants in public' rule that I had to follow, but the boys were exempt," I continued, enjoying the way Green's eyes glazed over. "It's not even that I would want to drop my pants in public. I did that a few times in high school and it really wasn't the thrill that everyone made it out to be. It's the simple fact that my brothers didn't have this rule and were allowed to drop their pants willy-nilly."

Green stared at me for a long time. "You seem to be bothered a great deal by this turn of events."

"It threw off my entire day."

"A day we were under the impression you were to spend in your home," Green noted. Instead, you sneaked out and somehow ended up at Eternal Sunshine Cemetery in Detroit. Do you want to explain how that happened?"

"Don't answer that," Neil interjected, shaking his head. "I've got this one. Detective Green, was my client under arrest this afternoon?"

"No."

"Was she breaking any laws by leaving her house in the middle of the day?"

"No."

"Was she breaking any laws by visiting the cemetery?"

"No, but it seems an odd place for an afternoon excursion," Green pointed out.

"The Grimlock family mausoleum is there."

"And they visit in February?" Green didn't look convinced. "That doesn't seem likely."

"There's very little snow on the ground," Neil pointed out. "What we do get falls for a few hours and then melts a few days later. We haven't had snow on the ground for most of this winter. It's been an odd weather pattern, certainly, but the Grimlocks hardly control the weather."

"And that explains your client's odd behavior?"

"I'm not a judge of behavior," Neil replied. "I'm a facts person, and the fact is my client wasn't under arrest. She was apparently under surveillance – which will be challenged in circuit court this afternoon, by the way – but she wasn't under arrest."

Green leaned back in his chair. "You're going to challenge my ability to watch Ms. Grimlock?"

"I am."

"How do you think that's going to go for you?" Green was back to cocky.

"Much better than it will for you," Neil replied. "The simple fact of the matter is that you're harassing my client."

"She's a suspect in two different murders," Green snapped. "She's been in close proximity to two bodies in two days. Don't you think that's a bit odd?"

"I think that investigating bodies is your business," Neil replied. "I think that stopping you from harassing my client is mine."

"Surveillance of a murder suspect is not harassment."

"I think we'll let a judge decide that." Neil patted my hand reassuringly. I honestly loved watching him work. He could get under people's skin even faster than I could. It was a gift I wanted to emulate. "So ... is that all? Can we get out of here?"

"You're not going anywhere," Green spat. "I haven't even started asking questions yet."

"Fine, but you should be aware that Ms. Grimlock is under no obligation to answer your questions. Each and every assertion you've lobbed at her can easily be explained away. I will bring up exactly that fact when I argue in front of the judge this afternoon."

"She's a murder suspect."

"Only because you refuse to do your job and find out what really happened," Neil said. "If I were you, I'd be much more interested in the person who called in the anonymous tip about the body in the backyard than Ms. Grimlock, who had no idea there was a body in her backyard. That's neither here nor there, though. You have no power to hold my client. If you try, I will have you in front of a judge for an emergency hearing before the day is out."

"It's almost five," Green sneered. "What judge do you think is going to grant you an emergency hearing?"

"That's for me to know and you to risk finding out," Neil replied, not missing a beat. He was getting into his stride. "My client doesn't have to answer your questions. Quite frankly, you overstepped your boundaries when you collected her at a cemetery that isn't in your jurisdiction. Because she wasn't under arrest, you had no right to force transportation in your vehicle. That will also be addressed in filings this evening."

For the first time Green seemed to realize what he was up against. He was in over his head, a guppy swimming with the sharks. I almost felt sorry for him when understanding washed over his features.

Green's eyes were cold when they locked with mine. "Is this how it's going to be? You're going to hide behind your fancy lawyer."

"I haven't done anything to require hiding," I said. "I was walking down the street with my boyfriend, enjoying the snow. Okay, I wasn't enjoying the snow. He loves the snow. I was merely humoring him because the key to any good relationship is compromise.

"We were minding our own business, talking about wedding plans, when some guy barreled into me and uprooted our lives," I continued. "I didn't seek him out. I didn't kill him. I don't know what happened, and I certainly don't understand why you seem fixated on me."

"Jed Burnham died a month ago," Green said. "He didn't die on that sidewalk."

"I believe you have video footage to the contrary," Neil said.

"The footage could've been doctored."

"Oh, really?" I tugged on my limited patience because I knew a meltdown would only hurt my standing. "You're suggesting I killed a man I've never met, hid his body for a month, somehow transported it to downtown Royal Oak and then doctored the surveillance video within moments of the event happening? How do I manage to make it through the day with the weight of this super villain cape pulling at my neck?"

Neil smirked as Green scowled. "She has a point. Your medical examiner says Jed Burnham died a month ago. He's still running tests, but he doesn't have a specific date of death."

"He'll get one," Green said.

"Perhaps, but Ms. Grimlock didn't kill him, so you're wasting valuable time," Neil said. "Besides that, I've seen the preliminary reports. Mr. Burnham appears to have died of a heart attack. Last time I checked, that's not murder."

"Except Ms. Grimlock had another body in her yard this morning," Green noted. "We don't have a cause of death on him."

"No, you don't," Neil agreed. "I've seen that autopsy report, too. He had no visible wounds or head injury. He also appears to have been dead for six weeks, even longer than Mr. Burnham."

I jerked my head up, surprised. "Six weeks?"

Neil nodded. "He certainly wasn't in Ms. Grimlock's backyard for the duration of that time. In fact, the medical examiner commented in his notes that the second body – who has yet to be identified or even reported missing as far as anyone can tell – was so well preserved that there was a good chance he was embalmed."

"Embalmed?" My stomach twisted. My zombie theory was looking more and more likely. "Huh."

"How did you get the medical examiner's notes?" Green asked, incensed. "Did you bribe someone? That's against the law."

"I merely went to the department office and asked," Neil said mildly. "They were quite helpful. They seem to be looking at both cases as medical mysteries rather than murder. When I informed them that I needed the files because you were trying to charge my client with murder they seemed a bit baffled. It seems they hadn't ruled either death a homicide."

He was good. I had to give him that. Neil's cool detachment and dedication to his job had Green practically frothing at the mouth.

"You are not privy to the inner workings of my investigation," Green snapped. "No matter how you argue, you can't change the fact that Ms. Grimlock had a dead body in her backyard."

"I believe we covered that this morning," Neil said, studying his fingernails as he feigned boredom. "That backyard area is shared by multiple residents. Ms. Grimlock is hardly the only one with access to the property."

"No, but she is the only one who has access to two dead bodies in as many days," Green fired back. "That makes her a suspect."

I opened my mouth to argue, something acidic on the tip of my tongue, but it died there when the door flew open without anyone knocking.

"Not the only one."

Griffin appeared in the doorway, his chest heaving as he gripped the door handle hard enough that his knuckles whitened. His wild eyes searched the room until finding mine. His expression was hard to read, but there was definitely anger present. How much of that anger was directed at me was hard to ascertain.

"What are you doing here?" Green hopped to his feet. "This is a closed interrogation."

"You can't interrogate her without arresting her," Griffin argued, standing toe-to-toe with Green and refusing to back down.

"And he doesn't have enough evidence to arrest her," Neil said. "That will also be addressed in my evening court filings."

"Wow," Green sneered, his eyes flashing. "It sounds as if you're going to have a busy night filing complaints against me. Three of them."

"Twenty-five," Neil corrected, causing Green's mouth to drop open. "My secretary is printing them now and transporting them here so I can file them in a timely manner."

"Twenty-five," I sang out. "You've been a very bad boy."

Griffin shot me a quelling look. "Aisling, don't make things worse." He turned his full attention to Green. "Mark ... ."

"Detective Green."

"Detective Green," Griffin gritted out. "You're acting as if Aisling is the only suspect you have."

"She is."

"No, I was with her downtown the other night and I share the townhouse with her," Griffin argued. "Why am I not a suspect?"

I realized what he was doing. "Don't even think of pointing the finger at yourself," I warned.

"Definitely do not do that," Neil agreed.

"I'm not," Griffin said. "I'm just pointing out that more than one person was present both times."

"It doesn't matter," Neil interjected. "Neither case has been ruled a homicide."

"What?" Griffin furrowed his brow. He clearly hadn't heard the entire conversation. "Then what is she doing here?"

Mark began to look worried. "She's a suspect."

"You don't have a crime," Griffin exploded, holding out his hand to me. "Aisling, come on. You're done here."

I spared a worried glance for Neil, but he nodded for me to go, clearly understanding that Griffin was about to melt down.

"You can't just take her out of this room," Green snapped. "I haven't released her."

"If you want to keep her you'll have to charge her," Neil pointed out. "Do you want to charge her with murder even though your deaths haven't been ruled homicides ... or even negligent accidents, for that matter? If so, I'll have her out of court in five minutes. I will also secure a restraining order against you in the process."

"You seem to think highly of your abilities," Green growled. "What makes you think a judge will side with you?"

"Because I clearly know more about the law than you." Neil pressed his hand to the small of my back and prodded me forward. "We're leaving now."

"We definitely are." Griffin gripped my hand tightly as he led me through the door, mustering a dark glare for Green as we left. He didn't hug me. He didn't stroke my hair and tell me it was going to be okay. Instead he flicked a pair of hard eyes to me and pressed his lips together.

"I'm sensing the love is going to be hard earned tonight, huh?" I was going for levity but it fell flat.

"You don't have to earn my love," Griffin replied. "You already have it. You do have to earn my forgiveness, though. You're in big trouble."

"But I didn't do anything," I protested.

"You promised to stay in the townhouse all day, but then climbed through a window."

"I didn't promise," I clarified. "I was very careful when you brought that up. I simply sidestepped the question."

"Oh, well, that makes it better."

I scratched my head as I considered the conundrum. "Are we really going to fight?"

"Yes."

"Fine. I'll need food first. I'm starving."

"I believe that's already arranged."

17

SEVENTEEN

We returned to Grimlock Manor rather than head home to argue in private. I wasn't sure if that was a good idea, but when I saw the expansive Mexican fiesta bar Dad had ordered set up for dinner I wasn't about to complain.

Griffin was mostly quiet for the duration of dinner, answering the occasional question from my father and brothers, but opting not to embark on any dangerous conversational tangents.

I stuffed my face with tacos until I was sure I'd bust, casting the occasional glance to my left in the hope that he would offer me a smile or reassuring hand squeeze, but Griffin was clearly peeved. That didn't bode well for me.

My father, as if sensing my distress, decided to wade into dangerous waters before Griffin finished eating. "This isn't her fault."

"I didn't say it was." Griffin remained focused on his plate. "I don't blame her for the bodies."

"What do you blame her for?"

"Sneaking out."

"Well, I don't want to make things worse, but you should've seen that coming," Dad offered. "She's not the type of woman who can remain locked in her own home for long stretches."

"I know exactly what type of woman she is," Griffin growled. "She's the type of woman who apparently wants to give me a stroke."

Dad chuckled, catching me off guard. "You two are going to have a fiery marriage. It's going to be fun."

Griffin finally raised his eyes and scorched my father with a dark look. "I don't think 'fun' is the word I'd use."

"Then you're not seeing the bigger picture," Dad said. "She couldn't stay in that townhouse, given the circumstances."

"And what circumstances were those?" Griffin challenged. "The ones where I told her that she had nothing to worry about because they didn't have evidence? They can't arrest her for doing nothing."

"And yet Detective Green is clearly going to try," Cillian said calmly, drawing Griffin's attention. "I know you're upset. You're still dealing with what happened to Aisling in December. As much as you try to be brave and pretend you're over that, you're not. None of us are."

"He's right," Redmond said. "We all got a nasty jolt of reality when she was hurt. We all worried we would lose her. You're not the only one who loves her."

"No, but I love her in a different way," Griffin argued. "I know you all love her. That's one of the reasons I can live with the overbearing nature of this family. It's the love that makes you bearable. Even when you were calling me Detective Dinglefritz and threatening to cut off my hands, I knew that it came from a place of love.

"The fact remains that I love her in a different way," he continued, causing my heart to constrict when his voice cracked. "I don't want to say I love her more, because that's not fair to you, but ... well ... I love her more."

"You don't love her more than I do," Dad argued.

"In a way, I do," Griffin said. "I refuse to get into this with you. It's not fair to you. It's not fair to me. It's certainly not fair to her. We're not grading on a curve here. There's plenty of room for all of us to love her."

"Then why are you being such a pain?" Dad asked. "She's been through a lot the past year. I used to think you were something she would have to survive, that you would take off. Now I know that's not true, but punishing her for something she didn't do simply isn't fair."

"I'm not punishing her, and you really don't have a place in this particular conversation," Griffin snapped. "I am not angry because of the body on the street. I am not angry because of the body in the backyard. She didn't cause that. She did nothing wrong."

"So you're upset because she sneaked out of the house?" Braden asked, taking me by surprise when he inserted himself in the argument. He generally prefers sitting back and watching Griffin and me argue. "That's what she does. That's part of her personality. If you're going to be angry at her for that, then why are you even with her?"

Griffin narrowed his eyes. "I'm with her because I love her. I am not trying to change her. I am not even angry that she sneaked out. Part of me expected that. I am angry because she lied."

"I didn't lie."

"Close enough."

"So, if I told you I was going to call Redmond and have him pick me up so we could visit the voodoo lady at the mall you would've been fine with it?"

Griffin tilted his head to the side, considering. "Fine? Probably not. I would've argued with you. But I wouldn't be angry. I wouldn't feel as if you punched me in the gut with a lie."

I stilled, dumbfounded. "You feel as if I punched you in the gut?"

"I don't expect you to modify your behavior to fit my needs," Griffin replied. "I think we do a pretty good job of meeting each other's needs."

"If this is about to go to a dirty place, I'm exercising my right to protect my needs and actually punch you in the gut," Dad warned.

Griffin ignored him, recognizing the blowhard nature of the words. "I love you the way you are. You may not think you lied to me because you were careful in how you worded things, but that's not how I want to live our lives. I don't want to spend all of my time ripping apart every little thing you say to determine if you could be lying. I would rather take you at your word."

"So if I'm going to run away from the police and enlist a brother to do it, you want me to tell you?"

"Yes."

"Huh. Would you have yelled if I told you?"

"Yes."

"See, I don't like the yelling." I grabbed a tortilla chip from the bowl at the center of the table. "I always try to avoid the yelling."

"Yes, well, that's part of my makeup," Griffin said. "You can't modify it. There will be times I'll yell. You need to get used to that."

"Okay, well ... okay." That seemed fair. Even I couldn't come up with a reason to push further. "I'm sorry. I thought you would melt down."

"She was also upset because you didn't kiss her goodbye," Aidan offered. "She pouted about it all day."

"I wasn't even with you all day," I challenged.

Griffin pursed his lips. "I see." He leaned forward so he could rest his brow against mine. "I will kiss you goodbye from here on out whether we're fighting or not. Does that make you feel better?"

Strangely enough, it did. "You won't make jokes about me thinking like a chick when you do it, will you?"

"Of course not."

"Okay."

Griffin pressed a soft kiss to my mouth, ignoring the way my father and brothers groaned. "We're still going to talk about a few things, but the crisis has passed. You can stop eating."

"Thank God." I dropped the half-eaten chip on my plate. "I think I might burst."

Griffin smirked as he shook his head, taking a moment to bask in the mirth before sobering and focusing on Dad. "I need to know everything you guys did today."

"Well, it wasn't much, but we got a few leads," Dad supplied. "Aisling claims that the first body had a symbol on it. We found it in the voodoo section of Eternal Sunshine Cemetery this afternoon."

"Is that what you were doing?" Griffin rolled his neck. "One of the uniforms I talked to when I was entering the police department said that Green believes you guys were trying to hide bodies or something. They searched the area where they found you, thinking that's where you were hiding bodies."

"I guess a cemetery would be a good place to do it, but Detective Green sounds like a real idiot," Cillian said. "The symbol represents a snake creature that supposedly takes over the dead. I'll do some further research tonight. Maya is working a double shift."

"I know you guys aren't going to believe me, but the more I think about it, the more I'm starting to wonder if Jed Burnham was hissing," I said. "I said it sounded as if he was smacking his lips, but he might have been hissing."

"Here we go." Dad pinched the bridge of his nose. "Zombies aren't real."

"I've been telling her that for days, but she won't let it go," Griffin lamented.

"You don't know they're not real," I challenged. "You're picturing zombies from movies, the ones that bite and spread an infection. I think we're dealing with a different type of zombie."

"And how do these zombies work?" Griffin asked, keeping his expression placid.

"I think someone is working bad mojo on bodies and causing them to rise."

"To what end?" Dad prodded.

I shrugged. "Maybe they're sending them after me. I'm still not convinced that Angelina isn't behind this. I told you how bad my insults were the other day. That can't be a coincidence."

"Yes, well, insult horror aside, I still don't think we have enough information to say it's definitely zombies," Dad argued. "I think it's far more likely that someone is using bodies, perhaps planting them in areas near you, because they want to distract you from something else."

"That first guy ran into me," I said. "He was walking. I know you have Braden's human puppet theory to consider, but I swear he was walking of his own volition. No one was carrying him."

"She right," Griffin confirmed. "He was walking on his own."

"Then perhaps something else is going on," Dad suggested. "Maybe someone in the medical examiner's office is involved."

"I can start checking on that tomorrow," Redmond offered. "I have a contact in the office, and she's more than willing to share information."

I made an exaggerated face. "This isn't the woman you failed to perform with on the terrace, is it? I'm guessing she won't help if you have nothing to offer her in return."

Redmond scowled. "If you bring that up again I'll shove your head in the toilet and start flushing."

"Do I even want to know what you two are talking about?" Griffin asked.

"No," my brothers answered in unison.

"I'll tell you later," I said, patting his hand. "You have to wait until we're done fighting. The story is like a reward."

"Now I'm looking forward to it."

"I think we're all going to have to wedge bouts of research into our days for a bit," Dad said. "Until then, I think it would be better for all concerned if you and Aisling stay here overnight, Griffin."

I jerked my head in his direction, confused. "Why?"

"Because your brothers and father can serve as alibis if necessary," Griffin answered. "On top of that, the police department can't get inside the gate to watch us. I'm sure they'll be out on the street – and now everyone will be under some sort of surveillance. It will be much harder for them to keep track of who is coming and going because they can't see through the wall."

"Oh." That sounded mildly interesting. "I guess I can live with that if Dad promises me an ice cream bar tomorrow."

"And why would I do that?" Dad challenged.

"Because I had different rules as a child and I'm traumatized by it."

Dad scowled. "Oh, geez. I'll never hear the end of this, will I?"

"Nope."

"Fine. You may have an ice cream bar tomorrow."

"And an omelet bar in the morning," I pressed.

"And an omelet bar in the morning," Dad conceded, causing Griffin to grin.

"You really know how to lay down the law with her," Griffin supplied.

Dad averted his eyes. "She's still recovering. She needs good food to do it."

"And people say I'm whipped," Griffin muttered.

"Eat your taco, Griffin," Dad ordered. "If your mouth is full you can't say anything stupid."

"That's never been the rule for me," I pointed out.

Dad winked. "That's because you're gifted."

He wasn't wrong.

GRIFFIN WAS USED to sleeping in my childhood bedroom. We'd spent enough nights here due to danger and serious injury that he bought a toothbrush for the bathroom and stored some clothing in the closet. It was almost like a second home for us, even kind of a vacation home because others cooked, cleaned and did our laundry.

I changed into sleep pants and a T-shirt, and climbed into bed, watching as he stripped down to his boxers before hitting the lights and sliding in next to me. I waited for him to say something, but when he simply stared at the ceiling and didn't speak I knew the onus was on me.

"I'm sorry I metaphorically punched you in the gut."

Griffin snickered. "I think it's funny that you refuse to admit you did anything wrong."

"I should've told you what I had planned. Does that make you feel better?"

"Yes."

"I will tell you when I next plan to evade the cops."

"That makes me feel even better." Griffin slid his arm under my waist and tugged me so my head rested on his chest, tucking the covers around both of us to make sure we stayed warm in the drafty room. "You didn't get much of a chance to tell me what you learned at the voodoo shop. Do you really think this Madame Dauphine is involved?"

"It's my best working theory. None of this started until after I ran into her at the store."

"And Angelina? Do you really think she's involved or is she just an easy scapegoat?"

I shrugged as I traced my finger down the center of his muscled chest. "It could be a coincidence."

"But?"

"But I've learned that true coincidences are extremely rare," I replied. "Do you really think the cops will follow all of us now?"

"I think they'll try," Griffin replied, smoothing my hair before resting his cheek against my forehead. "I don't know how your father will handle that, but it could make collecting souls fairly difficult. If any of your brothers get caught ... ."

"My brothers know a thing or two about evading the police."

"That should upset me, but it doesn't. The last thing we need is one of them getting arrested for being at the home of a dead person."

"Knowing Dad, he probably won't take any chances," I said. "There are ways for us to sneak out of here, too."

"Like?"

"Like the people at the home office can drop vehicles at the bar and we can exit through the back door and walk there."

"That won't work forever," Griffin pointed out. "Eventually Green will realize that you're sneaking out of the house."

"Probably, but it will work for a day or two." I tilted up my chin to study his profile. The room was dark, but the ambient light from the moon shining through the window allowed me to see his face. "I noticed you're not calling him Mark any longer."

"I called him Mark when I respected him," Griffin replied. "I don't respect him any longer."

"Because he thinks an innocent and sweet-tempered woman like me could be a cold-blooded killer?"

"Because anyone with half a brain would realize that his theory makes zero sense," Griffin countered. "The fact that the medical examiner hasn't ruled the deaths homicides makes me wonder."

"About?"

"Exactly what he's trying to accomplish. I'm going to run a search on him tomorrow, ask around."

"Wait ... do you think he has something to do with this?"

"Probably not, but I'll check anyway," Griffin replied. "He's far too fixated on you for this stage of the investigation. There must be a reason."

"Still ... I'm sorry. I know you considered him a friend."

"I considered him an acquaintance," Griffin corrected. "It doesn't matter. You're far more important to me than he is. We'll figure this out."

"I know. I have faith."

We lapsed into amiable silence for a moment, the sounds of the settling house lulling me until I felt Griffin's hands roaming my midriff.

"Seriously? I thought you were still angry."

"I'm over that," Griffin said, rolling me so I was on my back and he could stare down at me. "I'm ready to make up."

I couldn't swallow my smile. "Should I start begging now?"

Griffin grinned. "You read my mind."

18
EIGHTEEN

"Okay, I've unloaded our case schedule for the next two days," Dad announced as he strolled into the dining room the next morning. He arched an eyebrow when he caught Braden and me trying to wrestle each other out of the omelet bar line. "Are you two animals? Is there a reason you can't take turns to get your food in a civilized fashion?"

"I'm starving," I replied. "I'm still recovering, after all, and I need my strength."

Dad stared at me for a moment, his expression unreadable. "You can't have it both ways. Either you're 'totally fine' and want us to stop hovering or you're still recovering and need us to coddle you. Which one is it?"

"Um ... I need coddling over breakfast and I'll be fine for the rest of the afternoon."

"Will you listen to that?" Braden licked his finger and stuck it in my ear, causing me to yelp and elbow him in the stomach. "She's manipulating you, Dad. Lay down the law."

Instead of immediately responding, Dad flicked his eyes to Griffin, who sat at the table drinking coffee and perusing the newspaper. "Do you want to handle this?"

"They're your offspring."

"And that's my newspaper."

"Which I will gladly share once you handle this situation," Griffin said. "There's nothing in here about the body found in our backyard. Either the press is refusing to run it because there's no cause of death or the cops are purposely keeping it quiet."

"Which do you think it is?" Cillian asked, pouring himself a glass of juice as he grinned at Braden and me. "Aisling, if you move your hip to the left you'll totally overbalance him."

"Hey!" Braden was offended. "Why are you taking her side?"

I took advantage of Braden's momentary distraction and moved to my left, snickering as Braden toppled forward and hit the floor. "Nice."

"I'm taking her side because she's still recovering," Cillian teased. "I'll take your side when she's feeling better this afternoon."

"I think that's a good rule for everyone," Dad said. "Aisling gets her omelet first."

I pumped my fist. "Score!"

"This goes back to that whole 'you being spoiled' thing," Redmond reminded me.

I shrugged. "I can live with that. It's the separate rules that bother me."

"What separate rules?" Griffin asked, handing my father the A section of the newspaper as he switched to the sports section.

"I found out yesterday that I had separate rules from my brothers," I supplied, smiling at the omelet chef as she gestured toward the ingredients. "I want tomatoes, mushrooms, American cheese, onions and ham."

"No onions," Griffin interjected.

"No onions," I corrected.

"Why can't she have onions?" Dad asked.

"Because then I can't kiss her."

"Double up on her onions," Dad ordered, causing me to smirk.

"That won't stop me from kissing her," Griffin noted. "It just makes it more of a challenge ... and I thrive under challenging conditions."

"You're going to be a pain today, aren't you?" Dad poured himself a glass of orange juice. "It's obvious you two made up, though. I'm glad for that."

"We're both glad." I beamed at Griffin. "I've promised to tell him when I plan to break the law."

"And I'm going to try to refrain from yelling when she does," Griffin added.

"Sounds like a healthy relationship," Braden drawled.

"No one asked you." Griffin shot him a look. "Can't you behave for five minutes?"

"Don't waste your breath," Dad said. "I've been asking all of them that for thirty years."

"And sometimes we even take the question to heart," Aidan said, handing a grouchy-looking Jerry a mug of coffee. "Are you going to spend the whole morning pouting?"

Jerry didn't answer, instead grabbing the Arts and Leisure section of the newspaper from the pile in front of Griffin and plopping himself in his regular chair.

"I haven't read that yet," Griffin pointed out.

"I don't think he cares," Redmond said, exchanging a weighted look with me. We were all used to Jerry's moods. When he suffered, we all suffered.

"What's wrong, Jerry?" I asked, hoping his answer would be short and without the tempestuous sighs that set my teeth on edge.

"Why would anything possibly be wrong?" Jerry asked airily.

Uh-oh. I risked a glance at Aidan and found him making a face. "What's wrong with him?"

"He's ticked because he missed out on all the fun yesterday," Aidan replied. "He wanted to go to the police station, too."

"Oh, well, next time." I forced a bright smile. "At the rate I'm going I'll be hauled back there at least two times today."

"Not likely," Dad countered. "Neil and the other members of my legal team – all well worth the twenty grand I dropped yesterday, mind you – filed more than thirty injunctions against the Royal Oak Police Department by the time the courthouse closed yesterday. They won't come after you today."

I brightened considerably. "Does that mean they won't be watching us?"

"Oh, they're watching us," Braden said. "Redmond and I went for a run this morning."

"You don't run."

"We do around the block," Braden said. "We wanted to see how many cars we could find, so we did a small circuit through the immediate area."

"How many cars did you find?" Griffin lowered the newspaper, curious.

"Seven."

"That's one for each of us," Griffin noted. "They're not taking any chances."

I knit my eyebrows. "Can they follow you to work?"

"They'll follow me to the precinct, I'm sure, but I doubt they'll follow me out on cases," Griffin replied. "If they do, I'll have a talk with them. As for the rest ... are they going to catch you doing anything freaky today?"

"Define freaky," Redmond said.

"Whatever you were doing out on the terrace with your nameless chick," I interjected, grinning when Redmond groaned.

"Let it go, Aisling," Redmond ordered.

"I'm good."

Griffin snickered as he shook his head. "I still don't know what's going on with that story, but I'm pretty sure it's better that I remain in the dark. As for the cops, I wouldn't worry about them. They don't have the authority to arrest any of you as long as you don't do anything illegal in their presence."

"We're spending most of the day here," Dad said. "We're conducting research."

"I'm going to run a search on Green to see if I can find a reason that he would go after Aisling this hard," Griffin volunteered. "I doubt I'll find anything – I'm guessing it's pure laziness and ego that has him gunning for her – but I'm going to look all the same."

"We're going to research the symbol and Madame Dauphine," Dad said. "If we have to leave, I'll text you."

"That would be a nice change of pace." Griffin watched me as I sat down with my huge omelet. "Give me a kiss before you eat those onions."

I did as instructed, ignoring the way Dad squirmed in his chair.

"If you find anything, let me know," Griffin said once we were finished. "I'm going to see if I can find anything on Madame Dauphine. I'll bet she didn't file a business license under that name. If I get any information, I'll email it to you, Cillian."

"Okay." Cillian bobbed his head. "Something tells me it's going to be a long day in the Grimlock household if we're all stuck here with nothing better to do than mess with the cops."

"Something tells me I'm glad that I have to go to work," Griffin said.

Something told me they were both right, and that it was going to be one hell of a day.

BRADEN POKED HIS HEAD into Dad's office and flashed an impish grin.

"Dad, where did you hide those water balloons we bought this summer?"

Dad, who busily worked at his computer, didn't glance up. "Why?"

"Why do you think?"

"I think you're going to terrorize the cops."

"Good guess."

Dad sighed. "They're in the pantry in the kitchen, behind the oatmeal. I thought you'd never look there."

"Why do you guys have water balloons?" I asked, interested despite myself.

"Because Dad told us we were too old to play with them," Braden replied. "We had to prove him wrong."

"Yes, and after they terrorized the butler ... and me ... with them, what happened?" Dad queried.

"He screamed, 'Do I have to lock you in the basement,' and then he confiscated them," Braden replied, eyes sparkling. "It was totally worth it."

"I'm sorry I missed it." I shifted to face Braden. "What are you going to do with them now?"

"Throw them at the cops."

I made a face. "I know that. But you should fill them with special stuff."

"Like what? Yogurt."

I tilted my head to the side, considering. "I never thought of that, but it would totally stink."

"I don't care what you do with them," Dad said, "but whatever you do, take it out of this room. Cillian and I are working."

"Story of my life," Cillian muttered.

I took pity on him and sidled over, hunkering down so only he could hear me. "I'll video it and bring you a snack when we're done."

"Sold."

I followed Braden out of the office, following him to the kitchen where Redmond and Aidan were amassing ingredients. "Where's Jerry?" I asked, glancing around.

"He's upstairs pouting," Aidan replied.

"And this is all because he didn't get dragged to the police station with us yesterday?"

"You know how he hates being left out of things."

I did indeed. "Go get him. There's a very good chance we could at least get violently threatened for what we're about to do."

Aidan brightened. "Good point."

"Found them!" Braden was triumphant when he returned with the huge bag of balloons. "Aisling gave me an idea, by the way. Maybe we shouldn't fill them all with water."

Redmond's eyes lit with interest. "What do you mean? I thought we agreed it was cold enough that the water would freeze almost immediately and drive the cops nuts."

"We can do that with some of them, but I thought we might mix things up," Braden said, flipping through the pantry. "We could use things like olive oil ... and coconut milk ... and evaporated milk."

"Oh, I get what you're saying." A wide grin split Redmond's face. "Water is fun, but it will be even better if it looks like a really big bird took a dump on their cars."

Braden joined in the revelry. "Exactly."

"What a great way to waste an afternoon," I laughed. "We haven't done this since we were teenagers."

"You probably won't think that if they arrest us," Redmond pointed out.

"They won't. They'll be too afraid to do that. Neil has them backpedaling. If they arrest us for water balloons it will look like a nuisance complaint if they actually try to take me to court for murder. Neil is a master at messing with them."

"That's why we keep him on retainer." Redmond dipped into the cupboard under the sink. "What do you think laundry detergent will do?"

"I don't know, but I can't wait to find out."

TWO HOURS LATER my cheeks were pink from the cold as I wrapped myself in a blanket in front of my father's office fireplace.

"You should've seen their faces when Redmond hit them with the egg balloon," I said. "I thought the one guy was going to cry ... and then beat us with whatever stick was nearest."

"How did you get eggs in a water balloon?" Dad asked, his eyes lit with curiosity.

"They used a funnel," Cillian answered. "We've done it before. I just got an email from Griffin, by the way. He's managed to dig up some dirt on Madame Dauphine."

I shifted, intrigued. "Please tell me she's wanted for something in a different state and we can extradite her immediately."

"Technically we can't extradite anyone," Cillian pointed out. "And, sadly, I don't think you'll be happy with the information Griffin dug up."

That didn't sound good. "What did he find?"

"Sit down," Dad ordered, getting a good look at my face for the first time since I re-entered the house. "You need some tea to warm up."

I rolled my eyes at Cillian as he swallowed a smile. "I'm perfectly fine."

"Yes? Well, I've decided the coddling will continue if you're staying under this roof."

"I can leave."

"Not if you want your ice cream bar after dinner tonight."

"You fight dirty." I indulged him by taking the mug of tea he offered, and then raised an eyebrow when he settled on the couch next to me and tucked in the blanket at my sides. "Dad, I'm fine."

"You could catch cold," Dad noted. "You were outside a long time. I should've thought better about letting you play with your brothers."

"I'll be thirty in, like, two years," I reminded him.

"And we weren't playing," Braden added, strolling into the room. "We were waging war. Speaking of that, I really loved the pink food coloring you put in that one balloon, Ais. It looked as if a pink marshmallow exploded over that car."

"It sounds like you had fun, for which I'm glad, but now it's time to turn serious," Dad said as he finished tucking me in. "You sit there until I say you've rested long enough. Do you understand?"

"Oh, geez." I pressed my eyes shut. "I'm pretty sure I brought this on myself, so I can't even blame anyone else."

"I'm sure that won't stop you," Braden said.

"Good point." I turned my expectant eyes to Cillian. "What do you have?"

"An urge to watch the video you two made," Cillian said.

"Aidan and Jerry are uploading it to YouTube right now," Braden said. "I'm sure it will be a big hit. It's called 'Cops get creamed.'"

Cillian barked out a laugh. "Nice!"

"Get to the point, Cillian," Dad ordered, shooting Braden a warning look should he interrupt again. "What do you have on this Dauphine?"

"From what I can tell, she seems to be the real deal," Cillian replied, sobering. "Griffin is still trying to track her name, but she's shown up in a few reports between here and New Orleans. Always under the name Madame Dauphine, though."

"New Orleans?"

"Yeah, I picked up on that, too," Cillian said. "Whoever she is,

Madame Dauphine keeps telling people she was born there. And she seems to have spent a lot of time there."

"That makes sense," I said. "She's trying to make a living off the Marie Laveau mystique. How long ago did Madame Dauphine come into existence?"

"About five years ago."

"And we have no idea who she was before that?"

"Not yet, but Griffin is still searching," Cillian answered. "She has a few complaints filed against her. None of them are serious, but all seem to revolve around this curse thing she does."

"Curse thing?" Dad leaned forward. "Does she put curses on people for money?"

"In the interviews she's done with police in various towns, she claims no," Cillian said. "She claims that she removes curses from people."

"Who puts them there?" I asked.

"It doesn't say, but she denies it's her."

"So she makes a living removing curses?" Dad slid me a sidelong glance. "Perhaps she's smart enough to put the curses in place long before she enacts them. Maybe she knew who you were when you entered her store because she's been watching you longer than we realize."

"Or maybe Angelina put a curse on me and Madame Dauphine let her because she knew I'd pay to have it removed," I suggested.

"I guess that's a possibility, too." Dad rubbed the back of his neck. "I'm not sure what to make of all this. Are you sure Madame Dauphine has never been arrested?"

"I'm sure she hasn't been arrested under that name," Cillian clarified. "We don't know her real name."

"And until we do, we're operating in the dark." Dad slouched on the couch. "This continues to grow stranger."

"What was your first clue?" I asked.

Dad shrugged. "The fact that you keep swearing that zombies are coming for us."

"I haven't been proved wrong on that."

"Let it go," Dad muttered, rubbing his forehead. He looked tired, which caused me to be sympathetic.

"Do you know what will make you feel better?"

"What?"

"We have more balloons. I was thinking that we could toss in some pickle juice from the jars in the refrigerator to really make the cars stink."

"I've had worse offers."

"Does that mean you want to play?"

"I guess, but Cillian has to play, too. We need to make it a family affair."

"That's how we get our best ideas," I reminded him. "Come on. We found the perfect spot."

19
NINETEEN

Once we warmed up from our second bout of cop torture, we settled in Dad's office to pretend we were conducting research. Okay, Dad and Cillian were really conducting research. The rest of us are often useless when it comes to books and computers, though, so we drank hot chocolate and ate doughnuts while whispering.

"You're driving me nuts," Dad snapped. "You know what happens when you drive me nuts."

"Not one more word!" My brothers and I did our best imitation of Dad at the same time, wagging our fingers and bellowing into the room.

"If you do, you'll be crapping leather from my boots for the rest of your lives," Redmond added, causing me to smirk.

Dad pressed the heel of his hand to his forehead. "Oh, geez. I forgot how much I hated snow days when you were younger."

"We loved them," Aidan said. "We got to have snowball fights and build igloos."

"And make snow angels," Jerry added, wandering into the room.

"Where have you been?" I asked, looking him up and down. He'd disappeared not long after we entered the house.

"I had to check in with the bakery," Jerry replied. "I left Nadia in charge. You know what an iffy proposition that is. She likes to add vodka to every recipe."

"That's kind of a nasty stereotype," I pointed out. "She's Russian. That doesn't mean she's a drunk."

"She's not Russian, and she is a drunk."

"Oh." Hmm. I always thought she was Russian. "What's with her accent?"

"She's pretentious."

"Oh, that's why you hired her." I nodded knowingly. "She's very pretty."

"Yeah. She's okay. The straight male customers seem to like her. All two of them."

I smirked until I realized Jerry looked distracted. "What's wrong with you?"

"Well, some very interesting information fell into my lap, but I'm not sure I should tell you," Jerry admitted. "On one hand, I think you'd want to know. On the other, you're probably going to do something stupid if I tell you."

"Then you should definitely tell me."

"Don't tell her," Dad ordered.

Jerry pursed his lips as I batted my eyes in his direction. "Your father says I shouldn't tell you."

"Since when do you listen to him?" I challenged. "He once said you couldn't pull off the color peach without looking like a walking vagina. Do you remember that? I happen to think you look dapper in peach."

"Don't do that," Dad warned. "I didn't say he couldn't pull off peach. I simply asked him why he'd want to pull it off."

"I happen to think it makes me look approachable," Jerry supplied.

"At least you have a reason."

I exhaled heavily as I glanced between Dad and Jerry. I was bored, a dangerous proposition, and I wanted something to do with my afternoon. I had a feeling whatever gossipy tidbit Jerry stumbled over while talking to Nadia would involve an outing. I desperately needed an outing.

"I'll spend an entire Saturday letting you try out different wedding hairstyles if you tell me," I offered.

"You can't bribe him with hairstyles," Dad argued.

"Yes, she can." Jerry smiled. "I'm thinking something up, hair off your neck, and a tiara."

That sounded terrible. "I'm looking forward to your ideas."

"Great. As for what I learned, Nadia says that Kristin Nelson came in and she happened to mention that Angelina is at the Rochester day spa ... and she's getting the works, so she'll be there the entire afternoon."

Ding, ding, ding. We have an excursion winner. "Dad ... ."

"Absolutely not." Dad was firm, refusing to meet my gaze.

"Angelina might know something," I reminded him. "We know where she is. She's at the spa, which means she put her purse in a locker while she's getting the works. If Jerry and I were to, I don't know, splurge on a spa day we'd have access to that locker."

Dad slowly lifted his eyes until they locked with mine. "No."

"A spa day would make me feel better," I added. "A nice massage would relieve the tension I'm carrying in my shoulders, and a facial would clear up this problem area on the side of my nose. That breakout is also from stress."

Dad shook his head. "No. You've spent weeks telling me you feel fine. You can't go back on it."

Oh, well, if he was going to be a hard-ass, I'd have to bring out the big guns. "If we're at the spa we won't be able to play a rousing game of 'How Long Until Dad Cracks Under the Pressure?'"

Dad growled, resigned. "Fine. You're not going alone, though."

"I know. Jerry is going with me."

"And you're taking Aidan, Braden and Redmond."

I stilled. They weren't my first choice of partners for a spa day. "We should compromise. We'll take Aidan. You can keep Braden and Redmond."

"Hey!" Redmond glared at me. "I like a spa day as much as the next heterosexual guy who is in touch with his softer side."

"Awesome." I flashed him a sarcastic thumbs-up. "We'll take Redmond, too. You can keep Braden."

"I don't want to go anyway," Braden huffed, folding his arms across his chest. "You're not hurting my feelings."

"That's too bad. If anyone needs help with a unibrow, it's you."

Braden scowled. "I do not have a unibrow."

"That's right," Aidan said. "He gets it waxed every two weeks."

"Secretly," Braden hissed, slapping Aidan's arm. "That was a secret."

"No one in this family can keep secrets," Dad said. "If you want to go the spa, all five of you must go together. That's non-negotiable."

"And this is in no way an opportunity for you to rid yourself of your most annoying child for the afternoon, right?" I pressed. "It's all a way to protect me."

"Who is my most annoying child?"

"Braden," I answered automatically.

"Aisling," Braden said at the same time.

"Well, look at that." Dad flashed a bright smile as he dug in his pocket for his wallet. "It seems I'm going to get rid of my two most annoying children. How lucky is that?"

I accepted the credit card he relinquished. "I'm going to spend so much this thing will look tired when I give it back."

"I expect nothing less."

"I THINK DAD WAS talking about Redmond and Braden when he said his two most annoying children were heading to the spa today," I announced as we walked into the spa lobby. "That's the only thing that makes sense."

"Yeah. That's the only thing that makes sense," Redmond deadpanned. "It couldn't possibly be you."

"I'm his favorite."

"No, you're the one he's coddled for the past two months because of what happened," Braden corrected. "I'm pretty sure he's over that. It won't work any longer."

"I've got a hundred bucks that says I can get a cake bar out of him tomorrow night."

"Bring it on."

I flashed a smile for the woman behind the counter, a milquetoast blonde with a forgettable face and hair so shiny I could've sworn it glittered. "We need the entire works."

The woman — her nametag read "Carrie" — pressed her lips together. "Do you have appointments?"

"No."

"We generally prefer appointments."

I slapped Dad's credit card on the counter. The black MasterCard caused Carrie's eyebrows to fly up her forehead. "We need the works."

"Absolutely." Carrie's demeanor changed almost instantaneously, and the smile she flashed Redmond was straight out of the "I've Lost My Panties" playbook. "What can I do for you?"

"I want a facial and an hour-long hot stone massage."

"That's what I want, too," Jerry said. "I also want a pedicure."

"I'll take all three of those," Aidan said.

"Braden here needs an eyebrow wax, a back wax, a bikini wax and a stick removal for his bad attitude," I added.

"I'll take a massage," Braden corrected, scorching me with a dark look before leaning closer. "I'll take a facial and eyebrow shaping, too."

I manage to swallow my laughter before turning my attention to the long hallway that led to the back of the spa. "Are we the only ones here today?"

Carrie, who couldn't take her eyes off Redmond, merely shook her head. "We have a few other guests. You picked a good day for an impulse stop."

"Great." I'd been to this day spa a time or two — it wasn't a favorite, but it wasn't terrible — so I was familiar with the setup. "I want to start with my facial and then end with my massage."

"Sure. Whatever." Carrie absently waved her hand. "Whatever you want."

"Great." I grabbed Jerry's arm and dragged him toward the dressing room. "We'll be out in a few minutes."

THE PLAN WAS to go through Angelina's locker before getting our facials. We were interrupted by a guest we didn't recognize, so instead we found ourselves being steamed and plucked to within an inch of our lives before popping back into the locker room while we waited for massage rooms to open.

"Watch the door," I ordered, opening the nearest locker. It was empty. "It shouldn't take me long to find her stuff and go through it."

"Why must I always be the lookout?" Jerry groused, cracking the door and pressing his eyes close so he could stare in every direction. He made a terrible spy, but he was always entertaining, so things evened out. "I should be the one going through her stuff. You probably won't even recognize half of the things in there."

I was pretty sure that was an insult. I riffled through five empty lockers before finding one with a purse inside. The bag was Kate Spade – obviously a knockoff – and featured pink flowers. "This has to be hers."

Jerry glanced over a shoulder, wrinkling his nose at the purse. "That's fake."

"Even I know that," I said. "It's pleather."

"Ugh. I'm glad you're the one doing that then. I'm allergic to pleather."

"Who isn't?" I searched through the purse, yanking out a large plastic bag and widening my eyes when I saw the myriad prescription bottles inside. "Look at this. There's like ... eight bottles of stuff in here."

Jerry pursed his lips. "What is it?"

"It's probably for early onset menopause," I replied. "When we saw her the other day I noticed some hairs sprouting from her chin."

"That seems like a lot of medication for menopause," Jerry noted dubiously. "Are those all hormone pills?"

That was a good question. "I have no idea." I yanked my phone out of my locker and snapped photographs of the labels. It was none of my business, yet I couldn't stop myself from being a busybody. It was Angelina, after all. She deserved it.

Once finished, I placed the medication on the bench and continued my search. Sadly, everything in Angelina's purse was utterly useless. "Who needs this much lipstick?" I held up three tubes as I made a face.

"That's Urban Decay, Sephora and Marc Jacobs," Jerry said. "They're all good choices."

I slanted my eyes in his direction, irritated. "Whose side are you on?"

"Yours, of course, but you have terrible taste in makeup. Wet n Wild stopped being an option when we were ten."

"Whatever." I let loose with a growl. "There's nothing in here other than makeup and medicine."

"What did you think would be in there?" Jerry asked. "Did you think she was carrying around a confession? Perhaps a curse with your name on it?"

I shrugged. "I don't know. More than this. I ... ." I didn't get a chance to finish because the door behind Jerry – the door he conveniently stopped watching three minutes earlier – popped open to allow Angelina entry. She looked wiped, her face devoid of makeup, and it took her a moment to realize who she was dealing with and exactly what we were doing.

"What the ... ?" Angelina took a step in our direction. "Are you going through my purse?"

Whoops. This wouldn't end well. "Absolutely not," I lied.

"What is that?" Angelina pointed toward the pink bag.

"That is a knockoff."

"It's the real thing," Angelina hissed. "I don't buy knockoffs."

"It's pleather."

"It is not. It's just ... a new kind of leather. It feels different."

"Like pleather? You know pleather has a distinctive texture, right?"

"I am not having this conversation with you," Angelina screeched. "You're evil and you're breaking the law. I'm calling the police."

Oh, well, this was an interesting development. "You know what? I'll bet there's an unmarked car on the corner with a bit of pink froth on the hood. There are cops in there. In fact ... yeah. You should tell them what you caught me doing."

"And why would you suggest that?" Angelina was understandably suspicious. "This sounds like another elaborate prank on your part." Angelina jerked the purse away from me. "I don't trust you." She stalked toward the door, leaving the medication behind as she hoarded fury like a Keebler elf during a cookie shortage.

As much as I disliked Angelina – and that scale had absolutely no limits – the medication was probably expensive, so I tightened the sash around my robe and grabbed the bag before following. Angelina was already at the front door, refusing to change her clothes and instead bellowing a variety of insults in Carrie's direction. Redmond was still at the front desk whispering sweet nothings in her ear, so Carrie barely lifted her hand to wave. It was more of a half-hearted finger shift than anything else.

"Have a nice day."

"Oh, stuff it," Angelina hissed.

Redmond caught my gaze as I chased after Angelina. "What did you do?"

"She caught me going through her knockoff purse. I need to give this medication back to her even though she's evil. It wouldn't be fair not to do it."

"Oh, well, don't let her get close enough to grab your hair."

"I'm not new."

I forgot to put on shoes, swearing under my breath when my bare feet hit the cold cement of the sidewalk. Angelina was halfway down the block – walking in a robe and high heels – when I called out.

"Angelina!"

Angelina glanced over her shoulder, her expression twisted and hateful. "What do you want?"

I held up the bag. "You forgot your medication."

"You mean you stole my medication," Angelina huffed out, striding back in my direction. "I'm filing a police report about this. Don't think you'll get away with it."

I shot a glance at the police officers in the pink-stained car, both of whom seemed desperate to stare out the opposite window and pretend they weren't listening to the exchange. "Do you guys want to arrest me?"

Neither man so much as looked in my direction.

"I guess not." I forced a smile for Angelina's benefit, knowing it would drive her crazy. "Are you going through menopause?"

"What?" Angelina's eyebrows flew up into her forehead. "Why would you ask that?"

I shrugged. "You're growing a beard."

Angelina's hand flew toward her top lip.

"Beard," I stressed. "You're doing a good job at keeping up on the mustache."

"I will rip your hair out of your head," Angelina hissed, reaching forward.

I easily sidestepped her, biting back the urge to laugh when Angelina almost tripped over a seam in the sidewalk. "You should be careful. I'm sure the cold feels good to you given all of the hot flashes you're dealing with, but it will hurt if you hit the pavement."

"It's going to hurt when I put my fist in your face," Angelina gritted out.

Finally, the police officer in the driver's seat of the car couldn't ignore the potential for violence a second longer and opened his door, embarrassment tinging his cheeks as he exited the vehicle.

"Ladies, is there something I can help you with?"

"Who are you?" Angelina asked, frustrated.

"They're cops," I replied. "I already told you that."

"Oh, well, I want her arrested." Angelina extended a finger in my direction.

"On what charges?" the officer asked.

"Being a menace."

"You'll have to do better than that."

"I caught her going through my purse," Angelina announced, scowling.

"Is that true?" The officer turned his full attention to me.

"No." I shook my head. "I accidentally knocked her purse off the bench and she caught me putting everything back. I was not going through her personal belongings."

"Don't believe her!" Angelina screwed her face into a hateful expression. "She's an evil woman who has been obsessed with me since we were kids."

"I'm not obsessed with you," I scoffed.

"You want to be me."

"You're a skank. No one wants to be a skank. Well, the Kardashians are fine with it, but they're the exceptions." I hopped from one foot to the other, my cold feet aching. "I need to get back inside."

"Wait." Angelina glared a hole into the police officer. "Aren't you going to arrest her?"

"I don't have jurisdiction," he explained. "If she were in Royal Oak I would arrest her."

"If you don't have jurisdiction why are you even here?" Angelina was beside herself. "I'm just so sick of all of this. I can't stand you and your stupid family and all the weird things that happen around you."

I couldn't exactly blame her. Still, it was too cold to remain outside, so all I could do before fleeing inside was raise a hand in farewell. "Good luck with your menopause. The beard is hardly noticeable, although you might want to look into some bleach just to be on the safe side. If it takes you a few days, don't worry about it. You'll cover it up eventually."

Whew. That should make her feel better.

20
TWENTY

"What happened to your feet?"

Dad didn't look happy when he found me staring at the bottom of my feet in front of the fireplace shortly before dinner. Griffin was due to arrive any moment. I was in serious pain, and I needed a way to hide my stupidity.

"Um ... I forgot to put my shoes on before going outside."

Dad cuffed the back of my head. "What did you really do?"

"I'm not exaggerating. That's what I did."

"Oh, geez." Dad lifted my feet and knelt, studying the soles as he made disgusted sounds in the back of his throat. "You have frostbite."

"I don't think that's possible. I was outside for less than five minutes."

"Then you almost have frostbite, maybe more like frost burn," Dad said. "The bottoms of your feet are all red and leathery."

"They won't fall off, will they?"

"I doubt it."

"Well, that's the best bit of news I've had in hours." I wiggled my toes, grimacing as pain shot through my feet. "Why didn't someone remind me to put on my shoes?"

"Because putting on your shoes before going outside during a Michigan winter is common sense."

"Obviously not."

"You're my least favorite child right now," Dad muttered. "You know that, right?"

"I thought I was your most annoying child."

"Those two qualities are not mutually exclusive."

"Good to know."

Dad growled, shifting his eyes to the open door as Griffin strolled in. "Hello."

"Hey." Griffin furrowed his brow. He looked tired, as if the day stalked him, stabbed him and then mounted his head in a hunting cabin. "What are you doing?"

"Nothing," I replied hurriedly, jerking my feet away and tucking them under the blanket. "Dad has a foot fetish."

Dad scowled. "That's disgusting."

"And borderline incestuous," Griffin said. "What did you do to your feet?"

"Nothing."

"I think she might have frostbite," Dad volunteered.

"Oh, well, there's some good news." Griffin joined Dad on the floor and extended his hands. "Let me see."

"I blame you for this, Dad." I stuck out my feet and whimpered when Griffin grabbed them.

"Sorry," Griffin intoned, lifting my legs so he could see the damage for himself. "I think you'll live, but I'm dying to know how you managed this."

Griffin made a groaning sound as he stood, one my father mimicked to perfection as he pushed himself up, and blew out a sigh as he sat on the couch next to me.

"It doesn't matter," I said, grabbing his hand and flipping it over so I could study his palm. "You look tired."

"Oh, thank you, baby. Men love to hear that just as much as women do."

"I didn't mean it as an insult. In fact, I was going to offer to give you a massage after dinner. I think you need to relax."

"That's nice of you." Griffin patted my knee. "It's also suspicious. I can't remember the last time you offered to massage me. More often than not you trick me into massaging you."

"I had a professional massage today."

"Did your father hire people to come in and keep you out of his hair?"

"I wish I'd thought of that." Dad shuffled to his desk. "She suckered me into giving her my credit card so she could stalk Angelina at the spa."

I expected Griffin to be agitated because he wasn't informed of our spa visit, but all he did was smirk. "Fun. Did you get in a slap fight today?"

"Not even close."

"That's not what Redmond said," Dad interjected. "He said Angelina reached for you, but you managed to evade her."

"Did she slap me?"

"No."

"Then it wasn't a slap fight."

"Fair enough." Dad turned back to his computer. "Did you really spend four thousand dollars at the spa?"

"Most of that was Braden," I replied. "He needed a lot of work done. That unibrow is frightening."

"Really?" Dad didn't look convinced. "Braden says you needed special treatment to hide the hump in your back."

"I'll make him pay later."

"Of course you will."

I turned back to Griffin. "What were we talking about again?"

"Your slap fight with Angelina."

"Oh, it wasn't really a slap fight. Jerry found out from Nadia that Angelina was spending the afternoon at that day spa in Rochester, so we decided to go there. Dad gave me his credit card, and sent Braden, Aidan and Redmond with us because he was sick of hearing us talk."

"I was sick of you guys attacking the police with water balloons," Dad corrected. "Hearing you talk was a close second, though."

"We'll come back to the water balloon thing," Griffin warned. "What did you find out at the day spa?"

"That Braden gets his unibrow waxed every two weeks. Oh, and he has his back waxed, too."

"About Angelina," Griffin pressed. "What did you find out about her?"

"She's going through menopause."

"Really?"

I shrugged. "She had a boatload of medication in her purse. We accused her of having menopause. She didn't deny it. She also had three really expensive lipsticks in a knockoff purse, and she tried to have me arrested by the cops who followed us, but they just laughed at her."

"The cops followed you to the spa?"

"They did, although they tried to pretend they didn't, even though Angelina and I were going at it pretty hard," I explained. "They didn't get out of their car until Angelina tried to pull my hair. By then my feet already hurt because I'd forgotten my shoes, so I didn't spend much time messing with them."

"Oh, well, that was very smart of you." Griffin exchanged a weighted look with my father. "Tell me about the water balloons."

"That sounds like a line from a porno."

Griffin smiled as Dad scowled. "I don't think your father finds that funny."

"I just pretend I don't hear her fifty percent of the time," Dad said. "As for the water balloons, technically it's my fault. Most of them were bored, and I didn't see the harm in it."

"The harm in what?" Griffin asked, tracing his finger over my engagement ring.

"I let them torture what I assume was about half of the Royal Oak Police Department with a bag of water balloons and their imaginations," Dad replied. "They got a little creative. I found the pink food coloring amusing. The laundry detergent was ingenious, because it won't come off in this weather. I drew the line at the lighter fluid."

Instead of expressing outrage or disappointment, Griffin broke out in huge grin. "You attacked the police with water bombs all day?"

"Just in the morning. We went to the spa in the afternoon."

"Well, that sounds like a day well spent." Griffin brought my hand to his lips and kissed my knuckles. "Do you want to hear about my day?"

"Always." I shifted so I could rest my legs on his lap and share the blanket with him. "Did you miss me?"

Griffin smirked. "Always. Where are your brothers? I only want to go through this stuff once."

"I'll get them." Dad left us alone while he hunted the troops, giving Griffin a chance to kiss me to the point where I thought my lips might be suffering from frostbite, too.

I was a little breathless when we separated. "You really did miss me, huh?"

"Yes. I pictured you here, bored out of your mind, and pitied your father for most of the day. I'm happy to hear you managed to have some fun."

"I still missed you." I pressed my index finger into his cheek. "I'm sorry you missed the shenanigans."

"I'm sure you took video."

"It's already on YouTube."

We shared another kiss, ignoring Dad as he cleared his throat upon entry.

"Knock that off," Redmond ordered, smacking his hand against Griffin's arm as he walked past him. "There's no need to act like animals."

"That's rich coming from you," I shot back. "You tried to get naked on a public terrace the other night. Who's really the animal?"

"You," Redmond replied, wrinkling his nose. "You're a ... what's the most annoying animal on the planet?"

"An ostrich," Jerry answered, lifting the other side of the blanket and crawling under to cuddle next to me.

"No one cares about annoying animals," Dad barked. "Griffin has some information he'd like to share. You have been screwing around all day. It's time you focus on something important."

"I, for one, look forward to it." I beamed at Griffin, but he shook his head.

"You can ease up," Griffin said. "You're not in trouble, and I have no energy to fight. You don't have to lay it on so thick."

I blew out a sigh. "Good, because I was running out of material."

"I'm sure you were." Griffin turned somber. "So, I have some interesting news and I'm not sure how you'll take it. Before I share it, I want everyone to remember that we don't know anything yet, so there's no reason to fly off the handle."

"Did you hear him?" I asked my brothers pointedly. "He means business."

"I'm talking to you, baby." Griffin kept his tight smile in place. "I decided to run a state search because I had an idea. I thought maybe the two bodies we're dealing with weren't the first to be discovered under mysterious circumstances."

"That's a good idea," Dad acknowledged. "I didn't even think of that."

"I didn't until later in the afternoon either," Griffin admitted. "I wish I'd thought about it earlier, because I would've had time to make a few calls once the search results came in, but I can chase that tomorrow."

"Well, don't keep us in suspense," Aidan chided. "What did you find?"

"Fifteen other bodies."

"I'm sorry, but ... what?"

Griffin nodded, as if to hammer home the truth behind his words. "There have been fifteen bodies found in this area — we're talking Wayne, Oakland, Macomb, Washtenaw and Monroe counties — in the past three weeks."

I was quiet as I absorbed the information.

"In some cases, witnesses reported seeing the bodies move before they fell to the ground or were discovered later unmoving in a park," Griffin continued. "In one case, a woman swears the body hissed at her and tried to bite her neck before she clocked the individual with her purse. By the time police showed up, the body wasn't moving and the medical examiner found that he'd been dead for at least two weeks."

"That's almost exactly what happened to Aisling," Redmond pointed out.

"It is." Griffin's gaze was heavy when it fell on me. "Do you have something you want to say?"

I nodded. "I do."

"Well, let me have it."

"Okay." I sucked in a big mouthful of air before tossing off the blanket and hopping to my sore feet, ignoring the pain that shot through my soles as I pumped my fist in the air and wiggled my hips. "I was right!"

I did the dance of the ages, my "I'm right" dance, and didn't bother acknowledging the sighs and eye rolls permeating the room. When I turned back to Griffin, I found his lips curving as he watched me. "It was almost worth putting up with the dance to tell you that."

"You liked the dance," I argued, limping toward the couch. "Admit it."

"I prefer the 'I won' dance, but the 'I'm right' dance is a close second." Griffin lifted my feet so he could study them a second time. "Did that hurt?"

"It was worth it."

"How did I know you would say that?" Griffin's fingers were gentle as he lightly rubbed his hands over my sore feet. "While I'm not quite as enthusiastic about Aisling being right, I can no longer say with certainty that she is wrong."

"Ha!" I extended a finger in Dad's direction. "I was right."

"We don't know that," Dad cautioned.

"How can you say that?" I was understandably annoyed. "We have seventeen dead bodies discovered in the metropolitan region and all of them appear to have been wandering around after death."

"Perhaps there's some sort of weird virus going around that causes the exact same thing," Dad suggested. "Have you considered that?"

I honestly hadn't. "No, because it's zombies."

"Or it's a mutated virus," Dad shot back. "The simplest answer is almost always the correct answer, Aisling. You know that."

"That's not what you said when I told you the Easter Bunny was bunk right after my sixth birthday."

"Shut up." Dad graced me with a warning look before shifting his attention to my brothers. "I don't know what to make of this, but who here believes that we're being invaded by zombies?"

Dad used that tone of voice he used when asking if any of us had seen a snipe while camping in the backyard. To my utter surprise, Aidan and Braden raised their hands.

"Really?" Dad's frustration bubbled up. "Now I have three of you believing in zombies? Ugh."

"I don't know if it's zombies, but I think it could very well be something freaky and supernatural," Jerry offered. "Of course, there's always the possibility that it's a super virus like in *28 Days Later*, and we're all doomed. I'm not sure which I prefer."

"Ooh." I was intrigued by the *28 Days Later* comparison. "That's a good reference, Jerry. Those weren't zombies. They were infected people who kind of looked like zombies."

"It's not zombies," Dad snapped.

"You said yourself it could be a weird infection," I pointed out. "You can't backtrack now."

"An infection is vastly different from zombies."

"Except for the symbol I saw," I reminded him. "Did any of the bodies have that symbol, Griffin?"

"I asked, but I won't get an update until tomorrow," Griffin replied. "Right now we're in a holding pattern. All we know is that this isn't new and Aisling is hardly the only one affected. That's something I'm certainly going to bring up with Detective Green when I see him again."

"Do you think he knows?" Dad asked.

"I think he must have done a search for like cases," Griffin said. "If he hasn't ... well ... he's not half the cop I thought he was."

It was a sobering statement. "No matter what, he's not a quarter of the cop you are."

Griffin squeezed my hand. "You can chill, suck up. I'm not angry with you, and I actually found watching the 'I'm right' dance delightful. As for the other stuff ... I'm not sure what to do about it. We simply have to wait it out."

"Which means we're all stuck in this house for the night," Redmond said. "Does anyone else think that sounds like a psych experiment gone awry?"

Everyone but Dad and Griffin raised their hands.

"What do you suggest?" Dad asked, even though he looked as if the last thing he wanted to hear was an honest answer.

"I think we should go to the bar," Redmond said. "It's right around the corner and we can walk."

"Yay!" I clapped my hands, excited.

"You'll have to walk yourself," Griffin said. "I'm not carrying you."

"I'm strong. I'll figure a way to do it."

Griffin shifted his eyes to Dad, something akin to resignation passing between them.

"What do you think?"

"I think they won't shut up until they get their way," Dad replied, patting his hands on his desk. "Okay, after dinner and Aisling's ice cream bar, we'll go to the bar."

"Yay!" I clapped a second time, something occurring to me. "Can we have a cake bar tomorrow?"

Dad was apparently beaten down, because he didn't hesitate to bob his head. "Sure."

"Ha!" I pointed at Braden. "You owe me a hundred bucks, and I'm going to do the dance again at the bar."

Griffin chuckled as Dad rolled his eyes to the heavens.

"I think you've done the dance enough, baby," Griffin said. "Perhaps it's time to win with a little grace and dignity."

"Where's the fun in that?"

Griffin held his hands palms out and shrugged. "I don't know. Maybe you can discover something new, something you never knew existed inside yourself."

"Screw that. I'm dancing, and Braden is buying."

"Now that sounds like a plan," Dad said.

21
TWENTY-ONE

I ate so much I almost felt as if I was waddling as I walked along the sidewalk. It was cold, but because no one wanted to be the designated driver – I had a feeling Dad wanted to drink his woes away after being trapped in a house with us for the better part of the day – we walked the several-block distance.

My feet hurt, although I was loath to admit it. I kept my expression blank as I walked, willing the pain out of my head. After a few minutes, Griffin slipped ahead of me and stopped, gesturing toward his back.

"Get on."

I stared at him a moment, surprised. "You're going to give me a piggyback ride?"

"I can't stand it when you're in pain."

"I'm ... fine."

"Get on," Griffin repeated, sighing.

I did as instructed, almost moaning in ecstasy once the pain dulled. Dad slid us a sidelong glance as he walked, shaking his head as Griffin matched his pace.

"You know, I don't want to hear one word from you ever again about how I spoil her," Dad said. "I may spoil her. All right, I do spoil her. You're just as bad, though."

"It's easier to be hurt myself than watch her struggle." Griffin's breath rasped out with the accompanying cold weather vapor. "It's not so bad."

"I think you're whipped," Braden said, increasing his stride so he was right behind us. "It's a little sad. I won't ever be that way with a woman. In fact, whatever woman I finally settle with – if there is one, because I like playing the field – will wait on me."

Dad snorted, amused. "Please. You would be bored with a woman who did your bidding in five minutes flat."

"No way."

"You're the type of man who wants to be challenged, Braden, even though you don't know it yet," Dad said. "It's fine that you want to play the field. You have plenty of time. When you want to settle down, however, it will be with someone who challenges your mind."

"Puh-leez," Braden scoffed, rolling his eyes. "I want a quiet and demure woman. Aisling has taught me that the mouthy ones are way too much work. Look at poor Griffin, for crying out loud. He's carrying her to the bar."

"He's helping her to the bar so we can all have a drink and relax," Dad corrected. "There's a difference."

"Not in my book."

"You'll notice the difference one day."

I rested my cheek against the back of Griffin's head as I studied Braden. He irritated me no end at times, but I worried about him. He missed Mom the most. He might not realize it, but he was desperate for someone to love him.

"Dad's right," I said after a beat. "You're going to want a woman who doesn't kowtow to your every whim."

"That means a woman like you," Braden argued. "Why don't you ask Griffin – who can barely breathe under your added weight – how that's working out for him."

"Don't drag me into this," Griffin gritted out as we turned the final corner toward Woody's Bar. "I'm happy with my woman."

"Even though she climbed out the window to avoid the cops?"

"That doesn't bother me."

"You're a cop."

"And she's the type of person who does her own thing," Griffin said. "I happen to like that about her. She's always entertaining, and I'm never bored."

Instead of making fun of Griffin, Braden looked intrigued. "Do you think you'd be bored with someone who waited on you? I always pictured my eventual wife serving me beer while wearing sexy lingerie."

Dad and Griffin laughed in unison. Something about the way they looked at one another piqued my curiosity.

"Aisling is more the fuzzy sleep pants and T-shirt type, and she never brings me beer."

"I do so," I argued.

"When have you ever brought me a beer?"

"Well ... ." That was a good question. I didn't have an answer. "I do things for you."

"You do, but that wasn't the question," Griffin said, sighing as we hit the front door of Woody's Bar, the local pub owned by a family friend. "I asked when you ever got me a beer."

I racked my brain and came up empty. "Well, I'll get you one tonight."

"I'd prefer you had your own beer and didn't make a scene tonight," Griffin said, glancing over his shoulder and fixing the non-descript black sedan pulling into the parking lot with an unreadable look. "We have company."

Dad followed his gaze, scowling. "Do you recognize them?"

Griffin nodded. "Detective Green is in the passenger seat. I think that's Rick Roberts driving, but I can't be sure because of the way the light's hitting the windshield."

"Do you think they'll come in?" Dad asked.

Griffin shrugged. "It doesn't really matter. We're not doing anything illegal."

"Everyone needs to stick together," Dad ordered, earning groans from my brothers. "I'm sure two of you want to hook up with whatever pretty faces you can find tonight. You'll have to settle for collecting phone numbers. We're all leaving together. I don't want any crap if these guys try to pin another potential murder on Aisling."

"Fine." Braden shot me a look. "You're more work than you're worth. You know that, right?"

I watched him swagger away, a bit of guilt weighing me down.

Griffin slid his arm over my shoulders and tugged me through the entryway. "You're always worth it," he whispered, kissing my cheek.

I looked to Dad for reassurance, but Griffin had to say that. We were getting married, and his future sex life depended on my moods. Dad was a different story.

"You're worth it ninety percent of the time," Dad clarified. "The other ten percent I want to lock you in the basement."

That seemed fair.

The bar was busy for a Wednesday night, but several booths were open – including the large one at the center. Dad grinned as he headed toward the owner, Woody, and Griffin led me toward the booth. I opted to take an end seat, but only because it would be painful should I have to shift around my brothers during frequent bathroom breaks. Griffin seemed to understand, because he settled inside with little complaint.

Jerry and Aidan joined the booth party, while Cillian, Redmond and Braden wandered toward the pool tables. They were clearly looking for a game.

"I haven't seen Maya around much this week," I noted as Dad brought over several drinks. "Is something going on?"

"She's working double shifts because she and Cillian are hoping to go to one of those Upper Peninsula spas next week," Dad supplied, shoving a whiskey and Coke in my direction. "If this isn't settled before then, I'm not sure they'll be able to go."

More guilt flooded my gut as I looked over my shoulder and found Cillian. He seemed happy, gregarious while making boasts with Braden and Redmond as they readied to play. I hated the idea of him having to change his plans because of me. "He should go no matter what. This is my issue, not his."

Dad took the open spot on the other side of the booth and shook his head. "This is our issue because we're a family," he corrected. "He won't leave if you're in danger. Maya is kind, easygoing. She'll understand."

"She shouldn't have to understand."

"Then maybe we should work to fix this before it becomes a factor," Griffin suggested. Maya was his sister, so he didn't want to dwell on what she and Cillian would do during their spa trip. He liked to pretend their relationship was platonic. I understood, because my brothers felt the same way about him – at least at first – and he'd always been uncomfortable in their presence. At some point that had faded, although I wasn't sure when I first noticed he'd grown more comfortable.

"We'll start digging hard tomorrow," Dad said. "There's not much more we can do tonight. We need to learn more about those bodies."

"And that symbol," I added, my eyes drifting to the bar and landing on a familiar brunette. "I'll be right back."

I moved to get up, but Griffin grabbed my arm before I could. "Where are you going?"

I gestured vaguely, pointing at nothing and everything at the same time. "I'll be around."

"Angelina is at the bar," Dad supplied. "I was hoping Aisling wouldn't see her, but I can tell we won't be that lucky."

I heaved out a sigh, frustrated. "I'm won't bother her. Well, I won't kill her."

"That's exactly what you're going to do," Griffin argued. "Why?"

"Because she didn't answer my questions earlier."

"And she won't answer them now," Dad pointed out. "Maybe we should send Cillian over. She still has feelings for him. She might be more willing to talk if he asks the questions."

That seemed unfair to Cillian. "I think it should be me," I countered. "I'm the one who went through her stuff today. I owe her ... um ... something."

"I notice you didn't say that you owed her an apology," Dad prodded.

"That's because I won't apologize." I made a hissing sound as I got to my feet. "I need to talk to her. Don't worry. I promise to be on my best behavior."

Griffin arched a dubious eyebrow. "Is that saying much?"

"Not really."

I carried my glass to the bar, smiling brightly at Woody as I hopped onto the stool next to Angelina. She didn't immediately look in my direction. In fact, she seemed infatuated with her drink. I exchanged a brief look with Woody – who was well aware of our history and probably ready to step between us should things go wrong – before tapping my fingers on the countertop to get Angelina's attention. When she still didn't look in my direction, I groaned and swiveled to face her.

"Are you going to pretend I'm not here?"

"What?" Angelina swayed a bit as she turned. It took her a moment to register who she was talking to, and when she did, she glared. "Why are you here? Am I being punished for something?"

She was drunk. She also was tired, weariness invading her eyes as she rubbed her forehead. For some reason – and I would forever deny it if pressed – I felt bad for her.

"You're being punished for all manner of things, including being a skank," I announced, sipping my drink. Woody looked as if he expected us to start pulling hair and hurling insults, but he wisely remained behind the bar. "Aren't you going to call me names, too?"

"Is that what you want?" Angelina was blasé. "Fine. You're a whore. You've always been a whore and you'll always be a whore."

I preened under the insult. "Thank you."

"You're a whore who is getting married, though," Angelina noted. "How did you manage that?"

"He asked."

"Yeah, but ... why? You're a terrible person, and he's hot. He also seems nice, and people like him. Why did he choose you?"

"I happen to be a catch," I replied, lifting the small green straw out of my drink so I could suck from the end and then chew on it. "How long have you been here?"

"What time is it?"

"Almost seven."

"I've been here for two and a half hours."

"How long are you going to stay?"

"Until I can't feel anything."

Angelina's answer caught me off guard. She was a morose wonder, all pout and no bite. No fun at all. I preferred when she growled and tried to stab me in the heart with her fake fingernails.

"What's up with you?" I asked after a moment's hesitation. I wasn't interested because I cared about Angelina, I reminded myself. I was interested because she was my mortal enemy and she was clearly calling zombies from beyond the grave to stalk and try to kill me.

"What's up with you?" Angelina challenged. "Why are you here? Where's your fiancé?"

I pointed toward the booth. "Over there, with Jerry, Aidan and Dad."

Angelina brightened. "Oh, good. I love Jerry the fairy."

I frowned. Even when she managed to make me feel bad for her I still hated her. It was good to find consistency in her poor attitude. It kept my world afloat. "I have to hand it to you, whenever I start to think you might not be a terrible person you always find a way to rebound and be horrible. Don't call him that, by the way. I'll beat you up no matter how drunk you are if you do."

"Whatever." Angelina waved her hand in a dismissive manner. "I don't care what you think."

"I don't care what you think either," I pointed out. "I think we're even on that front."

"Yes, we're all kinds of even ... except you have a father who spoils you rotten, brothers who love you and a fiancé who thinks you walk on water. You even have Jerry the Fairy telling you that you're great."

I extended a warning finger. "I will rip your hair out of your head and shove it down your throat until you choke."

"No, you won't." Angelina flicked her eyes to me, causing me to shift when I saw how shiny they were. She was near tears, which is something I enjoy when I'm the one causing the tears. This was something else. "Why are you over here? Your family is over there."

"They are, but ... I need to know why you were in the voodoo shop." Angelina was in no shape for one of our regular sparring matches, so I decided to take her from the front instead of tackling her from behind. "Some weird stuff has been going on, and I need answers."

"Is that why you were going through my purse this afternoon?"

"I still maintain your purse fell and I accidentally saw things inside when I was putting them back. That was an accident."

"Oh, whatever!" Angelina made a face. "You're so full of it."

She wasn't wrong. "I need to know," I repeated. "The stuff that's happening ... it's really odd. I mean, like ... terribly odd. It's like science fiction odd. No, wait, more like horror movie odd."

"Well, you've had sex and you can't be the virgin who survives at the end, so here's hoping the masked killer slams a knife through your head if we're living in a horror movie." Angelina lifted her drink and took a healthy gulp. "Actually, living in a horror movie makes sense. I probably have you to blame for this, huh?"

"For what?"

"Everything." Angelina swigged her drink. "What kind of weird stuff is going on? From what I can tell, your family is into all kinds of weird stuff. You had that monster in your house a couple of months ago ... and then there was that weird mirror thing you killed. Are you fighting another monster?"

I graced Angelina with an appraising look. "You've always been a monster in your own right."

"Ha, ha." Angelina ran her finger over the lip of her glass. "You must be desperate if you think I'm involved."

"No, I'm suspicious because I saw you go into that voodoo shop the other day," I countered. "That woman is odd, and the weird things started right after that. Did you buy a curse or something? You're not trying to kill me off because you think I'm the one keeping you from Cillian, are you?"

"I know Cillian will never care about me like he used to," Angelina blurted out. "I know that I can't have him ... no matter how much I want him. A curse won't change that."

Well, at least she was thinking clearly. "So what are you doing with Madame Dauphine? Is she helping you raise zombies to go after me?"

Angelina knit her eyebrows, her face flushing with confusion. "What?"

Hmm. She didn't understand what I was saying. That was either a very good sign or an extremely bad one.

"Let's start this from the beginning," I suggested, flashing a fake smile. "Why were you at the voodoo shop?"

"I need medicine."

My mind hopped to the bag in her purse. "Are you trying to find a holistic cure for menopause?"

"I don't have menopause." Angelina's eyes flared with hatred, and for the first time since I sat down with her I recognized my longtime nemesis.

"Then what's going on?" I swallowed half of my drink as the unthinkable occurred to me. "Are you ... sick?"

"Not me."

"Who?"

"My mother." Angelina tilted her glass back and drank until there was nothing left. "She has cancer. The doctors say she'll be dead in three months. I was hoping – no, praying – that the voodoo lady would be able to help me. But I don't think she can. It's ... too late. The doctor says it's too late."

And just like that, my anger and dislike gave way to pity and compassion. How did that happen?

22
TWENTY-TWO

"What?"

I wanted to have misheard her. I wanted her to say it was a joke and she was just trying to make me feel sorry for her. I wanted her to do something – anything really – that would alleviate the big ball of sympathy building in my gut.

Instead a tear slid down her face, and I thought I was going to have to punch someone. Angelina was crying, so I couldn't very well punch her. Of course, that wouldn't stop me from trying to find a way around that pesky little detail. She was Angelina, after all. She'd earned more than her fair share of punches.

"She's dying. Breast cancer."

"But ... ." I searched my memory for the last time I saw Angelina's mother. It was years ago. "They must be able to do something."

"It's stage four. Metastasized. With more chemotherapy they might be able to prolong her life, but only for a few months. She doesn't want to do it because her quality of life would be poor."

I could see that. Who wants to linger when you can do nothing but lie in a bed and torture the people who love you? Even I couldn't find joy in that. "I'm ... sorry." I honestly meant it. "So you went to the voodoo shop for a magical cure?"

"I'm desperate. She's all I have left."

"What about your father?"

"My father is not like your father," Angelina said, pointing at her glass so Woody would refill it. "He left when I was in elementary school. I saw him once a year after that. Once I turned eighteen and he no longer had to pay child support, he took off. He's in Ireland now. He sent me a Christmas card two years ago. It was a photo of him and his new wife ... and young sons. It had a generic 'Wishing you the best this holiday season' message and a signature I couldn't even read."

Oh, well, that was just ... unbelievable. "I didn't know that."

"Why would you? It's not as if we ever talk."

"That's your fault."

"Yes, because you're completely innocent in the situation," Angelina drawled.

I risked a glance over my shoulder and found Griffin and Dad watching me, perhaps waiting for me to make a scene. They were engaged in conversation but very aware of my actions. "I'm not taking responsibility for the relationship you created," I said after a beat. "You started all of this."

"And you always finish it, don't you?"

She wasn't wrong. "I'm sorry about your mother. I never liked her – I figured she was the reason you were so evil – but I understand that you love her."

"I do love her," Angelina confirmed, smiling as Woody slipped a fresh glass in front of her. "She's difficult and almost always impossible to deal with, but I love her."

Given the way I interacted with my brothers, I understood that. "So what happens now?"

"I watch her die." Angelina was so matter of fact, so ravaged with pain, it tugged at my heart. "She's in the hospital until Friday. Then she'll come home for a few months. I had to hire a nurse to help because I can't leave my job for an extended period."

Angelina was a real estate agent, so she kept odd hours. "And then what? Do you just wait for her to die?"

"Yes."

I hated Angelina. That would never change. Still, the idea of her sitting by her mother's bedside and waiting for the woman to die sounded horrendous. I couldn't imagine going through the same thing with my father. But even if it happened, I had four brothers to share the burden, to lean on when things got rough. I also had Jerry and Griffin. Suddenly, my life seemed very full – as did my heart.

"Madame Dauphine couldn't help you?"

"Apparently not. She had some spiel about prolonging Mom's life, but I didn't believe her. I think I only went in there because I was desperate."

"And you're not buying curses to raise the dead to send after me, right?" What? I had to be sure.

"I don't even know what that means," Angelina growled.

"Forget it." I waved off my suspicion. Angelina was clearly dealing with her own problems. I was barely a blip on her radar screen. "For what it's worth, I'm sorry about your mother."

"Why? You always hated her."

"Yes, but you're obviously in pain. When I cause you pain, I enjoy it. This is ... different."

"It's final," Angelina noted, slurring just a bit. "It's final, and when it's over, there will be no going back."

As a reaper, I knew that very well. "Yeah."

"Except your mother came back from the dead," Angelina said, her red-rimmed eyes flicking to me. "How did you manage that?"

"I didn't manage that," I replied. "She didn't really die." I shifted on the stool, uncomfortable. "I can't get into specifics with you, but we only thought she was dead. She was kept someplace else for a long time ... changed ... and then escaped. She's not the same mother she used to be."

"And yet you have her. She's here. Maybe I could do the same thing for my mother."

I grabbed Angelina's wrist and dug my fingernails in, ignoring the way she cried out as I forced her eyes to me. "You don't want that!"

"That's easy for you to say," Angelina snapped, yanking her hand back. "You have your mother. You're not about to be forced into a lonely world by yourself. You have your brothers ... and your father ... and Griffin, who very clearly must be mentally ill to love you, but is hot and seems to adore you, so it can be overlooked. You also have Jerry the Fairy."

"I feel sorry for you, but I will smack the crap out of you all the same," I warned.

Angelina ignored the threat. "You'll never be alone. People love you even though you're terrible ... and you have stupid hair."

"My hair is awesome," I countered. "And ... I'm sure someone must love you."

"Only my mother."

"Well, adjust your attitude and see if that changes," I suggested. "As for what you said ... you don't want that for your mother. I know you can't see it right now – it hurts too much and you're clouded by grief – but sometimes dead is better."

"Do you believe that?"

"I do."

"Do you wish your mother never came back?"

Did I? I wasn't sure. "I wish the woman who came back was the one we'd lost. She's not. She never will be."

"But you have something of her," Angelina pressed. "You have her back. That has to mean something."

"It does, but not what you think. You can't understand because you're drowning in bitterness and regret, things that are eating you alive. Don't focus on that. Focus on spending time with your mother."

I grabbed the glass from her and handed it to Woody, ignoring Angelina's protests. "Get her a cab, Woody. Don't give her any more to drink."

Woody nodded before focusing on Angelina. "How about some coffee, huh?"

I didn't hang around for Angelina's answer, instead hopping off the stool and moving back to the booth. I ran into Dad halfway there, taking him by surprise when I gave him a bear hug and buried my face in his neck.

"What's this?" Dad's eyes filled with concern as he tilted my chin up. "What did she say to you? Do you want me to send Jerry over to pull her hair?"

I shook my head as I fought off tears. "Leave her alone."

Dad arched an eyebrow. "Leave her alone? Are you feeling okay?" He pressed a hand to my forehead.

"No. I'm not feeling okay. Leave her alone all the same."

"Okay." Dad smoothed my hair. "What's wrong?"

"I have it good."

Dad chuckled, amused. "You do, but that's no reason to cry."

"No, but it's a reason to be grateful." I forced a smile for his benefit. "Come on. I'll talk Woody into letting Jerry sing karaoke once he gets Angelina out of here. I promise that will be entertaining."

Dad returned the smile. "That sounds fine."

He probably wouldn't say that when he realized Jerry was on a Cyndi Lauper kick, but there were worse ways to spend an evening.

GRIFFIN LEFT ME in Dad's capable hands the next morning. We talked a bit about what I discovered regarding Angelina, but he wisely left me to ponder the meaning of life on my own before handing me off to Dad. They both seemed a bit worried over breakfast, but neither pressed me too hard.

Once we were trapped in a vehicle together and heading toward the voodoo shop, Dad changed his tune.

"I know you're upset about what Angelina told you ... ."

"I'm not upset," I clarified, cutting him off. "I'm just ... um ... surprised."

"No, you're upset," Dad argued. "You're upset because you feel bad for Angelina. That goes against your very DNA."

"She said some things."

"Like?"

"Like I didn't understand how it was to be her because I would never be alone," I replied, resting my cheek against the cold passenger side window as the cityscape blurred on the other side of the glass. "I never really thought about it before. She was evil and that's all I cared about. I never wondered what happened to her father. I never thought about her not having any brothers or sisters. Even that gaggle of horrible tarts she hung out with in high school isn't around. She truly is alone."

"And you never will be." Dad parked in a city-owned lot not far from Voodoo Vacation. He waited for me to join him at the front of the car before speaking again. "It's okay to feel bad for Angelina and still hate her at the same time. She's been terrible to you over the years."

"She called Jerry a fairy again and I didn't even punch her in the face."

Dad took sympathy on me as he slipped his arm around my shoulders. "That must have been hard on you."

"You have no idea."

"It's not your fault that she's going to be alone," Dad noted. "You didn't create the situation."

"No, but it's a mess all the same." We lapsed into silence as we walked across the parking lot. "I love you, Daddy." I don't know what made me say it, but I was overwhelmed by the urge and gave in.

"Oh, geez," Dad groaned, pinching the bridge of his nose. "I'm going to have to buy you something before we go, aren't I?"

I shook my head. "No. I just wanted to say it."

"Well, thank you." Dad gave my shoulder a squeeze before reaching for the store's door handle. "I love you, too."

Dad entered first, taking a long look at the display shelves and décor before focusing on the woman behind the counter. Instead of giving her the beady eye and terrorizing her – which is why I wanted him with me on this little excursion – he broke into a wide smile. "Evelyn?"

Evelyn? I wrinkled my nose as I glanced between faces.

"Oh my ... Cormack?" Madame Dauphine wiped her hands on a towel before sliding out from behind the counter and heading in our direction. She completely ignored me as she barreled past, throwing her arms around Dad's neck as he chuckled.

"I can't believe it's you," Dad said once he released her, a warm smile splitting his handsome face. "When Aisling mentioned that she thought the woman running this store was trying to emulate Marie Laveau it never even clicked."

"Well, I always enjoyed reading about her," Dauphine said, leading Dad toward the counter. I noticed she'd dropped the accent and faux

French phrases. "I just brewed a fresh pot of tea. Would you like some?"

"I would love some." Dad took one of the stools at the counter, completely forgetting me. "How long has it been?"

"Well, it was right before graduation," Dauphine said. "That was more than thirty years ago, right?"

"You don't look a day older."

"Oh, you always had the charm." Dauphine lightly tapped Dad's forearm as I openly gaped and glanced between them. "Do you want tea, dear?" Dauphine's expression wasn't nearly as friendly as she focused on me.

"I'll pass."

"Aisling, don't be rude." Dad's voice was low and full of warning. "Madame Dauphine is an old friend."

"Don't you mean Evelyn?"

Dad ignored me. "So how did you end up here? When we graduated, I thought you were heading off to New Orleans."

"Oh, I spent years in New Orleans," Dauphine said, handing Dad a mug of tea. "I love the city and the culture. I plan to go back eventually, but I got homesick and decided to open a shop here for a bit. I've been back about six months."

"You should've called me when you hit town, Evie. I would've loved to see you."

Oh, now it was Evie? Someone grab me a puke bucket.

"I wasn't sure if that was a good idea," Dauphine said. "Last time I saw Lily she tried to pull my hair out in one big clump. She never got over the fact that we dated before you two got together. I told her it was in the past, but she wouldn't believe me. And when I heard that she died it seemed somehow ... disrespectful ... to contact you."

What a load of horsepucky. Wait a second ... . "You dated each other?" Yup. I definitely needed a puke bucket.

"It was long before you came into my life." Dad spared me a dark look. "And, yes, we dated."

"For two years." Dauphine beamed at Dad, giving me the impression she'd like to pick up exactly where they left off. "It was the best two years of my life."

Oh, puke. I didn't say that out loud. "Puke." Okay, I couldn't keep my mouth shut and said it out loud.

Dad flicked my ear to quiet me. "Don't be a pain, Aisling. Evie is a good friend. There's no reason for your attitude."

"She sent zombies after me," I exploded.

Dad's cheeks colored as he flashed an embarrassed smile in Dauphine's direction. "Stop saying that."

"It's true."

"Yes, this isn't the first time she's stopped in. I've been a little confused by her motivations," Dauphine said. "First she was chasing some poor girl while accusing her of doing it, and then she accused me of some odd things."

"Poor girl? Angelina?"

"You just spent thirty minutes telling me how sorry you feel for Angelina," Dad interjected.

"I didn't use those exact words."

"Shut your mouth, Aisling," Dad ordered, his eyes fixed on Dauphine. "I'm sorry about her. She's had a rough couple of weeks."

"Yes, I read that in her aura," Dauphine said. "She's ... troubled."

Dad flicked his eyes to me. "Are you troubled?"

"Did you not hear the 'puke' comment?"

Dad made a face. "Ignore her. She's in a mood."

"She's your daughter," Dauphine teased. "I'll bet she's always in a mood. Although, to be fair, I didn't realize she was your daughter when I first saw her. I knew there was something familiar about her, but I couldn't put my finger on it. She looks just like you."

"There are four more at home who do the same."

"You have five children?" Dauphine's eyebrows flew up her forehead. "That sounds like a busy life. You and Lily must've had your hands full."

"Yes."

"And how are things since Lily passed?"

Dad and I exchanged a weighted look. "Different," Dad answered carefully, shooting a warning look in my direction before continuing. He clearly didn't want to share private family information with his good friend Evie. "It's very complicated. But that's not why we're here. We actually came for information."

"About zombies?" Dauphine's eyes lit with mirth.

"Something is going on," Dad said. "Seventeen bodies have been discovered over the past few months, and all of them suffered from the same malady."

"Which is?"

"They were dead and still walking around," I answered. "That means they were zombies. Laugh all you want, but I'm right."

Dauphine stared at me for a long moment. "Okay."

"While I don't share Aisling's enthusiasm for the subject, something is clearly going on," Dad said. "I don't suppose you can shed light on the topic?"

"I'm sorry, but I can't. I don't know anything about raising the dead. I'm a voodoo practitioner, but I tend to straddle a mainstream line. I considered dabbling when I was younger, but never really embraced the dark arts. You know that."

"I do." Dad's expression was thoughtful. "So, tell me what you've been up to the past thirty years."

And just like that, he completely shoved my zombie problem aside and focused on his own needs. The love I felt only minutes before evaporated.

"You're going to have to buy me ten things for me to keep quiet about this," I hissed.

Dad's expression didn't change. "Fine. Go ... look around ... while we catch up." He waved his hand to dismiss me.

"Ten expensive things," I pressed.

"Ignore her, Evie," Dad admonished. "She's not much of a morning person."

"She doesn't seem to be much of an afternoon person either," Dauphine noted.

"She's ... tempestuous," Dad said.

"She must get that from Lily."

"She does indeed."

Yeah. Puke, puke and more puke.

23
TWENTY-THREE

I lost track of Dad's conversation with his good friend Evie as I perused the store, picking a spot in the corner so I could flip through several books. Unlike the tomes at Grimlock Manor, the books in Dauphine's shop seemed to be old and focused on black arts. Of course, not twenty minutes ago she said she'd abandoned her interest in black arts years ago.

"I thought you said that you straddled modern times with your beliefs?" I asked when there was a break in the conversation.

Dauphine, who was in the middle of pouring Dad another cup of tea, glanced in my direction. "What are you looking at?"

"*The Secret to Unlocking the Dead*," I replied, reading from the front cover. "There's a bunch of stuff in here about raising the dead."

Dad left his tea on the counter and headed in my direction, lifting the book from my lap so he could flip through it. "This book looks old."

"It is old," Dauphine said, appearing at Dad's side. She brushed her hand over his arm, giving the impression it was an innocent act. I knew better. "I offer a multitude of books. It's part of the mystique."

"This book claims that raising the dead is possible," Dad noted, taking the chair across from me and focusing on the pages. "You indicated that wasn't the case."

"I didn't say it wasn't possible," Dauphine countered. "I merely said I didn't participate."

"So it is possible?" I asked, grabbing another book from the shelf. "How is it done?"

"I've never done it, but the rituals are fairly standardized," Dauphine replied. "Mostly it's done through blood magic."

"Meaning?"

"The person interested in the ritual paints symbols on the dead with their own blood and performs an incantation."

"And that's all it takes?"

"I believe it's more in depth than that – and the priest or priestess must possess a certain amount of power – but, yes, that's basically it." Dauphine gave me a challenging look. "I doubt very much anyone locally is doing it."

"I wouldn't be so sure," Dad said, shifting in the chair. "Aisling was approached by a man who hissed like a snake several nights ago. She punched him in the face, causing him to cease moving. Now, she punches like a man thanks to her brothers, but I've never seen her hit anyone with enough force to kill."

"One punch can kill if it's delivered in the proper manner," Dauphine pointed out.

"That's true, but the medical examiner stated that the man had been dead for at least a month," Dad said. "Then, two days later, she woke to find the police poking around her backyard because someone called in a tip about another body. Even though that body wasn't ravaged by the elements, the medical examiner believes he died six weeks ago."

"Really?" Dauphine didn't try to hide her interest. "I haven't heard anything about either case on the news."

"I'm sure the police are keeping the details quiet. They don't want to start a panic," Dad said. "There's enough craziness without people whispering about zombies overrunning the area."

"You mentioned other bodies were found," Dauphine said. "What do we know about them?"

"Not much. Aisling's fiancé is trying to get additional information. Hopefully we'll know more this evening."

"Fiancé?" Dauphine smirked in my direction. "What kind of man would put up with your attitude voluntarily?"

I opened my mouth, something snarky on the tip of my tongue, but Dad answered before I could.

"A good one," he said. "Griffin is doing his best to track information even though it isn't easy to come by. The bodies were found in different municipalities and counties. That means multiple jurisdictions are investigating, and we all know they don't like sharing information."

"No, that's definitely true." Dauphine rubbed her chin as she considered the situation. "You saw the one body up close, right?" She stared at me.

I nodded. "He was older. I would say in his sixties or seventies. He had a mark on his neck."

"A mark?"

"It looked like a snake with lines through it."

"The Damballah-Wedo," Dauphine mused. "That would seem to point to voodoo."

"We don't have anything that doesn't point to voodoo," I said. "In fact, this all happened after I stopped in your shop to find out what Angelina was doing."

"And I'm still not going to tell you about that," Dauphine warned, shifting from one foot to the other. She appeared to be lost in thought. I couldn't decide if she was trying to help because she wanted to slide into Dad's good graces or if she was simply putting on an act.

"I already know what Angelina was doing here," I offered.

"Really?"

"Her mother is dying. She's trying to find a way to save her, or at the very least prolong her life. You told her you could help."

"I said I could offer a little help," Dauphine clarified. "I didn't say I could stave off death forever."

"No, but you gave her false hope, and that's just as bad."

"I didn't get the feeling that you liked Angelina," Dauphine challenged. "Now you're acting as if you're fighting on her behalf."

"Oh, I can't stand her. That doesn't mean I think it's okay to take advantage of her when she's going through something so terrible."

"Aisling." Dad scorched me with a warning look before focusing on Dauphine. "Ignore her. She's ... conflicted."

"She's a reaper," Dauphine said. "I think all reapers are conflicted on matters of life and death."

"Aisling is conflicted because Angelina and she have a difficult relationship."

"She's my arch nemesis," I offered.

Dauphine rolled her eyes as Dad smirked.

"She'll be alone when her mother is gone," I continued, sobering. "It's hard for her. You shouldn't give her false hope."

"And who says I gave her false hope?"

"Well, you just said you don't dabble in zombies, yet you reportedly offered to prolong her mother's life. It seems to me you can't have it both ways."

"I never offered to prolong her mother's life," Dauphine clarified. "I simply said I might be able to make things easier."

"How?"

"That's really not my information to share." Dauphine forced a smile. I knew if my father wasn't present it would be a scowl. "Now, how else can I help you?"

"I'm not sure," Dad said. "We're chasing our tails here. Aisling is convinced it's zombies and I'm not so sure. I think it might be something else."

"Like what?"

"I have no idea, but zombies are far too fantastical."

"Zombies were considered normal a century ago," Dauphine pointed out. "It's only this country and modern times that seem to disbelieve the condition."

I arched a confrontational eyebrow. "Condition? It's not like psoriasis or menopause."

"Isn't it?" Dauphine's eyes flashed. "I think you're the type of person who wants to believe one thing. You won't open yourself to other possibilities. I'm sure you get that from your mother."

"Yes, because Dad spends all of his time hunting zombies and tying them up in the backyard so we can turn them into pets."

"Aisling." Dad made a clucking sound with his tongue as he shook his head. "I'm more reticent to accept the idea than she is."

"I think you're more open than you want to admit." Dauphine winked. "You're still handsome as the dickens, too."

"Oh, puke." I made a face as I stood, thankful the bell over the door jangled so I had something to focus on. The two individuals who walked through the door were disheveled, neither wearing a coat, and for a moment I thought they were homeless.

"Can I help you?" Dauphine asked haltingly.

The figures – a man who looked to be in his fifties and a woman who couldn't be older than twenty – turned in our direction. I noticed right away that their eyes were the same milky consistency as Jed Burnham's that first night. Oh, and the woman had a gaping chest wound.

"Son of a ... !"

Dad was on his feet before I could utter a curse, his hand sweeping out as he moved to push me behind him. I didn't consider myself the sort of woman who needed to be saved – not ever – so I ignored his efforts as I moved around the display case to get a better look.

"I don't understand." Dauphine's face drained of color as she stared at the man and the woman. "What's going on?"

"They're zombies, you idiot," I hissed, grabbing a jewel-handled knife from the shelf and tilting my head as I focused on the male zombie. "How did they open the door?"

"That's a good question," Dad said, giving the female a wide berth as he moved closer to me. He was determined to make sure I stayed out of trouble – something I overheard him promising Griffin in the hallway after breakfast. I bit my tongue to keep from pointing out that I'd already faced off with one of these things and survived.

"Evie, come here," Dad ordered, reaching for her arm.

The male zombie hissed, his grotesque gray tongue appearing between his lips. He stuck out a hand, trying to reach through the display shelf, but I easily evaded him.

"I'd like an apology," I announced. "You didn't believe it was zombies. What do you say now?"

"That we're in a very odd position," Dad replied, his eyes flashing.

"That's not the answer I'm looking for."

"Fine. You were right. Is that what you want to hear?"

"It will do for now." I narrowed my eyes as the female zombie moved closer to the shelf. If I didn't know better – and wasn't convinced that she couldn't see out of those milky eyes – I would have thought she was reading the bindings on the books. "What is she doing?"

"Looking for dinner," Dad replied, reaching for the knife. "Give me that."

"No. I found it first. I'm going to stab them."

"Give it to me right now." Dad's voice echoed throughout the room. "I am not kidding."

"Fine." I grudgingly handed over the knife. "If I get bit and die because of this, I hope Griffin makes you pay."

"If you die on me I won't care about anything like that. Now ... come here." Dad grabbed my arm and jerked me so I was behind him. "I'm going to stab him in the head."

"Okay, but don't be surprised if you get called into the police station as my accomplice." My attention returned to the woman as her hand floated over the books. Back and forth. Back and forth. When it dropped a shelf lower, her body stiffened – as if she sensed something – and her fingers wrapped around the spine of a large book. "What is she doing?"

"Stay back," Dad ordered, his eyes focused on the man. My father, in addition to being an avid reader and reality television hater, is an accomplished fighter. His movements were long and fluid as he stepped around the shelf and slammed the knife into the man's temple.

I watched, interested despite myself, as the man blinked through sightless eyes before dropping to his knees. He reached out with grubby fingers, as if trying to get his hands on me, but then toppled to the floor, a hiss escaping through his partially parted lips.

"Gross," I muttered, wrinkling my nose before remembering I'd been watching the woman. When I turned back to the shelf she was gone. Panic momentarily overwhelmed me as I imagined her creeping up behind me. Then the bell over the door jangled again, and she simply strolled out, a book clutched to her chest. Other than the festering chest wound – oh, and the way she lurched rather than walked – she looked like a normal shoplifter. "What the ... ?"

"Did she just leave with a book?" Dad was as confused as me.

"She stole a book?" Dauphine, who had been watching the interaction with something akin to detached interest, jerked her head up.

"Yes, you have a zombie shoplifter," I drawled. "Call the police, because I'm dying to hear you explain this one."

"Step off, Aisling," Dad snapped. "Now is not the time for your mouth."

"When is the time? I'm willing to wait."

"Do you ever shut up?" Dauphine challenged.

"No."

Dad ignored our bickering and strode toward the door, stepping over the body on the floor as he focused his attention outside. "We can't just let her go."

"No, by all means," I said. "I think you should hunt her down in a crowd of people, stab her in the head and take back the book. No one will even notice."

"Shut up, Aisling." Dad opened the door, but he didn't get a chance to step through it. Detective Green and another man, this one dressed in a uniform, cut off his avenue of escape. The look on Green's face was full of disgust, and it only grew darker when he caught sight of the body on the floor.

"Does someone want to tell me what's going on here?"

"I'm pretty sure he's talking to you, Dad."

"Thank you, Aisling," Dad gritted out, gripping the knife as he struggled with how to approach the situation. "I'm happy to see you, detective." Dad forced a smile, taking me by surprise. His reaction was something I expected from ... well ... myself. "We have a body. It's your lucky day."

Yeah. I definitely get that from him.

"SO HE JUST WALKED into the store with a young woman – one who was openly bleeding – and attacked while she stole a book and escaped?"

One look at Green's face told me exactly what he thought of that story.

"I think you should call Neil," I said, folding my arms over my chest when Green murdered me with a glare. "Oh, don't give me that look. You've been following me for days. You could at least be useful when we're being attacked by ... crazy people."

Even though I fully believed we were dealing with zombies, I knew better than to use that word in front of the police detective investigating me for a string of murders.

"And you expect me to believe that?" Green pressed.

"It's the truth," Dad answered, running a hand through his hair as he worked to calm himself. "I don't know what more you want from us. We were attacked and fought back."

"It's just that ... well ... this is the third body your daughter has been responsible for in the past week," Green noted. "That's a little more than a coincidence in my book."

"She's not responsible for this one," Dad argued. "I am. I shoved the knife in his head."

"Is there a reason you did that before calling us?"

"Self-preservation."

"I don't think that's going to fly in court."

"I guess we'll have to wait and see." Dad lobbed a weighted look in my direction. "Call Neil and have his team report to the police station. I think I'm about to be arrested."

Green didn't miss the gleam in Dad's eye – it was almost a challenge – but he immediately backed down. "We won't be arresting you at this juncture," he said. "We need to wait on the medical examiner and see what he says."

"He's going to say the guy has been dead for days ... or maybe even weeks," I muttered, sliding my eyes to Dauphine as she stared at the empty slot in the bookshelf. She'd been largely quiet since the police arrived. I couldn't really blame her. Explaining what happened made all of us look like idiots.

"I guess we'll have to wait and see, won't we?" Green sneered.

I ignored him as I shuffled to Dauphine, pursing my lips as I followed her stare. "Do you know what book she took?"

Dauphine nodded, her expression unreadable. "*The Book of the Dead.*"

I filed the name away to share with Cillian. "Do you still think that no one in this area is capable of raising the dead?"

"Obviously not."

"And you're not doing it, right?"

Dauphine turned slowly, the movement deliberate. "And why would I raise the dead to steal a book from my own shop?"

I shrugged. "I have no idea. If you did it, I'm going to find out. I don't care how friendly you used to be with my father."

"Does that bother you? My relationship with your father, I mean."

"You don't have a relationship with my father," I challenged. "You knew him way back when. Sure, I'm guessing you used to get naked with him – which is so gross I'll have to purge it from my mind with endless bottles of wine tonight – but you don't know him."

"You might be surprised," Dauphine argued. "I know him better than you think."

"I guess we'll have to wait and see on that, huh?" I held her gaze for several moments before turning. "If Dad isn't under arrest, does that mean we can go?"

Green looked pained, but he ultimately nodded. "Yes. Don't leave the area. We'll be watching you."

"Thanks for the heads up." I grabbed Dad's arm and tugged him toward the door. "We should stop and get more balloons on the way home." I smirked as Green scowled. "We need food coloring, too."

"Whatever you want." Dad ran his hand down the back of my head, his fingers shaking. "You were right, and I didn't believe you. I think that deserves a prize."

"Oh, I'm getting multiple prizes." I refused to give Dauphine the satisfaction of looking over my shoulder. "I'll want ice cream, too."

"Somehow that doesn't surprise me."

24
TWENTY-FOUR

I needed help carrying my loot into the house. Dad did his best to ignore the snickers and stares from my brothers as we hit his office, but it was difficult.

"Shut up," Dad ordered.

"Is there anything left at the mall?" Redmond asked, grabbing the huge stuffed sloth from the top of the pile. "Why do you have all of this stuff?"

"Because Dad has seen the light," I replied, dropping my bags in front of the couch and dramatically throwing myself on it so I could make sure I had my brothers' attention. "Zombies are real. I was right. You all were wrong. Suck it!"

Redmond arched an eyebrow as he dragged his attention away from the large bag I left on his foot. "I'm sorry, but ... what?"

"I was right."

Redmond lifted his eyes to stare at Dad. "She was right?"

Dad shrugged as he dropped the rest of my "I'm sorry you were right and I should suck it" haul by my feet. "She might've been right."

I extended a finger. "Don't do that. I was right."

Dad blew out a heavy sigh. "Fine. She was right. Zombies are real. They attacked at the voodoo shop."

"Are you okay?" Cillian lowered the book he read, paying attention for the first time. "You didn't get bitten, did you?"

I adopted a haughty expression. "They're not that type of zombie."

"There are different types of zombies?"

"Yes. There are the types we see on television, the ones caused by some sort of falling satellite or ancient ritual gone wrong, and there's the type created by crazy voodoo people to steal books."

"Steal books?" Cillian's voice ratcheted up a notch. "What kind of zombie steals books?" He turned to Dad for help. "She's making that up, right?"

"I wish." Dad rubbed his forehead as he sank into the chair behind his desk. "Why do you think she got so much stuff?"

"Because she's spoiled and you coddle her," Braden answered.

"When I was just spoiling her it was ice cream and a new coat," Dad said. "Once she was proved right and refused to shut up ... it was all this." He waved his hand at the bags.

"The cops followed us while we were shopping. I thought they were going to kill me at one point." I smiled at the memory. "That was after Dad stabbed a zombie in the head while another one disappeared with something called *The Book of the Dead*."

Cillian pressed the heel of his hand to his forehead. "I think someone should start from the beginning."

I shot my hand into the air. "Me!"

"No, me," Dad said. "You sort through your belongings and do ... whatever it is you're going to do with it."

"I got gifts for all of you, too," I said, smiling. I was nothing if not benevolent.

"You did?" Redmond was intrigued. "What did you get me?"

I dug in one of the bags and returned with a small package. "It's a pen with a buxom woman on it. When you turn it upside down ... her clothes come off."

"Sweet!" Redmond happily accepted the pen.

"I got you a new iPad." I handed the box to Cillian. "I got you a new leather coat, the one you had your eye on, in fact, and it's right over there." I pointed for Aidan's benefit. "I got Griffin a new coat, too. He's going to look very handsome."

"Wait a second." Redmond straightened his shoulder. "How come I only got a crummy pen?"

"I got you an Apple watch, too."

"Yay!" Redmond clapped his hands. "Hand it over."

"My credit card actually sighed at the Apple store," Dad complained.

Braden, who hated being at my mercy, was caught in an uncomfortable position. I met his gaze with an arched eyebrow and an evil smile.

"Do you have something you want to ask me?"

"I haven't decided yet." Braden folded his arms over his chest. "Okay, fine. What did you get me?"

I rummaged in the bag and came out with a pack of gum.

Braden groaned. "I should've known."

I stuck my hand back in the bag and came back with a large box. "And this."

Braden's face lit up when he saw the MacBook Pro. "I've been wanting one of these!"

"I know. I didn't forget."

"How much of your money did Aisling spend at the Apple store?" Cillian asked Dad, genuinely curious.

"Enough that I'm glad I have a black card." Dad opened his top drawer and pulled out a bottle of bourbon. "Now, if you're done comparing gifts, can we talk about something important?"

Cillian nodded. "I want to talk about the zombies."

"Fine." Dad launched into the tale, wagging a finger every time I opened my mouth to add a comment. He hurried through, refusing to embellish or take any verbal detours. When he was done, my brothers weren't nearly as wowed as they would've been had I told the story.

"You've got to be kidding." Braden was the first to break the silence. "So we're really dealing with zombies? I know we kept saying that they might be zombies because we didn't want Aisling to feel stupid, but now you're saying they're actually zombies?"

"I don't know that I would call them zombies," Dad hedged. "They're clearly reanimated corpses. I don't know how else to describe them – and trust me, I've tried to think of something for the entire hellish afternoon I spent shopping with your sister – so I guess we'll have to use the Z-word."

"And here I wanted to use the F-word," I said, earning a glare from Dad. "For best father ever," I quickly added.

"Shut up." Dad sipped his drink. "I have no idea what's going on. We've got book-stealing zombies. Weird symbols on bodies. It's just ... I don't know what to make of it."

"The important thing to remember is that not all of the zombies have gone after Aisling," Cillian noted. "Before three days ago, she didn't appear to be on anyone's radar."

"So who did you see that day?" Redmond asked.

"Just Angelina and Madame Dauphine." I slid a sly look in Dad's direction. "Speaking of Dauphine ... ."

Dad cut me off before I had a chance to blab. "I think we need to look in a different direction, although what that direction is I have no idea."

I rubbed my thumb over my lip as I regarded him. He was trying to keep me from opening my mouth about Dauphine – I wasn't stupid enough to miss that – but he had to know there was no way I could keep that to myself.

"Well, while you were showering Aisling with enough affection to make the rest of us hate her forever, I managed to come up with a few things." Cillian rested his new iPad on the end table as he turned his attention back to his laptop. "I scanned that symbol and performed a search. It came back with a ton of results, although most of them weren't in this area.

"When I narrowed the search to the Detroit area, I came up with some interesting findings," he continued. "As far as I can tell, that section of Eternal Sunshine Cemetery is the only one in this part of the state that caters to voodoo enthusiasts."

"What does that mean?" Dad asked.

"I'm not sure," Cillian replied. "The mausoleum at the center of that parcel belonged to an Oscar Santiago. I decided to run him because we didn't have much else to go on – and I like research."

"We know," Braden intoned. "You're such a geek that we're still floored that you're the one with a steady girlfriend."

"Women like men with brains," I countered. "They also like his hair. It's ... fancy." I fluttered my fingers for effect, basking in Cillian's grin as he turned back to the computer. "Oscar Santiago arrived in the Detroit area in the mid-1800s. There is some dispute over when. I couldn't figure out why at first, but I think I have now and I'll get there eventually.

"Oscar bought a barber shop in downtown Detroit not long after arriving. He worked for two years before sending for the rest of his family," he continued. "They were in Louisiana, for the most part, although a few were in Haiti."

"That would further the voodoo tie," Dad said. "Voodoo is accepted in much of New Orleans."

"And I think it was even more popular back then," Cillian said. "So Oscar opened a business and moved his wife and kids to the area. Because no one kept really good records back then, it's hard to keep track of all of his kids. He had at least eight, although four of them are believed to have died while under the age of ten."

I cocked an eyebrow. "Believed?"

Cillian nodded. "No one kept proper birth and death records back then. It's difficult to be certain. The mausoleum was built for Oscar, but his children started getting placed inside of it long before he died. Apparently they didn't rate names on their final resting places."

"Okay, he lost a bunch of children," Dad said. "Why is that important?"

"I'm getting to it." Cillian shot Dad a quelling look before continuing. "Oscar's wife made money for the family on the side. She was considered a high priestess, and doled out curses and holistic medical remedies for believers. All the believers congregated in the same neighborhood, by the way, so the Santiagos prospered in their new home.

"Oscar's shop was powerful, drawing everyone in the neighborhood for appointments or just to gossip in the middle of the day, and he worked for a long time," he continued. "In fact, some people claim that Oscar cut hair for more than one-hundred years."

"How is that possible?" I asked.

"Supposedly Oscar told people that he was going to live forever," Cillian replied. "He didn't hide his ambitions. He claimed his wife had the power to prolong his life as long as he wished. To do that, he had to drain the life essence of others."

Dad tilted his head, intrigued. "A wraith?"

"Not unless he was a different kind of wraith than what we're used to," Cillian replied. "No one ever described Oscar as looking different. He didn't have long talons for fingernails. He wasn't chalky white. Some people claimed he had a weariness in his eyes — and others swore that sometimes his eyes glowed purple — but otherwise people said he looked normal."

"That right there should be a hint that something was going on," Redmond pointed out. "The guy supposedly lived to be one-hundred and people said he looked normal. I don't think a lot of people lived to be one-hundred in those days."

"Here's the thing," Cillian said. "Oscar either moved to the Detroit in 1850 or 1900. No one can agree. His age was consistently called into question."

"Okay, why is that important?"

"Because he died in 2000," Cillian replied. "In fact, he died three minutes past the stroke of midnight on the first of January in 2000."

"Is that date significant?" I asked.

"A lot of religions attached power to that date," Dad supplied. "Some people thought the end of the world would happen when the clock struck midnight and the century marker rolled over."

"In which time zone?"

Dad shrugged. "I don't know that anyone ever said. It's not that important in hindsight. Back then it was a big deal."

"I was only eleven," I mused. "All I remember is everyone freaking out about Y2K."

"Which could've been a manifestation of the bigger religious fears," Cillian said. "By the time he died, Oscar had outlived his wife and children. Half of his children reportedly died before reaching adulthood. The other half lived long enough to procreate, but the limbs on his family tree are short lived."

I understood what he was getting at. "Was he killing his family members to prolong his own life?"

"Blood magic in voodoo culture is supposedly strong, so that's my first guess," Cillian said. "This obviously wasn't legitimate voodoo, though. They cherry-picked the voodoo tenets they liked and then added their own stuff. With his wife's help, Oscar killed his kids and grandkids to stay alive, living until he was more than one-hundred and fifty years old."

"That has to be bunk."

"I'd agree, but the books say otherwise," Cillian countered. "He lived exactly three days longer than his wife, who was also ridiculously old when she died. She didn't die of old age, by the way."

"What did she die of?"

"She was hit by a car. It was a hit and run. The perpetrator has never been found."

"Oh, well ... huh." I scratched my nose as I absorbed the story. "You're basically saying that the wife kept both of them alive, and when she died – not by natural means – no one had the ability to keep Oscar alive, so he died."

"Pretty much," Cillian confirmed.

"So how does that help us?" Aidan asked. "We don't know that what's going on now has anything to do with Oscar."

"No, but he had that snake symbol carved on his tomb," Cillian pointed out. "I don't know for certain that he holds answers for us, but I don't know where else to look."

"So how do we use Oscar?" Dad asked.

"For starters, I'd like to look inside his vault," Cillian said. "I want to see if he's ... um ... preserved."

Gross. "What does that have to do with anything?"

"He wasn't embalmed," Cillian replied. "Supposedly, Oscar left specific instructions to be embalmed because he wanted his body to hold together when he rose again. It didn't happen because the few people he left behind – the ones he didn't kill – didn't want him to rise again."

"Do we think he's going to rise again?"

"Not particularly, but I still want to see."

"Well, I can tell you right now that Griffin is not going to partake in a family outing that involves opening someone's final resting place to see if he's embalmed," I argued. "I'm pretty sure he'll draw the line there."

"That's why you're going to have to stay here and distract Griffin," Dad said.

"I won't lie to him."

"Then don't lie," Dad said. "I'll lie to him."

That was a much better option, but I wasn't keen to be a part of it. "He might understand," I hedged, earning incredulous looks from my father and brothers.

"He won't understand," Aidan said. "Listen, I don't want to break into a vault and look at an old guy either. If Cillian thinks it's necessary, I don't see where we have a lot of choices. You've crossed paths with three zombies and had a fourth wind up dead in your backyard. That seems to indicate an escalation."

"He's correct," Dad said. "I still don't understand how looking at Oscar Santiago's body will help us, though."

"I want to see if he has the mark on his skin," Cillian explained. "Like I said, the voodoo community is really small in this area. If someone is really raising the dead – and it looks like they are – we should be able to track down the right community with a little legwork."

I remained dubious. "And Oscar's body helps us how?"

"He was supposed to rise after his death," Cillian replied. "I initially wanted to suggest it to see if he was there. If he's not, perhaps we have our culprit."

I snorted. "What? He came back from the dead to go after me?"

"No, but maybe someone brought him back from the dead to find a reaper," Cillian suggested. "One thing I haven't told you about yet is the fact that Griffin emailed me a list of property where the afflicted bodies were found. All of them were within a block or two of reaper households."

"What?" Dad yelped, leaning forward. "Talk about burying the lead."

"It's still a theory," Cillian cautioned. "It could be nothing."

"Or it could be everything," I mused. "So you think someone –

maybe someone related to Oscar Santiago – is trying to find a reaper to help prolong life?"

"It makes as much sense as anything else we've got," Cillian said. "It wouldn't be the first time. Wraiths believe that we prolong their lives."

I wasn't sure I agreed, but I couldn't think of another direction to go, so I ultimately conceded. "Okay. I'll keep Griffin busy."

"And I'm sure you'll do it in a PG way," Braden teased.

"Shut up, Braden," Dad warned. "We'll tell him we're going to the movies after dinner. You can say you don't want to go and entice him – not by doing anything lewd, mind you – to stay behind while we check the vault."

"What if he asks questions? I promised I wouldn't lie to him."

"I'll leave that to your discretion," Dad replied. "As of now, all we need to do is get out of the house. He might try to stop us before we leave, but I doubt very much he'll chase us."

"Okay. It's a good thing I have a lot of new toys to distract him with. That shopping trip was a great idea."

Dad scorched me with a glare. "You're my least favorite child right now."

"Just wait until I break out the disco light bubble machine you bought me and show it to Jerry."

"Oh, geez." Dad slapped his hand to his forehead. "Could this day get any worse?"

As if on cue, the butler picked that moment to arrive in the doorway.

"Mrs. Grimlock is here," he announced.

I shot Dad a dirty look as I shook my head. "You totally jinxed us."

"I really did," Dad muttered. "Next time I'll glue my mouth shut before I ask that question."

"That sounds like a fabulous idea."

TWENTY-FIVE

"What is she doing here?" I turned an accusatory look to Braden. "Give me back that computer."

Braden clutched the new laptop to his chest. "I didn't invite her."

"No one invited me," Mom announced, breezing past the butler and into the room. "I invited myself."

"Why?" Dad asked, reaching for the bottle of bourbon to top off his drink.

"Because I miss my children." Mom sent a twisted, although somewhat warm, smile in my direction. "Who spoiled the crap out of you today?"

Everyone pointed at Dad in unison.

"Of course." Mom made a disgusted sound in the back of her throat. "What brought this on?"

"She's my daughter," Dad replied without hesitation. "I love her."

"Why really?"

"Because I was right about the zombies," I supplied.

Mom furrowed her brow. "The zombies?"

"Did you miss that part when you were here the other night? I can't remember."

"I know that you were rolled by a man who supposedly died a month before," Mom said. "Braden filled me in. Since when did we land on the zombie theory?"

"Since we visited Dad's old girlfriend at the voodoo shop and zombies attacked," I replied, averting my eyes to avoid the death glare Dad leveled in my direction.

"Wait ... you were attacked by zombies?"

"You were attacked by zombies?" Griffin flew into the room, his eyes wide as he looked me over. "Did you get bitten?"

"They're not that type of zombie," Braden said. "They're different zombies."

"I'm fine." I grinned as I reached for the garment bag that held his new coat. "I got you a leather jacket."

"I got him a leather jacket," Dad corrected. "In case you forgot, I bought everything you came home with."

Griffin scanned the pile of items on the floor. "Yeah, you definitely spoil her more than I do." He picked up the stuffed sloth so he could make room for himself on the couch. "What's this?"

"That's Steve. I thought he had a cute face."

"Steve the sloth?" Braden snorted. "You've always been terrible at naming things."

"I don't know," Aidan countered. "I always through 'Braden the butthead' had a nice ring to it."

"We all did," Redmond said. "Go back to what you said before, Aisling."

"What part? The part where I was right?"

"No, the part about Dad's old girlfriend," Redmond replied. "What old girlfriend?"

"I'd like to hear about that myself," Mom said, crossing her arms over her chest. "Is this the girlfriend you had when I came back to town?"

"No, older than that," I answered. "It seems Madame Dauphine is really an old family friend with ties to the area. What are the odds of that?"

"Wait ... you know who Dauphine really is?" Cillian asked. "Why didn't you lead with that?"

"Why didn't you lead with the important part of your story?" I challenged, ignoring the way Dad glared at my slip.

"What story were you telling?" Griffin asked, legitimately curious.

"That's not important," Redmond said smoothly. He always was gifted when it came to changing the direction of a conversation. "Who is Dauphine?"

"Her name is Evelyn. Apparently Dad dated her before he and Mom hooked up," I supplied.

"Evelyn Stapleton?" Mom twisted her face into a hilarious expression. "What a slut."

"You get that from your mother," Dad said dryly, causing me to chuckle.

"Why is that ... whore ... back in town?" Mom asked, her temper flaring. If I didn't know better, I'd say she was jealous. It was an interesting development, because she'd shown very little romantic interest in my father since returning. Not that I wanted my parents back together, mind you. The fact Mom was probably eating people to sustain herself made that an iffy proposition at best.

"She's running a shop at Woodward Crossing," Dad replied. "She appears to be minding her own business."

Mom turned to me expectantly. "Is she?"

"I just told you she was," Dad snapped.

"I'm asking Aisling," Mom said. "She understands better how women operate. I want to hear what she thinks."

"She was all over Dad."

"I knew it!"

"She was not," Dad protested.

"You're so naïve." I rolled my eyes. "She kept touching you, running her hands up and down your arms." I demonstrated on Griffin for emphasis. "She also purposely rested her boobs on the counter and kept leaning over so you'd have a nice shot down her shirt."

"That was her signature move," Mom complained. "That's how she passed freshman math."

"Touching someone on the arm is not flirting," Dad argued.

"Um, it kind of is," Redmond said. "Every woman I've ever picked up at the bar gave me the go ahead by touching my arm. She never actually said yes."

"I think that's the refrain of date rapists the world over," I offered.

"That's how I knew you were interested in me," Griffin said. "You touched me every chance you got."

"Oh, puh-leez," I scoffed. "We got naked before I ever touched you. Wait ... that came out wrong."

"We know exactly what you meant," Cillian said. "The arm thing is a dead giveaway. What can you tell me about Evelyn, Mom?"

"She was a skank."

"I'll need more than that."

"She was a dirty skank."

Griffin's shoulders shook with silent laughter as I slid him a sidelong glance. "What?"

"Your Dad is right. You get that from your mother."

"Don't make me take that jacket away from you," I warned.

"I didn't ask for a jacket."

"Everyone got presents."

Griffin glanced at the items my brothers held. "I guess so. What brought on this shopping spree?"

"I was right, and Dad owed me for calling me a liar about the zombies."

"I never called you a liar," Dad interjected. "I simply said that zombies weren't real."

"And what happened today?"

"We were attacked by zombies."

"So ... who was right?"

"Aisling, you've pushed things just about as far as I'll allow," Dad said. "Do you really want to test my patience?"

That was an interesting question. "That depends. Do we get a cake bar after dinner tonight?"

"Yes."

"Then I'm done pushing you."

"That's what I thought." Dad turned his attention back to Mom. "As for Evie, she's simply running a business. She spent the last few decades in New Orleans, but missed home."

"Right. She's just that innocent." Mom made an exaggerated face and held up her hand to cut off the rest of what Dad was going to say. "How was Evelyn with you, Aisling?"

"Oh, she pretty much hates me."

"Good girl. What did you say to her?"

"I don't trust her," I replied. "Angelina told me that Madame Dauphine said she could help her prolong her mother's life. When I brought that up today, she kind of danced around the subject. She was much more interested in hanging out with Dad than talking to me."

"Angelina?" Mom's forehead wrinkled. "What does she have to do with this?"

"I was just about to ask the same question," Cillian said.

"Oh, well ... ." I looked to Dad for help. I'd purposely kept the information about Angelina's mother from Cillian because I knew he had a soft heart.

"Angelina and Aisling had a long talk last night," Dad supplied. "It seems she wasn't going to Evelyn's shop to gather ingredients to curse Aisling."

"That insult snafu was just a coincidence," I added.

"Angelina's mother has cancer," Dad continued. "She has only a few months to live. Angelina was desperate, and went to the shop because she hoped Evelyn would be able to help her."

"Oh." Cillian's expression was hard to read. "That must be hard on Angelina. She doesn't have any brothers or sisters or anything."

"No, she's going to be alone," I said. "It's very sad. She's still a skank, though. You can't let her draw you in."

Cillian scowled. "I happen to have a girlfriend."

"I know."

"I happen to love my girlfriend."

"I know that, too," I said, "but Angelina is the type to prey on your sympathy to get what she wants."

"Like thousands of dollars' worth of gifts?" Dad challenged.

I ignored the question. "Evelyn claims she knows nothing about the zombies, and I'm inclined to believe her," I said. "She seemed as surprised as anyone else when the female zombie stole the book."

"So what does that mean?" Mom asked.

I shrugged. "It means we're going to do more research and see where we land tomorrow."

"Until then, it's time for dinner." Dad drained the rest of his glass. "The boys and I are thinking of going to a movie after dinner. Does anyone want to tag along?"

"What movie?" Griffin asked, oblivious to the look Dad and I shared.

"We're staying here," I answered. "I thought we'd watch a movie up in my bedroom."

"You don't want to go to the theater?" Griffin was surprised. "You love movie nights with real Red Vines."

"I do, but ... I think we need quiet time alone."

"Why?"

"Because she wants to get naked with you," Mom answered, blowing out a sigh. "Geez. Are you always this dense?"

I was trying to evade saying anything of the sort, but I could hardly deny it given the circumstances. "Yeah. I want to get naked."

"That was an overshare, Aisling," Dad growled.

"Then you should've led us into dinner sooner."

"Next time."

"Sounds good."

DINNER WAS A FESTIVE affair, and my brothers were good at manipulating the conversation so I didn't have to lie to Griffin. It was the last thing I wanted, and the thing I didn't tell my Dad and brothers was that if it came down to it I would probably tell the truth if directly questioned.

Mom followed me to the cake bar after I'd stuffed my face with roasted chicken and vegetables, watching as I loaded three slices on a plate. I wasn't paying attention so I almost crashed into her before I realized she was practically on top of me.

"What are you hiding?" Mom's voice was low, and when I risked a glance at Griffin I found him engaged in an animated conversation about basketball with Aidan and Cillian.

"What makes you think I'm hiding anything?"

"I can tell by the look on your face."

I seriously doubted that. "I'm not hiding anything. I'm looking forward to a quiet night alone with Griffin and a mountain of cake." While I didn't want to lie to Griffin, I had no problem spinning a good yarn for Mom.

"Don't." Mom shook her head in warning. "While I'm sure you and Griffin could make a fun game out of cake and ... whatever it is you're going to do in your bedroom that you don't want to mention in front of your father, I know you. You're hiding something."

I stared at her for a long moment. Lying seemed the correct way to go, yet I couldn't shake the fact that she might be helpful when it came time for Dad and my brothers to leave. "Do you really want to know?"

"Does it have something to do with that trollop Evelyn?"

I shook my head. "Whose uses the word 'trollop' these days?"

"Does it have to do with Angelina?" Mom asked. "I can't believe you're actually friends with her."

"Hey! I am not friends with her," I countered, narrowing my eyes. "I simply don't see a reason to attack her when she's dealing with so much."

"You don't even like her mother."

"No, but I know what it's like to lose a mother."

Mom stilled, her expression shifting. "Fair enough."

"I am not friends with Angelina," I said. "Never think that, because ... I'd rather shave my head bald and watch a marathon of *Keeping Up With the Kardashians* than spend time with that woman."

"I have no idea what that is, but I'll take your word for it." Mom darted her eyes to the others and back again. "So what are you hiding?"

"In a nutshell? Dad and the boys need to get out of the house without Griffin noticing."

"Why?"

"They're going to break into a vault at the cemetery."

"Why?"

"There was this old dude named Oscar Santiago, and he told people he was going to live forever – and if that didn't work he intended to come back as a zombie. Cillian read a bunch of stuff during his research, and now he wants to see if Oscar's body is in the mausoleum we saw at the cemetery."

Mom furrowed her brow. "That sounds just like him. He's always been a research fanatic."

"He has," I agreed, scooping a slice of red velvet cake onto my plate. Four slices of cake isn't too much, right? "Griffin has come a long way, but he won't like the idea of us breaking into a mausoleum."

"No. Probably not." Mom wet her lips as she slid Griffin a sidelong look. He was apparently oblivious to our conversation. "So ... you're getting married?"

The question caught me off guard. "If you're going to start railing on him ... ."

Mom held up her hand. "I'm not. I understand that you love him."

"I do."

"He's not who I would've picked for you."

"Yeah?" I cocked an eyebrow. "Last time I checked, parents don't get to choose who their children marry. They like to think they do – and they might've actually had a say in it during olden times – but that's not how things go now."

Mom's lips curved. "Olden times?"

"You know, like on *Little House on the Prairie*."

Mom snorted. "I forgot how much you used to love that show. You and Jerry would hurry home from school to watch reruns."

"That was Jerry more than me."

"Don't lie."

"Fine. I liked it, too."

"I know." Mom held my gaze. "If you love him – and it's clear you do – I only want you to be happy."

I didn't know if it was hearing about Angelina's plight – or how much I really disliked Evelyn – but I wanted to believe her. "I am happy. He makes me happy."

"Then I'm happy for you." Mom mustered a grin that almost looked legitimate. "As for the rest ... don't worry about it. I'll make sure your father and brothers escape without you having to lie to Griffin. I know that's what you're worried about."

"And how will you do that?"

"Trust me."

I stared at her. "I'm not sure I do, but I have cake, so nothing is going to ruin this moment. If you can help, great. If you ruin this, I will be forever annoyed."

"That seems like a fair trade."

"I thought so."

"Just sit back and watch my magic."

"Just keep your magic from the cake," I said. "I plan to run on pure sugar for the rest of the night."

"So ... you're eight again?"

"Um ... ten."

"Fair enough."

26

TWENTY-SIX

"Let's look at wedding stuff."

Mom took me completely by surprise after dinner when she directed me toward a couch in the parlor, dropped the huge pile of magazines Jerry collected on my lap, and pinned Griffin with a pointed look.

"You want to look at wedding stuff?" I was understandably confused. I thought she was going to create some sort of diversion so Dad and my brothers could slip out of the house. I hadn't expected this.

"Of course I do." Mom's lips curved as she adopted a wistful expression. "I used to dream about looking through bridal magazines with you before ... well, before."

I understood what she was saying, but it still felt odd. "Griffin and I were going to do that together."

"That's okay," Griffin said hurriedly. "I can go with the guys to the movies if you want to spend some time with your mother."

I knew it was difficult for him to offer. He didn't trust her. He worried she'd do something to me once she earned back everyone's trust. Instead of readily agreeing, though, Mom shook her head.

"This is your wedding, too, Griffin," she said. "You should be involved in the planning. In fact, it's really nice that you want to be involved in this stage of things. Most men would bow out. I want to look with both of you."

Griffin exchanged a quick look with me. "Okay. That sounds fun. Aisling has been a little reticent when it comes to looking at wedding stuff."

"That's because she was raised with boys." Mom's tone was pragmatic. "She's afraid they'll laugh at her."

I snorted. "They always laugh at me."

"Yes, but that's in a 'ripping on your siblings' sort of way. This is different. This is something she cares about – even if she doesn't want to care about it because it makes her look girlie – and she's terrified they'll somehow ruin it for her."

"Is that true?" Dad asked, hovering in the doorway. "Is that why you've been so weird?"

"Not completely," I hedged, shifting in my seat. "I've also been worried that I'll ruin Griffin's life. I don't know how I could possibly think that – what with all of the zombies hanging around and all – but I've decided to let it go."

"You have?" Griffin was dubious. "I'm not complaining if that's really your intention, but you've been a little ... standoffish about it."

"I just don't want you to ever regret choosing all of this."

Griffin's eyes softened. "There will be times I regret your father and brothers. There may even be times I regret Jerry. I will never regret you, though."

"Hey!" Jerry made a face.

"I will also regret the regrets after I have a meltdown," Griffin conceded. "As for the big picture, I will never regret that."

Mom looked directly at him, the angular planes of her face twisting. "I think I finally see what Aisling finds so appealing about you."

"He also looks really good naked," Jerry said.

Mom cracked a smile. "I'm sure he does. So, shall we look through some magazines and jot down some basic ideas?"

Griffin took me by surprise when he answered first. "Absolutely."

"I'm included, right?" Jerry asked.

Mom nodded. "We would never plan a wedding without you."

Jerry beamed. "Great. I'll go grab a notebook."

I looked to Dad as he watched, something unsaid passing between us. I knew this was the perfect way for him to escape. I also felt as if Mom was really interested in the process, although I couldn't help but wonder if that was wishful thinking. It was hard to wrap my head around.

Dad's smile was small, something meant only for me. He offered me a small wave and then stepped back into the dining room. He had a chore to complete – a gross one – but I knew we'd talk about this eventually.

"Where should we start?" I asked, leaning into Griffin as he got comfortable at my side.

"Colors," Mom answered automatically. "What colors do you want?"

"Oh, well ... I have no idea."

"Then that's where we'll start."

TWO HOURS LATER, what seemed like an innocent diversion had turned into a potential bloodbath.

"I don't want live music," I argued.

"Why not?" Jerry was petulant.

"Because a DJ is easier," I replied. "You can enjoy more than one type of music with a DJ."

"Yes, but a swing band is classy," Jerry pressed.

"No, a swing band is pretentious."

"You say that like it's a bad thing."

I glared at him. "Listen ... ."

"Don't argue," Mom ordered. She sat between Jerry and me, a glass of wine in hand, and honestly seemed to be having a good time. "There's no need to argue. This is a wedding. It's supposed to be a happy time."

"No offense, Mrs. Grimlock, but you need to stuff it," Jerry snapped. "I want a swing band."

Mom's eyes flashed with mirth rather than mayhem. "It's not your wedding, Jerry."

"It might as well be," Jerry said. "Aisling is my best friend. We've been dreaming about weddings since we were kids. This is a big deal."

Griffin traced his fingers over the palm of my hand as he listened. "Is that true? Have you been dreaming about your wedding since you were a kid?"

I shrugged, noncommittal. "I guess. In theory. Of course, that's when I thought I'd marry George Clooney."

"I'm better than George Clooney."

"You're a very handsome man with a face like an angel," I countered. "But you're not George Clooney."

Griffin poked my side. "I'll show you how much better I am than George Clooney later. As for music, I agree with Aisling. I don't want a swing band."

Jerry folded his arms over his chest and huffed. "Why?"

"Because my guest list is going to be made up of cops, and they won't find a swing band entertaining."

"I didn't even think of that," I mused. "You're going to have a lot of cops there. I wonder if that will make all the reapers Dad invites uncomfortable."

"Why would it?"

"Because nobody likes cops, man," Jerry replied. "Even when you're not doing something, cops make you feel uncomfortable. It's the way of the world. You can't fight it."

"Whatever." Griffin moved his finger to my ring. "I won't invite everyone at the precinct, but I have to include a few captains and lieutenants."

"You can invite whoever you want. Dad is paying."

"Yes, and I think he's actually looking forward to it," Mom said, flipping through a magazine. She seemed engrossed with the glossy pages. "I know you've been considering having a dress made, but do you know what kind of dress you want?"

"A wedding dress."

"I know that." Mom scorched me with an impatient look. "What kind of wedding dress?"

"Oh, well, a white one. But not too white. It makes me uncomfortable." The expression on Mom's face did not reflect motherly love when I risked a glance in her direction. "What?"

"I mean style," Mom barked. "Do you want strapless? Full arms? A bow in the back?"

"Oh." Realization dawned. "I definitely don't want a bow in the back. I also don't want full arms. I think I'd feel as if a cloud was trying to strangle me."

"It's nice that your head is in a good place, baby," Griffin teased, tucking a strand of hair behind my ear. "That's only going to make this process easier."

"Ha, ha," I intoned, rolling my eyes. "My head is in a good place. I need a simple dress. I will completely freak out if someone tries to get me into one of those dresses that make me look like a cotton ball."

"That's completely understandable," Mom conceded. "I'm sure we can find something you mostly like in one of these magazines and take the photo to the dress designer for a starting point. When do you want to get married?"

"Oh, well ... ." I exchanged a look with Griffin. "We both want to get married in the summer so we can have an outdoor wedding."

"That's a charming idea." Mom beamed. "So next summer, right? That gives us seventeen months."

"This summer," Griffin corrected, catching Mom off guard.

"This summer?"

Griffin nodded. "I'm not waiting seventeen months. We're getting married this summer."

"That's like four or five months?" Mom wasn't happy with the truncated timetable. "You're not pregnant, are you? That will kill your father."

I didn't bother to hide my scowl. "I'm not pregnant," I barked. "I know how birth control works."

"Yes, and you also knew how the parking brake on your father's Jaguar worked when you were a teenager and we all know how that ended. He spent months rebuilding that thing, and now he has an aneurysm if you even think of looking at it."

I wrinkled my nose. "I maintain that parking brake was defective and the fact that the car rolled down the hill and into the Dumpster was not my fault."

"If that's your story."

Griffin chuckled as the doorbell rang. "Do you want me to get that?"

"I will," I said, pushing myself to a standing position. "I need to run to the bathroom anyway. Don't let Jerry pick out anything frilly while I'm gone."

"I'll see if I can restrain him," Griffin said dryly.

I was in a good mood as I slid my sock-covered feet over the ceramic tile in the foyer, humming to myself as I considered the fact that I'd spent two hours with my mother and she hadn't said one passive-aggressive thing – or tried to eat the help. That's progress, right?

I opened the door, mildly curious about who would be visiting. Just about everyone I knew was essentially living here at present. My mouth dropped open when I saw the figures on the porch.

There had to be at least thirty of them, three or four already on the porch, and they were all shuffling toward the front of the house making a hissing that made me think of the world's biggest balloon springing a leak. I could only make out the features on the ones closest to the door, but the milky eyes were evident. I knew exactly what I was dealing with before the nearest one – a woman dressed in a sable coat with pearls draped around her neck – reached for me.

I reacted instinctively, slamming shut the door and flicking the lock before I cried out. Then, because it seemed like the thing to do, I slid the chain lock in place for added security before scurrying back to the parlor. When I slid through the door, Mom, Griffin and Jerry were exactly where I'd left them, all focused on a magazine.

"I think the napkins should be baby pink," Jerry said. "I've always loved that color."

"I don't like the idea of pink," Griffin argued.

"You need something soft," Jerry said. "Aisling is a girl. Girls like pink."

"I don't disagree that we need a soft color," Griffin challenged. "I merely think that we should go with a purple – something that matches Aisling's eyes. I think that would be pretty."

Mom smiled, amused. "Actually, I think the purple is nice. I ... ." She broke off when she saw the look on my face. "You don't want purple?"

I waved off the question. Wedding preparations were clearly done for the night. "Purple sounds great. We have another problem."

"What?" Griffin asked. "Did something happen? Did your father and brothers get in an accident?"

"I have no idea, but I'm assuming they're fine."

"Okay ... what's the issue?"

"The front yard is full of zombies."

Griffin stilled, his brown eyes searching my face as if trying to find a hint of amusement. "I'm sorry?"

"I'm not kidding," I said. "There are zombies all over the front yard. One rang the doorbell. Oh, and one of them is wearing pearls and a sable coat."

"That seems like a terrible waste," Jerry said, struggling to his feet. "What are we going to do?"

That was a very good question. "We need to check all of the doors and windows and lock this place down."

"Then what?" Mom asked, striding through the doorway and heading toward the foyer so she could look through the window panes. She leaned down, peering through, and jerked back when a pasty face appeared and hissed at her through the glass. "There really are zombies out there."

I was incensed. "Did you think I was making it up?"

"I'm not sure what I thought, but there really are zombies out there." Mom rubbed her chin as though considering a math problem. "They go down pretty easily, right?"

I nodded. "I don't think that means we should raid Dad's sword collection and start stabbing heads, though."

"I think that's exactly what we should do," Griffin said, heading for the stairs. "We need to arm ourselves."

Mom nodded as she followed. "He's right. Whatever we decide, arming ourselves is the most important thing."

I had my doubts. "But ... ."

"Aisling, we're about to be overrun by zombies," Mom said. "Pick a weapon now, argue later."

Ugh. If I had a nickel for every time I'd heard that sentence. I followed Griffin to the game room where Dad kept his sword collection, grabbing a light one, not overly long or broad, with a comfortable grip before heading back downstairs. Griffin, Mom and Jerry spent more time on weapon selection, but I didn't care what I stabbed our visitors with as much as I worried about what would happen when Dad and the others returned.

Griffin was the first to join me, a large broadsword in his hand. He almost looked happy as he swung the sword, testing its weight and feel. "Your father has a great collection."

"Yeah. It's not at all weird to have a sword collection," I shot back. "It's not phallic or anything."

Griffin spared me a look. "It's going to be okay, baby. I won't let anything hurt you."

"I'm not particularly worried about us right now," I said. "We're relatively safe. I mean ... as safe as you can be when zombies are ringing the freaking doorbell. What's that about? Zombies aren't supposed to ring doorbells."

"Maybe they wanted to distract you," Griffin suggested.

"Maybe ... but this whole thing is unbelievable."

"Oh, what was your first clue?" Griffin shrank back when I murdered him with a dark look. I love sarcasm as much as the next person, but now was so not the time. "Sorry. That was uncalled for." He leaned in and pressed a kiss to my forehead. "It's okay."

"I'm not afraid of the zombies, Griffin," I supplied. "They move slow and seem easy to take out. Sure, there's a bunch of them out there, but we'll deal. That's not what I'm worried about."

"Okay, what are you worried about?"

"Dad and my brothers," I replied. "They're going to pull in the driveway and not notice the zombies until it's too late. I don't think bites really do anything, but we don't know that nothing bad will happen if one of them is bitten."

Griffin dug in his pocket for his phone. "I'll call your father and tell him what's going on. Then he'll be ready for when they return."

"That sounds like a plan." I kept one eye on Griffin as Mom stared out the window, her face expressionless. "What do you think?"

"I think these things don't look overly difficult, but there has to be a reason someone sent them here, and I don't like not knowing what that reason is."

"That's the story of my life," I muttered, earning a smirk from Mom. I turned at the sound of footsteps, finding the butler scurrying in our direction. Oh, well, this would be easy to explain. "Everything will be okay."

"Oh, I wouldn't say that."

I didn't recognize the new voice right away, but when I tilted my head and stared at the doorway behind the butler I realized he wasn't alone. He had two people with him – and one of them was Detective Mark Green.

"Oh, well, this is just perfect." I briefly pressed my eyes shut. "And I thought the hardest thing we were going to do tonight was pick out a color palette for the wedding."

Jerry patted my shoulder. "Live and learn, Bug. Live and learn. Nothing ever goes as planned in this family."

He wasn't wrong.

27
TWENTY-SEVEN

"What's going on?" Green was positively apoplectic.

I fixed him with a dark look. "Do you knock?"

"He knocked at the back door," the butler volunteered. He was generally unflappable, but looked a bit unsettled. "I wasn't going to answer, but he was rather insistent. There appear to be ... people ... surrounding the house."

"Yes, I noticed that." I flashed a smile that I'm sure came off as more deranged than comforting. "Are you the only staff member left in the house?"

"One member of the kitchen staff remains. Annalise."

"Then take her upstairs and lock yourselves in the second-floor library," I ordered. "Barricade the door. I don't think they'll go after you, but it's better to be safe."

The butler nodded. "Fine." He disappeared through the doorway.

I ran my tongue over my teeth as I did my best to ignore Green and looked to Griffin for guidance. "Do you think we should stay or go?"

"I honestly don't know," Griffin replied. "This house is a virtual fortress, but there are a lot of windows. If those things want in, they can get in. We could try to close off the tops of the two stairwells and wait it out on the second floor, but that makes escape difficult if they overrun the barricades. We'd be trapped."

"We can get out from a few of the second-floor windows if we have to," I countered. "Some of them open close to trees. I did it all of the time when I was a teenager and rarely got caught."

"Well, that's comforting." Griffin snaked his hand around my waist and kissed my cheek, offering intimacy and solace as his mind worked at a terrific pace.

Green wasn't nearly as calm. "Does someone want to tell me what's going on?"

I flicked my eyes to him, annoyance bubbling up. "Not really."

"Your house is about to be overrun by something that looks a lot like people, but I'm going to guess they're not really people."

"Oh, you're just coming to that realization now? How slow are you?" I growled as I shifted closer to Mom and glanced out the window. "What's the news?"

"The horde doesn't seem to be growing," Mom replied. "They also don't appear to be dispersing. They're gathering toward the front door."

"Maybe they can't understand complex orders," I suggested. "Maybe it's impossible for the person controlling them to force a proper fight plan."

"That would be to our benefit."

The police officer with Green, a younger man who looked to be twenty-five, wiped a hand across his brow as he widened his eyes. "What are they?"

I sent him a pitying look – this wasn't his fault, after all – and forced a smile for his benefit. "What's your name?"

"Dennis Langstrom."

"Well, Dennis, it seems we're under attack from zombies." I grinned as Green's face went slack. "Now, I know that's hard for you to wrap your head around, but there's no other word to describe what's happening. It's going to be difficult for a bit, but you'll have a great story to tell your buddies when you're done."

"The good news is that you don't turn into a zombie if they bite you," Jerry offered. He looked nervous, which wasn't surprising, but he remained on his feet and didn't cause a scene by melting down. I considered that a win.

"We haven't tested that theory, so be careful," Griffin cautioned. "I still think we need to call your father."

I swallowed hard as I locked gazes with him. "We can try. The thing is ... um ... they might not hear their phones."

"I know they're in the theater, but they have to be leaving soon," Griffin argued. "They'll check their messages and know what's going on before getting here, which means that we only have to hold out for a little longer."

"Well ... ."

"They're not at the theater," Green scoffed. "We tried to follow them, but they blew past at least two theaters. They were heading toward Detroit when the detail I assigned to them lost their vehicle on Woodward."

Griffin appeared calm at the news, but I didn't miss the almost imperceptible straightening of his shoulders. "I see."

I lowered my voice. "It's not what you think."

"Really? I think you and your mother conspired to hide whatever it is your father and brothers are doing." Griffin's tone was icy. "You made me think you wanted to talk about the wedding when really you didn't want me asking questions."

"Um ... ."

"Oh, don't go all martyr," Mom ordered, turning to face us. "Aisling didn't want to lie to you. I offered to help. It's not the end of the world."

"Really? Then what are they doing?" Green asked.

"Yeah, what are they doing?" Griffin echoed.

I grabbed Griffin's arm and dragged him away, making sure to scare off Green with a warning look before whispering, "They're at Eternal Sunshine Cemetery. Cillian found some stuff on this guy – Oscar Santiago – who thought he could live forever. Apparently he was stealing life forces from his kids, which is not important right now, but still gross.

"Cillian thinks that he can find answers in his vault," I continued.

"I knew you wouldn't be happy about it, and I told my dad I wouldn't lie."

"You still tried to distract me with wedding stuff."

"That was Mom. And, quite frankly, I kind of liked the idea of sitting down to talk with her and you about decisions. It was an option I didn't think I'd have and when it fell in my lap ... ."

Griffin studied my face for a long moment. "Okay, let's not add to this insanity by arguing," he said. "I get that you didn't want to lie, but hiding the truth is basically lying."

"Not really, and I didn't intend on never telling you," I argued. "I just didn't want you to know beforehand because I knew you would try to stop them. I was going to wait until it was done and then tell you."

"And have a huge argument?"

"I made Dad wait outside Victoria's Secret this afternoon and I bought a bunch of new stuff with his credit card while he pretended he didn't know what store I was in. I didn't figure the fight would last all that long."

I expected the admission to further irritate Griffin. Instead, despite his best efforts, he cracked a smile. "I can't believe I'm willingly marrying you."

"You still want to, right?"

"I'm always going to want to. I think that makes me a sick man."

"I think that makes you the perfect man for me." I squeezed his hand. "I'm sorry. Cillian was convinced there was information there that could help us. I don't know if their phones will work inside a stone crypt. I'm guessing they turned them off so they wouldn't draw attention to themselves. The last thing they need is someone calling and a security guard hearing the ringtone. I mean ... they're breaking into a vault."

"And what do they expect to find in this vault?"

"Some dude who reportedly lived for one-hundred and fifty years and only died because his voodoo priestess was involved in a car accident right before New Year's Eve at the turn of the century."

"Oh, well, that doesn't sound weird or anything." Griffin dragged a hand through his hair. "I don't want to freak you out – that's the last thing I want to do – but have you considered the fact that we're not the only ones getting a friendly visit from the neighborhood zombies tonight?"

I stilled, dread rolling through me. "What do you mean?"

"Perhaps someone feels you're getting too close," Griffin replied. "And, by you, I mean your entire family. What if this is a way to make sure none of you ever discover what's really going on?"

I felt sick to my stomach. The thought that Dad and my brothers might be in danger from a zombie attack – and in a cemetery of all places – made me want to heave. I also wanted to punch somebody, but that seemed to be a counterproductive move. "We have to get over there."

"We do," Griffin agreed. "We need to try calling first." Griffin kept his hand on my shoulder as he led me to the group. "Jerry, try calling Aidan. See if you can get him on the phone. Make sure they're okay."

"All right, but ... what's going on?" The look on Jerry's face wasn't friendly. "Are they not at the movies?"

"They're not at the movies," Griffin confirmed. "As to where they're at, well, we'll discuss that later."

Jerry seared me with a hot glare. "You knew?"

"Not now, Jerry. We'll fight about it later."

"Oh, we'll definitely fight about it later," Jerry muttered. "I'm thinking that I'll get my way on the swing band after all."

"We're not getting a swing band." Griffin extended a warning finger. "We need to focus on the problem at hand."

"I don't see how the creatures outside will be that difficult if we fight as a unit," Mom interjected. "They're slow. There are four of us."

"Six," Green corrected. "If you're leaving, we're going with you. I want an explanation first."

"I don't have an explanation for you," I shot back. "Someone is raising zombies and sending them after me. I have no idea who or why. If I knew, this would no longer be a problem."

"Because you would kill the perpetrator?" Green challenged.

"Because we would arrest the perpetrator," Griffin corrected. "Believe it or not, I didn't fall in love with a killer."

"And yet bodies keep dropping wherever she turns up," Green shot back.

"Bodies keep turning up all over metropolitan Detroit," Griffin said. "You have fifteen other bodies found in various municipalities. They all appeared out of nowhere but seem to have been dead for some time. Those fifteen other bodies had nothing to do with Aisling."

"The two in my jurisdiction did," Green snapped. "She's clearly up to something. I believed that before I knew there were zombies wandering around her father's property."

"Open your eyes," Griffin hissed. "The other bodies were zombies. Wow, I can't believe I just said that."

I patted his back in a sign of solidarity. "I told you. You didn't want to believe me, but I told you. If things weren't so dire I'd do the dance again."

"Not now, Aisling," Griffin growled. "You'll do the dance once this is over. You'll be naked when you do it."

"It's a good thing Cormack isn't here," Mom noted. "His head would implode if he'd heard that."

"Aidan isn't answering," Jerry announced, his face twisted with worry. "I tried Mr. Grimlock and Cillian, too. All of their phones go straight to voicemail."

The news wasn't a surprise, but it landed like a mule kick to the gut. "We have to get to them."

"Where are they?" Green asked.

"Don't worry about it," Mom answered. "I have an idea, if you're interested."

"I'm always interested in a good idea."

"Can you still gain access to your father's keys for the Jaguar?"

I nodded. "He keeps them in his office safe. He doesn't trust Redmond and Braden not to take the car and cruise for women."

"That's very smart of him." Mom's lips curved. "The Jaguar is fast and maneuverable. You should be able to drive it through this crowd."

"And?"

"You and Griffin can take the car," Mom said. "It's in the garage, and I doubt there are any zombies in there. I will distract them on the front lawn, draw them in my direction until I'm sure you're safe and away from the property. Then I'll lock the doors and wait this out until you return."

"But ... ."

"She's not going alone," Griffin interjected.

"Of course she's not." Mom sent him a "well, duh" look. "I never once considered that you would let her leave. The Jaguar is small but both of you can fit."

"What about me?" Jerry whined.

"There's no room for you, Jerry," Mom replied. "You'll have to stay with me. I promise to protect you."

It was a nice offer, and I wanted to believe Mom would do whatever it took to keep Jerry safe. I wouldn't risk him, though. "There's room for Jerry to come with us if Griffin drives," I countered. "I can sit on Jerry's lap."

"Your father won't like the fact that you're letting Griffin drive," Mom pointed out.

"No, but something tells me he'll get over it."

Jerry visibly relaxed at the news. "That's the plan I vote for."

"We can put the swords behind the seats," I added. "That way we won't go into the ... where we're going ... unprotected."

"And where would that be?" Green asked.

"It doesn't matter," Griffin replied. "I think that's our best plan of action. The thing is ... ." He broke off as he faced down Mom. "I don't know that I can leave you here."

Mom smirked. "I can take care of myself."

"I know you can," Griffin said, "but you're Aisling's mother. If something happens to you, I'm not sure she'll ever get over it."

"That's a bit dramatic," I muttered. "I've already gotten over it once."

"No, you didn't," Griffin countered. "That's not the point, though. Leaving you here to fight these things on your own goes against everything I've ever been taught, everything I believe about myself."

"Griffin, I have been taking care of myself for a very long time," Mom said. "I will be fine. If you take Aisling and Jerry, they're your main concerns. You need to keep them safe."

"They're always my main concerns."

"That's kind of sweet," Jerry sniffed.

"Keep them your main concerns," Mom stressed. "I believe I'll have the better end of this deal. You're the one who could be running headlong into danger."

Griffin didn't look convinced, but he swallowed hard and nodded. "Stay safe."

"Keep my children safe," Mom said. "That's the most important thing. If I can manage to get away, I know where you're going. I'll be along when I can to help."

Even though I considered arguing further, I didn't. Instead, I opened Dad's safe, grabbed the keys to the Jaguar, and followed Griffin and Jerry to the garage. Green, who remained flabbergasted, put up an argument when he realized we were serious about leaving.

"You can't go out there."

"We have no choice," Griffin said. "We have to get to the Grimlocks."

"And what about us?"

"You let yourself into my father's house," I pointed out. "You were safe in your vehicles. I don't think you're in any immediate danger here. In fact, I'm starting to wonder if the zombies are here to make sure we don't leave."

"I've been considering that, too," Mom admitted. "When you're ready to leave, text me." She held up her cell phone for emphasis. "I'll draw their attention to the front yard, which should give you a window for escape. Don't waste that window worrying about me."

"We won't." Griffin grabbed my hand. "Come on, baby. It's time to blow this joint."

I snickered as I shook my head, the sound guttural and forced. "That was lame."

"I know, but it made you smile, didn't it?"

I nodded. "For now."

"We're going." Griffin cast one final glance over his shoulder in Mom's direction before disappearing into the kitchen. "Everything will be okay. Have faith."

I was trying. It wasn't easy, though.

ONCE INSIDE THE JAGUAR, doors locked and the seatbelt

fitted securely around Jerry and me as I sat on his lap, I exchanged a weighted look with Griffin as I held my phone.

"Are you ready?"

Griffin started the Jaguar, smiling as the engine roared to life. "Oh, this thing is going to fly, isn't it?"

"Try not to wreck it," I warned. "Even if we save his life, Dad won't have much of a sense of humor if this thing gets scratched. Trust me. I know. I'm still hearing about the Dumpster incident."

"I'll do my best." Griffin nodded. "Text her."

I did as instructed, waiting for the answering beep before giving instructions. "Wait exactly two minutes before you open the garage door and then punch it. The gate should be open."

Griffin's eyebrows jumped. "She opened the gate?"

"I guess." My stomach tightened as Griffin revved the engine. Things were about to get very real. Jerry shifted beneath me, pressing his cheek to my back. "Aidan is fine, Jerry. I would know if he wasn't."

"Is that a twin thing?" Griffin asked.

"It's an 'I can't take it if it's not true' thing."

"Then it's definitely true." Griffin squeezed my hand. "Thirty seconds."

We waited, the time seemingly passing in short bursts that felt like hours. When the two minutes elapsed, Griffin punched the button to open the garage door and floored the accelerator.

I scanned the yard as we passed, the faces nothing but a blur. I caught sight of my mother a split-second before Griffin escaped onto the road in front of the house. She stood in the middle of the yard, her sword busy as she slashed, her expression grim and focused. She looked sweaty and busy, but also unharmed.

"She'll be okay," Griffin said, shifting the car and increasing speed. "Everything is going to be okay."

"I know. Just go. We can't turn back, and I wouldn't want to even if we could. We have to get to Dad."

28
TWENTY-EIGHT

The Jaguar was sporty, sleek and fun on a normal day. While trying to race to a cemetery to save my family from possible zombie attack, it was cramped and painful.

Griffin never smiled during the drive, but he seemed energized when we parked, smoothly sliding out from behind the steering wheel and collecting his sword from the narrow spot behind the seats.

I was much less graceful, tumbling off Jerry's lap with a loud "oomph" as I tried to stretch the kinks out of my legs. "Never again," I muttered.

"Here's your sword." Griffin slipped my weapon into my hand, his eyes keen as they scanned the cemetery. "Redmond's Expedition is here, but I don't see anyone."

"Do you see any zombies?" Now that we were officially out of the house, Jerry's bravado had slipped and he looked terrified. He also looked resigned. He wasn't going to leave Aidan to fend for himself no matter what.

"Not yet," Griffin replied. "Do you remember how to get where we're going?"

I nodded. "We need to be quiet until we know what's going on."

"Then we'll be quiet." Griffin flipped his sword to his left hand so he could use his right to hold mine. I didn't have a free hand for Jerry, but that didn't stop him from crowding me as we slipped into the darkness.

The cemetery was quiet. Too quiet. I felt as if hundreds of eyes were trained upon me. Even if zombies were on the move, they didn't have eyes as much as murky orbs. It was disconcerting, and every noise I heard – whether the sound of our own feet scraping against the pavement or a rustle of wind through the barren branches – I jolted a bit.

"It's okay, baby," Griffin murmured, his lips close to my ear. I knew he was trying to make me feel better, but his words grated.

"You don't know that."

"I choose to believe it."

"Shh," Jerry hissed. "You said to be quiet."

"So I did."

We must have made a strange sight. Two men and one woman, all dressed in heavy winter coats but without hats and gloves – we clearly weren't thinking when we left the house – picking our way through a cemetery on a chilly February night. Oh, and we all carried swords.

Yeah, if anyone saw us they'd call the cops for sure. We had "crazy" or "cosplay" written all over us.

I remembered the way to the back section of the cemetery, releasing Griffin's hand when we approached. It was dark, so I had to rely on my ears rather than my eyes for the initial part of the approach.

I paused at the top of a small hill, squinting as I tried to spy any hint of movement. There were streetlights behind the cemetery, illuminating the small neighborhood there. They offered very little help to us, though, and it was only because I happened to be staring directly at the mausoleum that I caught a trace of action at all.

Griffin saw it at the same time, lifting his finger to his lips to warn us. Jerry and I shot him twin looks of disgust, but followed him, crouching low and sliding in close to a tree so we had at least a modicum of cover.

The moon, which was largely covered by clouds, peeked through a bit and revealed a scene that caused my blood to run cold. There had to be at least twenty zombies on the small hill, most of them surrounding the mausoleum that housed Oscar Santiago's remains. The horde made it impossible for those inside the mausoleum to escape in any direction.

"Oh, no." I exhaled heavily.

"I see it," Griffin gritted out, his tone grim. "It's still going to be okay."

I wasn't sure how he knew that, but arguing seemed like a bad way to go. "We need to get the zombies away from the mausoleum. That will allow Dad and the others a chance to escape."

"I know."

"We need to be quiet when we do it, because if we attract too much attention from the neighborhood it won't be good. We might accidentally draw bystanders too close. We don't want that on our consciences."

"I know."

His tone was starting to grate.

"I kind of want to pinch you," I whispered.

Griffin cracked a smile. "I know. I'm sorry. I'm thinking."

We lapsed into a silence for a few moments. I didn't want to hurry him, pressure him to make the wrong decision, but patience isn't exactly one of my virtues.

"We need to move faster," I added.

"I know." Griffin faced me directly. "I have an idea."

His face was flushed with excitement, causing my stomach to roll as I realized whatever he had planned would force us to separate. He wouldn't willingly drag me into danger, but he was readying himself to take on the mob by himself.

"What's your idea?" Jerry asked.

"I'm going over there." Griffin pointed toward another mausoleum, this one much smaller, to our left. "I'm going get on top of it and call the zombies over. I want you two to wait here until the coast is clear – or clear enough that you only have a few of them to deal with. Then I want you to get the others out and start back toward the parking lot."

I immediately balked. "That's the dumbest plan I've ever heard."

"I'll be fine."

"I won't leave you." I jutted out my lower lip and crossed my arms over my chest, being careful not to poke Jerry with my sword in the process. "It's not going to happen."

"You don't have a choice," Griffin said, his voice low. "I won't be far behind you. In fact, here." He pressed the keys to the Jaguar into my hand. "Put Jerry in the Expedition with everyone else. You drive the car. I know you'll wait for me. I promise I'll be right behind you."

Tears pricked the back of my eyes. "No."

"Aisling, I swear that I'm not about to fall on my sword and sacrifice myself," Griffin said. "I'm the most athletic. It will be easiest for me to get on the other mausoleum. Once I'm up there, all I have to do is lean over and start stabbing heads."

That was the most ridiculous plan of attack I'd ever heard. "No. I can't ... no."

"You left your mother," Griffin pointed out. "You trusted her to do the job. Do the same for me."

"It's not the same."

"Why?"

"Because I can't be without you."

"Oh, baby." Griffin rested his forehead against mine. "You're not going to be without me. I promise. This is the smartest plan of attack. If things go wrong, at least your father and brothers will be out. They'll be able to help."

"He's right, Bug," Jerry said. "We need to get the others out. To do that, someone has to draw them away."

Even though the argument made sense, I wasn't in the mood to agree. "Then I'll be the one to draw them away," I suggested. "I'm the one they want anyway. They might not react to seeing you."

Griffin tilted his head to the side. "What do you mean?"

"I mean that they've been cursed to go after reapers," I replied. "Those other bodies – those fifteen other bodies you told me about – they were all located near reaper homes. That can't be a coincidence.

"When the zombies attacked in Madame Dauphine's shop, they paid zero attention to her," I continued. "The one was interested in Dad and me. The other went for the book. Neither one of them cared about her."

I didn't add that I'd wondered several times since then if that was because Dauphine was involved in this mess. Dad didn't think so because he had fond memories of his good friend Evie. I wasn't willing to rule it out, though. She recognized me as a reaper. She told Dad she didn't realize I was his daughter, but given how much I look like him and her close personal relationship from decades past, that didn't make much sense.

"You didn't tell me that." Griffin's tone was accusatory.

"I didn't have time. Mom showed up for dinner. We were trying to pretend we weren't the type of family who breaks into vaults to look at bodies. I was very busy."

It was a serious conversation, but Griffin cracked a smile all the same. "I see."

"I need to be the one on the mausoleum," I argued. "They'll come for me because of what I am. Once you get my Dad and brothers out, you can take out the zombies and then we'll go to the parking lot together."

Griffin didn't look convinced. "Aisling ... ."

"If it was a good enough plan for you, it should be a good enough plan for me," I argued. "We can't guarantee that the zombies will go for you. They will go for me. They were created to do just that."

"I hate it when you have a point," he muttered, rubbing his hand over his chin. "Can you get up on the roof without help?"

"I grew up with four brothers," I reminded him. "I know how to climb things."

Griffin was reluctant, but as I watched him scan the scene a second time, I knew that I'd won.

"Okay," Griffin said after a beat. "You don't get down from that mausoleum until I tell you it's okay."

I bobbed my head in agreement. "Okay."

"Your word on it."

"I promise." I fluttered my fingers over his cheek, cold skin making contact with cold skin even as a small ember of heat flared between us. "It'll be okay." I parroted his words back to him.

"It will," Griffin agreed. "We're going to plan the perfect wedding. We're going to have a great marriage. No swing band, though."

"Definitely no swing band."

"I hate you both right now," Jerry grumbled.

"Be careful," Griffin intoned. "Don't do anything to endanger yourself. If you need me ... ."

"I'll call," I finished, forcing a smile for his benefit.

"Okay." Griffin pressed a soft but insistent kiss against my mouth. "I love you so much."

"I know." I grinned as I pulled back. "I love you, too."

THE WALK TO THE second mausoleum was nerve wracking. It took everything I had not to look over my shoulder, to make sure Griffin was watching my back and no zombies were creeping up behind me. I knew he was. I didn't question it. That didn't stop me from wanting to see it.

The zombies seemed obsessed with the Santiago tomb, which gave me plenty of time to hop on a headstone and jump to the mausoleum roof. It wasn't a normal mausoleum, the roof only about five feet off the ground compared to the Santiago mausoleum, which had seven-foot-tall ceilings. Once I was settled on the roof, a minor scrape on my wrist serving as an annoyance before gripping the sword in my hand, I looked in Griffin's direction for reassurance.

I couldn't make out his features. It was too dark. I could see his hand move from the spot above his heart to his lips, though. He pressed a kiss to his fingers and raised his hand in the air, giving me strength as I swiveled to face the zombies.

First I tried to whistle through my fingers. It was a trick Dad taught me when I was a kid. He regretted it soon after because I spent two straight weeks letting loose with ear-splitting whistles whenever I wanted to irritate my brothers. I ended up irritating Dad more than anyone else.

Sadly, it was too cold for the whistle trick, so I had no choice but to yell.

"Hey, jerkwads, I'm over here!"

At the sound of my voice, the zombies raised their heads. They didn't stop hissing or moving their feet, but something about their demeanors shifted.

"Come this way." I waved with my hand even though I was certain they couldn't actually see me. They were moving on instinct, a spell or curse fueling them. Nothing more. "You want to come this way, boys. Oh, sorry, I see there are a few girls. I didn't mean to be sexist. Come this way. That's right. Over here."

The more I talked, the more interest the zombies took in me, most of them immediately abandoning their attack on the Santiago mausoleum. "I have something shiny to show you."

The zombies didn't move fast, but once they turned to face my direction they didn't hesitate to begin their plodding walk away from the place where my family hid. They didn't so much as look back over their shoulders to see if anyone exited the other mausoleum. Now that they heard my voice, it was as if I was the only person in the world. They shuffled in my direction, single-minded in their attempt to track me, and opening the path behind them so Jerry and Griffin could get to my father and brothers.

I watched Griffin cut across the field, giving the zombies a wide berth. His eyes constantly tracked back so he could see me, his expression cold and immovable. I raised my hand, feeling a bit silly and sheepish, and waved so he knew I was fine.

Then I focused on the zombies.

I didn't hesitate as they grew close, kneeling on the right side of the mausoleum roof and shoving my sword into the first head that appeared. The sound was one I wouldn't readily forget, twisting my stomach as I attempted not to regurgitate the piles of food and cake from dinner.

I steeled myself and continued working, stabbing five heads before I realized that the falling bodies were cutting off the rest of the zombies from their approach. I switched sides, forcing myself to remain focused on the immediate enemy and trusting Griffin to get my family out of harm's way.

I stabbed another two zombies and then waited. The location of the mausoleum – on a small, rolling slope – prevented the zombies from getting closer because the fallen bodies blocked their path. I was essentially safe, but I also couldn't reach the zombies to decrease their numbers without risking toppling off the roof.

Griffin, breathless, jogged to a spot behind the zombies. They didn't immediately notice, but when I saw he was about to open his mouth I shook my head.

"Don't talk. Did you get them out?"

Griffin snapped his mouth shut and firmly nodded.

"I have a problem." As long as I talked, the zombies kept trying to get at me. They never even glanced in Griffin's direction. That was exactly what I wanted. "They can't get any closer."

Griffin opened his mouth again, but I shook my head to keep him quiet. "Don't ruin things. I'm the only one who can talk."

Griffin cracked a smile and rested his hands on his hips, his chest heaving as he fought to catch his breath in the cold.

"They can't get closer and I can't risk leaning too far over to stab them," I said. "I wanted to take out more of them, but I don't think that's possible.

"You need to point Dad and the others back to the cars," I continued. "Do you see that hill over there?" I pointed to a steep incline to my right. It was behind a stand of leafless trees. "I'm going to hop off the back of this mausoleum and go up the hill that way. Do you see how they're confused and can't climb? I'll easily be able to run from them."

Griffin looked as if he wanted to protest, but he could tell by my expression now was not the time.

"Get to the top of the hill," I ordered. "I'll draw them over to the left here and then jump off the back corner right here. Then I'll run up the hill and give you a big hug and kiss."

Griffin grimaced, unsure of my plan.

"It's the best way, and you know it," I pressed. "I probably won't be able to run up the entire hill – it's really steep – but I will be so far in front of them it won't matter. Go on. I'll be with you in three minutes. I swear."

Griffin exhaled heavily and then nodded, as he began running. I watched him turn his head every few steps, and smiled as he disappeared around the bend. I knew where he was. I knew he was waiting. All I had to do was get to him.

"Come here, you little maggots," I ordered, moving to the front left corner of the mausoleum and banging my sword against it, making a ton of noise to draw the horde. "Fresh meat! Come and get it!"

I did this for a full minute before turning and jumping off the back corner of the mausoleum. I didn't give myself a chance to think about it. I simply jumped.

I hit the ground hard but kept my footing, breaking into a run as I started up climb the hill. I was out of breath quickly, the cold squeezing my lungs. I was almost parallel to one of the maintenance sheds when I noticed more movement ahead of me.

Thinking it was Griffin, I increased my pace. I wasn't watching close enough. A figure hopped out from behind the shed and slammed a fist into my face before I registered what was happening.

The figure was dark, shoulders slouched, and the face covered with a knit mask. I was desperate to call out for Griffin, but I couldn't find my voice.

My vision grayed around the edges as I hit the ground, my head spinning as I desperately clung to consciousness. I realized I was in trouble – real trouble – seconds before my mind went blank.

My last thought was an obvious one: This isn't good.

TWENTY-NINE

I woke in a small room, the only light coming from a naked bulb at the center of the ceiling. I glanced around, rubbing my sore face where the punch landed and scowling. I'd been knocked out twice in two months. I was going to start getting concussion syndrome at this rate. I might as well be a professional football player if this was going to keep happening.

A hint of movement at the corner of the room caught my attention, and when I looked in that direction I found Madame Dauphine standing in the corner next to the cemetery's lawn supplies. She looked amused, for lack of a better word. She also looked agitated.

"I freaking knew it!"

I considered rolling to my knees, but that seemed like too much effort given the incessant throbbing in my cheek that I was certain would affect my balance for the next few minutes. We were clearly in the storage shed I'd walked past on my way up the hill. There's no way Dauphine could drag me farther than that. Once I didn't meet Griffin as he expected, he'd come looking for me. This was the first place he'd search.

"You knew what?" Dauphine asked, her voice laced with agitation. "What is it you think you know?"

"That you're a crazy old bat," I replied. "You'd better hope that Griffin finds me. He believes in law and order. If it's my father, you'll find out just how far your past relationship won't get you."

"Is that so?"

"Yeah. And, you'd better hope you don't survive long enough for my mother to find out what you've done, because she already hates you. She'll eat you for breakfast, pick her teeth with your bones, and then scatter your worthless carcass so her friendly wraith assassins can munch on what's left."

That sounded terrifying, right? There was no need to push things further. I did, though. That's my way.

"And, for the record, I'm pretty sure my mother eats people, so you're going to cry when she gets her hands on you. We're talking big, fat girly tears here. The kind those Lifetime movies dole out like candy."

Okay, that should do it.

Instead of trembling with fear, Dauphine merely shook her head. "Your mother is dead."

"No, she's not. The zombies you sent to the house weren't enough to kill her. Slow her down, maybe. Kill? Absolutely not."

"Your mother died almost eleven years ago," Dauphine argued. "I read about it in the newspaper. Honestly, I wish I would've found out sooner. That would've made things easier. Unfortunately, the news reached me only about a year ago."

She had to be joking. "Well, much like the things you keep raising from the dead, you can't keep a Grimlock down. She's back. She's been back for months."

"Is that a fact?" Dauphine didn't look as if she believed me. "I think you're simply talking to hear yourself talk. That shouldn't surprise me. I've only met you a few times, but you've done exactly one thing each and every instance. Do you know what that is?"

"Figure out that you were a psycho?"

"Talk!"

"Oh, well, I'm good at that, too." I sucked in a hissing breath as I touched my cheek. My face would be swollen and bruised tomorrow. I really hate that. "I have to give you credit. You pack quite the wallop. Who taught you to throw a punch?"

"I didn't hit you. That's hardly what I'm here to talk to you about."

"You didn't hit me?" That made absolutely zero sense. "Did you train one of your flying monkeys to do it? That was a nice trick, cursing a zombie to attack your store while we were visiting. It made you look like a victim. Unfortunately for you, I didn't fall for it."

"I didn't do that either." Dauphine looked bored with the conversation. "I would've done it if I'd thought of it, don't get me wrong, but it wasn't me."

I started to feel as if I wasn't getting a clear picture of the situation. That needed to be remedied. "What's your plan here? You thought you'd be able to take us out by separating us, huh?"

"I didn't care about taking you out," Dauphine clarified. "I cared about keeping you occupied. You've been a bit of a pain in my posterior for the past few days. I thought if I distracted you that I'd be able to achieve what I started without ending you."

"And what's that?"

"Immortality."

"Oh, geez." I made an exaggerated face even though it stung to move my facial muscles. "What is it with maniacal nitwits wanting to live forever? It's like you guys can't find some new goal. Have you ever considered that there's a reason people weren't meant to live forever?"

"And what would that be?"

"Because life is meant to be finite," I answered, not missing a beat. "You're supposed to embrace it. You're supposed to be afraid of death because you don't want to lose what you have, like love and family. You're not supposed to hold onto it like it's some big prize. You're not supposed to hurt others, kill others, to get what you want. You're not supposed to sacrifice people to give yourself something you didn't even earn."

"Now you sound like a Lifetime movie."

She wasn't wrong. "That doesn't mean what I said isn't true."

"And yet I still want to live forever."

"Like Voldemort?"

"Who?"

"You're probably too old to get the reference," I muttered. "Like in *Highlander*? You want to live forever, even if it means cutting off other people's heads."

"That's an interesting comparison, but I simply want power," Dauphine countered. "That's what we're looking for here."

"And you think reapers can somehow give it to you?"

"What do you mean?"

She was being cagey now. "I know that you've sent out, like, seventeen of these zombie things – that was before tonight, so the number will increase – and they've all been discovered near reaper homes."

The look on Dauphine's face was dark. "How do you know that?"

"The cops have the addresses where the bodies were found, and we have the addresses of where reapers live," I replied. "It wasn't hard to figure out."

Sure, Cillian figured it out because he's smarter than the rest of us combined, but Dauphine didn't need to know that.

"Is your father aware of this?"

"He is." I didn't hold back my smugness. "He won't be happy when he figures out it's you."

"I don't think he'll be happy regardless," Dauphine noted. "You've put me in an awkward position, Aisling. I was hoping to make it through this without tapping a member of Cormack's family. I wanted him to come through this unscathed."

"Because you want to jump his bones."

"I've always been in love with him. I won't deny it."

"It must really chafe your behind that he fell in love with my mother and forgot all about you," I supplied. "Did you pine for him? Did you grow bitter and ... stupid?"

"I'm not sure how you can sit there and call me stupid when you're the one locked in a storage shed."

"That's because you hid like a girl and punched me when I didn't expect it," I snapped. "Griffin was waiting for me at the top of the hill. Do you really think he's just going to throw up his hands and say, 'Oh, well, I guess I'll move on,' because I disappeared? He's going to come looking for me. And he won't be alone."

"I'm sure he will try to find you," Dauphine said, seemingly unbothered by my diatribe. "But right about now he has his hands full."

My blood ran cold. "What does that mean?"

"It means that we had to call on some additional ... I guess you'd call them friends ... to deal with the threat your family poses," Dauphine explained. "Had you left things the way they were, we would've been able to finish up our plans without involving you. Now we have to kill you. I'm not happy about it, but perhaps it will bring your father and me closer when it comes time to mourn."

"You really think that's going to happen?"

"I think your father has five children. You might be the only girl, and it will gut him to lose you, but he will have to carry on for the rest. He will grieve. I will help. By then the ritual will be complete. I'll get exactly what I've always wanted, I just didn't expect to use you to do it."

"And what do you want again?"

"To live forever."

"There has to be more to it than that." I shook my head, annoyance and disgust warring for top billing in my head. "You want his money, too." I thought back to her store. It was nice, in a kitschy sort of a way. It clearly wasn't bringing in big bucks. "You want to live forever, but you'll need money to do it. My father has that money."

"You're not as dumb as you look."

"I couldn't possibly be." I realized what I said too late to take it back. "That came out wrong."

"You should think before you speak," Dauphine suggested, turning her eyes to the door and tilting her head, reminding me of a dog listening for its master. "I think that's your biggest fault. It's too late to adjust your attitude now, but perhaps if you believe in reincarnation you'll get another shot."

"You seem pretty sure of yourself," I said. "Your zombies aren't fast or strong. They're not smart. They can't problem solve. My entire family – well, except for my mother, who is back at Grimlock Manor ripping apart the zombies you sent – is here. They will come for me. They won't let anything stop them."

"And now you're the one who sounds pretty sure of herself,"

Dauphine countered. "Your father and brothers, and that man you seem to care so deeply about, they will look for you. The undead have this place surrounded, though. They cannot cut their way through. By the time they do, you'll be dead and the ritual will be complete. If it's any consolation, you'll be giving yourself to something greater than yourself."

"You sound like a deranged fortune cookie," I snapped. "You're overestimating what your mob of undead freaks is capable of. They're like possessed dolls, and not like Chucky, because he was a badass. Those things out there are pretty far from badass."

"They will hold as long as they need to hold." Dauphine kept her eyes on the door, causing my suspicions to pop.

"Who are you waiting for?"

"It won't be long." Dauphine didn't even look at me as she responded.

"You're waiting for someone," I said, struggling to my feet. I gingerly brushed off my filthy rear end as I looked her up and down. "You said 'we' earlier. I missed it the first time – my mind is kind of slow thanks to the punch – but you said 'we.'

"You also said that you didn't hit me and you didn't unleash the spell that sent the zombies into your store," I continued. "You're working with a partner. Who is it?" I was practically salivating. "Is it Angelina? I'm going to be really upset if she fooled me with a fake 'dying mother' story."

"You need to stop with the Angelina obsession," Dauphine chided. "She is nothing but a pathetic girl trying to save her mother. She's not worth your time."

"Neither are you, but I'm still talking to you."

"That's because you believe I will free you," Dauphine said. "That's not really an option for me. You see, I need you to complete the ritual. I had other options, but you've forced a confrontation and I'm out of time."

"You keep mentioning your ritual. What is it? Why do you need me?"

"I don't need you particularly. I need the blood of a reaper."

That's when things clicked into place. "Of course. You're not so different from wraiths. They get a special boost from reapers if they can absorb the right souls. They're different from you, living more of a half-life, but you think you can use reaper blood to live forever."

"I think that Oscar Santiago was on to something when he tried his own experiment," Dauphine corrected. "The mistake he made was going after his own family. Do you know that it was his great-granddaughter who killed his wife? She knew she was next on his list and fought back. She ended him. Going after reapers should eliminate the problem of making enemies."

"Oh, I don't know. I think reapers are pretty much the worst enemies ever. Still, my mother will make you pay in ways you can't possibly imagine."

"Why do you keep saying that?" Dauphine fixed her full attention on me. "Your mother died in a fire more than ten years ago. I read about it."

"She came back."

"You're a reaper. You know that's not possible. Once crossing over, there is no escape from death."

"That's true," I conceded. "Lily Grimlock didn't die in that fire, though. She was burned. She was taken captive. She was held for a long time. She was kept alive by nefarious — and I'm guessing really gross — means. But she didn't die. She came back."

"Really?" Dauphine's expression was thoughtful. "I would very much like to compare notes with her."

As if on cue, the storage shed door opened. Dauphine's smile was serene as she turned, clearly expecting to find her partner. Instead, she found my mother, or at least the woman who had been my mother at one time. Neither woman looked happy with the predicament.

"What the ... ?" Dauphine scrambled to get away, heading toward me in an effort to put distance between my mother and herself. I was too smart to let her get close to me.

"Don't even think about it." I grabbed a rake hanging on the wall and slapped it against Dauphine's head. The blow wasn't hard enough to knock her out, but it did ring her bell.

"What's going on in here?" Mom asked, her tone prim. "I heard my name mentioned and thought now would be a good time to join the party."

"Where is everyone else?" I asked, thinking of Dad, my brothers, Jerry and Griffin. "Are they okay?"

"Your father is dealing with his attorney about five hundred yards from here," Mom replied, her eyes never leaving Dauphine's face. "Apparently they have a billing disagreement."

I furrowed my brow. "His attorney? Neil?"

Mom nodded. "It seems that faithful old Neil is involved in Evelyn's plan. He was the mastermind. She was the power. Your father is discussing it with him now."

That didn't sound good. "Discussing it?"

Mom ignored the question and remained focused on Dauphine. "How are you, Evelyn? The years haven't been kind."

"You should talk," Dauphine sputtered. "You're so pale you look like a ghost."

"There are worse things than dying," Mom said quietly, her gaze momentarily meeting mine. "What happened to your face?"

"I got punched. I thought it was Dauphine at first, but now I'm starting to suspect it was Neil. There's no way she could hit me that hard. I don't think she could've dragged me into this shed without help either. She's not very big."

"Well, I'm going to hit her that hard as retribution just to be on the safe side," Mom said. "What was her plan?"

"She wants to live forever."

"Like on *Highlander*?"

"Or *Fame*."

Mom snickered, although the amusement didn't make it all the way to her eyes. "I think you should head out. Griffin is helping with the cleanup. He's not far up the hill, but he's ready to melt down. When he saw I was heading in this direction I believe he first thought I was coming to hurt you rather than help."

"He didn't believe that. He knew. After what happened at Grimlock Manor, he knew."

"Well, it doesn't really matter, does it?" Mom forced a smile. "You need to go to your father and Griffin. They'll want to see you. No, scratch that. They desperately need to see you."

I spared a glance for Dauphine. She'd recovered a bit, was no longer cowering on the floor. She looked terrified. I couldn't muster any sympathy for her, but that didn't mean I wasn't curious. "What will you do with her?"

"What was she going to do to you?"

"Bleed me dry because she believes that she needs reaper blood to live forever."

Mom's smile was hideous as she hunkered down so she was at eye level with Dauphine. "Then I believe I will bleed her dry. We need to have a bit of a discussion first. You don't need to be present."

"But ... ." I was lost, confused. "How will you explain this to the cops?"

"I wouldn't worry about Detective Green," Mom said. "We had a long talk after you left. I believe he's going to put this case to bed rather quickly, and without bothering you again."

That sounded a little too convenient. "But how?"

Mom swore under her breath, exhaling heavily as she faced off with me. "Aisling, I understand you've had a trying night. I know you value human life, even when a particular human tries to hurt you. You get that from your father. This is an exception."

Was it? "She's still a person."

"And she's utterly dangerous," Mom said. "She would've killed you for some ritual that she wasn't even certain would work."

Wait ... would it have made a difference if she knew it worked? "Mom, hand her over to the police. You don't need to kill her."

"The police will have no idea what to do with her," Mom argued. "They'll think she's a crackpot, that she's crazy. She won't serve time in jail. If we're lucky, she might get a year or two in some lockdown facility. Then she'll come back. Do you want her to come back?"

"No, but ... ."

"Do you want her to go after Griffin? After Jerry? Do you want her to go after the children you and Griffin will share one day? They'll have reaper blood, too, Aisling. This woman is a threat as long as she lives."

I wanted to argue further. I wanted to find a way to spare

Dauphine, not for her sake but rather my mother's benefit. Finally, I heaved a sigh and relented. I'd killed to protect my family. I'd done it more than once, and in brutal fashion. Expecting Mom to do differently somehow seemed unfair.

"Okay, I'm going." I shuffled to the door, doing my best to ignore the terrified squeaks Dauphine emitted. "Don't torture her."

"We're going to have a talk first. Then, I promise, I will make it fast."

I figured that was the best I was going to get. "Good luck."

I didn't turn back as I exited the storage shed, instead pointing myself up the hill. When I reached the top, I heard Jerry and Griffin bellow my name in unison. Griffin was on me before I had a chance to catch my breath.

"Are you okay?"

I nodded. "I got hit in the face."

"You scared me." Griffin tightened his grip as he kissed my good cheek. I let him hold me, glancing over his shoulder to where Neil Graham rested on the ground. Dad stood over him, a dark look on his face. The lawyer didn't move. It looked as if Dad had exercised his own brand of justice.

"I want to go home."

Griffin stroked the back of my head. "You're going to the hospital first."

"I'm fine."

"You're still going." Griffin pulled back, cupping my head as he regarded me. "Then, if you're good, I'll get you some ice cream and tuck you into bed."

"Our bed?"

Griffin spared a glance for Dad and shook his head. "I don't think that will go over well. We'll head home tomorrow."

"Fine." I was resigned. Griffin was right. Dad wouldn't take it well if we disappeared. "I want heaps of hot fudge with that ice cream."

"Consider it done."

30
THIRTY

It was almost midnight by the time we made it back to Grimlock Manor. The yard was free of bodies – I had a feeling my Dad made a call to the home office and requested assistance – and Griffin managed to talk everyone out of accompanying us to the hospital while still retaining access to the Jaguar.

The house was dark, and I headed straight to my bedroom. Griffin detoured to the kitchen. I was barely in my pajamas and under the covers before Dad appeared in the doorway.

"Can I come in?"

I eyed him suspiciously. "That depends. Are you going to yell?"

"Not tonight." Dad stepped into the room. "I'm reserving the right to yell tomorrow morning. I need a good night's sleep to decide if I'm angry."

"Can we have an omelet bar?"

"Again?"

"You can never have too many omelet bars."

"We're having omelet and waffle bars tomorrow," Dad said. "I even got my hands on some fresh blueberries because I know they're your favorite."

"Sold."

Dad smiled as he circled the bed and sat on my side of the mattress, his fingers gentle as they moved to my face. "I'm sorry this happened."

The simple words surprised me. "You didn't do it."

"No, but the man I sent to defend you was responsible for this entire mess. I can't help feeling that I should've been aware of that."

"How?"

"I don't know."

I propped myself up on the pillows and locked gazes with him. "Do you remember what you told me when Angelina made Jerry cry at the homecoming dance junior year?"

"No."

"I was angry. I told you I should've seen it coming. I said I should've locked her in the bathroom, or drowned her in the toilet or ripped her hair out and left her bald. You told me that I'm not responsible for the actions of others, and that I did the only thing I could do."

"Which was?"

"Take care of Jerry."

"I sound like a wise man." Dad smiled. "That doesn't change the fact that I feel a bit blindsided. I should've seen what Neil was doing. There weren't any signs, but ... I still feel as if I should've gotten to him before he went after you."

"I think, at least from what Dauphine said, they made a point not to go after us right away because she wanted to forge a relationship with you," I supplied. "She thought she could finagle a way into your good graces and bank account."

"Well, that's ridiculous."

"It is." I pursed my lips. "What happened to Mom?"

"She handled Evelyn and left the cleaners to deal with the rest. She got Evelyn to admit to quite a few things, although the attack in the store was apparently all Neil. He was worried she would spill the truth. He wanted the book for himself, so he sent the zombies to retrieve it. He also placed the anonymous call about the body in your backyard."

"I'm not really surprised about that."

"Once I got over the initial shock, I wasn't either," Dad said. "Redmond called Madame Maxine when we were finished. She was ... reticent ... but admitted she thought Evelyn was up to something. She claims she didn't know exactly what Evelyn had planned."

"Do you believe her?"

"I didn't speak with her. It hardly matters now, though, does it?"

"I guess not." I rolled my neck, cringing when I felt the initial twinges that signified I would be sore in the morning. "Mom didn't want to stay?"

"She had a busy night. I believe she was tired."

"I know I've been the one fighting this, the one trying to keep her out, but she came through tonight. She came through six weeks ago, too. Maybe ... maybe we can try to let her come through more often."

"I've considered that," Dad said. "I'm not sure how I feel about it."

"It's up to you to decide, because I think it will be hardest on you and you've earned the right to make the ultimate decision. I'll agree with whatever you want."

"Oh, that has to be a first." Dad chuckled as he pushed a strand of my hair away from my face. "We'll talk about it in the morning. I would like to find a way for this to work for all of us."

"For what to work?" Griffin asked, striding into the bedroom with a package of frozen peas in his hand. He cast me a sidelong look before pressing the peas to my swollen face, and then focused on Dad. "Please tell me we don't have another crisis to deal with already."

"No, not a crisis. Aisling and I were simply discussing how to handle the Lily situation."

"Ah." Griffin stripped off his shirt before reaching for the button on his jeans. He didn't seem to care that we weren't alone. "What did you come up with?"

"We'll talk about it in the morning and try to make things work to the best of our ability."

"That doesn't sound like much of a plan." Griffin kicked off his jeans, leaving his boxers on as he crawled in next to me.

Dad arched an eyebrow. "Did you need to do that in front of me?"

"I'm tired and sore. You'll live."

Dad snorted. "Do you remember when you feared me? Good times."

"I never feared you," Griffin countered. "I feared you might turn Aisling against me, but I never feared you."

"That's disheartening."

"You did make me extremely uncomfortable, if that helps."

"It doesn't hurt." Dad grinned as he sighed. "The home office is taking care of Neil's body. I'm not sure what will be done with Evelyn's remains, but ... I'm sure it will be handled with the proper amount of secrecy."

"That's just what a cop wants to hear," Griffin muttered.

"Do you disapprove?" Dad asked, legitimately curious.

"No. It had to be done. I would've done it myself if it came to it. Mrs. Grimlock simply beat me to it."

"Given her history with Evelyn, it was her right," Dad said. "Plus, well, Lily fought off an entire horde of zombies. She kept you three safe. I can't find fault with her actions this evening."

"What about all of the bodies?" I asked. "Do you know where they got them?"

"No, and we can't get them back where they belong without making things public," Dad said. "I'm sure most of them had proper funerals and burials the first go around, so hopefully they're at peace. They'll be cremated this time. There's nothing more we can do."

"That seems kind of disrespectful."

"Do you have a better idea?"

"No."

"Then we can only do what we can do," Dad said. "As for the other issues, we'll discuss it over breakfast. I think the one thing everyone has earned this evening is rest."

"Sounds good to me," Griffin said. "I'm looking forward to whatever food surprise you have in store for Aisling tomorrow."

"An omelet bar and a waffle bar." I grinned even though it hurt. "I'm going to eat my weight in breakfast foods."

"That sounds delightful." Dad smiled as he stood. "Griffin told me what you did at the mausoleum. While I'm not a fan of you running off half-cocked and taking on the world without backup, I am proud of what you did."

"It would've worked if Neil didn't hide behind that shed and punch me when I wasn't looking. Dirty, rotten cheater."

Dad chuckled. "Yes, well, he won't be cheating anyone ever again. As for the police, your mother said she had a heart-to-heart discussion with Detective Green. I don't think they'll be sniffing around again, at least on this one."

"I'll ask around tomorrow to make sure," Griffin said. "I doubt that Mark will want to admit what he saw last night. He'll probably deny it to his final day because it will make him look nuts if he tries to spread the story."

"We'll watch him," Dad said. "I doubt he'll be a problem. You two should get some sleep. It's late."

My father looked tired. He so rarely did. Neil's betrayal weighed heavy on him. I felt the need to ease his burden. "I was thinking you could look at some wedding stuff with us over breakfast tomorrow."

Dad arched an eyebrow, surprised. "You want to include me in the decisions?"

"You are paying for it. Wait ... you're still paying, right?"

"If you ask me that again I'll disown you," Dad warned.

I held my hands up in capitulation. "I won't ask again. I want your input, though. In addition to paying, you're my father. You'll be giving me away."

"Really?" Dad was caught off guard. "I thought you might find that tradition antiquated."

"Nope. I'm yours to give away. Wait ... I think that came out wrong."

Griffin chuckled. "I think it came out exactly right."

I glanced at Dad and found his eyes glassy. "Don't cry." I was horrified. "I meant it as a ... I don't know ... respect thing. If you don't want to do it, you don't have to."

"Oh, don't ruin it." Dad rolled his eyes. "The last thing I want to do is give you away, kid. Part of me would like to keep you forever."

"That sounds creepy."

"I couldn't imagine giving you to a better man, though." Dad pressed a kiss to my forehead. "Now, sleep. We'll discuss everything over breakfast. I look forward to watching you eat your weight in waffles and eggs."

"We're both looking forward to that," Griffin teased.

Dad hit the lights on the way out, stopping long enough to smile and offer me a small wave before disappearing into the hallway. I waited until I was sure he was out of earshot before speaking again.

"Do you want to mess around?"

Griffin groaned. "Seriously?"

"Dad is putty in my hands tonight. We can totally get away with it. He let you strip in front of him and only said one passive-aggressive thing. That must be a new record."

"I heard that, Aisling!" Dad yelled from the hallway. Apparently he wasn't as far away as I thought. "Don't make me come in there."

"Just joking," I bellowed back.

"Make sure you keep it that way."

Griffin smirked as he glanced at me and lowered his voice. "How about we save the romance for when we're back in our own bed and your face doesn't look as if you've gone ten rounds with Rocky. How does that sound?"

"Boring."

"You'll live." Griffin rolled me so I could rest my good cheek on his chest. "You really did scare me tonight."

"That's starting to be the norm for us, huh?"

"Yeah. Knock it off."

I giggled. "Hey, Griffin?"

"What?" He was already half asleep.

"I really do love you."

I could hear the smile in his voice when he answered. "I know. Now sleep. If you open your mouth again, I'm going to fill it with something."

"You said you didn't want to mess around."

"I meant a pillow."

"That's not romantic."

"Neither is the bag of peas melting on my chest."

He had a point. "Goodnight."

"Sweet dreams, baby. You've earned them."

Made in the USA
Coppell, TX
04 June 2020